The Crystal Key

PSYCHIC SOLUTIONS, MYSTERY #3

PATRICIA RICE

Ariel

23:10 GAMECAM1: *LARGE ANIMAL IN PINE?*

Ariel Jackson-Ives frowned at the notation. Large animals did not normally occupy this sparse South Carolina piney wood. Imprecision could be life-threatening when one lived alone.

She brought out the binoculars, but in the darkness, she only saw branches swaying from a heavy weight. The pine was half hidden by an ancient oak. Her house security cameras didn't reach beyond the yard.

The game cameras in the woods were on a separate circuit that she'd installed herself, but the pine was too distant to see clearly.

Frustrated, she continued her routine, playing through the videos on each camera in order. The paths through the woods to the pond at night made for better entertainment than television.

23:15 GAMECAM2: *fawn losing spots*

23:46 GAMECAM3: *opossum joeys almost full grown; female carrying another litter?*

01:15 GAMECAM1: *no movement sighted*

At precisely 01:30 she double checked her security video and returned to work. The darknet was busy tonight. She followed a trail of illegal-cryptocurrency and sent the route to her contact.

At 05:00 she stopped for breakfast. As she buttered her toast and fried her egg, the game camera nagged at her. *What if there was a bobcat?*

Therapists had said she needed to regularly modify her routine if she ever wished to pass as neurotypical. *I could watch the video while eating.*

Ariel studied her toast and tea. She didn't like crumbs on her desk or sticky things near her keyboards. She finished her toast and egg, refreshed her tea mug, and carried it and her paper notebook to the massive computer desk filling half her front room. Carefully setting the mug on a coaster on a side table away from her keyboard, she switched on the feed from game camera number one, so she had a larger zoomed-up image.

05:32 GAMECAM1: *large branches moving*

That was slightly better, less imprecise. Perhaps changing her routine sharpened her mind.

She usually went to bed at 06:00, just as dawn lightened the sky at this time of year. But dawn would be a good time for a big cat to go on the prowl. She'd seen coyotes and foxes at dawn.

Her security lights went off on the east side of the house as the bright August sun rays hit them. Ariel enlarged the image on her wide-screen monitor. Definite movement. A flash of blue caught her eye. *Blue?*

Uneasy, she opened up all her house security cameras on the big monitor, then ran the game cameras on a second screen.

I'll have to tell Dr. Shaw I stayed up past bedtime. That's progress, isn't it?

06:33 GAMECAM1: *branches moving. More blue!*

At 06:35, her house security cameras all shut down, turned off by hands other than her own.

Ariel slammed the desk with her palms. *That bastard!*

Only two people besides her knew how to turn off those cameras. One of them had been missing for months—the one who knew her routine best, the one who knew she normally went to bed at 06:00. *The one who had installed her keypad and set the password.*

She'd thought he *understood*.

Furious, she loaded the gun she used on unruly wildlife. She swung the game camera positions to the path toward her back door. She knew how to protect herself.

As soon as the jeans-wearing Cajun staggered through the shrubbery guarding her yard, she snapped a photo with GAMECAM3 and shot it off to the two people who would have heard the alarm when her security went off. The third damned person she had trusted to send messages to was now at her kitchen door, punching in her security code.

2

If he thought she'd gone to bed, she had a little surprise for him.

She waited in the shadowy corner of the kitchen until the door opened, and she had a good view of his blue tank top. He was more brown and muscled than ever. With his hair grown out into unruly curls and his face metal removed, he was barely recognizable as the bald, tattooed soldier who'd entered her life over a year ago. Without compunction, Ariel shot him mid-chest with the full force of her water blaster.

All six-foot-two of giant rat collapsed like a decompressed accordion.

One

"EVANGELINE MALCOLM CARSTAIRS ON A *YACHT*!" SITTING ON A deck chair overlooking gray Atlantic waves turning pastel with dawn, Evie took a selfie of herself in the bright pink hot pants she had found in her Great-Aunt Val's wardrobe. Rather than downsize, her aunt had left Evie to recycle all the things she no longer wanted. Beat thrift store shopping. "I grew up in a trailer park and your family owns a *yacht*. I should probably go scrub the toilet."

"The head," Damon Jackson-Ives corrected. "And my adoptive father owns the yacht because he stole people's money. My real father was a desert rat."

A fact they'd only discovered a few months ago, but not one that changed their cultural divide. Their moral and emotional gaps were less simple to define given Jax was an honest lawyer and seeker of justice, and her family descended from a legacy of women who did what it took to survive. The months it had taken to reach this level of companionship had been entertaining.

Evie snorted at his description of his genius biological father and stretched out her leg so she could study her newly polished toenails. "Yeah, a desert rat who owned a silicon mine, a microchip company, and was both a lawyer and engineer. My daddy pounds nails for a living. And your *mother* was a political analyst. Mine reads crystal balls. Let's face it, dude, we are not compatible." Although they'd done a fine job of *compatting* in the yacht's luxurious quarters last night.

"Not seeing a large difference between political analysis and crystal balls." Setting aside his phone to sip his mimosa, Jax admired her preening display.

That he *noticed* her gave her a thrill. Intelligent men tended to disregard her as a petite flake—which came in handy upon occasion, admittedly. But a girl liked having her special man pay attention when she fixed herself up.

For their final yacht date, Jax was wearing funky linen trousers tied with a rope. And no shirt. Although she admired his sculpted muscles, she envied his ability to brown nicely in the sun. Her redhead's skin didn't. Which was one reason they were out here at dawn.

Wariness tinged his reply. "So, you're saying we should break up because your family isn't rich, even though my family is dead, and I'm nearly dead broke? If you're looking for excuses, we could go with your family having lived in the same town for four centuries while mine has no roots."

Well, yeah, when he put it that way. . . "You grew up with country clubs and *yachts*. I grew up with witches with attitudes. You could be a hotshot lawyer if you didn't hang around with me."

He settled back to sip his drink and presumably ponder her complaint. "My adoptive father stole his clients' funds. Your family holds witch parades and drives out a corrupt mayor, then supports a transgender candidate to take his place. And you are altruistically suggesting that we give up the best sex I've ever had, so I can have yachts and belong to a country club?"

Evie tried to wrap her ADHD-afflicted brain around that. "Well, if it's all about the sex, okay, we're good. A bad influence for Loretta, maybe, but kids have to learn adults make mistakes too."

"And now we're a mistake. You really know how to make a guy feel special." Jax reached his muscular leg over to her lounge and rubbed his toes up her naked leg.

Evie gave up. "I'm done trying to save you from yourself. I'll miss our weekend getaways now that the yacht has been sold. How is your dad doing these days?" Evie nibbled at her cranberry bagel, snapped photos with her phone, and toyed with the deck chair adjustment. Sitting still wasn't exactly a habit she'd ever developed.

Jax grimaced. "Stephen has sold the house, his cars, his partnership in Stockton and Stockton, and now the yacht. He thinks that will be enough to pay off the clients he owes, plus court fees and so forth. Living on social security and a pension will be good for him."

"I'm glad you agreed to be his character witness. Your aura is brighter for it." Evie breathed deeply of the salt air and admired the ball of gold rising over the surf while catching surreptitious glimpses of Jax's awesome pecs. She'd known he was no weakling since that first day she'd done her best to maim him last spring. Since then, she'd had time to learn just how those hard muscles felt up close and personal.

She tingled all over and wondered if they might have time for one more round before they had to go home. . .

Since the meathead was being his usual dutiful lawyer self and checking his overnight mail, she figured she ought to act like she wasn't a sex maniac, pretend she had a business, and check hers. It was just. . . she could do three things at once while he was concentrating on one. She slid her bare foot over to rub his and opened a message from one of her neighbors.

Jax leaned over and blew in her ear just as she whistled and sat up straight, nearly taking off his nose. She waved the phone at him. "Look! This might be a realio trulio case! *Her grandmother may not be her grandmother!*"

Undaunted, Jax nibbled her ear—until his phone sounded an alarm, then beeped. "Hold that thought." He flipped to his text messages, cursed, and showed her the screen image.

Roark! The last time they'd seen him, he'd been hightailing it out of town in pursuit of happiness or Sasquatch. Or maybe both. "What on earth is he doing?" Evie grabbed the phone to study the background. The big Cajun was creeping around Witch Hill? Why?

Jax was already out of his chair. "The alarm was Ariel's security being cut off. The image is from Ariel."

"How did she take that photo if her cameras are cut off? Why would he cut her security?" Following him up, Evie began gathering their breakfast dishes while her thoughts spun with worry for both Ariel and Roark. "He looks awful, but maybe that's just the shadows? Will she be okay?"

Jax returned the text with a brief word or two. Evie knew his neurodivergent sister didn't process long communication. The phone didn't beep back, and he cursed some more. No communication was worrisome—but not unusual.

"I'll clean up. You try to reach Reuben. He was pulling together more propaganda for the mayor's campaign late last night and may still be asleep."

Running down to the cabin, Evie did a hasty scrub of their dishes and dashed back to strip the linens while Jax paced and tried to wake up people who could reach Ariel faster than they could.

Ariel was as close to a non-verbal Crystal Child as Evie would probably ever meet. Her aura was crystal clear, and she was so sensitive to conflict that she'd retreated inside herself and might break like pricey glass if pushed too far. Psychiatrists had other words for her, none of them right.

She flung a shirt up at Jax, who wiggled it on while punching keys on the phone. The man could multi-task when needed. She threw the rest of their things into the Harley's saddlebags, gave the cabin a swift check, and joined him on deck. He grabbed her waist, kissed her as if he meant it, then dragged her to the gangplank. Well, so much for a last minute quickie.

This had been a fascinating summer, but idylls had to end. Her luck with men generally never lasted even this long—which made her wary, if only for their ward's sake. Jax had been too busy this summer setting up his new office to look for anyone more his type. That didn't mean Evie dared dream that the illusion would continue. Which meant she needed to assert her independence.

"If I had my own car, I could stay here and look into this granny case." If she had an actual job, maybe she wouldn't mind so much when he moved on. She ran to keep up with his longer legs.

"Buy your damned Miata. Loretta is a billionaire." Loretta being their ten-year-old ward. "She shouldn't be riding around town in a broken-down utility van or a bicycle."

Said the lawyer climbing on his Harley, Evie thought grumpily as she joined him. "I've saved the reward money and the allowance I receive from the trust. I have enough for a down payment without dipping into the kid's money."

"I know—she's family." He repeated the argument they had regularly over their orphaned ward. "But her *family* used to own three high-end cars." He climbed on and hit the motor, drowning out further argument.

But Loretta's parents had *earned* their wealth. Evie hadn't. She still felt guilty accepting the allowance, but buying groceries for Loretta and the tribe the kid now called her family cost more than Evie earned. As long as she spent the money on Loretta, she could handle it.

If she had any credit, she could take out a car loan. But dog walkers and psychic problem solvers had difficulty obtaining credit for some odd reason.

Afterthought, South Carolina, a town with a population smaller than some mega-church congregations, was inland, roughly halfway between Charleston and Savannah. On a quiet Sunday morning, it took them a little less than an hour to drive home.

"Reuben's van is gone." Jax leaned the bike against her Victorian carriage house and unbuckled their bags.

"Doesn't mean anything. He could still be at the mayor's. Check your messages." Evie hurried up the back steps of the huge old house her great aunt had left in her care. If Reuben wasn't here, who was watching Loretta?

Her mother, of course. Owner of the *Psychic Solutions Gift Shop*, Mavis greeted them with the wave of a spatula and the smell of burning pancakes. Reading crystal balls didn't include reading pancake recipes. "Just in time, dear. There are atmospheric disturbances over Witch Hill."

"Yeah, they're called Roark LeBlanc." Evie leaned over and gave Loretta a kiss on her braided hair. The kid was in her favorite seat at the breakfast banquette, frowning at burned pancakes covered in syrup and chocolate chips. "Throw them out," Evie whispered. "You should have told her about the frozen ones."

Running away from her pricey boarding school, the kid had landed on Evie's doorstep a few months back looking for her parents—who were spirits desperately clinging to their only child. Since Loretta was heir to their fortune, Jax, as their executor, had followed close on her heels. It had taken some untwisting of palpable disbelief to convince him that Loretta was another psychic Malcolm and belonged with Evie, the dog walker.

Having happily settled into Evie's chaotic family, Loretta added canned whipped cream. "Nah, these will do. Reuben's bubble was really twisted when he ran in and out a little bit ago. What's wrong?"

As an Indigo child, Loretta's declarations were often perceived as strange, but Evie interpreted the *bubbles* she saw as a person's soul. The kid was pretty good at nailing character. As part of Jax's former military intelligence crew, Reuben had a *lot* of issues to work through. Roark, his former partner before he vanished, was one of them.

"Roark showed up at Ariel's. We'll let Jax handle it. I think Sensible Solutions has a genuine case." Evie showed the kid her phone, then rescued the rest of the pancake batter from her mother.

Had Roark crushed his personal Sasquatch or the beast trounced him? And why in the name of the goddess had he gone to Jax's hermit sister?

"Shouldn't one of us go with him?" Mavis asked worriedly as Jax dashed back out.

"Ariel is less than five minutes away. If he needs us, he'll let us know." Shy Ariel did not need spacey Mavis fluttering around.

Solid as Gibraltar in her colorful caftan, her mother settled on a counter stool. "Your Aunt Ellen claims she's won a Cadillac. I'll believe it when I see it sitting in her driveway."

"Another one of those magazine giveaways?" Evie guessed. Her aunt's subscriptions provided the local library with all the magazines it could use and then some.

"Most likely. They're always sending her junk from some contest she's won. Pris needs to take the mail away from her. My sister is losing her marbles." Said the woman who'd lost her home because she didn't read mail that she'd psychically determined to be unpleasant. Mavis poured syrup on the pancakes Evie set in front of her.

Evie tried not to worry about Ariel and Roark while her family ate. She thought she almost pulled it off until her phone beeped with a text message. She grabbed it back from Loretta and opened the app.

HELP was all it said—from Jax's sister, who never communicated.

Two

ARIEL PACED THE NARROW STRIP OF KITCHEN BETWEEN ROARK'S sprawling dead weight on the floor and the table. The man was huge. His biceps had biceps. Broad brown shoulders covered five entire tiles.

She didn't like touching people, so she couldn't test his pulse. He didn't seem to be bleeding, but she couldn't lift him to see his front. She hadn't seen blood in that first glimpse before she shot him. Water couldn't kill.

He still breathed.

Reuben was Roark's friend, not hers. He hadn't answered her text. Jax was too far away. What should she do? Call an ambulance? How? She'd have to explain. . .

I can't. I can't.

The therapist said she should *try* anytime she told herself that. If she ever wanted to be typical. . .

Just calling a taxi was almost beyond her capability, even when she had an address. A phone call giving directions to this cottage hideaway plus a description of Roark collapsing. . . extended into the inconceivable.

Ariel crouched down, gathered her frayed nerves, and poked Roark's bulging upper arm. It was like touching leather over steel. He didn't stir.

Is he sleeping? He spent the night in a tree! I should smack him. He worried everyone sick after his phone lost contact—just like Jax. Men are despicable.

Ariel returned to pacing the front porch in hopes someone would miraculously appear.

Mitch Isa Turtle poked his head from his house, and she fed him the turtle food she'd special ordered online. She paced some more. Sick to her stomach from helplessness, she returned inside.

Had Roark cracked his head on the tile? No, he'd collapsed first. He was still breathing. In fact, he was practically snoring. Relieved that he was still alive, she escaped to her computer. What did she search on? Collapsed man?

Not finding anything in search engines, she went back to check again. Still breathing. For how long? It had been over an hour. She paced back to the porch. Was that dust rising down the road?

Relieved, terrified, overwhelmed, she retreated to the shadows of the porch as the van arrived with a speeding Harley close behind—help, at last. Sliding down the wall to sit on the porch planks, she tucked her knees to her chest and hugged her shins. She rocked silently while the men turned off their engines at the perimeter she'd set.

No people! No people, no people.

She rocked to soothe herself as they slowly approached. *Jax, Jax, Jax, okay.* She rocked harder as the tall Black man climbed out of the van and followed her brother. *Reuben.* She recognized Dr. Reuben Thompson, but she didn't *know* know him. She repeated his name to calm her overworked senses.

He's Roark's friend. He's Jax's friend. She rocked harder, banging her head against the siding.

"In the kitchen?" Jax asked, keeping his question simple, as the therapist had taught him.

Ariel nodded quickly, briefly. Her stomach knotted. She needed to go to her darkened room and close the door.

She'd almost killed Roark. Would she go to jail like Stephen, their adoptive father?

Now that someone was here to take charge, she texted Evie. Evie's family was weird like her. They'd understand. They'd make Roark better.

With the message sent, Ariel slipped into her computer-filled front room. She swallowed hard when she saw the men lifting Roark's lifeless length from the kitchen floor. She pointed down the hall to her tiny library office, then, like the coward she was, she retreated to her bedroom and closed the door.

A four-room cottage was much too small for this many people. Frantically glancing around, she grabbed her pillow and blanket. Opening her closet, she removed her spare pair of shoes and sank to the floor, closing the closet after her. *Better.*

Three

RESPECTING ARIEL'S PRIVACY, JAX LED REUBEN TO THE FRONT yard. Evie had arrived on her bike after his sister's summons. She was inside now with Iddy, her veterinarian cousin, examining Roark in hopes he didn't need a medical professional.

Ariel wouldn't emerge from her hiding place until everyone was gone.

While waiting to hear the verdict, Jax inspected the contents of the duffle they'd retrieved from the pine tree. Nothing in it gave away what the Cajun had been doing these past months. Of course, Roark was well trained in military intelligence and knew better than to carry anything that would identify him or anything he worked on. "He wouldn't have come here if he'd felt safe going to a hospital. What do we do if he needs a doctor?"

"Man won't go to no hospital, no way." Dedicated computer nerd and doctor of engineering, Reuben pulled a stylus out of his man bun and poked at the phone to Ariel's game cameras, the ones she'd apparently set up without anyone's knowledge.

Jax's sister was a fruit basket, but a damned smart one. She had a complete life out here in the woods that none of them knew about. She'd hate them trespassing on her privacy. Jax snatched the phone from his friend and tossed it inside to one of the computer tables.

"He was setting up a command post, man. I'm gonna figure out why."

Reuben retreated to the utility van containing his endless inventory of computerized equipment—including satellite internet.

Jax didn't think Roark would leave a trace for Reuben to find, but he was welcome to try. He paced impatiently. Both Reuben and Roark had been under Jax's command when all the crap had come down that obliterated their careers. The Cajun computer hacker was a damned good man, just a little messed up. Jax had no idea why Roark had vanished so hastily, or where he'd been these last months, but knowing Roark's abilities—Jax hoped he'd not left witnesses.

Evie emerged from the cottage with fresh water for the turtle. "Iddy says she thinks the leg wound was from a bullet, but it seems to be healing without infection. She's hoping his collapse was from exhaustion and maybe hunger, but she's no physician. Ariel doesn't keep much food on hand, but I've found some frozen bean soup and ham and set them on the counter. Once he wakes, maybe one of them will get a clue."

Jax knew the veterinarian was more normal than most of Evie's family. He'd just have to rely on her judgment for the moment.

"I should probably stay out here and wait for him to wake up. At least Ariel isn't afraid of me," Jax said in resignation.

"Ariel isn't afraid of anyone," Evie retorted. "If she'd had a real gun instead of a water gun, she could have blown Roark to heck. Your sister has a social anxiety disorder, not a yellow streak down her back. And given her intelligence levels, she has good reason to be anxious."

"You're not her therapist." Jax still had difficulty with Evie's confidence in her aura reading. He'd like to believe her, so he had an excuse to go into the office and file that case on his desk.

When his neurodivergent sister and a ten-year-old ward had suddenly been thrust into his care, he'd realized how much he had wrapped his life around work. Finding a balance between his career and family still didn't come easily even after all these months.

"You can't know she's not terrified," he argued.

"I've seen enough therapists to talk like one, but I've also seen Ariel's crystalline aura, and Loretta has seen her huge soul. Your sister is as tough as you are. Her brain is simply wired weird, like mine. I don't know how she'll deal with Roark." Evie glanced up at her much taller, darker cousin emerging from the cottage. "Are you sure we can't move him?"

Iddy shrugged. "He's been through a lot. I think he passed out, then just fell asleep. I'd let him keep sleeping. His feet are badly blistered. I suspect he's been doing a lot of walking to reach here."

"Where he feels safe." Evie turned to Jax. "Your friend. Your sister. Your call."

Knowing Roark's penchant for trouble, Jax grimaced. He'd have to trust Evie. "I don't like it. Ariel won't like it. But he's a good man, and I have a feeling we'd better hear his story before we take him anywhere he might be in danger."

Reuben emerged from the van. "Eh, boss, I got a few leads. Should I send them to Ariel as warning?"

Jax rubbed his head. "Do I want to hear this?"

His phone beeped. So did Evie's. While Iddy shrugged and headed for her car, Evie and Jax checked their messages. Reuben's text included a newspaper link.

Explosion rocks small town in rural Louisiana.

Oh yeah, that was Roark, all right.

Four

ROARK'S EMPTY BELLY ROUSED HIM. HE WAS USED TO THAT. Sleep helped. But an oddly sweet fragrance forced his senses to say *not right*. Waking more, he noted the texture of fluffiness. *Fluffy?*

Figuring a bear would have suffocated him by now, he wasn't too worried, just curious. He lay still, tuning into sounds. Water dripped. A computer beeped. That blamed critter down by the pond croaked. But he didn't hear people. Where the hell was he? He peeked at whatever was covering his bare chest. A pink fluffy blanket? *Pink.*

He didn't generally wake disoriented or hallucinating. He closed his eyes and scrolled back his memories. . . *Ariel*. She'd shot him.

He wasn't dead. He rubbed his hand over his chest. His filthy shirt was gone. Had she removed it? Roark didn't think that possible. Ariel didn't touch people, and she was half his weight. She couldn't have moved him. . . Where the frigging hell was he?

Sharp hearing had allowed him to survive Afghanistan and his childhood. He froze and tuned his senses wider. Still not sensing anyone nearby. How the hell could the woman not breathe?

Moving nothing more than his eyelids, he scanned the dimly lit room. Light filtered through one *pink*-curtained window. Shelves of plants surrounded it. Bookshelves lined the longer wall in front of him. He sat in a recliner tilted to make a bed. Behind him appeared to be more shelves.

It wasn't a prison box.

Relieved, he found a way to raise the chair upright. From this position, he could see his duffle. Discarding the pink bunny fluff, he got up—and realized he wasn't wearing jeans. His bandage had been changed. What the. . .

No way had Jax's prissy sister done that. He dug out a tank top and khakis. Then, considering the woman who'd smothered him in pink fluff, he added a denim work shirt. The cottage was air-conditioned. His travels hadn't been. He needed a shower.

He needed food. That had been his earlier objective, when the damned fool woman had shot him. With what? A stun gun?

Cautiously opening his door, he peered into the dimly lit hall. The door across from this one was closed. He'd spent a lot of time guarding Jax's fragile kid sister to make sure she'd adapted to her new abode. He knew Ariel routinely rose at two in the afternoon. Gauging by the sun, it had to be after noon. His opportunity to escape unseen was limited.

The cool wood floor felt better on his battered feet than his worn army boots. He still winced as he crept to the kitchen. Opening the refrigerator, he discovered all the makings for sandwiches on a shelf, waiting for him. Ariel wasn't that domesticated. Someone else knew he was here. That could not be good.

He dug into the cold bean soup, not wanting to make noise with a microwave. He slapped ham between bread and tore at it while quietly navigating the small kitchen to the front room—Ariel's giant play area. She'd been busy adding to her equipment since she moved in.

All the screens were dark, but a light gleamed on the laptop when he opened it. He hit a key and a selection of *guest* or *owner* popped up. He clicked guest and the window opened. . . to show images of the explosion in Whitesville.

He mentally cursed in three languages. *She knew.* Ariel already knew.

That's when he glanced at the clock on the computer screen. Four o'clock. The damned woman was awake and lurking. How much had she told the others?

Judging by the food in the refrigerator—*Evie.* And by the duffel and the chair—*Jax and Reuben.*

Game over. He needed to claim his van and get out of here.

He didn't want his friends involved. This was on his head alone. But how could he make them back off while he figured out what to do? He slugged from the bottle of water he'd found in the refrigerator and pondered his options. He didn't want to drag innocents into this.

He picked up a cell phone lying beside the laptop. It didn't have a password and opened to pictures of him sneaking up to the back door. The freaking, scary female had added her own cameras to the security system he'd installed. She was flaunting it by leaving the phone where he'd find it.

Score one for the frigging genius.

He checked the phone's contacts—the list included everyone he'd ever met in this town plus a few he hadn't, all neatly labeled as to who they were. Wickedly, he hit the one addressed to Ariel and typed **MERCI.**

She instantly texted back a link. She knew he was up. Of course she did. Roark hit the link. It opened a file of bank statements. Ariel had a genius for money—and hacking bank accounts. She'd been busy while he was sleeping. He studied his da's name and address on the statements and the sizeable sums of money flowing through the account. *Merde.*

Game on again.

Five

AFTER INTERVIEWING THE POTENTIAL CLIENT, EVIE SET DOWN her phone on the kitchen island and wrinkled her nose at her scribbled notes. "I don't think we'll make much money off this one."

Professorial Reuben leaned against the back door, munching a banana. Since he'd been working with Larraine Ward, the mayoral candidate, the fashionista had talked him into wearing more cosmopolitan slim jeans with a blazer and a collared shirt instead of his usual rags. The new clothes went with his man bun, but not so much with his scarred African features, although he'd replaced the bone in the bun with a stylus. PhD or not, underneath that polite veneer, Dr. Rube was still one tough gay dude. "Will the job look good as a reference?"

Evie crinkled her nose. "Guess that depends on what grandma was up to. According to Stacey Gump, after her granny died, she found multiple computer devices around the senior living apartment. They were set up under strange names and contained receipts and bills not addressed to Marlene Gump, her grandmother. Out of curiosity, she called any phone numbers she could find and got voice mail with her grandmother's voice. Granny died in Savannah. The other addresses were scattered around Georgia and the Carolinas. The granddaughter claims her grandmother had nothing more than a government pension and an annuity to live on and couldn't possibly afford different homes."

"Can the granddaughter afford to pay you?" Loretta asked pragmatically from her seat in the banquette, where she poked at a Game Boy.

"There's your father speaking." Evie spun around on the counter stool. Loretta's father had been an investor who made millions in his brief lifetime. The kid's finances were Jax's bailiwick. "Stacey Gump is heartbroken. Her grandmother practically raised her. Shouldn't we help those who are hurt?"

"What about the client's parents? They got money?" Reuben asked cynically.

"You want me to be crude and ask if granny left them any money?" Evie slid off the stool. "I should at least look at the apartment. Maybe grandma left a ghost behind. Can you take me into Savannah, or do I have to beg a ride elsewhere?"

"You just wanta snoop." Reuben threw the banana peel into the trash. "Shouldn't we be keeping an eye on Ariel and Roark?"

"They're adults. Do you really want to get involved in whatever Roark is up to right now? He didn't let us know where he was for a reason." Evie very much wanted to know what that reason was, but the information Reuben had dug from news files had been more scary than useful.

Before the storage building explosion in Roark's old hood, neighbors had reported gunfire and people running. No suspects apprehended. Search for bodies ongoing. That had been a week ago. She was just happy Roark had escaped.

"Not if he's blowing up things again. I can't let Larraine be associated with nothin' illegal, so a legit job is good. I can't believe the mayor race is actually *close*." Professor Reuben, the human garbage disposal, opened the refrigerator in search of more food. He didn't let disgust with the human race prevent him from eating—and never gaining a pound on his lean, muscled frame.

He emerged with a leftover pizza slice. "Who'd want a senile old coot to run the town?"

"Maybe a bunch of other senile old men who don't want a Black, trans-gender, fashion designer for mayor. People are weird like that." Larraine Ward had entered the town's special mayoral election with an agenda of change—not an easy platform to promote.

Evie had known Larraine's opponent since childhood. Hank Williams had to be pushing eighty and the very picture of rural conservatism. Worse, he owned the hardware store and everyone knew him. Larraine had her job cut out for her.

"People ought to vote for brains and big bubbles," Loretta pronounced. In the kid's lexicon, that meant generous souls—which Larraine Ward had, if anyone cared to notice. "If you're going to Savannah, can I go with you? School is starting in a few weeks, and my birthday is coming up."

Evie knew that. She also knew Loretta's parents had showered her with junk she didn't want on her birthdays, then bought her a school uniform and sent her to boarding school. She wanted to do better but wasn't entirely certain how. "We need to do a special girls' trip. It wouldn't look good to introduce ourselves to a client with a kid tagging along. It's hard enough explaining ghosts."

Loretta pouted but returned to her game.

Ignoring her comments about the mayoral race, Reuben shrugged and appropriated a can of soft drink. "I got time. We can play with ghosts. We can leave the chipmunk with Jax."

Evie snorted and hopped down from the counter stool. "Not likely, unless he can fit her in a briefcase. Gracie will come over. Give me a minute to change into something businesslike."

"You don't own anything businesslike," he shouted after her.

"I'll be eleven in a few weeks. I'm old enough to stay by myself," Loretta complained—to deaf ears. Heirs to a fortune required protection, especially when they were kids.

Evie didn't feel too guilty abandoning Larraine and the election for a few hours. Jax and his team had done their civic duty safeguarding the mayoral ballot by uncovering the town's rigged voting machines. Beyond that, there wasn't much she could do to make a small, conservative population wake up and see progress as a good thing. She'd leave that to Larraine's professional campaigners.

Right now, she needed a real job so she could buy a car. Maybe once people saw she could run her own business, she'd get a little more respect for her abilities. Doubtful, but Evie didn't like giving up hope.

She came down wearing one of Great-Aunt Val's shirtdresses from the sixties. It had probably been a miniskirt on tall Val. It came to Evie's knees, but the gold and orange pinstripes made her happy, and she'd found a wide belt that fastened with cool brass hoops. She'd even pulled her unruly carroty hair into a knot. She'd never had money or incentive to have her ears pierced, so she didn't wear earrings. Maybe she should think about that.

She texted to be certain Gracie was on her way, then stopped in the kitchen for approval. "Ta-da, businesslike." She spun around.

"You're wearing Keds," Loretta pointed out.

"Keds are the new cool. Gracie and Aster are practically on the doorstep. Talk them into going to the pool," she told Loretta.

"Let's get moving. Can we put dinner on the expense account?" Reuben juggled the van keys.

"If we had an expense account, we could. Otherwise, you'll have to pony up for a Big Mac."

"One of these days, you'll have to pony up for real shoes." Outside, he didn't bother opening the van door for her the way Jax and Roark did but let her climb in on her own.

Evie appreciated that he treated her as an equal, even if it meant clambering ungracefully into the high seat.

Reuben started the van and backed it down the drive. "All right, now tell me what you weren't saying in front of Loretta."

She wrinkled her nose. "I'm the one who's supposed to read auras, not you."

"Yeah, and I'd be one dead spy if I couldn't read a face as easy as yours. What was grandma up to?"

"Grandma was ex-FBI. Stacey is afraid Granny Marlene might have hid dangerous information someone wanted, and she may have been killed before she could get away. No one else is taking granny's death as anything except old age, so it could be awhile before she has the autopsy report."

"Well, shit."

Evie grimaced. That was more or less her thought, but beggars couldn't be choosers. They needed a job, any job. And Stacey Gump had promised a deposit.

～

Jax finished up his paperwork on the two land fraud cases he'd taken up against his old law firm and Afterthought's former mayor. He'd never meant to be a pencil pusher, but until recently, he'd never thought about anyone but himself either. So there was that.

Now that he knew his real father had lost his life trying to stop massive voter fraud, he had to try on shoes that size. Aaron Ives had been an engineer, an entrepreneur, a lawyer, and a family man—while single-handedly fighting for justice.

Jax, on the other hand, had blown up his military career and any hope of the diplomatic post he'd coveted. Instead, he'd landed a job in his adoptive father's cushy law firm, one that evidently turned a blind eye to criminal fraud by its partners—a job he'd ultimately had to quit. So he was starting over these days.

He had a lot of catching up to do.

His office phone rang and he checked caller ID, but everyone hid their names these days. He needed a secretary to screen his calls, except he could barely afford his rent. His savings account was dwindling by the minute. He let the call go to voice mail, then checked his computer to read the message.

A reporter. Evie and Reuben liked reporters publicizing their new business. Jax wasn't so fond of them. Why would a New Orleans newspaper contact him? He was pretty certain they didn't care that he'd just opened one more tiny law firm in the county seat of Nowheresville, South Carolina.

New Orleans.

Oh crap, if a newspaper reporter had connected him with Roark, then everyone else would too. Well, they didn't know where to find Roark—yet— or they wouldn't be calling Jax. That was one pretty damned good investigative reporter to make a link between two ex-soldiers. Roark had been flying under the radar since he'd left the service, but he did own the van. *Somehow.* Jax hadn't asked questions. The title may have led them to Afterthought and Jax.

He sent a text warning to Reuben, who flew as low as Roark. They'd both been busted out of the service for insubordination and worse, but mostly for revealing what officers hadn't wanted revealed. That was a hard story to explain to prospective employers.

Finishing up his files, Jax ran them over to the courthouse, then hopped on his Harley to pick up supplies and make a swift run to Ariel's. He needed to see if Roark was awake and coherent.

His sister. . . would probably shoot him when he walked in the door. It was Jax's fault that their adoptive father had to sell the comfortable nest she'd lived in most of her life. Roark could never have barged in on her in the mansion they'd grown up in.

Jax parked the bike under a spreading dogwood and texted Ariel to let her know he was outside.

Roark popped out the front door instead. He still looked haggard—as best as one could tell, given the dude's size and bronzed coloring. He needed a shave and a haircut. Jax had never seen him in anything except a military buzz that revealed his tats. He could understand why now. Roark's curls had him looking like a black sheep.

Roark pointed at one of Ariel's cameras. "She's even got audio, so if you've come to blast my hide, we haveta go elsewhere."

Jax waved at the camera. "Want me to punch him?"

His phone beeped with a text response from his reclusive sister. **LISTEN**

He showed it to Roark, who looked resigned. He sank down on the front porch, sprawling his legs over the steps and leaning against a post. Jax threw him a beer from his saddlebag. Aiming the spray at the weed-patch lawn, he opened one for himself and waited.

Roark took a deep slug, wiped his mouth, and didn't pretend he didn't know what Jax wanted. "Ain't pretty. It's family business."

Jax nearly snorted up his beer. "You remember *my* family? What's a little murder and fraud among friends?"

"Yeah, well, your real daddy was honorable, even if it got him killed. My daddy ain't honorable or dead, not for lack of tryin' on the dead part."

Jax waited.

Roark grimaced at the familiar tactic. He ran a rough hand through his thick curls. "My dad grew up t'inking it was okay to grift. His family was poor, his dad died in an oil rig explosion, his mom needed money for his siblings, you know da song."

"He danced for the money they paid." Jax quoted a line he'd heard his parents use. He thought it referred to Gypsies, Romani, whatever. Roark looked enough like one to qualify.

Roark snorted and chugged the beer. "Did a bit of dat, too, I expect. Good lookin' SOB. I don't know for certain since I wasn't born den, but I get the impression he cheated women, a *lot* of women, in his younger days. He's too fat and slow dese days."

"You're one of the results?" Jax asked cynically.

"Nah, he actually married my mom. My granny is a scary Vodou priestess, probably threatened to raise the spirits on his black soul. He settled down, worked on da rigs, came home and gave my mother a baby every year. Until he punched da wrong guy in the face and lost his job. Old story. He came home and started punching us—until I got big enough to punch back. Things kinda went to hell after dat."

Jax thought they sounded like hell before that happened, but he'd lived a privileged life. "How old were you?"

'Bout twelve, I reckon. We had our own garden patch and we ate good. I grew fast. You've seen the official records. I got baseball scholarships, got out, came home ever' so often to t'reaten to beat the crap out of him if he hurt Ma or the kids. She finally got one of her brothers and his wife to move in and look after da youngers so she could work. After that, she booted my dad out."

"And he went on to bigger and better things?" Jax guessed.

Roark shrugged and crushed his can. "He was outta my life. I didn't follow his. But recently, he apparently got syndicated."

Jax waited. He imagined Ariel was inside, frantically working through computer files, looking for Roark's father, even though the crafty bastard hadn't mentioned his name. Ariel wasn't as good at Google as she was at money, but she wasn't bad, either.

Roark glared, then reluctantly continued. "Me, I don' know who and what he did. But he was dragging in my brothers, and Ma got hot under the collar. I went down to persuade her to move to Texas with her sister, get the kids outta that hole where there ain't two coins to rub together, but she likes her job and being near family. The stink got so bad, my grandma threatened to put a hex on him. You don't wanna get on the wrong side of that woman."

"Stink?" Jax took superstition with a cellar of salt. But since meeting Evie and her auras and Loretta and her bubble souls. . . He probably ought to pay closer attention.

"Da was runnin' this dodgy phone bank in an old storage shed with a bunch of punks who could talk a good talk. My brothers said weed flowed like water, but all they were doin' was making sales calls. I sent the boys to Texas and called in cops. Cops poked around, shrugged, and nuttin' changed."

Jax pinched his nose. "So you blew it up?"

"*Mais, j'mais,* no. I tapped lines, connected dots. They had so many phone scams goin', they was losing track of dem all." He was slipping deeper into his native dialect with his fury. "Tellin' old ladies they won prizes if they sent a hundred bucks to cover shipping. They even had one selling *psychic* services. Evie woulda rolled heads."

"Evie would have pulled noses and cut phone cords and taunted them to the devil. You're the one who blows up things." Actually, Evie would have looked for ghosts to spook them, but that wasn't relevant.

"Did *not* do dat, no. Me, I reported dem to the phone company. When no one did nuttin', I cut the lines, warned everyone the cops were coming, and while the bastards ran like a *cocodril* on their heels, I told Da what would happen if he ever scammed anyone again. Told him I'd reported him to the FBI, which I MBA sorta did, except no one got back to me. We got in a fight but ain't no way he can win. So he pulled a gun. He got me once before I kicked it and punched him flat. Gun went off again and hit a barrel of fireworks. Place blew. I rolled out." He huffed and glared at the cloudy sky. "Don' know if Da did, but I got threats from his phone sayin' I'd never see Ma again if I didn't leave town."

"So you left?" Jax asked in incredulity. Roark never backed down.

"Dey blew up her chickens and her car. She and Gran ordered me out. I figgered something bad was going down besides Da's griftin', and I needed reinforcements, but I'm flat busted. I hoped I could get the van, and you could connect me with one of dem para-military units, give me time to make some cash before I go back in. Someone has to protect my family, and it ain't Da."

The front door crashed open. Ariel's long brown hair flew loose down her narrow back as she cried, "*Stupid!*" and flung a phone at Jax and glared at Roark. "Speak English." A second later, she was gone, as if she hadn't been there at all.

"Want to match all your siblings against my one?" Jax asked, opening the cheap phone she'd flung.

"Mine ain't crazy, just young and stupid. Dat. . . *that* phone you got was in my jeans. Is she washing my clothes?" Roark tried to look casual and didn't snatch it back.

It didn't take a second to locate an enormous file of phone numbers. "You stole this from the call center?" he asked. From Roark's look of defeat, he gathered Roark hadn't planned on sharing. What else was he hiding?

Jax sent the file of numbers to Reuben. It wouldn't hurt to check these out. Then he glared at Roark. "You're wounded. You're not going anywhere. Besides, your family can't afford for you to get blown away in some foreign war. You have one right here to fight. I already have a reporter from New Orleans sniffing around, so you're probably right and something or someone bigger than your father's grifting is going down. Better to clear the air with friends at your back."

Roark looked alarmed. "I ain't bringing trouble down on friends! Dat. . ." He grimaced at the security camera to show he'd heard—and respected—Ariel's command. "*That's* why I ditched my phone and traveled incognito. I didn't want anyone following me."

An MIT grad, Roark knew how to speak English, probably better than the university's Boston students. But he'd hidden his brains for so long, it was second nature to slip into country boy mode. Jax flipped through the list of numbers and other stolen documents, but none were immediately comprehensible.

He didn't want to endanger Evie and Loretta by bringing Roark back to Evie's place, but he couldn't abandon his friend. He, Reuben, and Roark had been through hell together. Roark needed them now. But the only places Jax could call his own were his office and this cottage—and the cottage was rented from Loretta's trust.

He handed the burner back to Roark just as his own phone beeped again.

He could almost hear the resignation in the single image Ariel sent—the recliner in her spare bedroom.

Jax thought he might fall over in shock.

Six

"Bleak," Evie pronounced as Reuben drove the utility van up the circle drive to the Azalea Retirement Apartments in the senior citizens' complex.

A six-story high-rise of cement blocks disguised by paint, a few rose-bushes, and half-dead azaleas, the building had undoubtedly been built early in a prior century.

"It survived decades of hurricanes," Reuben countered pragmatically, parking in a lot filled with cheap SUVs, trucks, and a few sedans. "But it ain't no luxury unit, for sure."

They entered a lobby of artificial plants under fluorescent lighting. The smell of disinfectant was strong. Evie assumed that was a healthy thing, even if living with the stink had to be depressing. The receptionist at the horseshoe-shaped desk noted their arrival in a guest book and directed them to the elevators. "Miss Gump is waiting for you upstairs. Are you relations?" She eyed Reuben with curiosity.

"Nah, I'm the family ghost-buster," Reuben responded, heading straight for the elevators. "Gotta get one of them cool blasters to carry," he muttered when Evie caught up with him.

She giggled at the image of Professor Reuben in his man bun and scar tattoos carrying a ghostbuster. "Just buy a great big scary looking black bag and pretend you're Will Smith."

"Yeah, I like that. I can put my equipment in that, slap bugs all over the room. Except I'm thinking once the perp is dead, electronics don't help much. Don't know what you need me here for." He looked stoic as the elevator rose to the fourth floor.

"You distract the client with intelligent questions while I go spacey and look for auras. We'll figure out a routine once we have some practice." Evie tried to tuck a straying strand of hair back in its pin, with little success.

"I like undercover better. You shoulda left me in the van." The nerdy spy looked uncomfortable.

"You're working with *Larraine*. You are no longer invisible." The mayoral candidate was movie-star flamboyant in the eyes of their rural town.

"Man, Larraine takes up so much space, even Will Smith would be invisible around her. You, on the other hand, make me look like a drug dealer pimping an innocent."

"I'm small but not a child." Evie smacked his hard bicep, then punched the doorbell to Apartment 421. She stood straight and smiled big when the door opened.

Marlene Gump's granddaughter, Stacey, wasn't any taller or older than Evie, and she was Asian. Evie mentally smacked herself for judgmental expectations of FBI families with names like Gump and held out her hand. "Miss Gump? I'm Evangeline Malcolm Carstairs from Sensible Solutions, and this is my partner, Reuben Thompson."

Judging from Stacey's hesitation, she'd anticipated someone different as well. To her credit, she shook hands and gestured them in. "I feel foolish calling anyone about this, but I found your name in Granny's computer. I have an aunt who lives in Afterthought, so I called, and she said you'd helped her. Then I read how you caught Senator Swenson and his son and thought maybe. . ." She gestured helplessly. "I really don't want people to know if Gran was doing anything wrong. I just want to know if we're leaving things undone that she might have wanted finished."

"And if we find pots of stolen money, you want to return it to the rightful owners, right?" Reuben asked cynically, scanning the shabby apartment with a jaded eye.

"I really don't think Granny would *steal* anything." Stacey looked uncertain. "I mean, she worked with law enforcement all her life. I think maybe she just got bored? It was weird enough to find all these cell phones and computer devices scattered everywhere. . ." She gestured at a maple dining table lined with laptops and notebook computers. "But I keep finding scraps of papers with addresses and names stuffed in odd places. And utility bills and credit card statements for other people."

Reuben headed straight for the hardware. "She got a land line? Voice mail? You got all her ID here?"

Stacey's face scrunched up with doubt and concern, but she followed Reuben to explain the file folders she'd created.

Evie preferred to stay connected to the atmosphere. She was sensitive to temporal displacement, and the apartment gave her cold shivers. The hair was literally standing up on her arms. "May I look around a little?"

"Of course." Stacey held her elbows and looked a little chilly, too.

They were on the fourth floor, and it was August. The apartment would be sweltering without air-conditioning, but the air didn't seem to be blowing. Evie glanced at the extra-large thermostat. It was set on 80, the way a lot of old people did. It was way colder than that in here.

Evie started with framed photographs packed in an open box. Photos of Stacey at various ages, occasionally with her parents, she guessed. Marlene's son must be Stacey's father, judging by the purely Southern name. Mama had the Asian genes. They all looked happy. None of the images included anyone who might be granny.

The furniture was boring enough to look as if it came with the apartment. Stacey had done a good job of cleaning out toiletries and packing up clothes and dishes. Evie wandered into the bedroom, closing the door so she wouldn't be overheard. The linens were still on the bed. Poor Stacey might be staying here while she worked. Money could be tight.

This room was even colder, but Evie didn't see any evidence of an aura. She bounced on the bed and opened her third eye.

Granny Marlene popped up beside her.

Evie nearly had a heart attack and fell backward on the hard mattress. Then she glared at the translucent apparition gleefully bouncing on the bed. She had a vague impression of graying curly hair, mom jeans, a red T-shirt over a stout figure—she didn't look like ex-FBI. There she went again with the biased preconceptions.

"You did that on purpose," Evie accused.

"You actually see me!" Granny crowed. "I didn't think that was possible. We had some spooks in the agency, but they bled when pricked. I don't. I tried."

"Hilarious. At this stage, I doubt if you could lift a knife. Want to explain what you were doing? Your granddaughter is concerned."

Granny bounced. Her aura spurted with surprise as she floated near the ceiling. "Hoo, this is pretty cool. Can I go through walls? Are you doing this to me?"

Good question. Evie had nearly no experience with new ghosts and hadn't a clue. She just seemed to attract spiritual energy. Did she make the energy coalesce? She knew her ghostly encounters drained cell phone batteries. Scientific experimentation probably wasn't happening though.

Granny Marlene vanished for half a second, then re-emerged. "Wow, an empty apartment is depressing. I can't believe I wasted so much time in this dump."

Evie sighed. Her last murdered ghost had been a tempest of barely coherent fury. Looked like this one had attention problems worse than her own. "What's with all the computers?"

Granny wafted in and out a bit as she spoke words more inside Evie's head than out. "Yeah, I may have left a mess. I figured I had a few good years to make it better."

She spun around near the ceiling and looked vaguely worried, as best as a translucent coloration could. "I was hoping my son might show up. He's not here, is he?"

"Not corporeal or otherwise. He probably thinks packing up an apartment is woman's work."

"He travels. He's probably. . ." Granny gestured vaguely, then shoved off the ceiling. She floated through the closed door into the hall. Evie refused to follow. It tended to be embarrassing when people saw her talking to thin air. She flipped through the last clothes in the closet—business suits that Stacey probably meant to donate. She'd read enough detective mysteries to know to hunt through pockets, but Granny had been meticulous about cleaning them out. Or her granddaughter was. That was probably how she'd found the weird bills.

Granny floated back again. "Cute guy. Is he available?"

"Not for Stacey. He's gay. Want to give me a clue where to start? Tell me what you were investigating?" Evie pulled out a dresser to check behind it. Cobwebs.

"Bad guys, of course." Granny's aura colors reflected uncertainty again. "My memory isn't clear. I used to have a great memory."

"But you have no physical brain anymore, just leftover energy, probably because you feel as if you've left something undone." Evie had been taught to be creative since birth. Reading tarot cards and crystal balls required an understanding of human nature, which her mother had. Evie—learned auras. Both required explaining things that weren't explicable. This ghost's aura was all over the place, in rotating pastels.

"I remember! I went fishing for phishers." Granny Marlene spun about some more, then darted into the closet.

"Fishing for *fish*? For *fishermen*?" Evie hoped Granny wasn't slipping too far into the other side just yet and losing her words.

"Thieving bastards scammed what's-er-name out of her annuity check, left her eating nothing but peanut butter all year. Social Security only pays the rent."

Peanut butter and fish. Evie wasn't following. She'd ask Stacey if she knew anything about annuities.

Granny flitted back and forth, her colors now cycling through various stages of anger. One thing Evie could say for Stacey's granny, there wasn't a muddy color in her. She was clear as a rainbow.

"Who scammed what's-er-name?" Evie asked, in hopes of coherency. She'd learned from her last ghost that spirits didn't seem able to recall names.

"I had to have the housekeeper fired." Evidently agitated, she whipped back and forth faster.

"Will I find information about this in your desk? Were you murdered, by any chance?"

"Get her out." Without further warning, Granny glimmered and was gone.

Who? Stacey? Shaken, Evie returned to the front room where Stacey and Reuben were arguing over his desire to haul all the technology to his van. She wished she could stash Stacey in the van, too.

～

"Can't do this," Roark muttered, pacing Ariel's front porch. "Can't live here like the damned turtle, hiding under a rock, doing nothing." He glared at Mitch Turtle, who'd dared to poke his head out to nose his fungi dinner.

"You helped Ariel and me to uncover our real father and his killers." Jax knew this was simplistic, but he and Ariel owed Roark, and Roark needed help. *Quid pro quo.* "Why shouldn't we return the favor? You'll be doing most of the work. You and Ariel are the computer whizzes, not me. Maybe you can teach her a few things. Who knows? You need a place to stay, and she offered."

Roark ran his hand through his curls. "Mebbe wit my. . ." He glared at the security camera. "Maybe if I live out here on the porch, run an extension to keep the laptop juiced. . ." He studied the wooden porch running the length of the bungalow. "I'd need my sleeping bag."

"Or you can climb in and out the bedroom window." Amused that his non-talkative sister had sent the brash soldier into a tailspin, Jax bit back any further helpful comment when Roark's burner phone beeped.

"We can't sleep twelve hours a day, bébé!" Roark shouted at the phone.

Well, he was probably shouting at the security camera. Ariel only sent texts.

Roark held up the phone. "She says she sleeps days. I can sleep nights. No problem. What about the other eight or twelve hours? Loan me airfare to your ranch. I can handle desert."

"The ranch has no phone reception, no wi-fi, remember? Tell Reuben and Ariel what you need, and they'll help. Once you've got the goods on your dad or whoever, we can all work to put him away. When you're out of danger, you can start making money to take care of whatever needs taking care of, all right?"

"None of this is all right! I just wanted food and to hook up to the internet for an hour. How da hell did I end up in a cage?" He waved at the camera as if to erase what he said. "Sorry, bébé. But I need space."

In Afghanistan, Roark had been kept in a cage and had developed pretty severe neuroses. But comparing the bungalow to a prison was a little extreme.

"Look, Ariel obviously trusts you. That doesn't happen often. She needs help adjusting to this place as much as you need a place to stay. You won't find a better hide-out with internet connections anywhere. No one visits except Evie's family, and they won't say anything. Send a list of what you need, and we'll see that you get it. You have Reuben to be your wheels. Try it for a few days, heal, see what happens."

Jax jiggled the coins in his pocket. His job was talking people into things, not understanding how they felt about it. He just knew Ariel wouldn't have offered the recliner if she hadn't wanted to. She was like him that way. They had both been raised privileged and selfish.

33

"Food," Roark said in resignation. "That skinny sister of yours nibbles like a mouse. Make groceries, and I'll cook for her."

"I'll bring a microwave so she can heat it up at midnight. Don't think she'll sit down for a real meal," Jax warned.

"She's got a microwave. She don' need any of us for anyting. Bring extension cords and a porch shade. I'll work outside."

"It's August! I'm steaming in my shoes just standing here. You'll melt." Jax couldn't believe he'd said that to a man who had survived the plains of Afghanistan.

"You sound like Evie. Go back to shafting shysters. I got t'ings to do."

Roark let himself back inside.

Jax's phone pinged. Ariel's text read **CRAB**.

"Takes one to know one," he told her security camera.

He'd send Roark a bucket of crabs to cook, and then he'd contact a few sources about that explosion, see how the investigation was going.

He didn't want a man on a Wanted poster living in his sister's house for long.

Seven

SKINNY. ARIEL LOOKED DOWN AT HERSELF AND SHRUGGED. *So, I'm skinny. He's tall. It happens.*

She usually ate at 16:00 and started work at 17:00. She didn't have time to fix a meal if she meant to keep her schedule. Besides, she didn't want to be in the kitchen while Roark was wandering about.

She should have shut out Jax and Roark the way she usually did, let them solve their own problems. But Roark's dramatic arrival had her feeling edgy—and vulnerable—and shot her routine to hell, so she couldn't think straight. He filled the house with his explosive energies. She needed space to *think*.

She hid in her room until she heard Roark in the shower. She grabbed cheese and crackers and flavored water from the fridge and took them to her computer desk in the front room. Then she pulled the pocket door between her and the kitchen. She could do this, one baby step at a time. As Jax had said, they owed Roark big time. And she owed Jax for finding her the perfect home.

She might be a nutcase, but she didn't lack integrity. She paid her debts. Besides, she enjoyed mysteries.

She'd pulled the stolen call center phone numbers from Roark's burner phone while he was sleeping. Using the numbers, she'd begun a painstaking search. The bank account had been relatively easy to locate once she worked out the area code of outgoing numbers. There weren't many banks in that region. And once she was in one account, she could trace transactions to others.

What any of it meant was questionable. But she enjoyed watching the spiderweb develop like an intricate puzzle.

Lost in the labyrinth she was creating, she nibbled cheese and shut out the world as she'd learned to do. If Roark was still in the house, he didn't intrude on her concentration.

At 18:06, her security warned of someone on the drive. She opened the computer screen on Jax unloading bags on the bench she'd designated for deliveries, presumably for her guest, since she hadn't ordered anything. She returned to work—until Roark trotted around the house to retrieve the bags. He was back in tank top and frayed shorts, looking like a muscular, bronzed gym rat.

He thought she was skinny. Fine. She returned to tracing slimy snail trails on the internet.

She looked up again when delicious aromas emanated from the kitchen. If he kept taking up space, she could not *do* this. She needed concentration. She gritted her teeth and focused. Despite the constant battering at all her senses, she did one thing extremely well—*focus.*

At 19:25, her phone beeped with a message. **SOUPS ON**

The back door slammed. Now she understood the need to throw something, anything, to express frustration. Except she kept her desk free of clutter, and throwing a monitor wasn't happening.

It was hours too late for dinner. Setting her jaw, she ignored the text and continued working—except her security alarm went off again. She flicked on the screen, revealing the bastard slipping around the house to the front door. Did he think she'd abandon her desk just because he'd *fixed dinner*? Would he barge in on the front room, thinking she was in the kitchen, eating?

He found an angle on the porch where the camera didn't reach, and she lost track of him, blast the wretched beast. That was *his* security installation on the porch. Had he planned that hidden corner? Was he spying on her even now?

She couldn't take the distraction of fearing he'd barge in on her. She picked up her phone and texted. **EAT AT 23:00**

He'd have to use his own equipment until then.

Some of these bank transfers were leading to *Savannah*. She couldn't stop now.

~

EVIE CLIMBED THE ATTIC STAIRS TO THE NEWLY FINISHED GARRET bedroom Loretta had insisted on. They'd used their combined allowances from Loretta's trust to add insulation and walls in the turret and installed a window air conditioner. Loretta was still deciding on décor, but the room was currently painted spring green because Evie found paint on sale and couldn't stand white walls.

The kid was happily ensconced in a maple poster bed she'd discovered in the jumble of furniture stored in one of the Victorian's packed bedrooms. A stuffed spider now hung from a bedpost, and a battered magenta teddy bear slept on the pillow. Instead of a nightstand, the kid had added a square oak, spindle-legged table she'd stacked with books.

Loretta's designer bedroom in her parents' home had been a pink fantasy out of Disney. She could have anything she wanted now, but with the independence Evie offered, she was establishing her own distinctive style.

"Don't make me come back up here to turn out your lights." Evie kissed her ward's head. "And you should get used to turning them off early to practice for school nights."

Loretta happily wriggled into her mattress and sheets. "Reuben fixed the lamp so it goes off at ten. I'm good. I like listening to the birds when the sun comes up."

"I hope that means you turn off the a/c if you're leaving the window open!" Evie had never had air conditioning, because she'd never had money. Paying for cool air seemed extravagant.

"It goes off on its own. Quit worrying. I want to finish this chapter before the lights go out."

Having been royally dismissed, Evie jogged downstairs and out to the back porch, where Jax and Reuben were settled in with drinks and nibbles. They used to do this in the cellar rec room, but since Roark had left, the energy had changed. And with Loretta tucked so far away, Evie preferred being able to listen for doors opening and closing, even if the mosquitoes ate them alive on the porch.

"Do we need to check on Stacey?" she asked as she grabbed a cold drink and settled into her aunt's ancient Adirondack chair. "Granny was most emphatic that we get her out."

Reuben gestured carelessly. "She said she'd leave after the rest of the boxes got carted off. She ain't believing in warnings from beyond. I told her those computers might be dangerous, but she's looking at selling them."

Evie reached for a chip and fretted about what she should have said.

"I've started tracking the names and addresses Granny left behind." Reuben sipped his beer and snatched a tortilla chip from the package. "A couple belong to women who've reported their identities stolen by phishers."

"Granny's ghost mentioned fishers, which sounds grammatically incorrect. Shouldn't it be fishermen or fisher people or something?" Ensconced in pillows, Evie sipped her iced tea. She was trying not to worry about Stacey sleeping alone in that apartment.

"Get the girl a real computer," Reuben complained, digging into the salsa Evie had made with the bushel of tomatoes one of her dog-walking clients had insisted she take.

"Phishers, with a PH," Jax explained from his matching chair, sans pillows. "They're internet scammers who send emails from Nigerian lawyers to steal your bank account or who fake company logos to get your passwords. I'd like to think they're feeding foreign villages and spreading the wealth, but Robin Hood doesn't exist."

Reuben snorted. "Phone scammers are usually American, because they need to speak good English, or what passes for it. Internet scams only require a modicum of grammar and an ability to copy graphics and can be anywhere. Those of us out on the darknet have slipped video bugs into some of their computers. They're just bro's smoking their assets or carting automatics in Caddies. Ain't no honor among thieves."

"You can *video* the villains?" Evie asked in incredulity, stopping before shoving a chip into her mouth. "Why can't you turn them in to the police?"

"Yeah, you wanna explain how you hacked a computer and took illegal videos? Tell 'er, lawyer man."

"Hacking is illegal. Evidence obtained by illegal means is not admissible in court. And the worst of the cockroaches are in foreign countries where US law can't touch them. Some of them have armed gangs for protection. If Granny was chasing those jerks, she was getting senile."

"*Granny* could have been the phisher who stole the IDs," Reuben reminded them.

"No way, her aura was crystal clear." Evie sipped her drink and tried to imagine how an old lady could use identities stolen off whatever the darknet might be.

Jax grimaced and set aside his beer. "Get the autopsy report and assure her granddaughter she died in her sleep or whatever and give it up."

"Stacey said her granny had a heart condition. The doc saw nothing suspicious, but they have to send her to the coroner 'cause no one was with her when she died, and the body was there a while. Happens all the time in those places." Reuben filled a bowl with chips, covered them with salsa, and added shredded cheese.

"Stacey could probably sue the home if they were supposed to have staff checking on her," Jax suggested.

Evie loved his intelligence and integrity, and he was a hero in bed, but he simply couldn't lose his uptight lawyer attitude. She poked his ankle with her bare toe. "Granny's ghost mentioned someone whose annuity check was stolen and a housekeeper she got fired. There was a Laura Evans who lived in the Azalea Apartments who complained about not receiving her pension money, and a housekeeper by the name of Carmela Jones was fired around the same time. If Granny mentioned both incidents, I'll guess there's a connection—and not a Nigerian one. I am not completely clueless. I can ask questions."

"Those old ladies talk like nobody's business," Reuben agreed. "But they got sharp memories. Laura Evans died this past year. And there ain't no Carmela Jones in any database anywhere. The social security number she used was a fake. Cleaning service didn't work too hard verifying it. Half their staff are illegals. So Granny might have complained, and the cleaning service fired a Jones, but the home has no record of it."

"And that doesn't explain all Granny's computers or the utility bills and bank statements of strangers. The pension annuity case might have been the reason she went over the edge and put her investigative skills to work, but how's an eighty-year-old retired FBI agent supposed to hack hackers, if that's what she was doing?" Evie nibbled her chip and tried to work her head around it.

"Lawfully," Jax suggested. "What did you find when you traced the names on all the bills her granddaughter found?"

"Far's we can tell, they're real people," Reuben responded. "Some died recently. Some are in Alzheimer homes. All of them got hacked or phished, and their info is floating out there on the darknet for pennies. I haven't traced them all. Weird thing is, Granny used VPN on all those devices. That means she didn't want anyone tracing *her*. How many grannies know to do that?"

"What's VPN?" Evie hated proving she was dumber than grannies.

"Virtual Private Network," both Reuben and Jax replied, showing off.

Jax did the explaining, keeping it simple. "You install it on your computer to keep websites and so forth from knowing where you are. It's used a lot more in other countries where they use it to fool networks into thinking they're in Australia instead of Asia, for instance."

"Huh." Evie nibbled at a chip but couldn't think of any good reason to use such a thing. But then, she had nothing to hide.

Reuben plowed his way through his chips. "Maybe we should pay some visits to the local addresses. Why'd she need real people? Not making much sense unless she was scamming."

Evie lit up. "There were a few Savannah addresses in there. Loretta's birthday is coming up. We can combine shopping and ghost hunting. I can take Loretta to the stores. Stacey gave me keys to the apartment. I can go back and see if Granny's ghost will talk some more. And we can check out some addresses while we're there, see what kind of places they are, and do some snooping."

Jax reached over and knuckled her head. "Google maps, Madame Psychic. Just look up the address and zoom in. An internet search will probably turn up neighborhood statistics and networks. Reuben can do that with one hand behind his back."

Evie smacked his invading fingers away. "How do you know this stuff? Shouldn't you be defending the innocent or something?"

"Until I met you, criminal fraud was my specialty. I kept R&R around for the hard work. I'm trying to stick to less dangerous stuff for Loretta's sake. You might want to try the same."

Evie grimaced. Much as she adored her macho man, she and Jax would never be on the same page. They came from different worlds, with different expectations. *Security* and *safety* weren't in her lexicon. "Not too many months ago, you thought me and my family were the frauds. If anyone can expose scammers, it ought to be me. I know how people think, and I can almost literally see right through the crooks. I want to go to Savannah. *You* stay here and babysit. Or I can take Loretta with us and go shopping."

"She's got a point, lawyer man. You grok bankers and brokers. We grok con artists and scammers. It would be cool if we could track some phishers to their nest and let the cops loose on them. Barring legal means, if we find anything, I can use ransomware to freeze computers and hack criminal bank accounts. No danger there. I'll go down and check out these addresses. Google don' know everything. Have the kid ready in the morning." Reuben unbent his lengthy frame from the porch steps and tossed his empty beer can at the recycle bin.

"You could at least wait until you have the autopsy report on the FBI agent," Jax shouted after him. "If the old lady was murdered, the crooks might be more than scammers! And look how Roark's fishing expedition turned out."

"Roark was dealing with his dad. Not the same." Reuben disappeared into the darkness. The doors to the cellar creaked and slammed after him.

Evie leaned over and patted Jax's hand. "Would you like it if we told *you* what cases to take?"

He growled, finished his beer, and appeared to think about it. Tossing the can, he stood, grabbed her by the waist, and lifted her from the chair. "I'd like to think I'd not take a dangerous case if you asked it of me, but that's theoretical. I just don't like you going off without me. Reuben is more careful than Roark, but his standards aren't mine."

Evie wrapped her arms around him and leaned her head against his shoulder. "Give me credit for brains to match yours, okay? I may not have book learning, but I know things you don't. And I'll never take chances with Loretta."

He squeezed her close. "I may know that intellectually, but sometimes, the gut gnaws. And I've seen you in action, remember? I don't want you jumping any more bad guys!"

"I only jumped you because you were cute." She kissed his ear, released him, and dragged him inside.

Moving Loretta to the attic left the second floor nicely unoccupied. And once Jax had moved into her bedroom, he'd bought a room air conditioner so they didn't swelter on hot summer nights. Maybe she'd keep him a little longer.

Her life had certainly improved since he'd showed up last spring. She just worried that he'd give up on her eccentric lifestyle once he recovered from the blows the Universe had delivered recently. *She* might bounce back, but Loretta was starting to count on having parents again.

"We ought to clean out the master suite in the tower, leave your room for guests," Jax suggested as they entered her childhood bedroom.

"What, and leave me no pine tree to climb down?" But Evie's heart did a little dance. Apparently, he hadn't tired of her eccentricity yet. Cleaning out Aunt Val's old room would take an army.

Eight

EVIE STUFFED HER WEEK'S EARNINGS FROM HER MOTHER'S
Psychic Solutions Agency in her back pocket. "We'll buy Loretta some school
clothes, maybe take the trolley around and see some sights—"

"Ghosts. You want to go downtown to see if you can find ghosts." Evie's
mother didn't look up from her tarot spread. "Any kid stores down there will
be pricey."

Evie picked up Psy, the Siamese cat, and bumped chins with him.
"Loretta is a millionaire! She can afford a few cute outfits if she likes." But
yeah, downtown was a lot more interesting than a shopping mall. "Does
Aunt Ellen have a Cadillac parked in her driveway yet?"

Mavis sniffed. "The contest said she had to pay a $250 delivery fee. She's
actually debating it. She can't even *see* well enough to drive. Honestly, I think
her brains departed with her eyesight."

The wind chimes over the door tinkled, and a stout matron wearing her
Sunday best—on a weekday morning—marched in.

Psy growled what sounded like *nassssty*. Evie's cousin Iddy, the vet, had
been trying to teach him to communicate, but cat minds were tricky. *Nasty*
could mean she had smelly perfume. Or *namaste*, for all Evie knew.

Recognizing the president of the church ladies, she agreed with the *nasty*,
though, and thought maybe she'd scamper out the back, until Mrs. White
spoke.

43

"We are having a mayoral rally at six for Henry in the reception hall. We simply cannot allow our town to be represented by a freak. We need to support our local businessmen. You'll be there, won't you?" Mrs. White demanded.

"Hank isn't a freak, dear," Mavis said absent-mindedly, still studying her cards. "But I agree that he's not much of a businessman." Evie's mother had a mean streak she hid behind her docile, gray-haired, caftan-draped persona. She was deliberately misinterpreting the message.

Hank Williams was Larraine's opponent in the mayoral race. The ancient hardware store owner was decidedly not the freak to whom the bigot referred.

Mrs. White looked in danger of losing her pleasant face. "I'm not talking about *Henry*. I'm talking about that hairdresser clown who will make Afterthought a laughingstock if it becomes mayor!"

It, nice. Evie rolled her eyes and bit her tongue. She knew better than to argue with people wearing auras so narrow it was a wonder they didn't suffocate from their own intolerance.

"Gloria is the only hairdresser I know. She's not running for mayor, and I don't believe she's a clown. Even if she was, she's a very good businessperson." Being in the crystal-ball-reading business, Mavis specialized in turning conversations on their heads. She peered over the top of her half-frame reading glasses to close her inane argument. "And really, dear, no one on this planet cares who's mayor here except us."

Marta White turned a few shades of purple and swiveled to confront Evie. "No one in their right minds will vote for a freak. Make sure your mother is there tonight. We'll put an end to this nonsense."

She huffed out.

Biting back a grin, Evie picked up one of the *Larraine Ward for Mayor* posters lying on the counter and taped it to the edge, facing the door so even the oblivious could see it. Larraine's photo showed a stylishly dressed, slender woman of mixed race, wearing a magnificent feathered aqua hat to match her aqua gown and a set of pearls bigger than any Marta White could claim.

Larraine owned the largest business in the county and had been born a Larry.

"Will you take these handouts to the meeting tonight?" Evie asked, knowing her mother's warped mind.

"Larraine promised to send over some without the photo, just listing her objectives. I'll leave those. The promise to bring a pharmacy to town will persuade half the congregation. Hank doesn't even have a platform. The cards are looking propitious." Mavis swept the deck off the counter and tapped them into a stack, then scratched behind Psy's ears. "Don't freak out that poor child by chasing ghosts, please. You know what happened the last time you did that."

"I'm not three any longer, Mom. The funny-looking guy with the eye patch is being hit by cars. I'll have a harder time controlling Loretta from complaining about the black bubbles of the people trying to con us into buying timeshares or whatever. Have fun with the church ladies." Evie skipped out before receiving any more useless parental advice. Mavis might occasionally glimpse the future, but a parent, she was not.

Which was where Evie got her lack of parenting skills. After her three-year-old self had darted into traffic chasing the pirate ghost, the city police had wanted to charge Mavis with child neglect. So she'd brought Evie back here. They'd survived. Loretta was smart. She would, too.

As soon as Evie walked back to the house, Loretta skipped down the stairs with her hair streaming loose down her back. "Can I have my hair cut, too? I'm too old to wear pigtails."

"We need appointments for haircuts and can do that right here in town. Why don't I stick a clip in it? Let's go back to the kitchen. There is bound to be something in the junk drawer." Evie waved at Reuben emerging from the cellar. "We're ready. Just give us a second."

"A second isn't ready," he retorted, loping for the van.

"Wonder what set his grouch off?" Evie yanked open a kitchen drawer, found one of Mavis's long hair clips, rolled Loretta's mousy brown hair up and clipped it in place. "Okay?"

The kid touched it dubiously but nodded. "But I still have bangs. Hermione doesn't have bangs."

"Hermione has mousy brown hair. You want a dye job as well?" Evie didn't bother locking the door as they ran out to the van. If anyone wanted to steal Great-Aunt Val's Monkees' album, she was all for it.

Loretta actually looked more like Harry Potter with her black-framed glasses, but Evie knew better than to suggest that to an eleven-year-old on the cusp of twenty.

Her ward actually seemed to be pondering the dye job.

"Think about new glasses frames. We need to find you a local optometrist." Evie diverted the kid as they climbed into the two-seat utility

PATRICIA RICE

van—not a kid-friendly place by any means. Maybe she *ought* to think about safety and get a real van with seat belts.

Loretta climbed in back to play with her techno-toys and Reuben revved up the engine.

"Where you want to do your shopping?" he asked, steering for the interstate.

"We should stop by Ariel's and see how she's doing," Loretta called from the back.

"What, you want to find Roark's body in the driveway with his throat cut?" Evie asked. "Let Jax referee that brawl."

Reuben was uncomfortably silent. He was a nerd who didn't talk much anyway, but Evie was sensitive to vibrations. She tuned in her third eye and read a lot of muddy water playing havoc with his aura. She trolled through looking for a source, but Reuben mixed his chakras badly.

"Are you upset because I'm in this seat instead of Roark?" she guessed, keeping her voice down so Loretta wouldn't hear.

"Nah, ain't upset. This a business."

"But Roark is supposed to be part of the business. He's the one you usually do security detail with. I'm not a tech like him." Evie watched his root chakra and solar plexus pulse with grays. Huh. Dented self-esteem and. . . she wasn't certain, but his courage was shaken.

"This job don't need no tech. We be fine. Just tell me where to let you and tadpole off."

Evie raised her eyebrows. "You're thinking to check out those addresses alone?"

He shot her a look of disgust. "This here van is a highly specialized piece of equipment designed to look innocuous. You think you and the tadpole peering out windows gonna reflect that goal? I know what I'm doing. You go shopping, and text me when you're done."

Ah, Evie began to see the nuances here. Roark was the badass who usually drove the van and handled the hardware. Reuben's skill was with the software, hiding in the back. And they had him acting as a chauffeur. Pretty huge come-down for a PhD in engineering.

"Y'know, I could get all uppity and women's rightsy and complicate your life right now," she warned. "But I'm a practical person. Loretta needs training and school clothes. You don't need a lot of help parking the van and

46

doing your thing just to collect info. But we need to stay connected. You can tap phone lines, but I tap lifelines. We have to work together."

He grimaced but eventually nodded. "I had to beat Roark up a few times before he got that cooperation thing. We'll figure it out." He cast her another dubious look. "You're *training* the tadpole?"

"If you have talent, you have to learn to use it or it goes to waste. I don't know a whole lot about what Loretta does, but I know to ask questions so she can work things out on her own." Which was essentially what Evie had done. Mavis couldn't read auras. She'd freaked when Evie had seen ghosts—and hauled her back to Afterthought where the rest of their weird family lived and could help.

"You need textbooks," Reuben decided. "A witch library with how-to manuals."

"I'm told there are such things, but if you haven't noticed, we're a little isolated. We're poor and not much inclined to travel either, so I have no idea where to find a book on witches. Our library certainly doesn't carry them." Evie had always wondered if there were others like her and her family in the world, but she'd not spent much time hunting.

"And you don't waste energy telling the world about your weirdnesses, so no other witch has got a reason to look for you. Makes sense. But we have to come to terms with advertising our skills, so you'd better be thinking about it."

"If the world wasn't so full of whackos, I'd hire myself out as a ghost-buster. But just mention the spirit world, and everyone who ever lost a loved one would be on my doorstep, and all the cynics would be poking fun. It's a tough balance." Occasionally, she did actually give the subject a thought.

"So, Sensible Solutions, it is, without explaining how we do what we do. Works for me, 'cause I ain't explaining what I do."

"You have to stop the illegal stuff sometime, don't you? How much of what you do will get you arrested?" Evie had spent a few nights fretting about the difference between hacking for information and hacking to steal valuables.

Reuben shrugged. "Unless I steal government information and post it on the web, they're not coming after me. Far bigger fish to fry, and they're lousy fishers."

Evie laughed. "With an F or a PH? Either way, it's good to know. But you're walking a fine line. I don't want you crossing where it's uncomfortable."

"That's a fine line too. Tossing those trolls attacking Larraine is probably illegal as hell, but I feel real good about it."

Remembering her tendency to trespass, Evie understood that. "Good thing we have our own lawyer."

She hoped Jax would stay around. Might depend on how much trouble they got into. Or how often.

~

WORKING WITH SOMEONE ELSE'S COMPUTERS WAS BEYOND frustrating. Roark didn't want to mess with Ariel's obsessive controls, but setting up his software in her computers required tinkering with the innards. . .

He needed to be in the van. Or back in the cellar where he and Reuben had set up a whole control room. His laptop had a ton of RAM, but he needed the speed of multiple processors.

And it was almost two o'clock. Ariel would wake shortly. *Merde.*

With most of his programs transferred from his laptop into one of Ariel's computers, he finished a data run, closed down, and logged out. He could hear the shower running, so he limped for the kitchen.

It was like living with a spook. A spooked spook. Like a fragile fawn, she shied away anytime he came near. Jax had explained her disabilities, but Roark wasn't a tip-toe kind of person. He respected her difference. He just couldn't handle it.

Until he could dig his family out of whatever hole they'd fallen into, he had to.

He made some of the funky herbal tea that Ariel liked, fried an egg, set it on some toast, and left it on her computer desk. She ought to eat before going to work.

It was too early to hit the sack. He'd have to use this time for collating data. But eventually he'd have to set up a VPN to see if Da's scammers had set up again. For that, he'd need a credit card.

That problem rumbled around in the back of his mind while he worked over the data collected so far. The porch was steamy, but the shade allowed him to see his monitor. He'd learned to work like this in Afghanistan. He could do it, even if he didn't like it.

He heard Ariel enter the front room. Resentfully, he tossed some slugs at the pampered, greedy turtle poking its head from his little house. Turtles ought to eat vegetables and feed themselves.

He crosschecked the list of phone bank calls against any that went to his father and brothers and removed those to one side of the matrix. The idiots knew nothing about security.

That still left him with hundreds of victims to identify.

He was lining up the phone numbers Ariel had related to bank accounts when he heard footsteps inside and the front door opened. Ariel had tied all her long sable hair with a zip tie. In one lush swoop, it fell over breasts concealed by a white shirt when she set an iced glass of tea on his makeshift desk.

Saying nothing, she returned inside. A text message followed. **BANK CROOKS**

At the same time, an email appeared in his computer mailbox. Roark sipped his icy drink, opened the email, and downloaded a matrix even more elaborate than his own.

He was more interested in the fact that the autistic angel had lowered herself to bringing him a cold drink than in the complicated intersections of banks and crooks. He assumed these names were *crooks*. Where did she get that language? Old movies?

He ran a few of the names through his networks, and his eyes nearly crossed.

She'd literally meant *bank* crooks. Half these names were associated with the banks in the region where his father operated. Leave it to Da to corrupt bank officials.

Nine

JAX SPENT THE MORNING WORRYING ABOUT EVIE AND LORETTA loose in Savannah. Reuben didn't have a caretaking bone in his body. The engineering nerd was all about the goal. That was great in a work environment—not so much around kids and danger-prone females.

As he finished up a basic contract for one of his clients, he tried to convince himself he was being sexist. Evie wasn't helpless by any means. She'd proved that often enough over these last—what?—five months or so. She didn't do things the way he did was all.

She was half his size and twice as breakable.

He gritted his teeth and shot the document over to his client. He jotted down his billable hours and wished for an intern to do the basic grunt work. Writing wills and contracts was way below his pay grade.

He didn't earn enough to pay an intern or even a secretary. Suing the former mayor put serious dents in his ability to attract paying clients. Suing a company owned by powerful politicians for unpaid royalties on his father's patents occupied too much of his time. He couldn't eat personal satisfaction. He needed to be thinking of expanding his business, not about Evie.

Considering taking lunch with the courthouse crowd, Jax checked the tracer app on Loretta's phone. The responsibility of taking care of a kid worth millions weighed on his conscience.

She was apparently right where Evie had promised to take her—an expensive children's boutique on the edge of the historic district. They'd probably do lunch next, and then. . . Evie would almost certainly take Loretta ghost hunting.

He buzzed Reuben. "Bored yet?"

"These are my people, bro," Reuben replied with a hint of puzzlement. "Granny was stealing the identities of middle-class ladies like my mom, living in those 60s housing developments with big houses and yards and broken-down fences and high taxes. Does that even make sense?"

"Little old ladies in big houses have pensions and savings accounts and no mortgage. Makes perfect sense, especially if they're widows. Rich ladies have brokers and lawyers and probably hungry families guarding their assets."

"But these ones are all white. I can't go in there and start asking questions without them calling the cops. I'm not picking up any signal from any of them either. No wi-fi, no phone calls. Maybe they're all dead."

"In which case, you need to get your ass outta there. But think about it— how old are these women? In their eighties like Granny Gump? Most of their friends and half their families have probably passed on. Who are they going to call? They're unlikely to own computers and are probably not driving or socializing much more than church on Sunday. They're lonely. If they had anyone watching over them, they wouldn't be prone to phone scams."

"Huh. Well, guess I'll go get lunch and wait for Evie to get herself in trouble. How long you think that'll take?"

"Long enough to feed Loretta, figure out Uber, and head for Granny's place," Jax calculated.

"She doesn't have a credit card for Uber."

"Loretta does. Go eat lunch with them. I'm going to touch base with Roark. If you see they're heading for trouble, let me know. We can be there in an hour."

"Yeah, drag Gator Man outta his funk and put him to work. I'm on that, boss." Reuben clicked off.

Jax wasn't Reuben's boss anymore. He wasn't anyone's boss. They were all having difficulty adjusting to civilian life and domesticity.

That didn't mean he wanted to return to the military and blow things up. But nine to five didn't suit any of them.

He started researching elder fraud. It didn't hurt to keep his hand in.

∼

"You have a good eye for what works for you," the salesperson cooed as Loretta emerged from the dressing room.

Evie translated that to *You look like a Goth rocker from a 90s horror flick, but I have bills to pay.*

Well-attuned to lies, Loretta turned to Evie for confirmation of her choice.

Evie held up a silky T-shirt with sparkles. "I'd go with red and black, or maybe even more daring, pink and black, for the wow factor. But you know me, I like color. And if you want torn jeans, we can buy them at the thrift store." And donate the enormous difference in price.

Evie found tight black capris with sparkly blue designs at the hem and added them to the stack. "No one will have anything like these."

"They won't go with red or pink." Loretta marched determinedly to the shirt rack for her size. "This will. This rocks." She pulled out a glittery blue tank top.

Evie mentally punched the air. The kid was finally becoming a kid and not a boarding school escapee. "Not colorful, but it goes with your dark hair." And Loretta's pansy-blue, indigo-child eyes, another place Evie wasn't going in front of the sales clerk.

After a little more trial and error, Loretta emerged from the shop with two casual school outfits and one nice Sunday dress—in navy, with silver stars.

"Shoes. I need shoes now." Loretta skipped eagerly along the shopping street.

"Food. I need food now. We'll look up shoe styles and stores while we eat." Evie led her to a café she'd already looked up, one high on organics and low on grease. This parenting business wasn't too difficult with Google as friend.

"Combat boots!" Loretta crowed over her chicken sandwich on a whole wheat bun, scrolling through a website. "In red!"

"Kiss is dead, or should be," Evie muttered, doing a hasty search. "High tops, in any color you want. They won't weigh you down if you have to run."

"Didn't think of that." Loretta went back to scrolling.

"Hey look, the grouch has found us." Evie waved at Reuben, looking very cosmopolitan in his blazer and man bun.

He placed his order at the to-go counter, then sauntered over to join them. "You win. Old ladies ain't me."

"Whereas old ladies are my bread and butter. The bad guys *stealing* from old ladies are you. We're learning." Evie nibbled at her tomato and mozzarella panini. She needed to buy some of this yummy cheese to use at home. "We're buying shoes first. Can you stand it?"

"They got my size? I been told my military dress ain't socially acceptable." Reuben swiped Loretta's untouched water glass and drained it.

Evie showed him the website for the discount store where Loretta had found the shoes she wanted. "I think there's an outlet nearby."

"Yeah, that works. I'm not dishing out my savings for pricey stuff." He nodded at Loretta. "You're a smart bubble witch. At those prices, you can have a pair in every color."

Loretta beamed. The kid needed family to help her learn normal—well, as normal as Evie and Company could be.

When Reuben's lunch was ready, they paid their bill and, carrying Loretta's bags, ambled to the van. As he drove them to the shopping center containing the shoe store, Evie scrolled through the notes and photos he'd taken. Granny's fake identity addresses were unexceptional to the point of boring. They still had time to explore more. Or go to Granny's.

An hour later, they emerged from the shoe store carrying three more bags.

"Business-like," Reuben was insisting as Evie continued her protests. "You can't wear ratty Keds everywhere."

"Red and black are cool colors," Loretta said soothingly, much as Evie had done with her earlier. "And you'll be able to run faster in comfort soles."

Evie almost choked on laughter. "Brat. I will not be running in Easy Spirit pumps. You just liked the name. And I'm paying you back."

Loretta's credit card had been maxed out with the day's shopping. Evie's pocket cash hadn't extended to cover both lunch and shoes.

"Carrot top will save them for good and not wear them," Reuben warned. "You'll have to hide the Keds."

They bickered like family all the way to the Azalea Garden Apartments. Evie thought Granny might be safer for Loretta than knocking on doors of strangers. "Training time, kid. You'll have to tell me if ghosts have bubbles."

They signed in at the lobby and took the elevator up to Marlene Gump's apartment. Reuben had actually remembered to bring a duffel for loading up all the devices Stacey had been reluctant to let go earlier. He'd talked her into it somehow.

"If you've already downloaded everything on her computers, what more can you discover if you take the devices back with us?" Evie thought they probably should have consulted Jax about liability clauses or something formal when removing expensive property.

"I didn't back up the entire system, just the documents. I should trace the history of usage, dig out passwords, see if I can trace her VPN calls. And I didn't back up the phones." Reuben sounded slightly disgruntled as he started to unlock the door.

The knob turned in his hand before he even inserted the key.

Urgently, he shoved Evie and Loretta against the wall. Staying to one side and looking like an action movie superstar, he kicked open the door with the side of his foot. Staying out of range of the opening, they waited. Nothing happened.

Reuben peered inside and cursed.

Evie peered around him, then pushed past.

The apartment had been ransacked. Granny's ghost was flinging herself in and out of walls near the ceiling. And Stacey Gump screamed against a rag in her mouth and rattled the chair to which she'd been tied.

HAVING WORKED OUT ARIEL'S COMPULSIVE SCHEDULE, ROARK had a crab salad and crusty hot bread waiting for her at four o'clock. He slipped out the back door before she opened the pocket door into the kitchen.

He listened on the back step as she exclaimed in what he hoped was pleasure, before he trotted around to the front. He'd run his laptop charger through the front window to a spare outlet inside. If he had the tools, he could run a wire through the wall and add an outside outlet, but he hoped he wouldn't be here long enough to need it.

A porch fan would be great to have, as well, but he settled for a battery operated one Evie had sent over. Her family junkyard of an attic had a little of everything.

He had to decide on an approach to shut down his father's re-opened phone farm. It would be most excellent if he could also retrieve the money of the victims, but that was secondary. Preventing Da from robbing anyone else and keeping his siblings out of prison had priority. And then he'd figure out who at the crooked bank was laundering the ill-gotten gains because his da was a clueless loser.

The sticking point here was that his expertise was computers and the internet, not phone lines and snail mail. His da's operation was way past old-fashioned but effective in scamming the naïve who still answered phones and believed anything anyone told them.

How had his father's operation generated phone numbers if they didn't access the darknet? Mail phishing, most likely. All Roark had to work with were the phone numbers of the victims and the bank account where the stolen money was funneled. He really needed to know more about the operation, but his brothers hadn't learned much about the financial end in their brief time there.

If he assumed they were using snail mail to compile phone numbers, then Da's crew probably stuck to simple contest and psychic scams that involved physical assets like checks and cards. Did they wipe checks to change the amounts? How were they using the credit card numbers? Buying gift cards? That and money orders were the usual. Once the thieves had those, the money was gone and there was no getting it back.

A regular deposit of money orders and suspicious-looking checks would alert any law-abiding bank clerk, but they'd obviously bribed at least one.

His da was practically running a community-wide mafia. Damn.

He wasn't used to prioritizing. He preferred running in with guns blazing. That hadn't worked so well this time. He should have known his da had more than one scheme running. But who knew it was illegal fireworks?

He'd already hacked the local police to see what they were making of the explosion. They had found no bodies and were calling it accidental. His grandma had probably told his ma that he was alive. No one had reported him missing. Sweet, da, real sweet. That meant they were gunning for him discreetly.

Ariel texted a polite **THANK YOU** for the lunch he'd left. The kid had been brought up right, with rich adopted parents and all the education and therapy money could buy—quite a contrast to his own upbringing. But she was an even bigger mess than he was.

Before he could work out a plan of attack, his dumb phone buzzed with Jax's number. "Yeah?"

"Evie and Reuben have encountered a situation. They can probably handle it, but I'm done for the day. You want to take a break and go with me?"

"As long as I don't have to get near no cops."

"I can't promise no cops. I'm pretty sure Evie called them already. But Reuben has the van. You can hide."

"Evie and cops that ain't your local sheriff? This ought to be interesting. Count me in."

Roark knew Ariel would work half the night and not even know he was gone, but he emailed her anyway. She didn't have to look at email if she didn't want to. He kinda wished she wanted to, but that was just loneliness talking. Once he had his family straightened out, all would be good.

Jax roared up on his Harley a little while later and handed him a helmet. Ariel hadn't responded to the email. Roark felt no guilt in leaving her. She was a force sufficient unto herself.

He was just happy to get out of prison.

Ten

"This simply isn't possible," the administrator of the senior living home, Lucy Murkowski, wailed. "We have security!"

Evie left Mrs. Murkowski and the police to work out how the thieves broke in. Loretta and Reuben were up to something with security cameras and bugs. She'd ask later. With the scene finally settling down, she took a detour down the hall and out of sight.

She bounced on the bed as she had before and opened her mind.

Granny sank down beside her. Brown muddied her formerly translucent root chakra. "I told you to get my granddaughter out."

"And Stacey's just like you and wouldn't listen," Evie countered. "I can't kidnap her. What can you tell me about the men who did this?"

Resembling a chubby, gray-haired gnome in her red sweater, Granny bounced and ended upside-down over the closet doors. She shoved off with her feet and hit the opposite wall before floating back down. Granny definitely had a bad case of ADHD. She made Evie feel normal.

"Don't know them. Never saw them before. I can't believe the stupid scumbag worked out who I am. The maid must have said something." She darted through the wall, presumably to check on Stacey.

The maid she got fired? Spirit energy was worse at remembering names than Evie. She tried to imagine ways of calming a hyper ghost, but she'd never been successful in calming herself. When Granny returned, Evie immediately asked, "*He* who? Who is behind this?"

"He keeps changing his ISP. I don't know. If I knew, he'd be in jail."

Dang, nothing was ever easy. Hearing Loretta calling for her, Evie tried one more time. "Is there anything you can tell me that might lead to whoever is behind this?"

"He uses illegals." Granny bounced out again.

This time, Evie followed her back to the main room where the director was still wringing her hands. Fiftyish, a dyed blonde with fake lashes and fake nails but an aura of compassion and bewilderment, Evie classified Lucy Murkowski under useless.

Granny snorted inside her head, confirming Evie's opinion. "Did she even mention the security cameras?"

"Reuben, did Mrs. Gump have security cameras, can you tell?" Evie tried to look qualified and efficient, but she'd worn comfortable clothes for shopping. Capris and T-shirt weren't businesslike.

Reuben gave her the evil eye, climbed on a chair, and removed a small camera from a kitchen cabinet. He stuck his finger through the hole in the back of the cabinet overlooking the dining area so she could see how it worked. So, he'd known and hadn't said anything. Danged secretive spy.

The policeman taking notes looked equally annoyed. "Why didn't anyone mention a camera?"

"Or all the others," Granny muttered. "Your guy knows where they are, doesn't he?"

Evie nodded in case Marlene didn't hear her mental answer. Spies liked to keep things close.

"The perps took the devices the cameras are connected to." Reuben handed the one over. "This might have a small memory chip but the backup is gone."

"The Azalea Apartments have security cameras in the corridors," the director said, brightening. "I'll call Fred, our security chief. He can tell you more about them."

To give him credit, the policeman didn't roll his eyes or swear at not being told this earlier. Or maybe he should have *asked* earlier. But this wasn't exactly a CSI scenario.

Loretta looked ready to bounce like Granny's ghost with the need to speak, but she'd wisely chosen not to mention bubbles. Yet. She was learning.

Granny's granddaughter rubbed her hands against her worn jeans and looked defeated. Evie gathered from her aura that she was angry and disappointed. Stacey had planned on selling the laptops. That didn't sound good for covering the costs of their investigation.

"Will insurance cover the loss? We have photographs of the equipment as proof of what is missing," Evie suggested to no one in particular.

Stacey brightened considerably.

Leaving the others to argue over insurance, Evie gestured for Loretta to follow her back to the bedroom. "All right, what are you seeing? In simple words, please."

Loretta bounced on the bed. Granny Marlene popped up, observing from the dresser—although floating a few inches above.

"Mrs. Murkowski has a weird bubble. It's a healthy color, but it keeps twisting up."

"Maybe when she lies?" Evie suggested. Teaching an Indigo child who sees things no one else can was a challenge. She could only go by her own experience.

"Maybe. It's not a big bubble, but I think she means well." Loretta kicked her legs so she could admire the new high-tops she'd worn out of the shoe store. "Stacey's bubble is sorta small. Does that mean she's not generous?"

"Or has lived a confined life?"

Granny snorted inside Evie's head. "My son and his wife made damned sure the poor kid led a narrow life. That's why I left everything to her. Maybe she can stretch her wings now."

Wow, a whole coherent sentence out of the ghost. Apparently it was easier to remember family. "Mrs. Gump agrees with your assessment," Evie told her. "Stacey has led a narrow life. You're learning!"

"You're talking to a ghost, like, right now?" Loretta's eyes widened in excitement.

"She's currently on the dresser. Do you see anything?"

Loretta studied the air above the tall dresser and shook her head. "The air is sorta wavery there, but I don't see any bubble."

"But now you know to keep an eye out for wavy air!" Evie watched Granny flicker in and out a bit. Then the ball of energy jumped down and apparently attempted pacing. She wasn't too steady. Apparently pulling together spiritual energy didn't allow much room for coordination.

Evie checked her cell phone to see if the battery was fading. The last live-wire ghost she'd encountered had seemed to pull energy from batteries and electricity. The cell was low but not drained, for the moment.

"Did she just move?" Loretta whispered, following the ghost's drunken, irritated path.

"Yup. Mrs. Gump, can you tell us anything about what you were doing with all those computers?"

"Catching con artists," Granny grumbled. "About as easy as seeing ghosts. What are you two anyway?"

Definitely more coherent but not useful. "Genetic anomalies?" Evie suggested.

If she was interpreting Granny's aura correctly, she was shooting her a glare. FBI agents probably didn't believe in things like spirit energy and psychics. She and Loretta must really be blowing whatever passed for a ghost's mind.

"Good for the soul," Evie countered the glare with just a hint of glee. "Broadens your perspective."

"Loretta, Evie," Reuben shouted from the front room. "Ready to go now?"

No, she wasn't ready. She'd never met a ghost who could carry on actual conversation. "Have you looked at the security footage yet?" she called back.

"Cameras, yes!" Granny shot through the wall again.

"Mrs. Gump was just the sweetest thing," the director was telling anyone who would listen. "I don't understand why she had all this security. I can't believe she was doing anything illegal!"

The room had started filling up. The policeman and some old guy in a blue security uniform were consulting over a laptop—probably the reason Reuben was getting antsy. He and Roark didn't handle authority well—which was why they got busted from the military.

Mrs. Murkowski was allowing a couple of old ladies to feed her cookies and sympathy. A slender, balding old guy looking like a professor in a tweed jacket—in August!—wandered about, examining the walls, as if he'd find real bugs or technical ones.

Reuben looked relieved at their appearance, but Evie wasn't ready to go. She tugged him into a quiet corner. "Have you looked at the security footage? Can you put back the cameras and set them to go to one of your computers?"

"After they all leave." He gestured in disgust. "I ain't got no authority here."

"Not when you talk like a gangster. Try talking like the PhD you are."
Evie thought about that. "Well, no, that would probably just spook idiots.
Okay, go wait in the van and plot what you can. Loretta and I need more time
to do our thing, and we need people."

"Jax is on his way." He held up his phone screen showing the text. "He
can legal them into order. I'll hack the wi-fi from the van."

"Coordination. We're getting better!" Evie watched him slip away, unnoticed. Fascinating how he did that.

Not sure how she felt about Jax showing up to take over, she tapped
Loretta on the head. "Okay, beansprout, you watch bubbles while I see what I
can stir up."

Since the kid had her eye on the plates of homemade cookies, she didn't
complain about the delay.

Evie joined the crowd around the director. A truly efficient manager
would have ushered out the extras to let the professionals work, then gone
back to her busy day. Was Mrs. Murkowski that inefficient—or trying to keep
an eye on what the police and security were discovering?

"Marlene wasn't sweet," the tall, slender man said, nibbling at a cookie as
if he didn't realize it was in his hand. "She was sharp."

Evie thought she heard Granny murmur, "You sweet-talking old goat."

Marlene was definitely not sweet. *Sharp*, remained to be seen.

"With all this security, did she suspect thieves?" Evie asked innocently,
accepting a gingerbread cookie from a lady wearing pearls and a waist-length
pink cardigan on her sturdy frame.

"She did." Gray curls bobbed on the lady leaning on a walker. "She said
the housekeeping staff harbored criminals, and we should all be careful. So I
keep my jewelry locked up." Not that she was wearing any.

"I called Ursula in HR. I've been assured all our staff has had background
checks," Mrs. Murkowski protested. "No one has reported criminal activity."

"Before your time," the professorial guy said. "Marlene had a housekeeper
fired for stealing some damn fool female's annuity. She's been on the prowl
looking for thieves ever since."

"Well, I'm sure she hasn't caught any or I would have known about it."
Mrs. Murkowski looked so indignant that Evie couldn't resist opening up to
read her aura.

Huh, yeah, something a little twisted there. Loretta was right. The aura of
compassion was still present, the bewilderment was stronger, and a cloud of

dark suspicion snaked through it all—or at least, that was how Evie interpreted it. She'd been known to be wrong. But given the situation and the director's protests, that seemed the most likely interpretation. Mrs. Murkowski knew or suspected something.

While she was at it, Evie took a look at the three old ladies and the gent. Well, dang.

All four were murky with distrust and fear.

~

ARIEL KNEW THE INSTANT HER GUEST DEPARTED. EVEN IF SHE hadn't seen Jax arrive on his motorcycle, she felt the sudden absence of. . . tension. Or atmospheric pressure.

She was weird as well as skinny. Old news. She saw Roark's email in her box and checked it, just in case, but it said nothing she didn't already know. She kept it anyway.

Determining there was nothing new she could access on Roark's case without more information, she returned to her usual work tracing illegal cryptocurrency transactions. She'd started with porn sites years ago, feeding the trails to law enforcement so reliably that they now requested her assistance. She enjoyed the work and it provided a nice nest egg.

She sensed another presence even before the security camera binged. This was more a mental presence than the atmospheric pressure of someone close by—which meant Priscilla, Evie's cousin. Now there was someone as weird as she was. Ariel acknowledged the intrusive tug by allowing Pris mental access to what she was doing.

Glancing at the camera view, she noted Pris wore red, white, and blue stripes in her wiry hair today. Ariel couldn't read minds and had no idea what the colors signified. They didn't really talk so much as reassure each other of their mental connection. She thought Pris might be lonely—or bored.

Today, her visitor was agitated, which was unusual. Ariel wondered how to calm her as Pris had mentally soothed her when she first moved here. Her routine didn't allow interruption during work hours.

She sensed Pris's cerebral tension almost as clearly as Roark's physical pressure. That couldn't be good. Pris was usually a pleasant *absence* of tension, while Roark was the extreme opposite.

Ariel tried to focus on her work, but these past days had already set her on edge. She had hoped that Roark's departure would allow her to return to normal.

Except, she really wasn't normal, was she? And yeah, she knew there was no normal but calling her *divergent* said the same damned thing.

She almost reached for the phone to call her old therapist, until she remembered they no longer had health insurance. Stephen retiring from his law firm had removed that safety net.

She squeezed her chunky monkey toy and rocked in her desk chair. Priscilla didn't go away. Her agitation became a question.

Pris was weird. Ariel understood weird. Could she hope. . . Understanding was out of the question, but perhaps, if she could help Pris somehow. . . They might be sort of friends?

She'd always dreamed of having friends. It didn't seem possible.

It wouldn't be possible unless she tried, the therapist had said.

Clenching her teeth, Ariel reached for her phone. **WHAT** she texted.

She sensed immediate relief. Having someone understand her terse messages was good, so she tried to relax a little.

MOTHER Pris texted back. Then she sent a series of images.

Ariel puzzled over the pictures of an array of junk mail like the stuff she routinely flung in the recycle. Hers was usually addressed to the previous tenant of the cottage, followed by "or current occupant."

This junk was specifically addressed to Ellen Broadhurst about prizes won. Priscilla's agitation increased.

SCAM? Ariel typed.

YES, HELP Pris replied. **DON'T TELL** she added.

Eleven

RIDING UP ON THE HARLEY, JAX SPOTTED THE INNOCUOUS utility van in the retirement home's parking lot and pulled in next to it. Within minutes, he and Roark had the lowdown on the computer theft from Reuben, who was cursing himself and apparently half the planet. Reuben scrolled through the limited footage he'd just copied from the client's security cameras.

"How did the *putains* get through the halls lookin' like dat?" Roark demanded, studying the brief, murky image of two men in black balaclavas—in August—entering the apartment.

"English," Jax said, repeating Ariel's demand with amusement.

Roark ignored him.

"*Insiders,*" Reuben concluded. "The home's security cameras were turned off outside that door."

That set off Jax's alarms. "I'm going in. You shouldn't have left them in there alone!"

"They're surrounded by senior citizens and a policeman eating cookies. Knock yourself out." Reuben went back to his studies, pointing out places where he wanted to install bugs, while Roark loaded up his tool bag of spy goodies.

Jax left them to it. He pulled out the lawyer card to get past the guardian in the lobby and swore at the slow elevator as it chugged to the fourth floor.

Loretta pounced on him the instant he entered the apartment. "I might be able to see ghosts!" she whispered. "But Evie is *talking* to one!"

Jax squeezed her shoulder and looked for Evie, finding her surrounded by old ladies all nattering at once. He shuddered and checked out the cop and security guard. "Fill me in later," he told the kid. "Go keep Evie out of trouble."

"Oh, she's the reason everyone is in here now, and why all their bubbles are shrinking. They're afraid!" She skipped off on that ominous note.

How did one raise a kid who can tell adults are afraid and wasn't worried about it? Mentally shaking his head, he joined the officials, introducing himself. Looking shaken, a young woman with vaguely Asian features was asking how long it took for a police report so she could claim the insurance. No one was giving her straight answers.

Jax figured it didn't hurt to drum up business, such as it was. "I'm Miss Carstairs' lawyer. If part of her job is to help you learn about your grand-mother, I can help you with the insurance claim. Did your grandmother have rental insurance? Have you asked the home if they have liability insurance? It sounds as if you were treated pretty roughly. Has anyone called a medic to see if you're okay?"

The men growled in annoyance. The females grew wide-eyed in appreciation.

Evie instantly arrived. Expecting that, Jax refrained from hugging her while on a business assignment but shot her a grin of triumph. She wrinkled her nose and didn't interfere as the young woman—Stacey Gump, apparently—decided she was distressed and now worried about her grand-mother's treatment and if the home shouldn't be investigated for negligence.

A woman introduced as Lucy Murkowski, the administrator, joined them, in accompaniment with a Mrs. Ursula Stanislaus, apparently from the company's Human Resources Department. Tall, fading blond, and strident, Mrs. Stanislaus caused hurricane winds all her own as she assured everyone the problem had been Marlene, not the home's employees.

The rest of the crowd followed, making private discussion impossible. Voices raised. Evie tugged at Jax's sleeve and nodded toward a tall gentleman hovering in the back. Without explanation, she slipped from the mob Jax had caused.

He did his best to keep everyone focused on the home's liability issues while Evie and the older gentleman slipped out the door. Jax wondered how long he should give her before he went looking.

Stacey crowded close enough to whisper, "That was grandmother's boyfriend. He said he had something he wanted to give me, but he didn't want to do it in front of the others. I think Evie has gone to fetch it. Should I join her?"

"She'll let us know if she needs us," Jax said with more assurance than he felt. Instinct roared for him to protect his own, but Evie wasn't really his. Evie was a free spirit who could never belong to anyone. He could only stay close and hope he was there when needed.

Evie returned without the old gent. She pulled Stacey aside, presumably for a report on anything she'd been given. Jax gave Stacey his business card in case she had any difficulty with the insurance claims. He'd learned the names of all the little old ladies so he could look them up later, if needed. The argument over the home's useless security footage wasn't going anywhere. Ursula was insisting that none of her staff would have turned off the camera. The equipment had to be faulty.

Figuring they couldn't learn anything more, Jax claimed Evie's arm and gestured to Loretta. Looking bored, the kid snatched the last cookie and fell in step.

"Some people have dull bubbles," the kid complained as the elevator took them down.

"Not everyone is as interesting as we are," Evie said with a laugh. She produced an old-fashioned flip phone from her pocket. "Mr. Charles said Marlene gave this to him in case anything happened to her. Oddly, he didn't seem to think dying counted, until Stacey got tied up."

"He was probably using it for free," Jax said cynically. "Does that thing even hold contact numbers?"

"It does. It's actually a very nice little device. Reuben will be happy. Check for security cameras when we step off." She exited the elevator, shoving the phone back in her pocket.

A good security system would have had cameras in the elevator. Jax didn't see any. He only noted one in the lobby. It wouldn't take much to enter the front door, sign in at the desk, enter the elevator and pull on hoods. . . He stopped at the desk and checked the guest register, left open for anyone to see. Using his camera pen, he snapped a photo of the current page, then signed them out. Most people didn't bother with that step, he noticed. The home had no idea if guests had left or not. That was a safety issue.

"Where's Roark? " Jax demanded of Reuben when they reached the van.

"He went in the back door with a few toys. Tell me this case is worth the effort because I sure as. . . heck. . . don't have much to go on." Reuben gave the computer screen with the hooded thieves a look of disgust, then produced clips of everyone who'd entered the building prior to the robbery. It had apparently been a shift change. The lobby had been filled with people.

Evie produced the flip phone. "Granny's emergency backup."

Reuben's eyes lit. "Genius, girl, give me that."

Jax sent him the guest book photo, and Reuben was a happy camper again.

While Loretta clambered into the van to resume her video game, Jax leaned against the open doorway. "So, do we know who Granny was investigating, presuming she's not the crook?"

"Keeping in mind that I have no idea how these things work—" Evie perched on the bumper. "Granny complained that whoever she was tracking kept changing his IPS or something like that."

"ISP," Reuben corrected. "Internet Service Provider. Not easy to change that unless you got a bunch of computers with different internet hookups. More likely, there's more than one scammer."

Evie shrugged at the correction and continued, "Marlene muttered about thieves and housekeeping, but I think she was after bigger fish."

"Phishers," Loretta crowed without glancing up from her game. "Fishing for phishers."

"That might explain the fake IDs to buy different internet providers for the different computers. I'll find out if she was using the addresses on the IDs." Reuben waved the flip phone. "It will take a while to track these contact numbers and see if I can trace any of her calls."

"The last batch was probably Mr. Charles calling his girlfriends," Evie warned with amusement. "Does that mean there's enough here to keep your holiness amused? Jax and I should probably check on Ariel if Roark's going to be here awhile."

"Oh, yeah, leave Roark here. I'd rather have you at my back on the way home." Jax straightened and held out his hand for Evie to take.

Reuben waved them off without looking up. Engrossed in her game,

Loretta simply called good-bye. She'd learned independence and entertaining herself from birth, Jax surmised.

"Can we check out those addresses Reuben drove by this morning? I'd really like to talk to those ladies." Evie climbed on the bike and hugged his waist.

How could he refuse with all those ripe curves pressed against him? "What about Ariel?"

She showed him her phone email. "She's taking on a case of her own. Tell her she needs to bill Pris for her time."

"Yeah, like I'm telling my sister anything about money." Jax kicked the bike into gear and followed Evie's directions to the suburban development Reuben had described.

"Reuben says this is the kind of place where he grew up." Jax rolled slowly through the older neighborhood. "Except he's from Florida. We should probably make him go home and visit."

"If you were a big Black gay PhD, would you go to Florida? He'd waste all his time spitting out crackers."

Jax snorted. She probably wasn't far wrong.

"There, the house with the shabby shutters and overgrown shrubs. Drop me off on the corner." After Jax stopped the bike, Evie kissed his cheek and jogged down the cracked sidewalk.

This place probably wasn't a lot different from the neighborhood where he had spent his first twelve years, before his parents were killed by a power-hungry sociopath. The houses were solid, just old and in need of maintenance. Some of the original owners had done a good job keeping up, others couldn't.

He kept an eye on Evie talking to someone through a screen door. A middle-aged woman emerged from a better maintained house across the street and glanced at him, sitting here on his bike. Neighborhood watch, good.

Never having been considered a menace by anyone—except Evie—Jax confidently parked his bike and strolled down the sidewalk. Aware that his slacks and collared shirt made him look more like a salesman than a thug, he nodded respectfully to the woman pretending to deadhead her roses.

He handed her his business card. "We've been alerted that Mrs. Decker may be a victim of mail fraud. We were hired to check on her."

He'd thought Granny had been investigating internet fraud, but Reuben had said these identities Granny had *borrowed* didn't have internet. But their identities had been stolen somehow.

The neighbor examined his card and nodded in relief. "She doesn't come out much since her hip surgery. We tried to look after her yard while she was in the nursing home, but we don't like to intrude. She has a daughter out in Oregon who stayed here for a while, but now it's just some visiting nurse service."

"Do you know the name of the service?" Jax asked as if just making conversation while watching Evie.

"Oh, they all sound alike, don't they? Home Health Care or something like that. They're here twice a week, like clockwork."

"That's good to know. A lot of people don't like to ask for help." Seeing Evie walk away from the house, he tipped an imaginary hat and strolled across the street to join her.

"She's waiting for the man to arrive with her million-dollar check," Evie said in fury, stalking toward the bike as fast as her short legs would go. "She has on her Sunday dress and best earrings and was certain they'd arrive today. She asked me in for tea and cake while she waited, wanting to share her excitement."

Evie didn't do anger well. Her cheeks were flushed and steam practically poured from her ears.

Jax held her arm and slowed her down. "So, if these are the dirtbags Mrs. Gump was tracking, you want to take off their hairy balls and shove them down their throats?"

Evie slowed down to breathe and lean into him. "And aren't you the sweet talker?"

Jax stopped by the concerned neighbor again. "Mrs. Decker is expecting a party and prize that won't be arriving. Do you think a couple of neighbors might stop by for a short visit to cheer her up?"

"A prize that won't—" Her eyes widened and her lips tightened. "I've heard her talk about those prizes. I'm glad her daughter hired you. We'll take care of this, thank you."

"Good neighbors are a blessing," Evie said more cheerfully as they waved and walked on.

When they reached his bike, she added, "Can we visit the other two as well?"

He glanced at the sun sinking behind the trees. "It's late and we can't save the world in a day. And bad things may have happened to Mrs. Gump for trying. Let's find out more from a safer distance, before they realize we're on their trail. I've picked up a couple of leads."

The roar of the Harley drowned out any of Evie's objections. At this hour, by the time they located the other women, anyone believing a million dollars would land on their doorstep today would already be disillusioned. Jax couldn't fix that. But he sure as hell meant to put a stop to the low-down low-lives who preyed on the lonely.

This felt better than whipping contracts out of textbooks.

Twelve

IT WAS DARK BY THE TIME REUBEN DROPPED ROARK OFF AT A GAS station to limp the last mile to Ariel's place. The van was in Roark's name. Anyone watching it might start putting two and two together, so it was best if he kept Ariel at a distance from his van.

Not that Roark thought his father was smart enough to trace him all the way to South Carolina, but he hadn't survived Afghanistan without good instincts, and his gut said Da wasn't working alone. Someone had provided his old man with those phone numbers. And the money leaving the local bank looked like a laundry operation. Banking alone was an aberration—Claude LeBlanc always dealt in cash.

The pale blue light of computer screens glimmered in Ariel's window as Roark walked up the drive. He stopped at her security camera and waved so she knew it was him.

These were the hours he was supposed to sleep, while she worked. But he'd never been much of an early-to-bed sort of guy.

He'd left her some gumbo to heat up. Using the keypad to enter through the kitchen, he checked to see that she'd eaten, then warmed up the leftovers for himself. He and Reuben had stopped for food in Savannah, but he had a few more hours of work ahead of him.

He could hear Ariel in the front room, tapping keys faster than seemed humanly possible. He didn't know how she saw the keyboard without lights.

He hoped she didn't mind him sitting in here while she worked, because the mosquitoes would eat him alive outside.

She buzzed a text while he ate—a phone number. Was he supposed to call it?

He ran a search on the number with his browser as he swiped his bowl clean with the last of the bread. Huh, the number was all over the place, probably a burner. What did she want him to do with it?

After washing out his bowl and wiping off the table, he grabbed his laptop and dared to creep down the hall to the back bedroom. The recliner was theoretically his bed. She'd said he could sleep while she worked. Not that he intended to sleep.

To the tune of crickets chirping outside and Ariel tapping away down the hall, he ran the texted number through the list of his father's victims. Bingo.

Why this one out of the thousands? Because it was a burner, an aberration? Burner numbers never hung around long enough to be stolen from wherever these thieves had compiled their numbers, did they?

What if. . . He sent the number to Reuben to check against the ones Granny had been using. They still hadn't worked out what the ex-FBI agent was up to, but if she was infiltrating rackets like his da's—or running them—a burner app would make sense.

Another text from Ariel followed with a different number. He tracked this one to the list of his father's victims as well, then ran another browser search.

This time, he got a clear name and address: *E. M. Broadhurst in Afterthought, SC.* One of his da's marks was right here in town?

And then he got an ugly knot in his gut. *Broadhurst* sounded familiar. Where had he heard that name? Afterthought was a very small town. The whole population could probably shelter in a Wal-Mart and set up housekeeping. He ran the address through Google maps, then did a street view—a small brick home not too many blocks from Evie's Victorian. *Evie.* She had aunts and cousins out the wazoo. Wasn't one of them—

He texted Jax with the name and a query.

Jax texted back: **EVIE'S AUNT ELLEN?**

Oh crap-a-doodle. *Da was scamming Evie's aunt?*

Why the burner number? What did Ariel want him to do? Why didn't the damned reticent female *talk*?

~

ARIEL HAD LITTLE GRASP OF THE REAL WORLD AND PEOPLE outside her computer bubble. She had no interest in social media or world news. *Numbers* fascinated her. She had traced all the calls Priscilla's mother had received this past month. She'd uncovered repeated calls from what Roark called a burner app—someone was hiding their identity and location.

Her mind poked around the edges of the problem. According to her research, scammers often used mail fraud to harvest names and addresses of lucrative victims to sell on the darknet. Once those identities were out there, they could be used for stealing credit cards or entire identities, building driver's licenses and passports. Roark's father could be perpetrating those crimes. Or just stealing money from old ladies. Hard to say.

She almost felt better now that Roark had returned and was working on the problem. He was trying hard not to disturb her concentration. He didn't understand that she was sensitized to every movement, every sound, every change in atmospheric tension. He couldn't help that. She was the one who had to learn to deal with it.

It had been somewhat simpler in the larger house she'd grown up in. There, she could burrow away in a far corner when the housekeeper arrived or her adoptive parents were home. This bungalow was much too small to escape without hiding in the closet under blankets with earphones on. She couldn't work like that.

So she practically *heard* his frustration with the lack of information she'd provided. *Heard* wasn't the right word, but there really wasn't a word for her extreme sensitivity.

Her dilemma was that she'd told Pris she wouldn't tell anyone. That seemed counter-intuitive. How could she help without calling in people who knew more than she did? What did Pris think Ariel could do? Evie's cousin already knew her mother was being scammed. Was Ariel supposed to divert the phone calls? She didn't know how to do that.

Roark's tension—frustration?—died back a little. He must be working on something.

She returned to tracing cryptocurrency in the exchange his father's bank account used. She might not know a lot about human nature, but she knew the kind of people playing with bitcoins were not little old ladies liable to be scammed by con artists. Someone was buying the cryptocurrency with good old-fashioned cash.

An email arrived in her box. Emails were usually long and contained too many time-consuming words. She ignored it. Sometimes she read them over lunch, but that was one hour and thirty-three minutes away. And she wanted to check her game cams then.

Her phone buzzed with a text. Irritated, she glanced down at it.

READ IT, Roark demanded.

Frowning, she saved her work and turned to her iPad to open her mailbox.

The email contained a long list of instructions and a script.

"*What?*" she cried, rather than throw her valuable device at the wall. Then in two ticks, she tapped back a vehement **NO**.

Roark rolled back her pocket door and stood there in all his masculine immensity, bulging biceps, tattoos revealed by his skimpy tank top, his black curls tousled and falling in his face. Damn, he wasn't like any male in her sheltered world. He exuded. . . pheromones, she decided. The whole room reeked of male pheromones. Hiding in her closet would not help.

"I can have the calls forwarded here," he said in a deep voice that sounded like a growl. "But I cannot sound like Aunt Ellen."

"Why?" she cried, unable to explain her lack of understanding.

"To set the bastards up and nail them. What, did you think I'd just trace the number and go shoot the scumbag? It could be my father or brother for all I know."

Ariel buried her head in her arms as the deluge of words washed over her. She *knew* this. She comprehended the words. *Voices* simply didn't fit in her head.

She took ten deep breaths as the therapist had taught her. She processed his words one by one and nodded against her arms. With difficulty, she forced herself to speak. "I can't. Can Pris?"

"Possibly. She's your client. You talk to her. She doesn't strike me as much more talkative than you." He closed the door and left her alone.

Thirteen

"HOW DID YOUR POLITICAL MEETING GO LAST NIGHT?" EVIE asked as her mother entered the kitchen on Wednesday morning. She threw an egg on the griddle and popped bread in the toaster.

"Transformational." Mavis boosted her solid frame onto a counter seat with a grunt. "I brought Larraine with me."

Picturing that scene, Evie laughed. "The conflict between southern hospitality and bigoted horror must have blown their minds. How did that work out?"

"Most of the younger ladies politely asked questions about Larraine's mayoral platform. The older ones went for the easy target of women not being qualified to deal with an all-male council." Mavis sipped from the coffee she'd carried in with her.

"I bet *that* stuttered to a halt pretty fast once they remembered Larraine used to be a Larry. I'm imagining their heads twirling trying to process whether a woman in a man's body can deal with men, of if they just gave up and admired her jewelry." Evie plopped the egg and toast on a dish and set it in front of her mother with utensils. "Maybe familiarity can breed understanding instead of contempt."

"Can we talk about my birthday party now?" Loretta asked from the breakfast nook. In her old-soul wisdom, the Indigo child accepted Larraine as just another adult. "Can we go to Disney World?"

"You just went to Harry Potter World a few months ago. That's enough expensive travel. Besides, we couldn't take all your friends to Disney. Don't you want to have a party with friends?" Leaning her hip against the counter, waiting for the next wave of breakfast diners, Evie scooped up a spoon of her peaches and yogurt.

Loretta's eyes widened. "We could have a real party? And I could invite everybody?"

Jax came down the stairs in time to catch this. He'd just showered and shaved and smelled masculine delicious, as well as looking suavely professional in his collared shirt and tie. The man disguised his superhero self extremely well, presumably to prevent scaring off clients. Suppressing a sigh of incredulity that he actually liked sleeping with *her*, Evie threw the prepared eggs into the pan and began scrambling them. ADHD had its benefits. She'd make a great short-order cook.

"Who is *everybody*?" Jax asked, filling the coffee machine.

"All my friends." Loretta scooped up her cereal, hunting down the strawberry bits. "I never got to have a real party."

Evie raised a questioning eyebrow at Jax, who shrugged. "Her parents took her out to eat and bought fancy gifts."

Her parents had died after Loretta's tenth birthday. Evie winced and vowed to give her ward anything she wanted for this party. "So, what kind of party did you have in mind?"

"I'll be eleven. That's too old for ponies and bounce houses."

"Huh, I didn't think anyone ever got too old for those." Evie tested Loretta's declaration. Sometimes, kids twisted what they wanted with what they thought others wanted.

"I am," she said most emphatically. "And my friends are."

"You might want to determine who's on the guest list," Jax suggested, *sotto voce*, as he fixed his coffee.

"ESP, I already know," she whispered back, dishing up eggs scrambled with veggies and cheese and handing it to him.

Loretta had enchanted a wide range of people in her few months in Afterthought. Indigo children had that ability—when allowed to express themselves, instead of being bundled up in uniforms and forced into niches too small for their expansive souls.

"Could I still have birthday cake?" Loretta asked uncertainly.

"Definitely. Three kinds, if you like, plus all the ice cream everyone can eat. We could probably even make homemade ice cream. Adults like that." Evie leaned against the counter to finish her peaches and think about what she would have loved at that age, just starting middle school and wanting to be a grown-up. "How about music? Would you like a dance party?"

Loretta's crystal blue eyes grew wide. "Could I? With real music?"

"Real music as opposed to what?" Jax had to ask. "Croaking frogs?"

Evie swatted him. "DJ or a band?"

"I could have a real *band*?" Loretta asked in awe. "A real one? Like on YouTube?"

"The Home Boys play parties," Mavis suggested, finishing her egg and toast. "But you'd have to book them pretty fast. Half of them leave for college in a few weeks."

"But I don't dance." Loretta's face fell.

"At your age, no one does." Thinking of all the guests Loretta would undoubtedly invite, Evie had a brainstorm. "We can bring in a line-dancing instructor!"

Loretta looked as if she'd died and gone to heaven. Evie memorized that look. In a few years, the kid would be a teenager and scorn everything suggested.

Reuben arrived just as Evie made her suggestion. "Line dancing? You ain't gonna get no Black folk around here line dancing."

Evie threw a biscuit at his over-sized nerd head as he reached in the refrigerator for the orange juice. "Bigot. Truth is, getting anyone around here to dance is a challenge. People just drink and watch. And they need to be drunk before they can be persuaded onto a dance floor. Since we're not serving alcohol at a birthday party, we'll leave it to the kids to work out."

"It's like folk dancing." Loretta didn't sound perturbed by the argument. "My gym teacher likes folk dancing. Do you think she can teach us line dancing?"

With his head in the refrigerator, Reuben replied, "I can teach you line dancing."

Evie grinned and winked at Loretta. "Larraine loves dancing."

~

SIX MONTHS AGO, JAX HAD BEEN LIVING IN A HIGH-END CONDO, driving a classic XKE, and working toward a partnership in an uptown

Savannah law office. The woman following him out on the porch, leaving everyone else to wash the dishes, had completely flipped his life on end.

"You're out of sorts," Evie said, leaning into him with a hug and kiss. "Can I help?"

And there was the reason he was now living in a Victorian money pit and riding a Harley and working with farmers in the back of nowhere. Jax hugged her harder and claimed a more satisfying kiss.

"What color is my aura today?" he asked once they stepped back so he could don his helmet. He still took Evie's so-called abilities with a cellar of salt, but she was eerily accurate too often to ignore.

"Your fifth chakra is a gray-blue, very unusual for you. Are you horribly unhappy to give up your fancy law job for us?"

He never knew what she was seeing when she studied him like that. With her carrot curls and wearing orange short shorts and a T-shirt proclaiming *Everyone was thinking it, I just said it,* she looked like an empty-headed teenager. No one would realize that behind the costume hid an all-knowing Sibyl.

"Protective coloration," he decided, ruffling her hair. "You can get away with asking questions like that and people simply think you're off-the-wall instead of damned scary."

"Pris has the corner on scary, and you're avoiding the question. Will you have time today to follow up the leads about the nursing home and services, or should I have Reuben take me back to Savannah where I do my thing? Does that have anything to do with what's bothering you?"

"I'll do some preliminary research when I have time. And I take back anything I said about buying a Miata if you plan on using it to poke around places harboring potential criminals. I'm the expert on danger, not you."

She brightened. "Ah, there we go! You want to be out playing superhero instead of pushing papers. You can do both, you realize. Just compartmentalize and choose only cases that push your buttons. No one here is asking you to be rich or ambitious."

"You are a dangerous female." Jax left her grinning like a Cheshire cat. Living with Sibyl had its moments.

Choose his cases. Nice thought, except clients weren't battering down the door to offer him the ones he wanted. He wanted the cases suing the former mayor, Arthur Block, for the assorted land frauds he'd perpetrated that had almost cost Evie's family the property that had been theirs for centuries.

He parked his bike in the alley behind his office. In a way, not having his pricey Jag made life simpler. He didn't need a secure garage or even a regular parking space.

After leaving his helmet in his office and checking his lackluster email, he walked over to the county courthouse—another example of his simpler life. Not having to drive half an hour in traffic to reach his office or the courthouse gave him extra time for more interesting pursuits.

Like finding out how many people wanted the former mayor's ass in a sling and which ones hadn't hired attorneys yet.

Admittedly, unless ex-Mayor Block had good insurance, there wasn't much money in this case. And suing the town wouldn't win anyone's heart. But a lot of people like Evie's mom had lost their homes to an eminent domain that had failed to produce the pharmacy promised. There ought to be reparations.

Suing the town to get the pharmacy seemed reasonable. So he looked up that file as well. Suing for his father's patents was satisfying, but he didn't know patent law. He needed fraud cases.

Once he'd satisfied his curiosity and itch for action, he returned to his office to work on Evie's case. Reuben could probably handle this, but Jax had had a client who'd sued a nursing home recently. He'd won him a substantial settlement and learned a bit about the industry in the process.

Like Evie, he couldn't hack computers, but he could talk to people.

She'd been calling him the Hulk and the Magician since they'd met. More recently, she'd called him a superhero. He didn't know what she was seeing that he didn't, but her appreciation restored a modicum of the self-confidence he'd lost in these past years of turmoil.

At his computer, Jax composed a letter to victims of the town's eminent domain disaster, then another to the unrepresented people flattened by the former mayor's development company fraud. He'd never had to hunt business before. If he had to do it now, it would be the kind of business that interested him.

Then he turned his attention to Savannah nursing homes. He knew most were businesses run by experienced people who meant well. And they employed hundreds of caring, skilled workers. But the baby boomer generation was providing a boom in the retirement home industry, and the more people employed, the higher the chance of hiring bad apples. Throw in the profit motive. . . corners got cut.

Reuben had sent him the names of the rehab home and the home nursing service working with Mrs. Decker, the lady expecting a million-dollar prize. The companies were, probably not coincidentally, the same ones a Mrs. Lopez and a Mr. Wong had used, two of Marlene Gump's stolen—or borrowed—identities.

The rehabilitation home was a small, private one, not one of the big corporate entities he'd dealt with. Rats. That complicated life.

The home-nursing service was owned by the same people, Sunshine Healthcare—not surprising. Once a company obtained government approval for accepting Medicare, they could expand quickly—if they had financial backing. This place wasn't publicly listed, so financial documents weren't easily attainable.

He started with the names on Sunshine's corporate papers. His old law firm hadn't canceled his access to the expensive research services they used for investigation. One of these days, he'd have to afford the subscriptions on his own, but for now, he took advantage of his old firm's carelessness.

Once he'd compiled a file on each of the corporate officers, Jax sent the dossiers to Reuben to compare with what he was digging out of Marlene Gump's computer files. Contrary to Evie's problem-solving approach, most investigations were tedious grunt work—

Plus good memories for making connections, Jax decided a moment later as he ran across a name he recognized: Lucy Murkowski, the administrator of Mrs. Gump's retirement apartments was listed on the board of directors of Sunshine Home Healthcare Services.

Come to think of it—there was Ursula Stanislaus, the HR director. Was this a completely employee-owned business?

The sticky web tightened.

Fourteen

ROARK APPROPRIATED ARIEL'S DESK CHAIR THE INSTANT SHE went to bed. Bent up in this cramped tiny chair, his injured leg as well as his back ached, but it was better than the porch.

He could hear her tossing and turning in her room, probably as uneasy as he was with this cage they were trapped in. He needed to be out and about, slapping mics on walls and phones, tracking his father and his buddies. . . but that required funds he'd blown by going home in the first place. He couldn't even ask Reuben to help him out. The dude had to earn his own way and didn't need an albatross weighing him down.

So Roark had to think like the computer prof, except technology wasn't an easy way of infiltrating his da's gang. Computers didn't feature in their lifestyle. Still, he might work out how to get his hand down the throats of the puppet masters pulling his father's strings.

He'd learned intimidation at an early age and at the hands of an expert.

First, though, Roark set up a social media account for one of his dimwitted cousins who didn't own so much as a dumb phone. Using that account, he "followed" all his family to keep an eye on how they were doing. His sisters were pretty active. They didn't seem to be making funeral arrangements for Da or even visiting him at the hospital, so he must have survived the explosion.

His family posted enough to keep him apprised of what his brothers were up to. It wasn't enough. His brothers weren't stupid and didn't tell everyone everything. But online, the only concern seemed to be about him. He couldn't help them there. Better that Da thought him dead. And their conjectures that he was hiding in the swamp or hiring special forces to invade amused him.

Next, he began the tedious task of identifying his father's victims from their phone numbers. As he suspected, all of the victim information was out there on the darknet. He narrowed down the ones to investigate further by checking their zip codes for the wealthier zones. Then he ran their credit reports, using the account Ariel had apparently set up and paid for. He didn't want to know her reasons for checking people's credit. If he and Ariel could do it, the puppet masters could too. The victims with money in the bank would be the ones they pursued hardest.

From the variety of numbers used, he deduced his da's scammers had burner apps and VPNs. Those prevented Roark from tracing their numbers and phones. Somebody knew their tech. If even the FBI couldn't track these criminals, he was nuts to try. But he had all the time in the world. They didn't.

Beside him, Ariel's cellphone pinged a text message. He picked it up and hesitated only half a second. He'd listened and watched her hit her security code enough times to guess she was using Jax's birth date. He tried it and the phone opened so he could read the message from Pris. Apparently Evie's cousin was either desperate or didn't realize Ariel slept all morning.

BOYFRIEND! the text exclaimed in all caps, followed by angry, weeping emoticons.

That might make sense to the Enigma Twins but meant nothing to Roark. Since Ariel was already prepared to make mincemeat of him, Roark typed back: **ARIEL SLEEPING. SHE TELL YOU PLAN?**

That stopped her cold. Oh well.

He set up a search/comparison for the scammer phone numbers he was collecting, then began checking each number individually in hopes at least one might slip up and use their real number. Roark knew the IQ levels of the people working for his da. Half of them had barely made it through sixth grade. They existed on charm and good looks.

Which made him uneasy in lieu of Pris's message. One of the prime phone and internet scams was dating app fraud. With a good template, his father's buddies might pull off an internet email fraud, but their specialty was sweet talking, which required phone calls. He'd learned that much from his brothers. At least they weren't pulling any of the intimidation calls where they threatened their victims—that they knew of.

Pris's mother had landed on his da's list with the magazine scam. That made her an easy mark for his other cons. Roark had added her to his investigation because her credit report showed she had substantial unused credit and a decent savings account.

He wasn't too surprised when the security alarm buzzed half an hour later—he'd heard the bike coming up the drive. He glanced at the camera. Evie's weird cousin leaned against a bicycle and waited. She wore all black today but her hair was all red. He was gonna guess that meant she was flaming mad.

Bored playing with numbers, he sauntered out to the porch. "Well, did Ariel tell you our plan?"

She narrowed her eyes and studied him. When he'd first arrived in Afterthought, Roark had thought Evie's cousin spacey. There wasn't an ounce of vagueness to her today.

"You block me," she announced, sounding suspicious. "Only my family can do that."

Roark shrugged, not having any idea what she was talking about. "I don't have time for games. Do you want help or not?"

"Some jerkoff is sending my mother photos of himself next to a Cadillac and text messages about how much he enjoys talking with her." She quit there, as if expecting him to understand.

"Can you send us the photos?"

She nodded and continued to wait expectantly.

Roark grimaced. "Your best alternative is to smash her phone and get her a new number."

"She's addled but not dumb. She'll realize a new number cuts her off from the jerkwad."

"And you think Ariel can stop fraud that even the FBI can't stop?" Yeah, so, he was curious. "That's what you want? For her to *catch* the jerkwad?"

"I want him fried in oil and prevented from stealing from any more naïve idiots." Pris was adamant. The flaming red hair practically glowed.

Yeah, she was related to Evie all right. Roark propped his shoulder against a porch post. "Boil one, and two more pop up. It's whack-a-mole. The alternative is to protect your mother. Forward all your mother's calls here. She'll guess something is wrong in a day or two, so we're taking chances on timing. We'll need someone to pretend to be your mother answering the calls. I can't do that."

"And Ariel won't. But I want these creeps *stopped!*" She glared at him.

Yeah, so did he, but not if he endangered Ariel and her family. Once his leg was healed. . . "I can't do that," he told her flatly. "Even the feds can't do that. We can just save your ma."

"I'll be back when Ariel is awake." Without further explanation, Pris climbed on her bicycle and rode off.

Roark rubbed his head and tried to decide if beyond-all flaky was better or worse than criminally charming. Mostly, he decided, families were weird.

An hour later, a photo came through. Roark glared at it in disbelief. There stood his father from twenty years ago, the young, curly-haired man Roark resembled—photoshopped onto an ad for a new Cadillac. Holy Mother Mary and Jayzus, which one of the reprobates had learned Photoshop?

All he'd have to do was drive into Afterthought in a Cadillac, and he could have Evie's Aunt Ellen eating out of his hand. Or calling the cops.

He'd have to shave his head again.

~

HE'S ON MY COMPUTER.

Ariel grimaced and tried to shut out the vibrations of her unwanted guest by stepping into her shower. All those male pheromones made her skin itch. She tried to scrub away the sensation but she only heightened her awareness.

By the time she'd dressed, she could tell Roark had abandoned her computer and was in her kitchen, permeating the air with the scent of frying bacon. The man exploded her senses.

And he refused to honor her schedule. She didn't eat until she'd been up for two hours.

Warily, she eased into the hall. She couldn't sense him in the house. With a sigh of relief, she entered the kitchen to find a fried egg and bacon on toast keeping warm, plus a sliced avocado wrapped tightly. Avocado! She hadn't ordered anything so exotic. Unwilling to allow an avocado to go to waste, she added that and a tomato to the egg sandwich, fixed her tea, and checked her game camera on her phone while she ate.

But making notes of animal activity wasn't anywhere as interesting as wondering what Roark was up to. Besides, the only animal she saw in mid-afternoon was Himself, pacing the woods, chinning on overhead branches like a restless bear, reminding her that she should be exercising instead of eating.

She finished her egg sandwich, returned to her room to brush her teeth and take her medications, did her exercises, then at exactly 15:00, went to her desk. She checked her phone for messages first—

And went ballistic.

Flying out the front door, she found Roark established in his porch cave and threw the phone at him.

The beast caught it with ease, flicked it on, punched in her code, and *checked her messages!*

If she wasn't usually incoherent, she was now.

"Bébé, your *ami* got trouble. I'm just helpin' her. She's coming out in a bit so we can fix t'ings."

She snatched the phone back and hit settings and began resetting her code.

"Don't do no good, *cher*. I can still hear it. You just put in your birt'day instead of Jax's. If it helps, I'll give you my phone's code. If we gotta work together, we might as well make ourselves useful."

He could hear *the buttons? I cannot do this!*

She picked up Mitch's food bowl of insect pellets and flung it at him. Without a word, she returned inside, leaving him to his sweltering cave.

Even she knew that was mean. He'd fixed her breakfast. He was staying out of her way, living in discomfort for her sake. The man had been driven from his home by criminal bullies who *shot* him and threatened his family. And she got mad because he. . . What had he done? *Listened* to her passcode?

How was she supposed to react to that? If she had a therapist any longer, she'd email and ask. Talking to a therapist had always been torture anyway.

Burying her face on her arms, she tried to think through this on her own.

Pris arrived before Ariel could gather all her straying thoughts and orga-nize them into a sensible pattern. At least Pris understood, sort of. Ariel rested her head and let Evie's cousin find her mind.

The image Pris formed in Ariel's head of the man and the Cadillac made her wince. She had no good means of relating to others, but even she recog-nized what this might do to Roark.

Reluctantly, she picked up her violated phone and checked her messages again. The man in the photo resembled a dissipated Roark, one with bags under his eyes and rounded shoulders instead of broad, muscular ones. The photoshop job was crude.

A message popped up from Roark: **RE-ROUTING**

She wished she didn't know what that meant but she did. Re-routing phone calls had been part of his Plan, the one she'd rejected. She returned to her front door. Roark sat on the step next to Pris, working on his burner phone. Ariel expelled a sigh of relief. Pris must have agreed to read the script.

I wish I could do it. She'd love to bring down criminals, too.

"All right, your ma's phone calls are now coming to me." Roark handed the phone to a wary Pris. "Is there a time when the scumbag usually calls?"

"When I'm not around," Pris replied in disgruntlement.

Recalling the phone calls she'd traced, Ariel corrected, "oh-ten-hundred to twelve-hundred, fourteen-hundred to seventeen-hundred."

Pris looked puzzled but Roark nodded. "It's fifteen-one-five now. We wait. We have two choices here."

Ariel and Pris both looked at him with impatience.

For Ariel's sake, he spoke slowly. He held up one finger to Pris. "One, we can tell the jerkwad your mother died."

"Bad, bad hoodoo," Pris said, shaking her head.

"Yeah, my granny would agree." He held up a second finger. "We play him, try to trace the call, or get a phone number or anything personal."

"That one," Pris agreed. "I'll play the death card later, if needed. Or maybe just say she's in the hospital. Then I'll smash her phone," she added grimly.

Ariel would have started with phone smashing. Rather than sit around, she returned to work. She didn't know what to say while they waited. She kept an eye on the security camera. Pris was weeding the neglected shrubbery. She couldn't see Roark in his cave.

Pris's phone rang at fifteen-five-five, right before Ariel normally ate. Except she'd already eaten. She gritted her teeth, looked at the computer screen she hadn't finished working, and dragged herself out of her chair. She *had* to hear this.

They had the phone set on speaker, and Pris sat next to Roark on the front step. He nearly made two of her. Ariel felt a weird tug of. . . she couldn't identify the emotion swamping her at seeing the two of them together, but she didn't like it. She watched as he opened his laptop to the script he'd prepared.

The man on the phone's accent resembled Roark's, except more slurred and seductive than Roark's crisp tones. "How ya doin', *cher*? Are you stayin' cool?"

"I have a cold," Pris said stiffly, following the line Roark pointed at. "Where are you now?"

"*Pauvre ti bête*, sorry to heah dat! When I get dere, I fix you a hot toddy like my grandma used ta make, and you'll be right as rain in no time."

Roark pointed at another line and Pris read, "When will you be here?"

"Well, I ran into a speck of trouble down heah in Atlanta. Someone stole my wallet. Dey're out using my credit cards to buy big screen TVs and da like. I'm talking to da police now, but it will be a while afore I can get new cards, 'specially since I gotta shut down my credit reports to keep dem from stealin' my ID. It may be a few days."

Ariel whistled. That was quite a ruse. Roark glanced over his shoulder and his expression was black as night. She thought maybe he'd wring the scammer's neck if he could.

In a hoarse voice, Pris read the line Roark pointed at. "That's awful. Does that mean you're not coming?"

That Roark had a response for everything the scammer said pretty much proved this was a routine call. Where had he come up with that script? Ariel waited to hear the response.

"Aw honey, I know you wan' dis car. It's a beauty, I gotta say. Leather seats, smells great, and the sound system. . . you're gonna love cruisin' wit dis. Mebbe you take me for a ride when I get dere, huh, cher?" the suave voice drawled.

Maybe we'll take an axe to your head. Ariel knew better than to say that aloud, but the expression on Roark's face said she was reading his mind.

Pris, on the other hand, looked cool, calm, and collected until Roark signaled her next line. She glared at him, then coughed up a giggle. Pris wasn't much of a giggler. The script said *giggle*?

Undeterred, the caller continued. "Hey, bébé, I was thinkin', if you could just wire me a few hundred, I could be dere tomorrow. I got all da papers, but I need to fill it up wit gas and have it cleaned up pretty for you. You been such an angel puttin' up with dese silly delays. Mebbe I'll get my cards back, and we can go out and eat somewhere fine. You pick a place, okay?"

Hmmm, wire fraud and not bank fraud. They'd need someone on the other end to spot him. Except he probably wasn't actually in Atlanta, was he? How did that work?

Pris followed Roark's finger on the laptop screen. "I don't know how to wire money. But my daughter showed me how to transfer money with my phone. Do you have a phone?"

The drawling voice hesitated—looking for the right reply in his script? Little old ladies probably didn't often offer to have funds transferred directly from their bank account. How was Roark planning on making that work?

Most phone money apps required a phone number or an email address or both. Would they work with a burner app? Possibly, since the apps accepted texts just like any other number. But the guy would have to add the money app to whatever phone he was using. . .

Ariel listened to the rest of the exchange but her mind was already traveling to the ways the money could be traced from whatever bank account they meant to use to a phone app to a real phone and bank account. . .

Pris had reached the final "I can't wait to see you" before Ariel tuned back in again.

"And anyone believes this crook will actually show up after he receives his money?" Ariel asked angrily, then shrank back against the door when both Pris and Roark turned to stare at her.

Had she really said all that?

Before she could flee, Roark handed her his phone. "Victims do, all the time. You can buy the scripts online or watch YouTube videos on how to do it. And the police files are filled with reports of senior citizens or lonely widowers or whatnot, losing thousands to *boyfriends* or *girlfriends* they've never met, or on prizes they never receive. This scumbag is working both."

"Mom's already sent the prize company hundreds for fees and delivery, and I'm not sure what all." Pris crumbled a pellet from Mitch Turtle's supply. "They probably have her credit card number and bank account by now. I talked to the bank, and they can't do anything unless she puts me on her account, which she won't do."

Ariel looked to Roark, hoping he'd understand her unspoken question. She didn't know how she'd managed the first one. She'd shocked even herself when the words had poured out with her anger.

He cocked his head. "It's possible they haven't hacked her account. I think we're dealing with phone grifters, not hackers. It's a slower process draining it out a few hundred at a time. I'm gonna guess dat. . ." He grimaced and corrected himself. "I'm guessing the final step will be to take a check in exchange for the 'papers.' Then they'll wash the ink, put in an amount they've established she has in the account, and clean her out with a forged amount."

"Mama just collected insurance money on a truck that got stolen. She hasn't been able to drive in ages, so she didn't plan on buying a new one. I was trying to persuade her to go to the eye doctor with the money." Pris stood up. "What do we do now?"

"Once I trace the call, *you* will alert the bank, the police, and maybe the FBI. I'm not doing anything. I don't exist. I'm one of Evie's ghosts, invisible." Roark shut his laptop and stood, towering over Pris on the lower step. "Best keep Ariel out of it too. She's no kind of witness. I'll send a few bucks through that app. With luck, when he doesn't get what he wants, dirtbag will quit calling, for a while."

Deflated, Ariel watched Pris ride off. They weren't going to catch the crook?

Roark nodded at the door, waiting politely for her to go in first. She noticed her head came above his shoulder. And then, in embarrassment, she ducked inside.

"We'll know whether the call comes from Nigeria or New Orleans shortly. That's my da's photo, but that wasn't him on the phone. They have a bunch of scum feeding those lines to a bunch of people who will never see that Cadillac."

He let the door close behind her, leaving her alone in the front room.

She didn't want to be left alone after that news. His *dad*?

Fifteen

"It wasn't heart failure," the low voice sobbed through the phone.

Handling six leashes as she walked her clients' dogs around Witch Hill, Evie juggled the phone closer to her ear. She definitely needed to invest in ear thingies. "*Stacey*? Are you all right?"

"They're saying Granny committed *suicide!*" Stacey's voice was a little louder but still tear-filled.

Remembering Granny's bouncy ghost, Evie was going to say that was a big NO. "You have the coroner's report?"

"After the robbery, the police had it expedited. She died of ethylene glycol poisoning. I looked it up, and I remember her telling me she thought she had a touch of flu. I was still in New York so I told her to call her doctor right away, with her heart condition, she shouldn't take chances." She hiccupped on a sob.

"All right, I'm taking notes. Do you know if she called her doctor?" Evie had nothing to take notes on, but her memory was good. She turned the dogs back home and jogged to urge them on. Poison flu? How did this compute?

"I don't know. The police are searching the apartment again, but I've cleaned everything out, and now they're looking at me with suspicion. She could have suffered for days!"

Evie was no medical expert, but bouncy Marlene's spirit didn't appear to have suffered too much. Shouldn't ghosts reflect the means of their death somehow? The last one she'd encountered had been in a fury at being shot. Granny ought to at least be angry or ill or something. Or maybe not.

Someone had *killed* that smart old lady? "I thought you said suicide? Why would the police be looking at you with suspicion?"

"Because I'm not white? Because I emptied her refrigerator, and they seemed to think food is how she killed herself? I don't know. Do I need to talk to your lawyer person?"

Lawyer person—Jax. Jax had been chatting up her client, of course. That's what lawyers did. "Let me talk to him first. He's expensive, and we don't want to go off half-cocked. Call her doctor, if you know who it is. Let's see if she visited him. I'll get right back to you."

Her junk pile of a mind finally called up ethylene glycol—*antifreeze*. Iddy had sent warnings to the owners of all the pets she treated cautioning them not to leave antifreeze out where the animals could drink it. How much of the stuff did it take to kill? Surely no one would drink the nasty stuff straight? Well, animals did.

She clicked Jax's number as soon as Stacey hung up. "Granny was murdered with antifreeze. Now what do we do?"

"Antifreeze? Administered how? Did she drink soft drinks? Eat Jell-O? I've heard of it taken in Gatorade. Does anyone drink that stuff anymore?"

She could tell he was taking notes and typing into his computer at the same time. She loved the way he turned his full attention to her problem. That almost felt like. . . respect?

She dropped off her first doggy client and pocketed the cash with a wave instead of her usual chat. Hurrying down the street, she juggled phone and leashes and avoided pedestrians and bicycles. "Don't know how it was ingested. Fruity water. Alcoholic drinks. I drank something called a grasshopper once. Horrible, sweet green stuff. That could have been straight antifreeze as far as I'm concerned."

"We need the coroner's report and security camera footage for the week she died. Who was there last? Check with Reuben to see if he's discovered any cloud account where Granny might have stored her backups. Do the apartments have nurses on staff? Would she have called for help? Do the cops know Stacey is inheriting all Marlene's worldly goods? They're trained to suspect the worst."

"They're saying suicide for now. Stacey was in New York. But if the stuff could be kept in fruity water. . ."

"You may have a murderer for a client." He swore in what sounded like several languages.

Evie didn't think Marlene's worldly goods were enough to kill for, but admittedly, she hadn't looked into them either. She'd been working on stolen identities, not murder.

"I need to talk to Granny before she fades," she warned. "As time goes on, the spirit has less energy and becomes less connected to reality. Besides, I need to help her pass on."

Jax cursed some more. His military background had taught him phrases she'd never heard—or he was very creative.

"I'll take you. Don't you dare go with Reuben by yourself. Chances are good if Stacey didn't kill her, then the real murderer was in the room with us the last time we were there." He clicked off.

Well, that was helpful. As she delivered the rest of the dogs, Evie made a mental list of all the people in the room when they called in the cops. The apartment had been pretty crowded, but aside from the residence and HR directors, Marlene's friends were all elderly. Why on earth would any of them murder her? Stacey had the best motive.

No point speculating. Evie rang Reuben next. She was really starting to enjoy this phone. She'd avoided cellphones, not just because she couldn't afford one, but because observation was her skill and phones a distraction. But now that her cases had moved beyond Main Street, she couldn't observe anything relevant there, so she wasn't missing out. She called and clued Reuben in.

"Yeah, I found the victim's cloud account." He sounded as if he was eating while typing. "I'm still digging around for her passwords. Ms. Gump was one wily old lady and knew her way around computers. This phone the old guy gave us even has a burner app. I've been concentrating on it, thinking her secrets were on here. Kinda weird giving it to the old guy like that, as if she expected someone to kill her."

"Or he stole it after he killed her," Evie added pragmatically. "Although why a killer wouldn't steal all the computers, too, is problematic."

"Pigs get fat, hogs get eaten. Let me know when you're ready to head out. I'll look into Stacey's finances while I'm at it." He hung up.

Pigs get fat. . . No one had noticed a missing spare cell phone. They might have been alarmed had the thieves got greedy and taken all the computers. But Stacey hadn't known about all the computers. . . Maybe there were others.

Evie knew her leapfrogging mind was good at puzzles, but right now, her thoughts resembled a cyclone.

She called Roark as she was walking up to the house. After filling him in on Stacey's news, she asked, "Are you following the activity at the Gump apartment?" He'd wired the front room and phone and ought to have some notion.

"The grandkid's sleeping there," Roark answered laconically, as if occupied with another task. "She's been giving a lot of stuff to Goodwill. Some of the ladies stop by and bring her casseroles and ask for trinkets in the old lady's memory. Kid's smart and hid all the good stuff, so they're toting off junk, best I can tell."

"No suspicious characters snooping around?"

Roark snorted. "All little old ladies and gents, and they all snoop. Dey been asking about furniture. The Nazi came and asked when she thought the kid would be out so she could have da place cleaned. Some gloomy Gus called to ask about da funeral, sounded like her dad."

"I'd like to meet the dad. Marlene asked about him and was disappointed he hasn't shown up. Do you have time to look him up or should I ask Reuben?"

Roark hesitated. "How much you want me in on dis gig? I don't want to muscle in on your job. I might haveta leave again."

"We're a team. That doesn't mean we don't have lives. Reuben is practically living with Larraine these days, handling her internet campaign. Doesn't mean he can't do the team's work too."

She didn't need Roark's aura to know he was in a funk. The Cajun usually exuded energy and take-charge confidence. He was operating on rote and with something else on his mind now.

"*Mais oui.* I'm messing with some other t'ings, but you let me know what you need, and I'm on it. I'll check out dear old dad. Need me to go with you to talk to Granny again?"

"Jax says he's going. We'll see what happens." Feeling better that her team was back together again, Evie bounced into the kitchen.

Only then did she remember the promise to find a band for Loretta's party.

Five cowboy-hatted, denim-wearing strangers were crowded into the banquette while Loretta served them cookies from the freezer.

～

Jax knew he'd walked through the looking glass when he rushed home to take Evie to Savannah on a murder case and found her serving barbecue to a boys' band in the backyard. He grabbed a sandwich from the picnic table to steady his reeling senses and stalked Evie down in the kitchen.

"Did the party start without me?" He reached in the refrigerator for a beer.

"Loretta wanted to study their bubbles before she'd hire them. *She* hired them, mind you. She's taking this party business seriously, like a little executive. I think she has spreadsheets."

"This is the kid who drew up forged legal papers making you her guardian that would have stood up in court," he reminded her.

Evie rolled her eyes. "Don't think I've forgotten! I still have them, in case the ones you filed fall through. Anyway, those poor boys are sitting there being interviewed by an almost-eleven-year-old, and I had to reward them somehow." She handed him a bowl of coleslaw. "Vegetables."

"Mayonnaise." He slathered some slaw on his barbecue anyway. It wasn't mayonnaise.

"Oil and vinegar, smarty. So go talk contracts with Pete. He's the drummer and their business manager. We can talk to ghosts after dark. That's more interesting anyway."

"Where's Reuben?" Jax bit off a hunk of sandwich and practically drooled at the spiciness.

"He was out there earlier, getting the group's play list. He's probably downstairs working out the dance routines for each song by now. His mother made him take dancing classes when he was a kid. In *Florida*. I wish I could have seen it. Salsa and line dancing and a skinny Black nerd—my mind might explode." Evie forked up barbecue and slaw from her plate rather than bother with a bun.

Jax could imagine it. Reuben had the athletic, lanky build of a dancer. He had a harder time imagining the professorial nerd performing a tango. "Is he looking after Loretta tonight or going with us?"

"He's not happy being seen in what he perceives as a white folks' home. He has Roark's eyes and ears on the apartment, and he's probably better off working through Granny's files here than watching me go bug-eyed there. You're the good interviewer, but you better check with Reuben to see what all he's uncovered today. I've been feeding the hordes and haven't had a chance."

Jax was accustomed to deciding on his own tactics. Learning to work with Evie's convoluted game plan was a challenge. But when she bumped his hip with hers and kissed his cheek, he decided the perks were more interesting than a corner office and private parking space. He went in search of Pete, wrote a contract on a napkin, and shook hands for a signature. Definitely not the legal grind he'd learned at Stockton and Stockton, or in the military.

High-fiving Loretta, who was in kid heaven with all the attention, he took the cellar steps down to Reuben's lair.

Wearing a pen in his topknot today, the nerd had set up a story board the way they had back in the day when they were tracking terrorists. An image of Marlene Gump was in the center. A range of senior citizens from the residential home lined one side, with strings and notes running back to Marlene. On the other side were blurry photos of people Jax didn't recognize. He studied those notes while Reuben finished on the computer.

Jax recognized the names of Mrs. Decker, Mrs. Lopez, and Mr. Wong as the identities Marlene had usurped. According to Reuben's notes, all three had been in the same rehab center associated with the residential home. Evie had met Mrs. Decker, who had gone home with the assistance of a home nursing service. Mrs. Lopez was now in the assisted living portion of the residence, in the wing designed for patients with dementia. Mr. Wong was deceased. As best as he could tell from Rube's notes, Marlene had been toying with various scammers by using those identities, but he didn't know if she'd traced any bad guys.

Reuben had taped a list of former patient/residents from Marlene's files on the wall.

Below them, he displayed employee photo ID tags—*which bore the same names as the former residents*. Weird. Jax didn't think the patients were actually employees. The ID photos on the badges were all of people much younger than the ages associated with the patients.

Employees had *stolen* the names of the patients? The deceased or demented ones, anyway.

Reuben finally signed off and came over to point at the employee ID tags. "All employed by Sunshine Home Healthcare Services, which operates the residential living home and the associated nursing home and home health services."

Jax pointed at the list of senior citizens. "And these?"

"Victims of identity theft. Some reported to police. Some victims Mrs. Gump must have dug out on her own because they're dead or *non compos mentis*. She had proof that some of Sunshine's employees were using stolen IDs. If the thieves knew about the information she'd compiled, she had enough enemies to murder her a dozen different ways."

"They're all illegals?" Jax studied the faces on the employee tags. A diverse collection of ethnicities and ages, there was nothing that screamed *illegal* beyond their stolen names.

"Or they have a record or a past they want to hide. Maybe they're running from abusive spouses. Who knows? Except using stolen identities pretty much guarantees every single one of them works cheap and keeps their mouths shut if they see anything questionable."

"Like housekeepers stealing mail with credit card and bank information? The seniors we met the other night are perfectly capable of trusting anyone who enters their apartments. They probably leave the mail on the kitchen table and their wallets at their bedside." Jax wriggled his shoulders in discomfort as he studied faces. He didn't like sending Evie into a place riddled with criminals or desperate victims.

"That seems to be the direction Mrs. Gump was going. She didn't have much in the way of evidence that anyone had actually been robbed of anything except the identities regularly showing up on the darknet. My gut says she was working it from both sides, trying to infiltrate the gang and find the leader."

"Then she wasn't trying to steal from the demented by using all those accounts?" Jax studied the information beneath the names of the victims from Marlene's computers. She'd had all their bank accounts, investment accounts, credit cards. . . She could have wiped all those people out.

"No evidence of it. Her bank account just had regular deposits from pensions and an annuity and distributions from her IRAs. She could have used any of those credit cards to feather her nest, but there was no sign that she did. Most of her victims wouldn't have noticed. You saw her place. She wasn't living in wealth."

"None of these employees using the stolen IDs are feathering their nests with their ill-gotten identities?" Jax pointed at the ID tags.

"Not so's I can tell. They're just using the names to work and collect paychecks. So far, I ain't found one of them living in anything more than poverty."

"So, the ones using the stolen names and social security numbers are all housekeepers and janitors and the like?" Jax studied the rest of the wall. "Who's paying their payroll taxes?"

"I'm not finding any payroll reports that match the stolen identities on the Sunshine ID tags. Sunshine's payroll reports mostly includes management. Let's estimate they employ a thousand lower-level people with stolen IDs who make over a thousand a month each. Not paying FICA alone would save the company nearly *ten grand a month* on the employer portion. If the company is fraudulently deducting FICA from wages, and not paying the government, that's twenty grand in their pockets—a *month*. And you know they're not providing health insurance or pension savings or any other perks. That's practically felony theft on its own."

Reuben pointed at another line of names and faces. "Here's where the money goes."

Jax studied the images. The photographs appear to have been cut from a website or financial report. All white, all ages, all in executive attire. "Management?"

Reuben grimaced. "I'm not positive those photos belong with those names, but they're listed as the board of directors and officers of Sunshine in the handouts they give to prospective clients. There's a host of directors and managers and whatnot under them, like Murkowski and Stanislaus that we met, but no ID tags like the regular employees. I just have their names from the FICA reports. No scrimping on taxes there. All legal and aboveboard."

Jax studied the officers and directors. "Huh, I can see why you think Granny's apartment is in a white folks' home. Do they just accept white residents? Hard to get Medicare approval that way."

"Not for me to say, but I'm staying clear. The only place I'd fit in there is as janitor, and I'm not doin' that." Reuben pinned a photo under Marlene's image. "This is her son, Professor James Gump, Doctor of Philosophy at some obscure college in upstate New York. And I'm going to stick my neck out here and say—government agent. He doesn't stay in one place long enough to really have a teaching job but shows up in scenes where the feds have a presence. The college is just a name on a resume."

"Followed in the family footsteps, did he? Any indication where he is now?"

"Not upstate New York." Reuben pointed to another row of names, some accompanied with pictures. "I'm going to start digging here. This is Sunshine's upper management. Mrs. Gump was compiling dossiers, but they're not thorough. She had next to nothing on the CEO and CFO. From what I've seen, those names were just made-up for marketing."

"Do you have Ariel and Roark checking finances? And someone needs to compile lists of patients and residents who have died or departed for any reason."

"You think they may have murdered others? For why?" Reuben grimaced as he thought about it. "Can't imagine anyone else getting nosy the way Mrs. Gump did, but yeah, if they kill one nuisance, there might be others. Will do."

Jax headed for the stairs. "You're good with Loretta's party? You didn't sign on for the favorite uncle role."

Reuben actually smiled. "Larraine said she'd better be on the guest list. We're going to show those kids how to boogey."

Jax was relieved to see the solemn nerd displaying signs of life. "And their parents. I'm thinking parents will show up to keep an eye on their darlings and for free entertainment. Evie's family doesn't exactly fly under the radar."

Reuben looked a little more sober. "Unlike us."

Jax winced. "Truth. But we're not spooks anymore. We need to adapt better than Prof Gump unless we want to abandon our families the way he did."

That meant Roark, too. He was healing. How long would he be willing to stay out of trouble with Ariel? If past experience was an example, the Cajun was building up an impressive amount of steam that needed an outlet before he exploded.

Sixteen

EVIE CLIMBED OFF THE HARLEY IN FRONT OF THE AZALEA Retirement Apartments, removed her helmet, and ran her hand through her hair. "We can't exactly sneak up on these wheels, can we?"

"Or with a Miata." Jax hooked the helmets to the bike. "I could help you find a junker and soup it up."

"Really? You work on cars?" She slipped her hand around his hunky biceps as they strolled up the walk. "You are a man of many surprises."

"Perhaps a legacy of my engineering father. He used to work on an old Camaro." He opened the door into the air-conditioned lobby. "Does Stacey know we're coming?"

"Yup. She's expecting a long, lawyerly talk. I'll do my thing while you keep her distracted." As they signed the guest book, Evie noticed a faded aura blending into the wallpaper that was definitely not Granny. She didn't dare tune out while everyone at the desk watched.

But when they reached the elevator wall, she tugged Jax's arm. "Wait a sec." She took a seat on a bench and bent over to rummage in her tote.

The aura hovered anxiously. *Anxious* seemed to be the spirit's key color. Hoping no one noticed a woman digging in her purse, Evie opened her extra perception.

Female, she was fairly certain. An older spirit, no longer bothering to cling to worldly elements like body or clothes—just pure energy. "How may I help you?" she asked while pretending to examine the contents of her bag.

The energy seemed tentative and uncertain. That wasn't unusual. Spirit energy normally withered down to a core focus, something left undone or unsaid or unsolved, in Evie's experience. But this one seemed to understand that Evie might see her. "Did Marlene send you?"

A quick nod, a flicker of relief, no words. So ghosts could talk to other ghosts? Good on Granny!

"I can send you on to join your family, if you like," she murmured, as if talking to herself.

"Look? First?" The voice was little more than a mental whisper but conveyed the message.

Evie translated that as unwilling to leave until they looked at something first. Typical. "Lead the way." Holding her cell phone as if that had been the goal of her search, she stood up again.

Jax watched warily, rightfully so. Even Evie knew talking to thin air was peculiar. The aura drifted toward the elevator just as the doors opened and several people stepped out. The aura passed through them, leaving them shivering. Evie tugged Jax into the now-empty car.

Since they'd already ascertained there were no cameras in here and no others joined them, Evie felt free to speak once the doors closed. "Did you know Marlene Gump? The lady on the fourth floor?" She rubbed her bare arms to warm the goose bumps.

The aura oscillated a little before finding speech. "Yes. Helped me."

Evie tried to contain her interest. Mostly, she offered old spirits an energy gateway to whatever was on the next plane. She'd been doing it since she was a kid but understood little. But then, she'd been confined to Afterthought's ghosts.

Here in the city, she had more opportunity for study.

She's learned better than to ask for a name. Names seemed to disappear first. Instead, she asked, "What floor?"

Again, the hesitation. She was fairly certain she heard "Five." She pressed the button and squeezed Jax's arm in appreciation of his silence.

On the fifth floor, Evie followed the faded aura down the hall to an office in a corner. The name plaque read *Savanna Johnson, RN*. The ghost passed through the door. Evie couldn't do that.

No one answered her knock. "What's the protocol on entering an empty office?"

"If it's unlocked, go for it. We can come up with an excuse later. Locked, forget about it." His aura reflected more curiosity than fear. He even turned the knob for her.

The door opened. With delight, Evie entered a cluttered office spilling over with files, what appeared to be medical textbooks, and an assortment of junk vases and knick-knacks. A cabinet of first aid supplies looked like a yard sale jumble.

She winced. She wouldn't want even her finger bandaged by this person. She looked for the aura and found it growing brighter in the dusky gloom. Dust-caked blinds looked as if they hadn't been opened in a decade. Perhaps no one actually worked here.

"Mine," the spirit whispered, hovering near the desk.

Had Savanna Johnson died and this was her ghost? Had the home not had a nurse since then?

Puzzled and curious, Evie appropriated a Kleenex and used it to open the top drawer. The spirit seemed to shake its head negatively. Evie touched the handles of the rest of the drawers until she reached the bottom and received a positive response.

Macho Man stood watch at the door while Evie rummaged through candy bars, potato chips, and the detritus that normally gathered at the bottom of a purse, like old lipsticks and Kleenex—until she finally reached an object that screamed This Does Not Belong.

She removed the brown velvet jewelry case and opened it—a diamond solitaire. "Yours?" she asked the now happily glowing aura. Surely if the nurse had died, her heirs would have cleaned out her desk?

Remembering Reuben's description of all the people poking around Granny's apartment—maybe the resident nurse had *stolen* a dead patient's ring? Especially if the relatives weren't right there to stand guard, like Stacey. The place might have a culture of appropriation.

"Granddaughter's. Return?" the spirit whispered, again tentatively.

Without knowing a name. . . "What was your apartment number?"

The aura grayed to hesitating gloom, then spun around to locate an emergency exit map on the wall. "Me."

A translucent finger pointed at a room midway down the fifth level hall, on the right side that overlooked the front lawn. "Room 552?"

The spirit didn't have an answer for that. It just waited expectantly.

Instinct had her asking, "Was Marlene looking for this?" Evie held up the ring box.

The aura nodded definitively. "Got caught."

"She got caught looking in here?" Before she died, presumably. That was worrisome.

The aura nodded. "They locked door."

But it wasn't locked now that Granny was gone. Unable to get more comprehensive answers, Evie pocketed the ring box, opened herself to the energy, and assisted the now-relieved spirit to the next plane.

Absorbing all that foreign essence always left her drained. She leaned on Jax as he helped her out of the office.

"Text Reuben to wipe that security camera," he muttered as he hurried her down the hall. "That looks an awful lot like theft."

"The ring belongs to the former occupant of 552, who wants to leave it to her granddaughter. We should stop and ask the current resident if she knew who had the apartment before her."

Evie sent the text to Reuben while Jax pondered the wisdom of her demand. Yeah, she knew it would expose them. But she was into asking questions.

Jax was more nefarious. "I'll have Reuben see if he can find the home's resident lists. They probably have files. Let's not clue anyone into our activities if we can avoid it."

"I don't like carrying around a stolen ring," she complained as he half-dragged her back to the elevator.

"You'd still have to carry it even after you knocked on doors. You just want to chat."

Well, yeah. She needed a better handle on a facility that had a thief for a nurse and residents who helped themselves to anything that wasn't nailed down.

~

"MY GRANDMOTHER'S DOCTOR SAID SHE CALLED HIM ABOUT FLU-like symptoms. He told her antibiotics wouldn't be effective, and she should take aspirin and stay hydrated, that he could send her an electrolyte solution, if she wanted, but she refused." Stacey sobbed into her tissue.

"Suicides don't call for medical help." Jax kept their client distracted as Evie slipped off to talk to Granny.

The ring escapade fretted at his thirst for justice. Evie had essentially stolen a ring—at the behest of a ghost? But it was the possibility that a nurse had stolen it first that had his gut clenching.

Stacey stopped sniffing to think about that. "You think it was accidental?"

"Unless she had dementia, not accidental." He hated saying that, but she had to understand the danger here.

Stacey froze. "You think someone *deliberately* put anti-freeze in her food?"

"Drink would be more likely, I'd think. Sweet stuff, like Gatorade." Jax tried not to pace.

"She kept soft drinks and such in the refrigerator to serve her friends. How would anyone know which bottle to poison if they meant to kill her?" She didn't seem any happier with the idea of murder.

"If the residents are in the habit of sharing bottles of drink, someone might have deliberately handed her a doctored bottle when she was visiting elsewhere. Or an alternative—there was one case where a woman murdered her husband by feeding him poisoned gelatin in the hospital when he didn't die from the first dose."

Stacey looked horrified. "Granny had *fruit gelatin* packages in her pantry. She knew better than to eat wasted calories, but she still made the stuff. Could someone have poisoned her salad?"

Hell, he shouldn't have mentioned that. "Did you throw out any salad when you cleaned the fridge?"

She shook her head and wiped her eyes, but she finally seemed to be thinking again.

"If the doctor told your grandmother to drink more, the killer could have kept handing her poisoned bottles. I doubt there was anything you could have done even if you'd been here. Did the coroner's report mention the contents of her stomach?"

Jax wondered what Evie was doing in the back bedroom with Granny's ghost. He didn't even know if Stacey understood what it was that Evie did. It wasn't as if he could explain. *He* still didn't quite believe it but walking right to that ring had raised his hackles.

Stacey shuddered. "No. The detective just barged in and asked to see the kitchen and got angry when I told him I threw out everything except the unopened cans and packages in her pantry, which I gave away."

"What else was in the fridge?"

"Old packages of condiments and bottles of drink. I even drank some of the water! Why would any of those nice old people kill my grandmother? She was helping them!"

"You knew she was helping them?" Jax didn't glance at the camera Roark had planted. At some point, they needed to collect the equipment before the apartment was leased to someone else.

"Gran said the staff was always pilfering small things. She had a way of tracking down the culprits and demanding them back. She never really adjusted to retirement, but her heart was bad, and she couldn't do anything any more active. I asked the doctor if she suffered much before she died. He said the poison probably just exacerbated her condition, and that she probably died peacefully." Stacey rubbed her face and appeared a little more relieved reminding herself of that.

For Stacey's sake, he hoped that was the case. He was no doctor though. "Is there anywhere else you can stay? There is some possibility that someone here stopped your grandmother from finding something more incriminating than trinkets."

She shook her head. "I moved to Atlanta a year ago. I suppose I could call Goodwill and see if they'll haul off all the rest of this stuff, but I was hoping I could sell some of it. I'm freelance, and money is tight."

Jax knew that feeling. "And your grandmother left you everything? Didn't that include IRAs or life insurance or anything?"

"Once the coroner releases her body and gives me a death certificate, I can use her insurance to arrange a funeral. Even though I showed them her will, her broker and banker won't talk to me until I have the certificate. I found bank statements in her desk, so if no one has stolen the balances, I'll have a cushion against hard times. I won't be rich by any means."

"You haven't hired me as lawyer, and I don't think you need one yet, but I'll see what I can do to expedite matters." Jax texted Reuben and asked if Marlene Gump had anything beyond bank accounts.

Evie drifted back to the front room. She tried not to look spacey when she was conversing with the spirit world, but Jax could tell she wasn't really *in* the room when she headed for the galley kitchen. A cabinet door slammed and the room turned several degrees chillier.

"All of them?" she seemed to mutter, opening doors on empty cabinets. "Did you think you were Miss Marple?"

Stacey stopped talking to watch. Jax just kept texting with Reuben, who had finally accessed Marlene's cloud and her security cameras. Apparently, the number of people visiting Granny in the week before her death included everyone but the governor. Granny was a busy lady.

"Power drink? Who brought it?" Evie asked, opening the empty trash can. "Who usually drank it?"

"Is she talking to Gran?" Stacey whispered. "Could I talk to her?"

Jax would like to say, *hell if I know.* But he was a professional. "Hard to say. Each case is different. We shouldn't disturb her." He felt like a shill for a phony medium, but it sounded as if Evie was learning a few things. He hoped.

"Yes, I understand. I'll tell her. Did you have anyone else working with you? Give me their room numbers."

"Spirits apparently don't remember names," Jax explained in a whisper.

"Wait a minute. Let me grab paper." Evie glanced around frantically.

Jax pulled a notebook from his jacket pocket and handed it over with a pen.

Evie flashed a smile of gratitude and began scribbling. "Ok, ok, if all this is in your files, we'll find it. The burner *phone*? Not an app. Ok, ok, right."

She stopped talking, leaned against the counter, and closed her eyes wearily. "Do you have anything to say to Stacey?"

Stacey straightened eagerly.

"Ok, yes, but that's rude. I'm sure he's busy with important work." Evie shook her head. "Will do. You need to let go and move on though."

Evie slumped, and Jax caught her, half carrying her to the sofa. Stacey stayed frozen where she was.

"Give the kid some kind words," Jax whispered in Evie's ear. To Stacey, he said, "Bring a glass of water?" He hastily added, "From the faucet."

Evie sipped the water, recovering her strength. Understanding how much these encounters took out of her, Jax watched worriedly. She wasn't just talking to walls but lending her strength to some inexplicable energy so the spirit could communicate.

Remembering what she'd said about drawing from batteries and other energy, he checked his phone charge. Way down. He pulled out his back-up battery.

Evie finally set down the glass and looked at her client. "Your grandmother says she loves you, and she's sorry she left you with this mess, and that you should probably go home and stay safe. I think she's right."

Jax suspected that was a stubborn expression setting Stacey's pale lips.

"What was the part about being rude?"

Jax could almost see Evie's thoughts whirling, but she was always honest, in her own way. He'd hear the rest later. He waited to see what came out now.

"Your grandmother is irritated with your father for putting job before family. I won't repeat her exact words because spirit communication is as much emotion as intellect. But she wants him here instead of you. He was supposed to collect her computers and finish her case." Evie sipped more water before continuing. "Personally, I think you need him to find your grandmother's killer and not us."

"My father? My father teaches philosophy. What would he know about computers and killers? He can barely use his cell phone."

Remembering what Reuben had said about the professor, Jax bit his tongue.

Evie wasn't so polite. "Your grandmother says he's working with the feds, just like her. He has resources we don't."

Looking incredulous, Stacey kept shaking her head. "No, that's impossible. After Mom died, he needed distraction, started taking visiting professor seats, speaking at conferences, just to escape the empty house. If you knew him, you'd understand. He's presiding over a conference in some small European country right now, or he'd be here."

A lamp crashed to the floor.

They all stared.

When nothing else went flying, Evie shrugged. "I don't think your grandmother agrees. Even if you can't call him, you should probably stay elsewhere. Your gran was on the trail of a rather large gang of criminals. You don't want them suspecting you're a danger to them too."

"Me? I don't know anything? I—"

Jax interrupted. "One of those nice old people may have spiked your grandmother's drink with antifreeze. Go home. Call an estate sale company to deal with the rest of the furniture. The cost of their commission isn't worth your life. Lock up and hide the keys. I'll email you a power of attorney to sign and handle the estate for you. Evie isn't the police. She can't protect you more than that."

The air filled with an old-fashioned perfume Jax recognized from his late, adoptive mother.

Granny giving her blessing to his suggestion?

Good Lord, he sounded like a psychic medium groupie.

Seventeen

ROARK ROVED RESTLESSLY THROUGH THE WOODS AFTER DARK. He should be sleeping. Or tracking his father's villainy. Or his brothers' activities. But he was a physical man and needed physical outlets. He'd caught up with a few old girlfriends over the summer. They'd had a little fun, but he wasn't eager to make them permanent. He hadn't enjoyed his home's narrow parameters when he was a kid, and after traveling the world, he certainly couldn't handle the limitations now. Marriage and babies were not his goals in life.

So, yeah, maybe he was a hypocrite. He was learning to enjoy the weird mindsets of Afterthought, so all small towns weren't alike. Maybe cotton fields were better than swamps. Besides, two big cities were just a short drive away. All he needed was transportation.

He jogged around the nearly dry pond a few times, working his injured leg muscle. Then he chinned himself on a few branches. The mosquitoes didn't bother his Cajun hide, but the knowledge that the enigmatic female on her computers could watch what he was doing had him on edge.

Over this past year, he'd observed Jax's fragile sister from a distance with fascination. Elegant, contained, graceful, and super intelligent—Ariel was everything he'd dreamed of growing up. Of course, no one from her country club set would ever look at a rough nobody like him—but Ariel didn't seem to need *anyone*.

And now that he was living with her—he'd learned that she was an irritating witch. Yeah, she had issues. Didn't everyone? He accepted that. But she'd spoken *an entire sentence* today. That proved that she *could* communicate. She simply didn't want to be bothered.

She preferred sitting in the dark and silence to living.

Now *that* was a severe irritation, wasting all her beauty and brains.

He chinned himself a few more times in frustration. There wasn't any way he was sleeping while his blood was running hot. But after passing his sap-sticky hands through his thick hair and dislodging enough debris for a robin's nest, he conceded a shower might help. He needed to shave these damned curls but he traveled light and only had his straight edge.

He knew how to be silent. His life had depended on it too many times. He actually preferred silence. That's when he could hear the sounds of the earth and people breathing. The one true advantage of small towns was the relative quiet. Cities where the noise never stopped were painful.

He thought Ariel might be a little like that. So he showered as noiselessly as he could and tried not to disturb her as he prepared their midnight snack.

Sitting at the kitchen table, nibbling half a sandwich, he opened his laptop. He'd already looked up Professor Gump, no surprises there. Reuben had been spot on. The prof was a spook.

He hunted down a few of the Sunshine officers out of curiosity and habit. The HR director was from Russia. He had her pinned as FSB in disgrace, but that was instinct. He couldn't read Cyrillic if he hacked it.

He checked to see if anyone had sent him anything new and interesting to work on. Tracing Pris's call had been a dead end leading to a cheap dumb phone, as he'd suspected. Still, knowing the location of the call was his hometown in Louisiana—and not Atlanta, where the caller purported to be—had given them evidence that they were on the right track.

Give him enough time and incentive. . . He could figure out a hack with that money app. It niggled at the back of his mind while he concentrated on other things.

Ariel had sent him a collection of bank statements from the Sunshine employees Evie was investigating. Weird. If he didn't know better, he'd swear banks had hired Ariel to hack their security. If she was anything like Jax, she hacked first, then warned the banks of their security breaches.

Why had she sent him these instead of his father's case? He scanned the statements first, looking for anomalies. He compared the names on the accounts to the staff chart Reuben had compiled—all upper management. Routine salary deposits, odds and ends of trifling deposits. No big entries of any sort—just the usual middle-class paycheck-to-paycheck survival. These clods were definitely working for the feels, not the money or glory.

Reuben the PhD had established a cloud account for the Gump files. Roark uploaded the bank statements there and looked to see if anything new had been added . Solving a puzzle was just a matter of fitting the pieces together—once they had all the pieces. They were just establishing the framework.

Apparently Ariel had grown bored with Pris's case and moved on to Evie's. As he watched, his mailbox filled with credit reports on the same employees he'd just looked at. These were a little more interesting. Comparing the property value of the houses people owned to the mortgage payments to the bank accounts. . . Unless they all had rich uncles, something did not compute. A tiny $40,000 mortgage on a $400,000 house was highly unusual for a young person. A $360,000 down payment?

Substantial down payments had to come from somewhere.

One or two people may have inherited parental homes but half of management? Did Ursula's used car salesman husband make that much money? If so, he was a crook.

The only thing that made sense was they were being paid under the table. So much for working for the feels.

He made a list of closing dates on the more suspicious loans and sent them to Ariel, asking if she could find large deposits in those accounts around that time. They hadn't all bought houses at once but over a period of the last ten years.

He didn't know why he was doing this instead of working on his father's case. Maybe because the only way to stop phone scammers was to blow them up, and even that hadn't stopped his da.

So, how did one stop a phone scam? His hometown police evidently weren't concerned.

Now, if he was on the receiving end of his da's calls. . . How could he arrange that?

Once he'd set Reuben to digging on Evie's case, Roark researched phone scams. The videos of gangs in Jamaica and entire call centers selling investments in Israel, all built around ripping off Americans by the billions of dollars, set his teeth on edge. Having grown up poor, he could almost get with the program of robbing the rich and stupid but not when the stolen money was buying guns and drugs and Rolexes. And since there were far more working people than wealthy. . . It wasn't the rich being robbed.

His father and his homeboys had the same excuses as these international gangs. They couldn't find work, or minimum wage didn't pay the bills. They had no money to feed their families. . . Why not skim a little fat off wealthier cows?

But people like Pris's mother had worked hard for those dollars and didn't have a lot to spare. Why should she lose the savings needed for eye surgery so Da could buy a Cadillac?

Watching these videos gave him ideas. His father's operation was small. He had somehow obtained thousands of phone numbers, enough to keep a few local boys employed. But they needed a steady array of victims to keep the money flowing. If he could dam up the river of cash. . .

That might buy him some time to get his hack in place.

Lost in work, he forgot Ariel's' timetable—until the pocket door slid open, and she was there, looking as startled as he felt.

Damn, the woman looked good. Even when hunkered down where no one could see her she wore a fancy tailored white shirt and slim navy shorts that emphasized her lean length. She'd tied her long dark hair in a sleek ponytail looped off her neck. His mouth practically watered.

Refusing to flee, Roark pointed at the sandwich he'd made for her. "I have an idea. Listen while you eat. Tell me what you think."

As if that were happening. . . But he needed to talk this out. He was used to lots of company—his huge family when he was a kid, his fraternities at school, his military units after graduation. . . He needed people.

Ariel's crystal-gray, long-lashed eyes widened in alarm. Then, warily, she studied him, studied the food, then studied his laptop. Apparently deciding he wouldn't bite, she gingerly settled into her usual chair and opened her paper notebook to take her game notes.

That didn't stop him from talking.

By the time he'd lined up his plan, Ariel had covered her ears, and her eyes practically spun in their sockets—but she was listening.

∾

ARIEL PRESSED HER FOREHEAD AGAINST HER ARMS AND LET Roark's river of sound sink into her fractured brain. She grasped his point easily—he wanted to stop his father's villainous depredations.

The rest—relied on complications beyond her comprehension, other than that the smallness of his father's operation made it possibly possible.

Her guest sat there in that damned tank top, looking all bronzed, muscled, and confident—so much so that her heart raced, and she didn't dare look his way again. She had to *think*.

How did normal women handle this rush of hormones? That's what it must be. She'd never experienced this level of—lust? She'd read the books, understood hunger and sex were primitive human urges. She fed herself regularly so an empty stomach didn't interfere with her work. But sex. . .

She was twenty-four and had never even had a date. Lust had never been on her spectrum.

Roark wanted a response. What could she say?

It took her a few minutes to process all his words and formulate a sentence. She'd rather divert a river of bitcoins. Numbers made sense. People didn't. "Divert *how many* phones?"

He took time to slow down and explain again. "Probably two dozen to start with."

She dared peer up at him again. She grasped *two dozen*. "How?" She hated sounding uncertain.

"We'll need the cooperation of the victims, so not easily." He waited for her to process that.

She nodded, understanding from the difficulty Pris had separating her mother from her phone. "Why?"

He lifted one finger. "Tie up the thieves' time by asking stupid questions when they call."

Ariel grasped the frustration that would cause if the conmen spent hours without scoring a dime. Some might quit and walk away.

Roark held up a second finger. "Set up a bank account with a small balance. Pretend we're victims and send them checks. If they're stupid enough to use snail mail, we'll catch them picking up the mail. If they ask for card numbers, we'll bumble about and give them wrong ones, make them call back."

She grimaced. "Stupid."

Ignoring the commentary, he held up a third finger. "Once we have solid phone numbers, we robo-call them, keep their lines tied up."

Ariel shrugged. Small operation, she remembered. But that wouldn't catch the crooks, just drive them crazy. She waited.

"Once we're locked into their actual phone accounts, we text alerts or leave voicemail telling them their phones are no longer secure."

Ariel straightened, wide-eyed. She could get inside a computer with that kind of message, but a phone? "How?"

"Reuben has the software. We just need to provide solid numbers."

"Why?"

Roark rubbed his big nose as if looking for a simple explanation. He finally shrugged those lust-inducing shoulders and talked. "Scammers running the insecure-phone fraud normally convince their victims that, for a few hundred dollars, they can save their data and/or clean out the phone." He waited.

Ariel nodded. She'd been reading up on scams.

"What I want to do is tell the thieves that the police are monitoring their phones, and they need to take them to an address I'll set up, to exchange them for new ones."

"Preposterous," she scoffed. But he looked so very eager. . . And she loved it when this man looked at her with hope and confidence. It made her tingle in inappropriate places. She knew she was super-smart about numbers, but she had limited understanding of human behavior. "What do I do?"

"Identify the best targets—elderly, alone, money in the bank." He said it slowly, watching her every second, looking delighted with himself—and maybe her, just a little bit?

Ariel nodded. She could do that.

"I already started that, but I need more. Once I have a list of people agreeing to divert their numbers, I'll need people to man the phones."

She couldn't do that. She glanced at her game camera notebook. She hadn't noted one single thing this evening. She itched to check the videos and update her notes. What if she had missed something significant? But the clock said she should return to work.

She hadn't really noticed the sandwich she'd nibbled at. She was grateful Roark saved her the time needed for preparing food. She hated to leave it behind. She hated messy food near her equipment.

"Eat," he said softly. "I'll leave you to think about it. I've got one more trick up my sleeve if the bastards don't give up. If hacking doesn't work, we'll whack the moles."

She had no idea what he was talking about, except he wanted her participation. Her therapist had said she should expand her boundaries, try new things. She watched him go, wishing she could go with him, like a regular person.

Instead, she finished her sandwich and returned to work late, like a regular person.

Eighteen

EVIE CURLED UP ON JAX'S BROAD, NAKED CHEST AND TOOK comfort from his heat and strength. He might not stick around, but she enjoyed this luxury while she could. "Marlene could have lived another decade or two and brought down a gang of thieves, but they eliminated her like so much trash!"

The night silence settled around them. Even the old Victorian lady quit squeaking and groaning as the worst of the day's heat slowly dissipated in a breeze. Evie took comfort in knowing others slept safely beneath her roof. She loved having a family of her choosing.

"Marlene had a heart condition. She knew that and took her chances anyway. I don't like you investigating killers. Did she tell you anything useful that you can just pass on?" Jax stroked her back.

Stroking helped her focus. Evie sighed and squirmed as she tried to recall unclear messages from the dead. "She said she liked power drinks because no one else drank them. Apparently, the neighbors had a habit of helping themselves to each other's refrigerators."

"So anyone could have laced her glass or bottle and assumed only Marlene would drink it. We still have no proof that she didn't ingest something intended for someone else. We need the full coroner's report. I have Reuben on it."

"On TV, they know all this instantly." Frustrated, she turned on her back. "The killer could be in the Bahamas by now."

"Stacey hired you to find out what her grandmother was doing, not to find a thief and a killer. You need to tell her Marlene was after nursing home thieves—then walk away. It's not as if she can afford more."

Evie punched his ribs. He didn't flinch.

"Granny was after more than petty thieves. You know that. I can't let them get away with murder. I can't let them keep robbing the helpless. It's just not in me. You and the others can move on, if you like—"

He turned on his side and pinned her to the mattress. "You talk to *ghosts*. You have no skill at tracking thieves and no means of defending yourself against killers. Figure if you keep investigating, we're all right there with you. If you don't want us to investigate, then you can't either."

"Well, that's one way of being sure you'll never get rich and leave us." Evie kissed his hard jaw.

One thing led to another, and the discussion was abandoned for better activities.

But in the morning, Reuben served up a plate of clues to feed their curiosity.

"Room 552 belonged to a Mary North, who died unexpectedly last spring. Relatives raised a stink about missing jewelry, but they had no proof that she hadn't sold it or given it away. Marlene Gump, however, claimed the nurse, Savanna Johnson, was selling it on eBay. The account was gone by the time the police investigated. The police report was pretty sloppy and inconclusive. With no photos to go on, they didn't even subpoena eBay. Except for the diamond, at most, the jewelry might have been worth a few hundred, not enough to look hard for the thief."

"But the memories of those pieces would mean more to her children than money." Evie let Reuben fix his own breakfast. He usually ate healthy but inhaled enough food to require a full-time cook. That wasn't her. "Do you have the name of Mary North's granddaughter?"

"Emailed it to you last night. She's in Kentucky. What will you do—send her an anonymous package? You've removed the only evidence the police might have had." Working at keeping his athletic physique, he slathered his toast with avocado paste and sprinkled on bean sprouts she grew on the windowsill.

"If the police didn't search that office earlier, they won't now. Anyone could have planted that box. What did you find out about the nurse?"

"She's as old as some of the residents. History of drunk driving. Out on leave after knee surgery. Her eBay sales almost cover her liquor bill. That's if she's really Savanna Johnson. I've found no evidence to the contrary. Driver's license, employee ID, and high school reunion photos on Facebook all add up."

"She might not be part of the ID theft ring. Management may just be guilty of hiring cheap help. I imagine a good nurse is expensive. One with a DUI record, probably not. It's pretty obvious they aren't concerned with keeping decent medical help on staff." Hearing voices coming down the stairs, Evie mixed up the whole grain pancakes Loretta preferred.

"Is fifty too many people?" the kid was asking, holding up her iPad to Jax as they entered the kitchen together.

Looking lawyerly and relaxed in his open-collared shirt, with his jacket dangling over one broad shoulder, Jax studied the list. "Impressive. I think your bank account can handle it. The question is, can Evie?" He looked up and winked at her.

She felt that wink all the way to her toes. The man was sin on wheels. She feared that a man with all that happening for him would abandon them one day when he found a better paying, more interesting position. He had ignored her worry last night. She didn't know what to make of that.

"Any of the neighbors on the guest list?" Stifling her quivering hormones, Evie poured batter on the griddle.

"All of them," Loretta said eagerly. "I didn't think it would be polite to make them listen and not let them dance too."

"Sunbeam." Reuben patted her approvingly on the head. "Larraine said she'd take you to her stylist if you still want your hair cut."

This was how life should be, Evie thought—neighbors thinking of neighbors, not *stealing* from them. What kind of unhealthy influence caused people to turn nasty?

"Maybe we ought to hold a wake for Granny, invite all the residents of Azalea Apartments, and serve only power drinks in her honor." She flipped the pancakes and added Jax's eggs and bacon to the griddle.

"Only if that's what the coroner's reports says she ingested. Miss Marple may need Gatorade and gelatin salads if she wants to catch a killer." Jax prepared his coffee.

"Soda crackers, ginger ale, and purple something or another," Reuben said, adding fruit and yogurt to the blender. "Coroner called for more tests. She lost a lot of stomach contents before she died."

Evie wrinkled her nose in disgust imagining how. "That's enough cheery news. Let's talk party!"

~

AFTER HER MORNING DOG WALK, EVIE RETURNED HER MOTHER'S golden retriever to the shop, then picked up Psy the Siamese and draped him over her shoulder. "Gossip hour. What will you be discussing today?" Her mother built business by holding court at the Oldies Café before lunch.

Mavis didn't like turning on the a/c, so the loud strains of *I am Woman* drifted in the open front door from the café.

"Your Aunt Ellen has gone crackers." Mavis took off the apron she wore while mixing her herbal concoctions and tucked her graying hair back in its pins. "She's convinced a handsome gentleman will be delivering a Cadillac she won in a contest she never entered. We need to pry her out of the house more."

"You need to convince her to see an eye doc before the scammers empty her bank account. Once she has the cataracts fixed, she can drive and get out again." Evie picked up the feather duster.

"Maybe we ought to find her a handsome man first," Mavis said dryly, taking the dog's leash and heading out. "Larraine called and said she's taking Loretta to the stylist this afternoon. You should go with them."

Evie knew that was a ding at her own unruly mop. After her mother left, Evie pulled on a carrot strand and studied herself in a scrying glass. Maybe her new job required a more sophisticated look? That might take dyeing her hair to something less clown-like.

One of her mother's regulars came in for her hibiscus tea, and Evie forgot about hair.

She had the shop dusted and a few more dollars in the register by the time Mavis returned. Her phone rang at the same time—coincidence or Pris? Evie checked the screen—Pris. Her cousin was too spooky. Heading for the door, she pushed answer.

"We need all the phones you can find," her cousin announced without preface.

"And hello to you too." Evie waved at her mother and headed home. "How you doin'? I'm thinking about cutting my hair."

"Phones, lots of them." Pris ignored the pleasantries. "You should have at least four at your house. Iddy can offer two, plus her mother's. I don't suppose Aunt Mavis has entered the twenty-first century yet?"

"You don't suppose correctly. Will land lines work? What about City Hall? I'm sure this is for charitable purposes, right?" Evie knew better, but her cousin needed to visit Planet Earth occasionally.

"City Hall will let us use their lines? This isn't your idea of a joke?"

"We used them to raise funds for the school's robot team last year. Our charming ex-mayor has an entire phone bank in the conference room. Tell them it's a non-profit fundraiser and you're in. No one really cares anymore. No mayor and no city council chair and old Hank running the show— they're all still in shell shock."

"PTSD," Pris corrected. "Call them, will you? The more phones we have, the faster we can shut down these scammers." She hung up.

Evie called Jax. "Stopping thieves is a charitable event, isn't it?"

"Sure, why not? Are you making enough money to need a tax deduction?"

"Ha, very funny. My radar says Pris is trying to rein in her crazy mother. Pris talks to Ariel. Do you have sister radar? Or do we just assume Roark is somehow involved?"

"If anything is going on, blame Roark. He can't be left unoccupied for two minutes. Need any more legal advice?"

"You are the bestest, most loveliest, most special lawyer in the universe. I may even fix you supper. How's your day going?"

"I shipped the ring to its rightful owner, maybe picked up a new client who wants to sue former Mayor Blockhead for investment fraud, and had an interesting encounter with a fellow attorney who thinks I should butter my bread on the other side."

Knowing the town's infrastructure, Evie processed that easily. "Ted Turlock wants you to drop the Block suits and help him work for the defense."

"You are positively uncanny. Are the smoke signals saying that your former mayor came into money? I might sell my soul if the price is high enough."

That's what worried her occasionally. Jax was used to an expensive lifestyle involving Jags and yachts and country clubs. No sense worrying about what she couldn't change. "No smoke signals that I've picked up. There's rumors Block is selling off property to cover his legal fees. You just want to know what's making the other side nervous. I don't understand politics, but I'll keep my ear to the ground."

"I'm picturing that position and thinking lewd thoughts. Talk to you later." Jax cut the connection.

Evie laughed. Reaching the house, she trotted down the cellar stairs where Loretta played Pac Man on an antique machine. Reuben, on the other hand, had set up a space-age command central in a U-shaped desk covered in electronic equipment.

The desk didn't hold her interest, but her eye caught on a new wall of suspects. She stopped to study the lists of names. "Maybe I should pick a few of these people and study their auras."

"You'll be lucky to find a clean one in the bunch. That's Sunshine's entire resident *and* employee list, including the ones they call independent contractors. Management has surrounded itself with suspicious black knights and helpless pawns."

Evie wondered if the residents were all pawns or contained a few of the black knights. "If you can determine all that with computers, that renders me useless. Should I just go bake a pie?"

Disappointed, she studied the connections between the Sunshine employees. Her team was good at following the money. People were *her* specialty. Well, and observation, maybe, and pies. And driving, if she had a car.

"Nah, we're being methodical, building lists first, looking for weak links. Fewer people we have to interview, the less likely we'll be noticed. I took a look at Stacey's finances. They're pretty clean. Good size student loan but daddy's paying on it. Her free-lancing pays the bills. No Jimmy Choo's on her credit cards."

"So she probably can use cash, but she's not desperate enough to kill her grandmother, we hope."

Reuben shrugged. "About the size of it. Now, your Mr. Charles may be a person of interest. He appears to be related to one of the managers and has occasional large deposits from various people unconnected to anything we can find. Nothing major though."

"Maybe he sells dead people's stuff on eBay too." Evie studied the index cards with red stars inked on them. They all appeared to be managers of some sort. "What's with the stars?"

"Roark determined they took large payoffs in the form of down payments on their houses. Makes for interesting bookkeeping which might matter to the IRS. Ariel is running down the sources of the funds, but they're buried deep in cashier's checks from years ago. My theory is that they're laundering money from the account where they stash their ill-gotten gains from under-paying taxable W-2 wages and whatever other scams they have happening."

Money and banks flew right over Evie's head. She'd never had any until recently. She focused on the index cards, looking for the people behind the money. She grinned hugely when she found a connection she liked.

She tapped the card of Ursula Stanislaus, wife of Dmitri, the HR employee who'd been in Marlene's apartment. She had a red star. "Her husband sells used cars. I think I'll pay him a visit."

Both Loretta and Reuben stopped to stare.

"Are you going with me to have my hair cut?" Apparently understanding Evie wouldn't be available all day, Loretta was the first to break the silence.

"Give me the time and place, and I'll work it into my schedule." Evie waved a hand airily.

Rather than argue, Reuben started typing into his phone. Evie knew what that meant. He was notifying Jax. A girl couldn't do anything around here without an army noticing. She didn't mind. An army couldn't stop her once she made up her mind. It was the making up her mind part that was iffy.

"Four o'clock, at some place in Savannah. I'll email the address." Loretta dug out her phone.

"Perfect. The car dealership is there too. Maybe I'll have a Miata to pick you up in." First, of course, she needed a ride. She couldn't ask Reuben for one. He was better occupied here.

It was Thursday. Iddy would be working. Her sister Gracie had a kid to look after. Pris. . . Who knew what she did. But she'd owe her once she got City Hall lined up. Evie punched in her spooky cousin's number and got voice mail as she climbed out of the cellar. She left a message, then started scrolling through her contacts. She'd only bought the phone a few months ago. Since she usually saw everyone in town every day, she seldom needed to call anyone. Her list wasn't long.

Jax must have been busy because he wasn't texting screams.

How much would an Uber cost? Did Afterthought have anyone driving for Uber? She began poking around to find out.

Not until she walked down the drive to the front of the house did she realize someone was knocking at her door. Not just any someone but one who could have stepped right off the cover of a romance novel. *Wow.* Jax was good-looking and hunky in his muscular military lawyer way. This guy. . . was romance sexy. Towering lean, longish dark hair, Euro-stylish in linen and polished leather, hand in pocket as he frowned at her purple door adorned with whatever amulet Mavis had thought necessary today.

Retrieving her tongue from the roof of her mouth, she called, "May I help you?"

He turned long-lashed dark eyes in her direction and looking relieved, jogged down from the porch to meet her on the lawn. "I'm looking for Damon Ives-Jackson. This was given as his last known address?"

"You know that makes you sound like a bill collector, don't you?" Actually, his accent was too delicious to sound anything other than sophisticated. Italian? With a faint Scottish burr? Was that even possible? Evie did her best to slip into aura mode while he found a counter answer to her challenge.

His aura had the orange-yellowish streak peculiar to Jax when he wasn't riled. . . and Conan Oswin, one of his California relations. She was almost prepared when the stranger replied.

"Sorry." He produced a business card. "I'm Dante Alfonso Ives Rossi. Damon and I have a common ancestor with the Oswins, cousins of his?"

"So they claim. I'm not the ancestry expert. How may I help you, Mr. Rossi?" Evie was torn between summoning her cousins to admire this specimen of male resplendence or warning Jax to hide.

But there didn't seem to be any harm in the stranger's aura, so she stupidly stared and waited.

He shrugged a little uncomfortably in his linen jacket. "It is a long story. If you could simply give me a means to contact him?"

Cellphone already in hand, Evie snapped his photo and sent it to Jax with the message— **ANYONE YOU KNOW?**

"Won't you take a seat on the porch and have some iced tea while we wait to see if he's available?" She gestured toward the shady wrap-around covered porch that gave the Victorian its charm.

Since she hadn't introduced herself, he looked a bit wary. As he ought to be. She could hear Pris's truck puttering down the road already. Her cousin and her mother would have picked up the stranger's presence and sent an all-points bulletin to all the family. They were weird like that.

"Help yourself to any seat. I'll be back in a minute." Evie hurried through the cluttered front room to her great-aunt's eccentrically colorful kitchen. She kept pitchers of tea on hand. A quick glance in the freezer found brownies. She zapped them while gathering a tray of glasses and ice.

By the time she returned to the porch, Pris was leaning against her truck, Iddy had her raven on her shoulder and a leash full of dogs heading this way, Reuben had moseyed out to take a gander, and Jax was pulling up on his Harley. Even her sister Gracie was strolling down the walk with six-year-old Aster in tow. Poor Mr. Rossi wouldn't know what hit him.

She set the tray down on the table nearest the wicker chair he'd chosen. "Have you ever lived in a small town, Mr. Rossi?"

"I spent most of my school years in Edinburgh and Napoli, so no, unless one counts the archeological sites I work on. They barely count as towns, though." He sipped the icy tea and watched Pris watching back.

"Well, you're about to have a small-town experience—" With a dollop of Malcolm weirdness, but Evie didn't mention that. "—so settle in and make yourself comfortable." She took a chair on the other side of the table and poured tea for herself.

Jax strolled up, looking casual with his tie loose and lacking his suit coat. The resemblance was quite uncanny between the two men—square, stubborn jaws, dark eyes, large Roman noses. . . Yeah, Evie would buy the family ties. They both had a sun-bronzed coloring that she was pretty certain was natural and not the product of a tanning bed.

"Did you get my message or are you just coming to stop me from going to Savannah by myself?" she called cheerfully.

Jax pulled out his phone to check his messages, proving he was responding to Reuben's warning about the used car dealer and hadn't seen hers yet. He snorted at the image she'd sent and cut across the lawn to climb the stairs. He held out his hand to the stranger. "I'm Damon Jackson; call me Jax. Dante Rossi? Conan said you've been corresponding." He poured himself a glass of tea.

Mr. Rossi set aside his tea to shake hands. Reuben took that as a signal all was well, clumped up to grab a brownie, and leaned against the porch rail in the background. Evie's cousin and sister consulted on the sidewalk. Given the stranger's good looks, Evie knew the outcome of that discussion. They all strolled up to join the party.

Leaving off their Malcolm names, Evie introduced her family.

Starting to look amused, Mr. Rossi acknowledged the intros. "I did not expect a royal welcome. And the queen of this court? I do not believe I caught your name, Your Highness." He bowed in Evie's direction.

She grinned. "Given names possess a dangerous power in the fairy court. You may simply call me Eve."

"Ah, one of the ancient ones! My Scots relations will appreciate this knowledge. I thank you for the reception, Queen Eve."

Jax placed a proprietary hand on her shoulder. Evie patted it. "You might want to take Mr. Rossi into the library before my family drools down his pretty jacket. I turned the fan on in there."

"While you escape in that menace your cousin calls a vehicle? Not a chance."

Pris didn't argue the description of her mode of transportation but helped herself to a brownie and perched on the porch rail. Today, she'd added a blue streak to her raging red hair dye. She'd had her normally frizzy brown hair cut punk style short and glossed it with product that made her look like a nineties' rock star. Even the newcomer was assessing her warily.

"You call City Hall yet?" Pris demanded.

"After the tea party. Go smash your mother's phone until we can get organized." Evie knew Pris was tuning into brain waves but hadn't quite got a handle on what was happening. Good to know she wasn't the only one.

Iddy, the veterinarian, poured tea and let her raven hop down on the back of Mr. Rossi's chair. He didn't flinch. Iddy was the embodiment of every modern witch Evie had ever seen portrayed—long black sleek hair, willowy tall, and self-possessed. Only she wasn't pale like a good witch should be. She was a healthy ruddy color from her father's Cherokee origins. She was pretty certain Iddy was ticking Mr. Rossi's buttons. Both tall, dark, and lean, they'd make a handsome couple, if Iddy didn't have her raven pluck the poor man's eyes out.

"The bird can follow you when you leave, but it won't hurt you while you're here, unless Iddy orders it, of course." Evie felt it was only fair to offer explanations. Strangers didn't often understand, but he couldn't say she hadn't warned him.

"Ah, I have a cousin who talks to animals," Mr. Rossi said, surprisingly.

"And that's one of the reasons I'm here. The Oswins tell me you know a family of Malcolms. . . Jax."

Evie laughed. Jax squeezed her shoulder again.

"I wouldn't want to reveal names of the fairy court," Jax said dryly. "Why do you need to know?"

For the first time, Rossi looked a little flustered. "One of my. . . Malcolm. . . cousins had a premonition, and I've learned not to ignore her warnings."

Nineteen

JAX TRIED TO STAY LOOSE AND UNCONCERNED, BUT HIS GUT
instincts kicked into high alert at Rossi's warning. "I thought you and Conan
were talking artifact thieves, not weird cousins."

He noted that Evie and her family were nibbling and drinking as if they
hadn't heard their guest's warning, but he was fairly certain that Evie was
checking auras, Pris reading minds, and Iddy probably had the dogs sniffing
for danger. As far as he was aware, the best Gracie could do was mentally fling
cookies at them. The aunts might show up any minute.

He was starting to appreciate this weird psychic shit fantasy.

Rossi rocked his glass back and forth on the arm of the wicker chair. "I
am talking theft with Conan. I could use some. . . how do I say this?
Because of my cousins, I know there are. . . energies. . . beyond current scientific comprehension. I have the cousins working through our family tree,
looking for relations who might have the time and the right ability to help
me in my research of a particularly peculiar cluster of pre-Roman-era
artifacts."

An *archeologist* believed in woo-woo energies? Jax bit his tongue and
listened.

"Your cousins have psychic abilities?" Evie translated.

Rossi nodded in relief. "Yes. And because they were focusing on finding
your branch of the tree, one of them picked up. . . I'm a scientist. I don't

know how to explain. Spiritual connections? Like a guardian angel watching over you? Does that make sense?"

"Nope," Iddy said. "Guardian angels don't watch over witches, or we would be living in an East Hampton mansion like our Puritan brethren instead of hiding in the cotton fields."

"Iddy is an idiot." Pris finished her tea and set the glass on a tray. "Our guardian angels don't let people like us hang around stiff-necked, wealthy aristos. Except they're called spirit energy, not angels. What does this one say?"

Jax didn't think he'd heard Pris string this many words together since he'd met her. She was wound up about something—was she reading Rossi's mind and not liking it?

"Not anything that makes a lot of sense," their visitor admitted. "The message I've been told to pass on is that there is more than one way to kill, and the obvious isn't always the answer."

"Good reminder," Evie said, helping herself to another brownie. "Even if we find the person who put antifreeze in Granny's Gatorade, that person was probably prompted by larger powers who don't care if people die from depression because of their thievery or of neglect from their carelessness. You came all this way to tell us there's something rotten in Denmark?"

Jax hid his smile. Evangeline Malcolm Carstairs looked like an empty-headed Barbie doll. It was sometimes hard to remember that she had a mind that sucked up every bit of knowledge she encountered like a giant information vacuum. And then she processed that information through her extremely eccentric thought processes and came up with flashes of true brilliance. Or psychic idiocy. Hard to tell the difference some days.

Rossi grunted and shrugged. "Well, no, I came in hopes I could find someone interested in working with me in Italy. My family was highly entertained to learn there was a pocket of Malcolms living in near invisibility in the New World. Given their unusual abilities, Malcolms usually stay in touch with family, even the ones in China. Your branch's ancestors appear adept at covering their tracks."

Oops. Jax saw the connections here. A branch of the Ives family he hadn't known about had tracked him down through their genealogy expert. His California cousins had apparently married into a family with odd abilities. It wasn't a far stretch to assume they were a distant branch of Malcolms and had started tracing Evie. He watched to see how Evie and her family took this.

"You're spying on us!" Pris scowled.

Ignoring her cousin, Evie sipped her tea with unconcern. "Our ancestors were called witches and fled for their lives in the 1600s. Your branches who communicate must have traveled much later, when burning at the stake wasn't an option."

"I'd be interested in meeting more of our family," Pris said, surprisingly, although she still scowled. "But my mother has gone bonkers, and I have to keep an eye on her."

Evie held up her cellphone to her cousin. "There, I've texted the non-mayor's secretary, and she just wants to know what date you want for your benefit."

Jax was almost as bewildered as their guest looked.

"Bonkers?" Rossi finally asked. "Is there something we might help with? My cousins like to meddle, so if there is something you need. . . ?"

"Unless you can pour acid through phone lines or air waves, probably not. Evie, make him welcome. I need to set up a sting." Pris set aside her glass and jogged down the drive to her truck.

That probably indicated Pris couldn't find any bad *mental energies* in their visitor.

"I'm sure all of you have better things to do than entertain a stranger. Is there a hotel nearby? I really would like to take a look around now that I'm here." Rossi set his glass down too.

Jax glanced at Evie, but he already knew her response.

"If you don't mind a guest room off the kitchen, you should stay here." She got out of her chair. "Afterthought doesn't have a hotel, and going back and forth from the city gets old. I'd like to know more about this family I didn't know existed. I should call Great-Aunt Val. And my mother and aunts would love to meet you."

Afterthought had a motel. Their guest simply didn't appear to be the sort to live with bedbugs, although Jax supposed an archeological dig might be worse than camping. Well, if Rossi had come to spy for his family, he might as well be subject to the full effect.

"I've only discovered that I have an Ives family, so I'm interested as well," Jax added. "If you don't mind entertaining yourself while occasionally being pestered with questions. . ."

"I have my own questions, so yes, I'd be delighted to accept your hospitality, if you truly don't mind." Rossi politely rose when Evie did.

Evie motioned him back. "I'll just go in and remove Loretta's latest collec-

128

tion of books and put on fresh linen. You need to be warned that the household contains a precocious almost-eleven-year-old who will converse eloquently on both Harry Potter and souls in the same breath. Be careful what questions you ask."

Iddy and Grace excused themselves as well, leaving Jax to quiz the stranger.

Before he could start, Rossi spoke first. "Now that the ladies have departed, I can give you the full message. I've been told that someone here is dealing with a dark energy that has no conscience, that you have a friend who is dealing with this entity also, and that Conan says they're both diving into a dangerous underworld—the real kind, not the metaphysical. He recommends you pull them back."

Jax mentally swore. Been there, done that, and there was no chance of stopping them, if he meant Evie and Roark. He might as well stand in front of a cyclone.

He picked up the tray of empty glasses and nodded at the door. "Looks like I'll have to help Evie find that car she wants so she has a reliable means of escape."

Or of getting into trouble, but she could do that with or without a car.

SITTING ON THE PORCH, WORKING IN COORDINATION WITH Reuben on an AI script that he hoped might clog up his father's call center, Roark heard his cellphone ringing in the kitchen. Damn.

Before he could untangle himself from his laptop and one of Ariel's, he heard her answer. His eyebrows soared, and he settled in to listen. She'd stolen his password as he had hers, so that was fitting. But Ariel *talking*?

He glanced at the time. Ariel not only talking but doing so during her two o'clock shower/exercise hour signaled a significant departure from routine.

He wanted to see if she would throw his forgotten phone at him or just go back to her rut. If he tried, he could probably hear what she was saying, but without hearing the other side, the conversation would still be a mystery. It wasn't as if Ariel was doing more than her usual curt one- or two-word replies.

His curiosity remained elevated as he heard her crossing the front room.

She walked lightly and the floor didn't squeak, but he knew when she reached the door and braced himself.

No way in heaven or hell could he brace himself for the sight of Ariel in a short, red, silk robe, with her luxurious hair wet and wrapped in a white towel. A neglected part of his anatomy stiffened at just the sight of her long bare legs and slim ankles. Her toes scarcely registered while he followed the parting of her loosely tied robe. He was one-hundred per-cent certain she had no idea what she was doing to him.

"Pris." She dropped the phone in his lap. "Phone bank."

Phone bank? He jerked out of his stupor and sat up straight. " A real phone bank?" he asked into the phone, watching Ariel disappear into the house.

The phone replied. "City Hall. Need a date. Make it soon. Mom is heart-broken that Cadillac man hasn't called. Oh, and we're being warned about dark energy gathering."

Roark had been calculating how quickly he could finish his AI program but the warning crashed through logic. "Dark energy?"

"Talk to Evie. Guy came all the way from Italy to tell us what we already know."

Deciding talking to Pris about the metaphysical was less than productive, he went straight for the goal. "How many phones and can we find people to man them?"

"Talk to Evie. I don't do people." She hung up.

If he weren't in this for himself, he'd say screw Pris and her crazy mother. But she'd just offered him the big golden key to his target. He needed to get cracking on the Phase One version of his software. He carried the phone into the house.

Earlier, he'd baked granola bars for Ariel to nibble so she didn't have to eat until she was ready. He set them out and had her tea prepared when she returned, fully dressed in a loose-fitting sundress that swished below her knees. He'd really liked that silk robe.

"I have to talk to Evie and Jax about the phone bank. Are you interested or do I take it outside?"

"Interested." She picked up a granola bar and her mug of tea and settled at the kitchen table with her notebook and phone.

His phone rang with Jax's name before he'd had time to call. "You developing ESP, too, dude?" he put it on speaker.

"Nah, Evie said you needed help with your magic trick. I'm checking to see how many people you want and to let you know my cousin Conan has been poking around in our cases. I'm pretty sure he has some fed connection. He's warning us that these scammers have gang ties. Bringing them down isn't a joke."

Ariel cringed but stoically drank her tea and made her notes. Roark knew he shouldn't impose on her like this, but she was capable of throwing him out if he got too obnoxious. So he had to assume she was interested.

"Well, considering Ariel is following money laundered through bitcoin exchanges and mortgages, we've already worked that out. Da's operation is peanuts to what we're seeing. We'll just make his part of the gang a little less profitable, encourage the bums to find a better job. Let *him* feel the wrath, since I'm guessing he's just a minor cog in a very large engine."

"Keep Ariel out of this," Jax warned.

Ariel stuck her tongue out at the phone.

"You just received a childish FU. Shall I teach her how to say it properly?" Roark bit into a granola bar. Jax had been his superior for years, but times changed.

"She's listening? And not hiding her head under her arms? Huh."

Ariel added a finger gesture.

"Need to Facetime this, man. That's another up yours. Any more brotherly words of wisdom?"

"Just be careful who you rope into whatever you're planning. I have to help Evie buy a car."

Jax switched off.

Ariel finished a note she was jotting, then picked up her phone to text.

Roark's phone binged. "I'm right here, y'know."

She made another finger gesture and finished her tea. I WANT TO DRIVE.

The message had gone to both him and Evie, not Jax.

"You can't even ride a bicycle! Tackle the basics first, see how you handle the road."

She picked up her phone again and added, A BIKE.

After he got past the utter impossibility of Ariel outside the house, wheeling down the road into who knows what, Roark loved the idea of teaching her to ride. Classic scenarios of holding her in the seat by her tiny waist immediately sprang to mind. Except he was flat broke. She wasn't.

"If you're paying, text Reuben to run over to the hardware store and find you a used 24" with good gears and wide tires."

"Email him," she ordered curtly, heading for her office. "Put it on my account."

She had an account? Man, he needed to know this managing female a *lot* better.

~

IN THE BACK OF REUBEN'S UTILITY VAN, EVIE SHOWED LORETTA cute hair styles on her phone. Jax had insisted on accompanying them to the used car lot, and Loretta had wanted to ride along—so Evie didn't miss the hair appointment. Poor Reuben got dragged along for the ride.

It was becoming increasingly obvious they needed a family car, not a Miata. A boring sedan no one would notice on a stake-out, she told herself. Not that staking out ghosts seemed like a good idea.

"You didn't give me much time to check out the used-car dude," Reuben complained from the driver's seat.

"I'll check his aura and know if he's honest. You can sit in the van, do your thing, while Jax kicks tires. What does tire kicking accomplish?"

"Not much these days. I think I've located a couple of good deals we should check out after you're done messing with this guy's head. Since you don't seem to mind Japanese made, what about a Toyota?" Jax showed her a small hybrid sedan.

"You can modify that? It's only four cylinders!" Evie had done her home-work—she'd interrogated a local mechanic.

"Muscle car, baby." Reuben added his two cents.

"We're not buying antique cars," Jax stated with ominous undertones. "They don't make engines like that anymore, and they suck gas."

"Your XKE was practically antique," Evie countered. "You can't rebuild modern cars. They're all electronic."

"Turbo-charged, four cylinder," the professor said from the driver's seat. "Camaro will do it."

"A Camaro is *not* inconspicuous. Muscle cars are out. I can add a turbo-charged engine to a beat-up Ford, if speed is what you're after. Better yet, a Civic or Subaru. High quality and no one notices them."

Reuben steered into the used car lot owned by Ursula Stanislaus's husband, Dmitri. Evie had no clear idea of what she expected, but she supposed an open mind was best. As he preferred, Reuben stayed with the van to research used car dealers, while Jax and Loretta climbed out.

The lot wasn't a large, fancy one. The office looked like an old gas station. The cars were of the ancient, cheap variety that one bought without much credit or trade-in, right up Evie's alley. She spotted a red Mustang immediately and headed that direction. Jax caught her elbow and steered her toward a brown Civic.

A short, plump man ambled from the office. "Welcome to Savannah's Best Cars. Can I help you folks?"

Evie pinched Jax's bronzed arm to shut him up. "I don't have much money. So I'm just sorta looking. I need a safe car that won't break down in intersections."

Already sweating in the August sun, the balding man stuck out his hand. "Dmitri Stanislaus. To whom do I have the pleasure of speaking?" He had only the slightest hint of an accent.

Playing it safe, he aimed his hand between Jax and Evie. Jax grabbed it first. "Just call me Jack, and this is my wife, Ivy. She's set on choosing her own car."

Oh, listen to the smooth-talkin' lawyer sounding all hick and everything. *Jack and Ivy.* Evie snorted and aimed for the Mustang again, while *Jack* and Dmitri had a little manly discussion clarifying that she wasn't trading in the van. Once she could hide behind the Mustang's open hood, she peered around to check out Dmitri's aura.

Not pretty. Not pretty at all.

Well, he was a used car salesman. What did she expect? To make any money in this business, one had to lie by omission, if nothing else.

Now that she knew his base colors were, well, pretty base, she could keep an eye out for changes. "What about this one?" she called, staring blankly at the shiny engine.

Loretta scrambled into the Mustang's front seat and scanned the dashboard. Knowing the kid, she was probably hunting for the VIN to look it up on her phone.

Dmitri hurried over to extol the virtues of a Ford engine.

Jax shoved his hands in his pockets and shook his head behind the dealer's back. Evie let Dmitri ramble, sized up his lying aura, and asked, "Would you let your wife drive it?"

That took him aback for a second. Remembering his wife as being the tall, glossy Ursula, Evie could understand his hesitation. She bet his wife drove a shiny BMW.

"My wife would look good in this," he assured her, avoiding the question. "So will you!"

Evie shooed Loretta out of the way so she could sit in the driver's seat and admire the fake new car smell. "Does your wife stay home? Or does she have to work and need a safe car?"

"My wife works hard," Dmitri said proudly. "She buys her own car."

Considering Ursula was a Russian immigrant who'd already reached the level of a red star manager who apparently received cash kickbacks, Evie bet she did work hard. . . at something.

"We're saving to buy a house, so I can't really spend this much." Telling the truth had always been optional in Evie's experience.

Dmitri's aura brightened. "We bought our first home a few years ago. It feels good to have your own place. Maybe you want to look at this nice car over here? It's not as pretty, but it's a good car and will cost you less."

Loretta flashed the phone report on the Mustang. It had been reported totaled by the insurance company just six months ago. Figures.

Evie was kinda liking the nasty little man who loved his home and his wife. She didn't want to believe he knew the Mustang had been totaled, even if he was lying through his pretty false teeth. Evie hopped out and followed him to the Civic that Jax had already picked out. Jax quirked his eyebrows in an I-told-you-so gesture but remained silent.

The Civic was boring. She wasn't handing over her driver's license to a professional liar so she could take a test drive. Reuben's text ended the so-far uninformative nattering.

URSULA ON HER WAY

Oh cool. She could interrogate arctic blondie—who swore her staff wouldn't do anything illegal.

Twenty

Roark's dumb phone rang with an unknown number. He missed his smart phone, but they were too easily traced. If the feds were warning him off this case. . . What the hell had his da got himself mixed up in? Or was Conan's warning just referring to Evie's case? Hers involved murder, after all.

Always curious, he answered.

"Eh, bébé, I worrit about you!"

Roark blinked, checked the number, and put it on speaker. Pris hadn't stopped the call forwarding? Roark opened the front door and waved the phone at Ariel. She didn't look up until the scammer spoke again.

"How dat cold? You takin' care?"

Roark smiled evilly. They'd only sent a few dollars through the money app to this creep, making it look as if Ellen had missed a decimal point or zero. He offered the phone to Ariel, who vehemently shook her head but watched him avidly.

His hack wasn't ready, and this guy already had the app, so he couldn't play him with the new version he was adapting. *Think fast.* Roark settled in a spare desk chair. "Who is this?" he asked in a nasal whine.

"Ah, pardon me. Is Ms. Ellen Broadhurst there?"

"No. You're supposed to leave a message." Roark dragged out the petulance for fun. He already knew where he was headed.

"I wish to speak to her, not leave a message." The scammer had lost his smooth charm. "Is she there or not?"

"She can't come to the phone. Are you her boyfriend?" Roark channeled an officer he'd had once, a wimp with the mind of a gnat who demanded respect for his minimal stripes.

"Eh, mebbe. When will she be home?"

"She won't. If you tell me your name, I'll have my other aunt call. I have better things to do." He hoped that sounded suitably ominous and waited to see how it flew over. If nothing else, he might end the nuisance calls entirely.

"Whacha mean, she won't? I got this prize I'm supposed to deliver. Has anything happened to her?"

Roark saw the big glittering hook hidden in the fake concern and decided running the line for a while might be fun. He flashed Ariel a smile. She handed him the spare phone she used for her game cameras. A second later, a text came through. SAY SHE'S DEAD?

MY INTENT he typed back while he wasted a few precious minutes of the asshole's time. "Prize? What kind of prize?"

Satisfaction tinted the response. "A Cadillac. Ms. Broadhurst meant to send $295 for delivery, but only $2.95 came through. We were supposed to drop it off tomorrow. If the money can be wired now, there's still time for delivery."

Slick. The asshat had already assumed Ellen was out of the picture and was moving on to his next mark. How many times had the *putain de merde* pulled that maneuver? Well, at least he'd avoided the bad hoodoo of actually declaring her dead.

Losing his whine, Roark adapted an eager voice. "I'm sure Aunt Ellen meant to send $295. Tell me where to wire it, and I'll see that it's done."

"That would be great." The charmer was all business. "Your aunt used a money app to send the $2.95. Do you wish to use that again? Or would Western Union be easier?"

"If the app didn't work, let me wire it." The nephew would not have access to his aunt's bank account for the app, but Western Union would take anything, so this seemed plausible.

Roark hooted once he had the wire info and hung up.

Ariel looked at him crossly. "Better dead."

"More effective for ending the calls, yeah, bébé. Not better for catching a crook." He carried his equipment from the porch to the kitchen so she could keep her routine dinner hour.

While she settled at the table with the chef salad and garlic bread he'd prepared, Roark got busy looking up officialdom near the designated Western Union office—on the outskirts of New Orleans. Figuring that office had been chosen for a reason, he went over the heads of the local authorities and sought higher ups.

He'd debated doing this earlier, only he'd been raised to be wary of officialdom. But this con was beyond reprehensible and into bloodsucker territory. It wouldn't hurt to try the official way while he was stuck here, where no one could find him.

Ariel ate and watched him worriedly as he located names and phone numbers. "Dangerous?" she asked once he sat back to ponder alternative channels if the cops failed him.

Jax had warned they were dealing with "dark energy." Roark translated that as some form of mafia. So, yeah, dangerous. He really shouldn't be courting risk while sponging off Ariel. He'd have to earn his fair share of Evie's case so he could get out of here.

But this one small fish shouldn't be a problem. He'd make the calls where she couldn't hear him, so she could rightfully say she wasn't involved. "I'll have to go into town to wire another three bucks. Shall I ride back your bike?"

She threw a piece of ham at him for ignoring her question. "Not distracted."

He threw it back. "Waste of good food, bébé."

She threw a crouton and carried her bowl to the sink.

He could walk out, like any mature adult. Or he could retaliate, because it was more fun. Interacting with Ariel so seldom happened—

He reached into the closet where he now knew she kept her water gun—and shot her squarely in the middle of her pretty white shirt.

~

"Should we check on Stacey while we're in the city?" Evie played with the power button on the used Honda she'd suckered a dealer into letting her test drive overnight.

Jax almost wished he hadn't talked up the pricier model, but the safety features sold him. He'd seen Evie drive. She was good, but she had to have been trained by a stock car driver. On her part, Evie had reluctantly accepted that Loretta's funds might partially pay the cost of security for their ward. Even she could see the practicality of sturdy construction and an engine that wouldn't quit on an isolated two-lane.

The Honda's leather seats, metallic blue paint job, and power mode gear probably sealed the deal. Hitting the highway would be the final test.

Jax stretched his legs in relative comfort and grimaced at her question. "You think you can pry more out of Marlene? You do remember Dante's warning?"

"Now that her hair is appropriately styled for an eleven-year-old, Loretta is happily helping Reuben and Larraine choose her birthday present, so she's safe. If you're worried, you can stay outside and watch for demons in the parking lot."

That was Evie being humorous. For all he knew, demons existed. Jax could name a few potential candidates. If psychics and witches were real. . . Why not demons? He'd start believing in Roark's voodoo queen grandmother shortly. "If I knew what a killer looks like, I would, but I don't. And neither do you. You just said Ursula had a martyr complex. Do I watch for burning stakes?"

The episode with the HR director had been averted when Jax had warned that having Ursula see them at her husband's car lot could be risky. Evie had insisted on watching from around the corner as Dmitri gave his wife the day's deposits. Jax hadn't seen anything suspicious.

"They all seem so murky," Evie complained with a sigh. She dodged in and out of late rush hour traffic. "Dmitri's aura reflects his love for his wife, over top of a river of lies. Ursula has zero compassion in her aura, and is equally dipped in deception, but she has the hots for her dirtbag husband. Ghosts and auras just aren't enough. I need *real* detective skills."

"A ghost warned you to get Stacey out and helped find a missing diamond. True crime requires all the help we can bring to the table. Piecing the puzzle takes instincts you can hone over time." He hoped, because he was enjoying the challenge.

He wasn't enjoying worrying about Evie in danger or that he was actually believing in ghosts. Life was complex.

It was dark by the time they reached the Azalea Retirement Apartments. Instead of a serene nighttime lobby settling in for slumber, they entered chaos. Jax held his arm in front of Evie to prevent her from dashing in before he could recon the situation. She ducked under his arm and strode up to sign the guest register as if half the residents weren't crushing the desk, screaming at each other.

Maybe her ADHD allowed her to take in all the arguments at once. Jax preferred taking them one at a time. Apparently, so did Lucy Murkowski, the director. Looking overwhelmed, she had retreated behind the protection of the big front desk.

"She stole my ring!" an overblown dyed blonde in stained scrubs shook the skinny arm of an Hispanic woman wearing a housekeeping uniform. The terrified maid chattered in Spanish.

"Savanna is the thief here," shouted one of the women Jax recognized from the gathering in Granny's apartment. "Everyone knows it."

"Ladies, ladies, please, let's settle down. . ." Murkowski practically wrung her hands attempting to separate the feuding residents.

"Without evidence, there can be no punishment," the tall, balding professorial sort Jax identified as Mr. Charles pronounced, to no one in particular.

Several other residents hovered in the background, loudly discussing other incidents of theft, and blaming anyone in sight.

Jax wanted to hand the director a backbone. Instead, he stepped up and crushed the wrist of the well-endowed blonde wearing scrubs and smelling of beer, forcing her to release the terrified maid. "Unless you are an officer of the law, you are assaulting this woman and can be arrested."

The frightened receptionist was on the phone, probably not calling 911. As Jax figured, a minute later, a thin man in his fifties with a head of iron-gray hair stalked from the office hall to yank Lucy Murkowski aside. Jax recalled the images from Reuben's wall and identified him as Bill Bibb, one of Sunshine's board of directors and VP of something-or-other at the home. What the hell was he doing here at this hour?

In the melee, Evie had slipped out of Jax's sight. She chose Bibb's arrival to scream.

Recognizing her operatic shriek, Jax swirled to locate her. Everyone in the lobby shut up and did the same.

For her car shopping and hair stylist expedition, Evie had chosen to wear purple knee-length shorts and a bright green T-shirt with purple writing that said *I do what the voices in my head tell me*. Her hair had frizzed in the August humidity and formed a halo of orange and red in the fluorescent lighting. She was holding both hands to her temples and staring wild-eyed at the crowd. Between her looks and the scream, she'd transfixed all onlookers, including the unamused VP.

Jax eased closer, keeping an eye out for sudden movements. He should sell Evie's services as a riot-quencher. Everyone silenced as she began to speak.

"Mary?" She rotated slowly, looking over everyone's heads. "Mary, is that the name you prefer?"

Jax refrained from rolling his eyes. Mary North had been the ghost she'd already sent on—and Evie's ghosts never used names. She was faking it. He kept a close eye on the blowzy blond in dirty scrubs. He'd bet good money, which he didn't have, that was the nurse who had stolen the diamond, Savanna Johnson.

"Is she seeing a ghost?" Abandoning her boss, Lucy Murkowski sidled up to Jax, whispering as she watched.

"Spirit energy, I think she calls it." Jax liked the sound of *energy* better than *ghost*.

"Mary. . . *North*." Evie bobbed her head and stared at a corner of the ceiling. "Ring? A ring of people? Mushrooms?"

Jax watched the drunken nurse frown and stagger a bit as she glanced toward the nearest exit. The Hispanic maid eased against the desk in fear.

"Ring, diamond? Stolen?" Evie wrinkled her pale brow in puzzlement and tilted her head as if listening. "Nurse? A *nurse* stole it?"

"I told you so," one of the little gray-haired ladies shouted. "Savanna steals from the dead!"

The riot of shouting began again, and the nurse shouted right back, swinging her fist and heading for the exit. Jax checked, and the gray-hired VP had vanished back down the hall, leaving the mayhem to his employees.

Lucy Murkowski gasped. "What do I do now? I can't call the police about a ghost."

"Check the nurse's employment record? And don't believe her if she blames a maid," Jax suggested, before catching Evie, who was doing a good imitation of a faint.

Appearing to support her, he led her back to the elevator, leaving the hubbub behind. "Cute. And here I almost thought you'd be a good riot quencher."

She chuckled. "I can, but it's no fun."

Since he'd seen her leading a mob of townspeople waving flaming brooms, he knew this had just been a tame episode. "Accusations and suspicious behavior won't get the thief arrested. Did you catch a glimpse of the VP who wandered in?"

"Yeah, very dark aura. Could be your cousin's *dark energy*. Can we arrest anyone on suspicion of evil?" She punched the elevator button for the fourth floor. "And the nurse is stewed in a lifetime of guilt and has a serious problem in her third chakra, dark enough to be cancer. I can tell her to see a doctor, but I can't have her arrested. Although cancer is punishment enough. This aura business isn't all it cracked up to be."

"You need to know the people to know what their aura reflects. And getting to know guilty people is not a safe way to go." Jax would have laughed hysterically if he'd heard himself talking like this even six months ago. He simply couldn't discount Evie's perceptiveness any longer.

He didn't like her silence as they left the elevator and headed for Granny's apartment. He was very afraid that he'd just planted an idea in her head, and now that she had a car of her own. . .

"I should go the car loan route," she said, surprisingly, as she knocked on the door. "I need to develop my own credit."

"A loan takes too long and you risk losing the deal. You can pay Loretta's account back with interest, and you can give the estate as reference the next time."

Marlene Gump's door opened, and a six-foot quarterback with spectacles blocked their entrance. Blessed with thick salt-and-pepper hair and a stern jaw, he didn't speak.

That didn't deter Evie. "Stacey's father, I presume? Good to meet you. It's about time you got here. Marlene has been frantic trying to protect her granddaughter."

"My mother is dead. Her remains are with the crematorium. I've sent Stacey back to Atlanta. If you're the investigators she hired, your services are no longer required. How much do we owe you?" He pulled a checkbook out of his inner coat pocket.

He dwarfed Evie, but she didn't seem to notice. "Authority, excellent." Evie beamed at the lout and shook off Jax's warning grasp on her elbow. "Marlene says she sent files to her old office, to a woman she refers to as the Stuffed Shirt With Tortoise-shell Glasses. If you're satisfied now that your mother was murdered for what she knew, perhaps you would be so good as to look up those files. Her computers were stolen before we could acquire all the relevant information."

The professor looked over Evie's head to Jax. "You're the lawyer? Then you know accessing federal files is against the law."

Jax put his hands in his back pockets, rolled back on his heels, and offered his best slick Savannah good-ol' boy attitude. "I also know that Marlene Gump was no longer employed by the feds, that she left her files to her grand-daughter, who allowed us access to them. If you want to go after criminals, find the ones who stole those computers. If you actually want to work this case, then we have added considerably more information to those files that you might wish to see."

Professor Gump frowned. Before he could speak, Evie tilted her head back and beamed at the ceiling. "Hey, Granny, happy now?"

A wind swept through the hall, slamming open the apartment door. Shoving past the professor, Evie walked in as if invited, chatting with an invisible entity. "Yeah, his aura is uptight, but it's protective. You shouldn't call him a chip off old Gibraltar. Is that his father?"

Professor Gump rubbed his wrinkled brow and stepped aside.

Evie often had that effect on people.

Twenty-one

HE'D SHOT HER WITH HER OWN WATER GUN.

Instead of going back to work, Ariel had had to curl up under her desk and rock until her jumping nerves settled. If she scared him, good. Served him right. He'd scared her.

But after Roark limped into town to do whatever he had to do, she'd practiced breathing and calmed down a little. She knew—rationally—that he'd only escalated what she had started by flinging food at him. What on earth had got into her?

She wished she had some way of locking the pocket door between the kitchen and her front office. She was furious enough to shove a desk in front of the opening and bolt the front door while he was in town, but she'd promised him a place to stay. Besides, he knew her security codes. The man was impossible.

She needed him out of the house. She simply could not deal with a huge presence sucking up her air and vibrating her home's bones.

And then he rode back on a ridiculously beautiful girl's bicycle, looking so pleased with himself that she wanted to. . . and no way could she, which made her furious all over again. Just the thought of coming close enough. . . Caused raging hormones and made her want to hide in the closet.

The bike sat there on the front porch, right next to Mitch Turtle's house,

143

calling to her. She could unbolt the front door and test the bicycle for herself, but Roark was still out there, tapping away on his laptop. The blasted man had parked temptation on her doorstep and waited for her to fall for it.

When she finally returned to her desk chair and opened her work, he sent an email. She paid no attention. Instead, she sought to burrow herself into the fraudulent bitcoin account in search of the owner.

Her phone binged with a text. She tried to ignore it, but it ate at her. What if it was Jax?

Frustrated at not being able to hack through the account's security, she finally poked her phone.

VIDEO LINK was all the text said, from Roark, of course. Now she itched to open the email to see what in heck he meant.

How did he do this to her? Her concentration was phenomenal. It was how she'd accomplished everything she had so far. Sensory deprivation had its advantages.

Roark needed turmoil to thrive.

Which, of course, sent her down the rabbit hole of doubt. Stupid therapists. Was she thriving?

Until Roark had come along, she had thought so. She was living on her own, paying her own way, and had even learned to deal with deliveries and telephones. If she could learn to ride a bike, she might even some day visit Iddy at the pet store. Eventually, she might. . . Well, meeting anyone for coffee or tea was probably out of the question. Noisy, busy cafés were excruciating.

So, she didn't need the stupid bike anyway.

To prove he didn't bother her, much, she opened the email. It simply included a link. She could handle that. She clicked, and a video from a bad camera angle appeared on her screen. It appeared to be a drugstore with narrow aisles and crowded shelves, but she supposed that could be the angle of the lens. It focused on a counter with a clerk wearing a shabby white coat. The clerk came and went as Ariel watched.

It took a minute before she realized this wasn't a clip but a hack into an actual, functional camera.

She couldn't remember the last time she'd been inside any sort of store. Watching from a distance like this was—not frightening. She always kept the sound off on her computer. She tested to see if the camera picked up sound but it apparently didn't. That was fine. She didn't mind just watching.

Of course, the game grew old, as most games did. For a while, the variety of characters stopping to buy everything from beer to hair dye was amusing. The store obviously didn't attract a high class of clientele. Shorts and T-shirts were about as dressy as they got. A few of the men didn't go that far. Some of the kids were barefoot. The "no shoes, no shirt, no service" warning didn't apply here.

She left the video running in a corner of her screen and returned to her work. Could she create her own scam letter and entice the bitcoin account holder to reveal his password? But if he used a random password generator, as she suspected, that wouldn't work.

Deep in thought sometime later, she jerked out of her focus at the beep of her phone. Annoyed that anyone disturbed her at this hour of the night, she glared at the text. **WATCH NOW**.

Focused on her own investigation, she almost disregarded it. But now that she'd been pulled to the surface, a gnat in her brain buzzed, and she opened the video wider.

A broad-shouldered young man in cut-offs and tank top loomed over the clerk and counter. He had a six-pack of beer and pointed at the cigarette cartons behind the counter. What kind of drugstore still carried cigarettes? The same clerk she'd observed earlier added a carton to the purchase and rang it up. Instead of taking cash, the clerk handed the customer a stack of hundreds, and pocketed a bill of his own.

What?

She wasn't good at reading expressions. Besides, she couldn't really see the customer's face until he turned to leave and walked off camera. Other than noticing he was young and didn't appear surprised or anything else as he stuffed the cash in the pocket of his frayed cut-offs, she simply couldn't understand what she was watching.

WHO? she typed.

PRIS'S WIRE TRANSFER

Wide-eyed, Ariel studied the screen. This young hunk had nothing better to do than steal from old ladies? To buy *cigarettes*? And no one stopped him?

Another email popped into her box. Now curious, she opened it to find a second link. This was a good way to infect her computer, but it came from Roark, so she clicked it.

A second camera angle opened, this one outside the store, aimed at the front entrance, sidewalk, and a piece of the parking lot. *How did he do this?*

145

Remembering her own game cameras and their accessibility, she assumed he had a contact inside drugstore security. He'd pulled strings.

This camera revealed the hood of a white police car by the curb. She could only see a bit of the official stripe, so she couldn't read what town. An officer was standing by the door, watching the parking lot, one hand on his holstered gun. Beyond him, she could only see legs on the other side of the car. One set of muscular legs was wearing cut-offs. The other appeared to be wearing uniform trousers.

Frustrated, she texted Roark. **WHAT'S HAPPENING?**

CHECKING ID

A minute later, an email popped up in her box. *They can't arrest him for picking up wired cash, but I recognize him. He's a cousin working with my da.*

Irritated, she typed back, *He took more money than you wired!*

Day's earnings, less clerk's commission for not questioning.

The kid had stolen all that money from people like Pris's mom, and the police couldn't arrest him? That just wasn't right. *What do we do?* She emailed back, enraged.

Roark pounded on the front door. Should she let him in? She had to. He was the only one who could stop these miscreants. Biting her lip, Ariel opened the door and absorbed the impact of male musk, bronzed shoulders, and wicked white smile. She wanted to slam the door again, but he pushed through as if he owned the place. His over-the-top confidence was maddening.

"I have a dude following Omer once the cops let him go. We need the location of da's new phone bank. Proving charges ain't easy. Blowing them up doesn't work. We need to take out their money and the leader." Roark paced the limited space by her front window.

Ariel retreated behind her computers. "They're stealing!"

"People wire that money willingly. You want to persuade Pris's mom to go to New Orleans to testify he didn't deliver the Cadillac?"

"*You* could." Agitated, she didn't know what to do with her hands.

"I sent three bucks, hardly a federal charge. We need to trace the money and the connections, find the big spider in this web. I know for certain sure that Omer and my da are bit players." He switched gears and opened the door. "Want to try your new bike?"

She wanted to crawl under the desk and bang her head again.

~

"YOUR MOTHER SAYS YOU SUCKED YOUR THUMB AND WET YOUR bed as a kid." Evie sat cross-legged on the floor of Granny's now empty apartment.

"Every kid does at some point. I'm not falling for the ghost crap. Tell me what you're really after." Professor James Gump sipped from a whiskey tumbler. He didn't offer them any. Judging by the emptiness, he'd probably left only one glass for himself.

Not that Evie would have accepted a drink from the uptight old goat. He was worse than Jax. "I want your mother's killer caught and whoever is stealing from these nice old people stopped. You have a dark, muddy gray in your first chakra. Do you have a heart doctor?"

Or he lacked a heart, but that wasn't polite to say. Loretta would probably say he had a walnut for a soul.

The old fed all but rolled his eyes and looked over her head to Jax. "I've seen my mother's files. She had very little evidence of anything more than petty theft between the residents—hardly a federal case."

"She recorded hours of chicanery between the conmen and people they thought were incompetent." Jax had his aggressive lawyer voice on. "All the victims passed through at least one of Sunshine's facilities. The scammers knew everything about them. Some of the residents had already lost their savings before your mother took over their identities. The directors of Sunshine are laundering large amounts of cash. She simply did not have the means to track the money or the conmen. You do. Read the files we'll send you. Follow the money."

"If you've been hacking personal accounts, you can be arrested, and your evidence is worthless." Stone-faced, Gump leaned against the counter.

Evie wanted to poke him with a sharp stick, but she spoke evenly. "I'm calling Stacey to tell her to make sure you go to a doctor. Your heart could explode, and where would she be then? She needs you. And Marlene says if you have us arrested, she'll haunt you until you die. She's passing back and forth through you right now, trying to catch your attention."

Marlene was saying a lot of other things, too, but Evie refrained from name calling. Mother and son must have had a rocky relationship.

Gump determinedly drained his glass. His thick hair ruffled in the non-existent wind.

"I'll take my chances. Send me the files. I make no promises."

"Your mother said you once cheated on your chemistry exam, and she made you tell the teacher and take an F. She says that didn't go on your official record so no one knows it but her and the teacher, and he's dead. I really don't think she'll rest until you stop these criminals." Evie stood up and dusted off her capris. "She also says Bibb is outside the door, and Mr. Charles is peering through his keyhole, watching."

A knock interrupted any reply. Evie answered the door for them. Marlene hadn't actually said all that since she couldn't recall names. Evie had just relied on impressions. The ghost really was agitated.

The vice president of Sunshine's board of directors frowned down at her. Evie decided she might start wearing high heels. She frowned back. "May I help you?"

That obviously left him flummoxed. He looked over her head. "Mr. Gump. I hope you have found the premises satisfactory and are now ready to cede the lease so we may rent it out again. We have a waiting list."

"We're paid through the end of August." Professor Gump didn't move from his relaxed stance leaning against the kitchen counter. Except his aura was on high alert. Good actor.

"We would like to clean and repaint the apartment before renting it again. It's part of the lease agreement." Mr. Bibb's aura was ominous. Black hearts were black hearts. That still didn't mean he was a killer.

"My mother was *murdered* here, Mr. Bibb. Until the police tell me there is nothing else they need, you will not be cleaning or painting. I could sue."

Evie was a trifle irritated that they continued talking over her head. Just before she put a spoke in their wheels, Jax intervened. "I've taken a look at the lease agreement. Professor Gump is within his rights to hold out until he's prepared to close out the apartment. If the police need longer, you'll no doubt be hearing from them. Is Sunshine improving security to see that nothing happens like this again? The melee we witnessed below indicates not."

Jax, at least, put a hand on her shoulder and attempted to steer her out of the way. Acknowledging her existence was good. Moving her, not so much. She stomped on his toe. He yanked his shoe before she could do much damage.

"Marlene wants to know what happened to the security deposits on Mrs. Lopez and Mr. Wong's apartments after they were moved into the nursing wing, and Laura Evans, after she died." Evie crossed her arms and glared up at the VP.

Bibb's aura couldn't get any gloomier, so she couldn't detect guilt or lies. She was totally useless except as a biting gnat. She needed to find a new job.

"I'm sure they were returned to their families or applied to their rooms at the home. I do not do the bookkeeping. That's Mrs. Murkowski's job. Now, if you will excuse me. . ." He turned to leave.

"Mrs. Murkowski doesn't do the bookkeeping. I had to inquire of a Henry Bibb pertaining to my mother's deposit. Your son, I assume?" the haughty professor asked.

"My brother. He works for the corporation, not for me." Without giving them further chance to question, the VP swung on his leather heel and walked off.

"He lies for a living," Evie said with a sigh. "Just like Ursula's husband. Interesting." She glanced over at the door across the hall. "Do you have anything to add, Mr. Charles?"

Still murky with distrust, Marlene's tall, balding boyfriend opened the door. "Marlene never mentioned a problem with security deposits."

"Mrs. Gump was suspicious by nature. I just thought I'd throw her questions into the pot. Have you found out anything interesting lately, Mr. Charles? She appears to be a little upset with you."

He looked nervous. "She was the jealous sort. I've been talking to some of the other ladies lately. You really see her ghost?"

"Oh, for heaven's sake." Professor Gump stood up and slammed his glass down on the counter. "Will all of you just leave? This ghost nonsense is preposterous."

Jax caught Evie's waist and shoved her toward the door. "It's late. We need to go home and make sure Loretta has someone watching her. It's good to see you again, Mr. Charles. Hope you're staying well."

"Well as can be expected at my age. Are the police saying anything about who might have harmed Marlene?" The older man lingered in his doorway.

The empty whiskey tumbler went flying.

Evie smiled over her shoulder at the professor, who'd totally been taken off guard. "Your mother thinks you might want to talk with Mr. Charles. He was the one who had her backup phone. Good-night, professor. I'll warn your daughter about your heart problem."

She walked out of Jax's hold and headed for the elevator.

Marlene had muttered a few choice words about Mr. Charles and the expense of keeping all his girlfriends, and they hadn't sounded like jealousy. They'd sounded a whole lot like they needed to be looking into the old man.

Twenty-Two

"NEW GLASSES!" LORETTA DEMANDED FRIDAY MORNING, bouncing on the breakfast banquette so her new shoulder-length hair swung freely. She wore her thick bangs clipped to either side, presumably until they grew out to Hermione length. "Larraine says I need square, black frames."

"I've made an appointment at the eye doctor for Monday. I'm thinking the lens are more important than frames." Evie accepted the fashion designer's wisdom on frame types, although she would have argued for crystal blue cat-eyes to match her Indigo ward's aura and eyes. But she liked color and Loretta liked dramatic black. Each to their own.

It was hard not to be judgmental when that was essentially her profession. Happy colors felt good. Black did not. How could she not judge a person on that basis?

Evie was still pondering the impossible when Reuben arrived bearing printouts of spread sheets and photos. He dropped them on the counter while he investigated the contents of the refrigerator. "Are we or are we not working for the Gumps? I'm gonna quit putting in time if we're not getting paid. I've got a raccoon to roost out of an attic and an inquiry about ghosts in a Charleston townhouse I should check out."

"You'll just leave a murderer out there and thieves stealing identities and emptying bank accounts? Shame on you." Evie handed Loretta oatmeal with a raisin funny face and a cinnamon beard, with apple slices for hair.

151

"And that's how you stay poor." Reuben produced cheese, eggs, and bagels and set them on the counter with his papers. "How you plan on paying for that car out there?"

"With my good looks." Evie fluttered her lashes and settled on a stool to eat her oatmeal. She was having second and third doubts about the car. It was a boring sedan. It had gone zero to sixty well enough. At least, it hadn't rattled. But it wasn't a Miata by any means.

And if she gave up ghost sleuthing, she really didn't need a car. Or to worry about whether it would work in a stake-out.

She just hated, with every ounce of energy in her—and she had a *lot*—to give up on those old people.

"You got a car?" Loretta was out of her seat in a flash, racing for the back door. "Why didn't you tell me?"

"Just borrowed it," Evie called after her.

The screen door slammed on her reply. Evie picked up the papers Reuben had left for her perusal. "You think all of Denmark is rotten?" As far as she could tell, these were profiles on all of Sunshine's board of directors. She picked up the one on Bill Bibb simply because she already knew he was rotten to the core. And there she went, judging by color.

"I'm thinking it's not just the employees living under stolen IDs. We need fingerprints or facial recognition or something, but the whole board of directors smells like dried and freeze-packed shit." Reuben fried his own egg and toasted the bagel.

"Wow, and they all look so pretty, too." The photos were all white males except for Ursula. Interesting. How did she get in the mix? Where was Lucy? Was she new? "So everyone on the board also holds a position in the company? Like, they actually work for a living?"

"Closely-held corporation. They're officers, directors, employees, and stockholders, possibly promoted through the ranks, just like any good mafia."

Looking as if he'd just walked off the pages of a male model magazine, their guest emerged from the back bedroom. The Italian was too tall and slick for Evie's tastes, and along with his streak of annoying Ives' aura, there was another questionable streak of red—just like Jax's. She'd learned enough about Jax to know his anger was at himself and maybe at the world's injustice, but she didn't know Dante Rossi. So there, she wasn't actually judging him. Yet.

"Good morning, Mr. Rossi. Breakfast is informal. If you can fix your own, please help yourself to what you need. Otherwise, I can whip up simple requests." Evie spied on his aura while she ate her oatmeal. She ought to feel guilty for studying people without their knowledge. She didn't.

"Dante, or Don, please. I learned to cook for myself or I'd starve on a dig." He peered into the refrigerator. "I sincerely appreciate your hospitality. I don't often have the chance to make myself at home."

"You don't have a place of your own?" Reuben assembled his concoction.

"An apartment I barely sleep in and an old villa I never visit." He juggled an egg, a loaf of bread, and the butter. "Miss Broadhurst says there is a cemetery on something called Witch Hill with a family graveyard that I might find interesting?"

"The stones are deliberately concealed in herbs and flowering weeds, but they're there if you look carefully. They date back to the 1600s. Do your Malcolms have a genealogist like Jax's family?" Evie washed her bowl in the sink.

"Several. It's rather essential given their eccentricities and need to consult with each other on the best use of their various talents. I can put you in touch with them, if you like. Miss Broadhurst has asked if I might work with a phone bank to bring down miscreants. She's a bit. . ."

"Intense?" Evie offered helpfully. "Don't let her put her mental voodoo on you."

Dante looked up from buttering his bread and raised an elegant eyebrow. "Interesting. But if I can be useful while I'm here, I'd like to try."

"Pris said I could help too." Loretta slammed back into the kitchen. "Can we go for a ride in the new car? I like the blue."

"I may take it back," Evie warned.

Unconcerned, Loretta scooted back on the vinyl bench to empty her bowl. "Pris says we're meeting at City Hall tomorrow, 'cause it's closed to the public on Saturday."

Jax walked in on that explanation. He frowned but kissed Evie's cheek.

He smelled so good that she could forgive his disapproving frown. She kissed his newly shaven jaw. "I don't know how Roark is planning on stopping. . . miscreants." She savored the lovely word. "But I'm all in for it."

Reuben took his usual seat across from Loretta. "He's writing a program that will hack phones, if we can persuade the scammers to download it. Then we can freeze their devices, which will obliterate their contact lists, force them to buy new phones. and slow down their depredations—unless they have backup. We need something more complex, but there isn't enough time."

"Roark hopes to add a phone locater to the app eventually. For right now, he assumes he only has contact numbers from his father's operation. Locating their hang-out shouldn't be difficult." Jax accepted the oatmeal Evie handed him and stirred in milk and honey. "Having them arrested is another story. People need to press charges."

"I take it you wish to catch a criminal consortium?" Rossi toasted his bread in the frying pan as Reuben had.

"Scammers," Reuben replied, with his mouth full. "Plain and simple."

Evie left them to discuss Roark's sting. She'd help tomorrow where she could, but she didn't understand much of it. She couldn't *see* people over a phone any more than she could understand them by reading Reuben's documents. It was becoming increasingly apparent that her services were useless in providing evidence so justice could be done.

Discouraged, she left the others to clean up and picked up her doggie customers for their walk. It had felt really good helping bring down Mayor Blockhead and his attempt to steal her family's land. And she was glad she'd been able to help Jax uncover the voting machine *miscreants*. But she was fooling herself to think they could stop anything apparently as pervasive as scammers. These were organized gangs!

She couldn't imagine Bill Bibb and Ursula carrying automatic weapons, but they wielded their power well without guns. Of course, she didn't think they were the common garden variety scammer like Roark's dad. They might have similar victims, but Sunshine gave new meaning to organized crime.

Happily imagining barging in on a Sunshine board of director's meeting with a dozen poltergeists and hexing them all, Evie walked the dogs up Witch Hill and let them loose to sniff and chase to their doggie delight.

To her amazement, Ariel appeared over the hill, wobbling on a wide-tire bike down the woodland path.

She halted at sight of Evie. Her normally blank expression slowly opened to a revealing grin. "I practiced all night."

"Pretty good, but you can break your neck riding over those tree roots. Where's Roark?" Evie knew better than to approach Jax's younger sister. Ariel had issues and had to be left to make her own decision to advance.

"Plotting." She seemed prepared to retreat, but Mavis's golden lab ran over to sniff her, and she hesitated.

154

"Honey is friendly. You can pet her. She's too dumb for Iddy to teach communication, but she knows better than to lick you to death." Evie rubbed the ears of an old beagle and kept her distance while Ariel and Honey got to know each other. She didn't think Ariel any better at communication than the dog, but petting and licking worked on some level.

She'd like to know more about Roark's plotting, but she figured Ariel couldn't explain. Instead, she nodded at a place near Ariel. "You're almost at the cemetery wall. I like to go through and look up the names of my ancestors. There are some really old plants in there, too, if you're interested."

Ariel nodded uncertainly. "Thank you." Apparently having as much stimulation as she could endure, she tugged the bike around. "See you." And she pedaled off.

Evie whistled to bring Honey back. Whatever magic Roark was wreaking on Ariel was working to drag the hermit out like this. Maybe he had a little of his voodoo grandma in him.

Maybe he should bring in his grandma on his sting. Hex the miscreants!

Would hexing work on Sunshine's board of directors? How superstitious were they? Wouldn't a gaggle of gangsters be paranoid already?

How far could a good hex go?

ROARK PACED THE WHOLE TIME ARIEL WAS OUT OF SIGHT OF HER game cameras.

They'd been up all night while she learned to balance on her new bike, practicing on the relatively flat road. She'd even allowed him to hold her up, which hadn't helped his frustration at all. Her waist was tiny, but she had breasts under those stiff shirts. He was thinking he should go back to sleeping in the woods.

And then, instead of going to bed as usual, the damned female had taken off on her own!

Jax would chop him into sushi if anything happened to his kid sister.

Roark breathed a sigh of relief when she returned into view of the camera. Now he could work again—if only he'd quit watching Ariel. She was too slender, but in that tailored red shirt with all that long black hair. . .

Stop it, stupid.

She didn't even bother to check on him when she came inside. She went directly to her room to shower, leaving him with boring code and a cockstand that wouldn't go away.

He needed to use her computers while she slept. He couldn't waste time on a ten-mile hike to work off steam.

Cursing, he sent a copy of his telephone-hack program to Reuben to test and started writing scripts for his phone bank helpers. Pris was rounding up victims willing to have their phone calls forwarded. She was probably using mental hoodoo to convince them.

While he worked, he kept his fake Facebook page open to see if anyone posted about his thieving cousin Omer but nothing came up. A minor arrest would go unnoticed by city newspapers. He did a quick check of newer social media, but his kin hadn't progressed beyond the old programs. No gossip anywhere.

He'd have to hope the officials he'd sent sniffing would follow through—not something he trusted them to do from his experience. He figured the Whitesville cops were well paid to leave his da's operation alone, so he'd set the state to snooping. But they were limited in local cases.

He sent Jax a query about the feds. If his Gump client was federal, would he be interested? Probably not. Damn.

Even if he caught everyone in da's gang tomorrow red-handed, he couldn't arrest them. All Roark could do was annoy the devil out of the asshats and slow them down.

A text came in from Evie. His eyebrows soared at the message: **HEX THE SCAMMERS**

Evie was weird, but she usually had a clue. How did one hex his dad?

He'd question why the hell he was doing this except Pris's mom nagged at his conscience, and he wanted to keep his brothers clean.

Follow the money then. He opened up Ariel's files and applied his mechanical mind to dollars and cents instead of gigabytes.

While investigating the scammers' profits, he stumbled on a way to replenish his own bank account—if only he had one.

Twenty-three

EVIE RETURNED HER DOGGIE CLIENTS TO THEIR HOMES, THEN DID her stint at the Psychic Solutions shop, giving her mother a chance to grab an early lunch and enjoy her gossip routine. She sent Loretta off to her very first sleepover to plot her first day of school—and probably her birthday party. Jax and Reuben were busy with their own projects.

Which gave Evie the entire afternoon to herself. She ought to be wearing her *Danger Will Robinson* T-shirt. Instead, she poked through Great-Aunt Val's sixties wardrobe and found a perfectly respectable dress that hit her knees—Val was considerably taller and the dress would have been far less respectable on her. The dress dripped with lace and came in an ice blue that Evie would never have worn on her own, but for her purposes today, it was perfect. She brushed her hair into submission, tied it back, then pinned and combed it tight. She even wore her new baby heels.

Then she mapped out her targets. She'd not had the opportunity to drive in Savannah often. She sometimes drove her aunts' cars to take them to medical offices or shopping, but Mavis didn't own a car and had no interest in doctors or stores. So Evie had to plot the order of her visits.

First up was the used car dealer to return the car they'd let her keep overnight. The Honda was pretty, but the luxury model made her uncomfortable. She didn't need leather seats.

She'd loved driving the Subaru Jax had sold. It had been small, and she

157

could easily adjust it for her short legs and height. The mechanic she'd consulted had assured her the unique engine got better horsepower and matched acceleration with some of the priciest cars on the market. And the dealer had a used one in stock—in black. Black could look sexy. Loretta would love it. And it was cheaper than the Honda, so she wouldn't owe as much.

Yeah, the Subaru wagon had a few miles on it, but Evie settled behind the small wheel, smiled, and drove it off the lot later than she'd anticipated. She might have to cut the remainder of her visits short, but she could justify this car in her head far better than the fancy one.

And it had heated seats for winter, so there—plus cargo room in back for hauling groceries and dogs.

The next address in her phone's GPS was Sunshine's home care office. She had to assume clients would normally call for services, but she needed to *see* people, not hear them. So she marched in the front door holding a folder of fake resumes she'd printed out in her mother's shop. Since the majority of Sunshine's employees seemed to have fake IDs, why not?

Inside the lobby was an assortment of hospital-type supplies: walkers, beds, wheelchairs, and things she'd rather not think about. She went up to the counter but no one appeared. Swell. Behind a stack of brochures advertising the agency's products, she found a bell and tapped it.

Eventually, a lank-haired young woman looking in desperate need of sleep or a cigarette appeared. "Yeah?"

Evie didn't waste energy checking this one's aura. It was probably dead. "Yes, Mrs. Stanislaus said you might have an open position. Is the manager in?"

"Nah."

Narrowed eyes indicated otherwise. Having checked the employee charts Reuben had drawn up, Evie already had the manager's name. She'd seen a high-end BMW in the parking lot. It wasn't as if she had anything to lose by making an idiot of herself.

She rapped the counter and called, "Mr. Peterson? Mrs. Stanislaus sent me."

Lying Girl snarled. "He's busy."

"He'd be less busy if he hired me." She didn't add "instead of you." She didn't want a bar fight. Yet. Evie pulled out her phone and opened her contacts. "I'll call him, shall I?"

"Wait here. Don't say I didn't warn you."

Not being of a trusting nature, Evie slipped around the counter and followed at a distance.

"She says Ursula sent her," Lying Girl whined from an office at the end of a long hall. "If I lose this gig, I can't pay rent."

"You know you can always come home, honey," a masculine baritone said, a trifle impatiently. "I'm sure Ursula doesn't mean to take your job. Send her back."

Huh, family operation from the sounds of it. Evie slipped back to the counter and pretended to peruse a pamphlet.

The clerk returned and kept a bland face. "He says go back, but he doesn't have any positions available."

All she really wanted was to see J.P. Peterson, Home Health Care president, Sunshine director, and according to Reuben's research, ex-con embezzler. If his aura was as black as Bibb's, she'd at least have established a pattern.

Apparently Mr. Peterson, unlike many of Sunshine's directors, had served his time and was now a responsible citizen—he'd kept his real name. But if he was working for crooks. . . he was probably employing his old tricks somehow. Hard to find honest jobs with his record.

J.P. Peterson did not stand when she entered and not because he was a young, woke feminist. Bad etiquette placed him in the category of *not a Southern gentleman*. Balding blond hair, weak chin, rounded shoulders, he bent over his laptop like any good Scrooge counting his coins. A keyboard and large monitor occupying half the desk gave new meaning to the cliché of keeping two sets of books.

"May I help you?" he asked with the same impatience he'd used on the clerk. His daughter?

She really hadn't planned this far. She worked best with improv. Mostly, she needed a few minutes to go ditzy and examine his aura. That required distraction. Pity she didn't have Gracie here to levitate that soft drink can—

"Mrs. Stanislaus said you were interested in a bitcoin account." Evie set her folder of useless resumes on the desk at just the right angle to topple an overfull pen holder. The holder was too lightweight to knock over the soft drink can, but it spilled pens and pencils. "Woops, sorry about that."

They both grabbed for the toppled utensils. Evie scooped up a flash drive and hid it in her fist as she returned pens to the container. Peterson grabbed for an escaping Mont Blanc and knocked the soda can over all on his own. *Blessed be.*

While he cursed and frantically sopped up the sticky nastiness with Kleenex, Evie opened her inner eye.

He was as muddy with lies and guilt as Ursula, the HR director. Murky forest green in his heart chakra indicated a load of resentment and low self-esteem. Dark blue lurked in the throat region—*fear of the truth*, interesting. Peterson was a toady for someone pretty powerful. That didn't make him a killer.

Evie produced wipes from her purse and helped clean up the gummy residue. "Good thing it didn't fall on your keyboard," she said cheerfully.

He muttered an obscenity and immediately examined his keyboard—while Evie studied his computer monitor. A spreadsheet with great big numbers involving many zeroes. Cleaning the keyboard abruptly shrank the spreadsheet window to reveal half a dozen other open windows—all bank accounts at different banks. Yeah, definitely a Scrooge, a frightened one.

Evie stood. "I can see you're busy, sir. Why don't I just leave my card and you can call me when you have time." She removed a card from her purse with her fake name and a burner number. She was learning technology from the best.

On the way out, she waved gaily at the sullen clerk. The stolen thumb drive burned a hole in her pocket. She wanted to take it straight back to Reuben, but as long as she was here. . .

She didn't dare take the direct approach at her next stop, in case Peterson started calling around, asking questions.

She drove to Sunshine's assisted living facility where she told the clerk her mother had been diagnosed with Alzheimer's and asked about the facilities.

Their office sent out a chirpy salesperson to show her around. Evie had memorized a list of technical questions that chirpy couldn't answer. Eventually, she caved and took Evie back to an office.

The desk chair was empty but a plaque read *Kurt Calder, VP of Patient Relations.* Recalling Reuben's investigations, Evie knew him as Sam Reilly, ex-con counterfeiter with a host of outstanding fraud warrants. She'd find a new ID if she were him, too—and counterfeiting IDs and credentials for his co-workers would be right up his alley.

She had time to wonder about the master mind who had brought these criminals together under one respectable-looking umbrella.

Calder/Reilly entered with a hearty smile, a tanning-bed bronze, and five o'clock shadow. "Miss Rose, my assistant said you have some questions."

"About a million." Evie offered a watery smile. "I never thought I'd be putting my mom in a home." That was also a lie. She'd thought about it often, with great glee. Mavis had days when Evie feared she needed to be locked up for her own good. But her mother would only lead the patients in a revolution and bust out.

Evie encouraged Calder/Reilly to spread out all his books and pamphlets and laptop videos. While he yapped, she tuned in to his aura.

Like all his partners, he was murky with guilt. No surprise there. He did seem to have a shred of compassion—a family he protected maybe? Jealousy and an ugly line of narcissism marred any softer colors. And a murderous red lurked near his heart. She tried not to judge, but she didn't want to know him better.

Just what had she accomplished? Calder left no flash drives on his desk. He wouldn't leave her alone to question any of his employees. She couldn't tour the facility stumbling about with her eye open to auras.

She needed to work there. That wouldn't be easy if all hires came through Ursula. She needed more experience at being an intrepid sleuth willing to don a disguise and do stupid things.

A tour through carefully chosen rooms and a nearly empty rec room gave her little opportunity to question anyone. If she were any good at planning, she'd have arranged for someone to call Calder and drag him away.

She did note the names on employee badges and patient doors. The names didn't ring any bells, but one never knew what would be useful.

They returned to the patient services office where, frustrated, Evie was about to say she'd have to bring her mother in for a visit, when Calder received a message that called him away.

Yay, Universe!

The outer office was empty, leaving the file cabinets unguarded. Evie was lousy at reading stacks of material, but where opportunity beckoned—her camera led the way.

STILL EXHILARATED, TERRIFIED, AND ON EDGE BY HER DARING break from routine the prior night, Ariel woke up Friday afternoon uncertain how to proceed.

Roark had *held* her on the bike. *Touched* her. And she'd liked it, sort of. It had been tremendously over stimulating. She'd needed the solitary bike ride to soothe her rattled nerves—far preferable to head banging, she decided.

Oddly, meeting Evie and her dog had helped. Maybe she should get a dog. Or start simple, with a kitten. Would Mitch Turtle mind?

Those thoughts as she showered didn't help her past the fact that Roark was out there, waiting for her.

She didn't like this man/woman thing. It was nerve wracking—because parts of her liked it too well. And while Roark seemed interested, he wasn't the kind of man who'd hang around forever playing babysitter for a nutcase.

Routine was necessary or she'd need more medication. She'd wasted most of her work hours yesterday. She didn't have time for crawling in a hole and soothing herself.

GO AWAY she texted Roark while she dressed. She hoped he understood. He'd been extraordinarily patient last night in teaching her to ride.

Determined to help him in return, she sipped her tea in the blessedly empty kitchen, checked her game cameras, and returned to her desk early, bearing a piece of toast. She had wipes to keep her keyboard clean. She could change, just at her own pace.

Roark had been in her files. Once, she might have been angry, but she was learning to work with him. Her therapist would be proud.

He'd sent her an email flagging the bank account that seemed to be receiving some portion of his father's ill-gotten gains with the message, *We can reset the automatic transfer.*

He could. . . uh. She emailed back: *to what?*

To go to our account. Victim's account. Scammers Anonymous. Anywhere.

Theft, she retorted. But her mind whirled as she used a hack she'd developed to open the account labeled Whitesville Fishing. She could change the transfer information on any account in this bank—but eventually, someone would notice, and she'd get caught. She didn't want to lower herself to the same levels as the criminals she investigated.

Right before her eyes, she watched a few hundred transferred from Whitesville Fishing's checking account to a related savings account named

Whitesville Phone Bank. Had his father really opened a savings account? Not if he was unfamiliar with how banks operated, as Roark claimed.

What did that accomplish? she emailed back. *He still owns it.*

Nothing. Yet. Let's get paid.

That almost sounded suggestive. She watched as half the small sum vanished from the new account through a bank transfer to an email address that Ariel recognized as Pris's.

Stealing from thieves. Cute.

Reparations. Fun. He included a link. *More Fun.*

This silly game wasn't accomplishing anything, unless she reported the hack to her bank clients. She checked the link anyway.

A video of an old crone draped in black shawls appeared, accompanied by eerie drumming. The woman was creating a hexagram in multi-colored powders on a stone surface in what appeared to be a cavern. Unlit black candles adorned each angle of the pattern. Shouldn't that be a pentagram?

A voice-over in sepulchral tones whispered, "A hex upon you, upon your cohorts, upon your gonads, upon your evil ways."

The crone looked up directly into the camera through sunken dark eyes and heavy wrinkles. "Thy will be done." She cackled, snapped her fingers, and the candles flamed on.

He was planning a costume party?

Dramatic, Ariel typed back, adding a sarcasm emoji.

My granny, the voodoo queen. We filmed her one Halloween.

And?

She was almost starting to enjoy this. . . not quite a conversation. She didn't converse well, but typing gave her time to think and didn't require that she read expressions or body language.

Adding to app.

Which made no sense in her world but apparently did in his. She waited but there was nothing more. She texted Pris to check her bank account for a partial refund from the scammer. It would be up to Pris to decide whether to return it to her mother.

Pris texted a surprise emoji back.

Uneasy with Roark's circular thought processes, Ariel returned to tracing bitcoin wallets, focusing on the ones that seemed to relate to his father's network. She couldn't figure out all the connections. The bank account

Roark was robbing only received small deposits, not enough to represent a large operation.

Those deposits got transferred to larger corporate accounts that received credit card deposits. The average daily take would feed a village but not buy any yachts. She assumed a certain amount of cash got skimmed off the top, if Cousin Omer was any example.

She couldn't trace cash, although a quick study of the Whitesville Bank's accounts showed more cash transactions than a normal bank would average. But that could be cultural. It spoke of an underground economy that avoided taxes.

She'd traced some of the transfers out of the larger account to an offshore account. More went to the bitcoin wallet she couldn't hack. Without being able to see into the wallet or offshore accounts, she couldn't tell if they were receiving additional funds from elsewhere. She suspected they did.

She returned to investigating the transactions in the bank accounts of the scammers' victims. Aside from the normal checks the owners wrote, there were a number of cash transfers to a variety of different banks. Most people, especially elderly ones, didn't use direct online transfers. That made her suspect the transfers weren't legit. It would take a while to trace them, though.

If she was right, the scammers had gained access to the victims' checking accounts and were slowly siphoning off the balances. Not all of them. Some of the poor suckers were still spending large sums on what appeared to be gift cards, given the round numbers. Others had debit card deductions and automatic payment on credit cards the thieves might be using. She'd have to dig into credit cards, but they were more troublesome. That would take a while.

She developed a spreadsheet of cash transfers from the victim accounts to half a dozen accounts that appeared to be fictitious business names—including Whitesville Fishing. It probably wouldn't help, but she emailed the spreadsheet to the security offices of the banks involved.

An email popped into her inbox. No longer resisting, she opened it. Roark had posted another link and added *download to the camera phone.*

The link took her to an unsecure website for moneytransfer.org. He'd set up a website? With what? Stolen credit cards?

With a sigh, she downloaded the app from the unsecure website. If it infected her camera phone, it wouldn't go to anyone else.

A perfectly normal money transfer app appeared, looking like any mobile bank wallet. She wasn't about to give it her own bank account. She typed in the bank information for Whitesville Fishing.

Apparently controlling the app, Roark created a transfer sending money from the Fishing account to Pris. Once the transaction completed—

The cackling granny video popped up, hexing her.

Then her phone froze.

Twenty-four

JAX PROUDLY DEPOSITED HIS VERY FIRST CLIENT PAYMENT IN THE bank. He'd earned a hefty salary at his old firm in Savannah, but that wasn't the same as earning every cent he billed his own clients.

He could pay office rent with that check. He'd need a lot more clients before he could hire a secretary. It was a shame Evie's multitudinous talents couldn't be better employed in his office, but she would spend more time analyzing his clients than filing. And asking her to do bookkeeping. . . She'd probably paint the walls.

The sex was too good to mess up by working together—in an office, anyway. It was a shame he wasn't independently wealthy so he could spend more time chasing haunts with her.

Which reminded him to check on the standing of his case against DVM Electronics. The voting machine company had so many suits against them now that they couldn't last much longer. He wanted the royalties and his father's patents before they filed bankruptcy. He'd had to hire a patent attorney who understood those archaic, complex laws.

"We can settle," Jax said, back in his office and speaking to his lawyer. "But only if we get the rights back on the patent. They can't be trusted not to start another company and continue the fraud."

A knock sounded on his outer office door, and he hurriedly ended the conversation while checking his security camera—Professor James Gump was in the hall, reaching for the doorknob.

It was never good to have a federal agent at the door, if that was what he was.

Phone still in hand, Jax let the stiff-rumped professor in. "Good afternoon, sir. To what do I owe this unexpected visit?"

Gump perused the nearly empty reception area. "Striking out on your own isn't easy."

"From that, I gather you had me investigated and should know why I left Stockton. Do I invite you back or do you simply want to warn me off?"

"Invite me back. A man who isn't afraid to stop highly-placed political figures who could destroy his career isn't a man easily warned off." Gump strode for the back office as if he'd been invited. He settled into the old-fashioned leather Morris chair with a sigh.

Jax checked his phone time and gestured at the mini-bar he'd set up on his credenza. "Not quite five o'clock, but if you'd like a bourbon. . ."

The professor nodded. "With water, if you don't have ice. I'm supposed to be cutting back."

Jax cracked ice out of his mini-fridge. It wasn't possible to survive a summer surrounded by cotton fields without ice. "Stacey nag you into seeing a physician or just practical policy?"

"The power of suggestion should never be underestimated. I had a little episode last night and went to urgent care. They made a few recommendations and urged me to see a cardiologist. I want to know how Miss Carstairs recognized the symptoms."

Power of suggestion. . . Evie could very well have the ability to instigate heart attacks, but she wouldn't. She'd simply been reading Gump's *chakras.* Anything else was on Gump.

"That's not why you're here." Jax handed Marlene's son a tumbler and settled behind his desk with water. "Evie gave you free advice. It was your choice to take it."

Gump glowered and sipped his drink. "I've been looking at the material your crew compiled."

"Evie's crew," Jax corrected. "I'm just their attorney."

"You were once their military officer. You can't tell me they operate without your direction."

Jax laughed. "I can and I will. R&R *never* followed my orders. They're tech geniuses who think all the world is a video game with codes they can crack. What is it you want from them?"

"They've already done more than enough. None of their evidence is permissible in court. It will take us months to compile a legal case. If you want to save them a lot of grief, divert them elsewhere. It's extremely dangerous for private citizens to poke around in the criminal underworld—as my mother discovered, to our great loss."

Ah, so the man was definitely a fed. Jax sat back in his chair and shrugged. Terror might twist his gut at this warning, but Evie and R&R would never stop unless they saw justice done. And he wouldn't stand in their way, no matter how much he wanted to. "We've already been warned."

"And yet Ms. Carstairs is poking around Sunshine offices as we speak. Hacking computers and using illegal research bases is one thing, personally stepping into a viper's nest is another."

She was doing *what*? Jax controlled his shiver and wished he'd poured bourbon for himself. Instead, he stoically defended her. "As you've seen, only Evie can do what Evie does. Without her, we would never have known what your mother was investigating or that she'd been murdered."

"If she isn't part of the solution, then she's part of the problem. I'm not buying ghosts. You need to pull her out of Savannah and leave the investigation to professionals."

"The same professionals who ignored Marlene's warnings and allowed her to die? Why would anyone trust you?" Jax hadn't believed in ghosts either, but whatever Evie did, it worked, however weirdly.

Gump drained his glass and stood up. "If we take up this investigation and any of you interfere, I'll have you arrested for obstructing justice. The bar won't look lightly on a federal charge. I'll see myself out."

Well, so much for hoping Gump might help.

～

SITTING ON THE HOOD OF EVIE'S SHINY BLACK SUBARU IN ARIEL'S driveway, Roark bit into his sub sandwich. He grimaced when Reuben held up a digital notebook and shouted in excitement at the info downloading from a flash drive.

"Holy craptastic, look at this dirt Evie dug! How did a retired old lady federal agent end up in a nest of gangsters?" Reuben's scarred black face was transfixed in awe.

If anyone dug dirt, it should have been R&R, not an amateur.

But as long as he was stuck here. . . He had some weird notion that if Ariel got used to all of them hanging around, she might join them. Proved his stupidity.

"Oh, c'mon now, Reuben," Evie called from Ariel's porch, where she was feeding Mitch Isa Turtle bits from her dinner. Evie had no compunction about disturbing their hostess. "You know Granny suspected they were rotten before she moved in there. She wasn't ready to retire."

Roark appreciated that Evie and Reuben kept him clued in on the team's work, even though he'd been pursuing his own goals. But he suspected Jax had been the instigation for this particular visit. The lawyer was wrapped in a black cloud even he could see.

"Get over heah were we don' have to shout and bother our hostess," Roark ordered.

Evie grabbed his sleeping bag from the porch and dragged it over to the car so she had a place to sit. "Ariel knows how to turn off cameras. You just don't want her to hear."

"Not if I gotta fight wit' her brother. He's got his official face on." Roark bit into his sandwich and waited expectantly.

They'd all arrived in Evie's new car so as not to connect Roark's van with Ariel's hideaway. Roark took that as a good sign that they were still a team. He wanted a team to keep Ariel safe.

"What have you done that requires fighting?" Jax had a way of sounding unperturbed even when he was in a rage.

"What color is he right now?" Roark asked Evie.

She spaced out half a second and scowled. "He's in protective mode and boiling hot mad. What did you do?"

Roark raised his hands. "I didn't do nuttin'. Sounds like you the one been out swattin' wasp nests."

"That's what I've been trying to tell you, oaf." Reuben hit him with the notepad, then settled on the blanket beside Evie, who guilelessly inspected her sandwich's interior as if she'd done nothing but paint fingernails all day.

Roark had only known Evie for six months, but even he knew better than to believe that innocent pose. "Don' make me work when I'm eating. Just tell me what got y'all out here." He sipped his beer and practiced outwaiting Jax.

That was easier when he knew he hadn't done anything wrong for a change. Or not too much wronger than usual.

Reuben wet his whistle with the beer before answering. "She stole a flash drive that contains what is probably the accounts for just one of Sunshine's multifarious operations. Apparently Peterson, the ex-embezzler, is their book-keeper, accountant, whatever. He enters their accounts into spreadsheets. I haven't had time to dig, but the accounts on that drive add up to a few million bucks. They're moving money into real estate, setting up investment companies, laundering cash into legit-looking operations."

"So, what, we're gonna bring down the mafia all by our little lonesome?" Roark grokked Jax's grim expression now.

"Send the drive to the feds and back off," Jax advised. "Gump is on it now. If you can't get any more out of Marlene's ghost, then you've gone as far as you can."

Roark snorted. As if that would happen in Evie's universe. White-hat Jax really didn't comprehend the cosmos of witchy women. Roark had grown up with his grandma. He got it.

Reuben didn't appear disturbed by the admonition. "If we're not getting paid any more, I can buy handing it over. Larraine's campaign is hitting full speed, and she can use more help."

Even though he knew it wasn't happening, Roark figured he could do his part to support a former officer who'd always had his back. "I could use some help in blowing up my da's operation. I'm pretty sure the feds aren't nowhere near him."

Evie nibbled on a piece of chicken she'd pulled off the sandwich she was systematically dismantling. "I'll do what I can to help you tomorrow, but I can't see ghosts or auras through phones. I like your voodoo video though. Mavis said it wouldn't fool an expert but it's appropriately scary. She ordered some of those flash-on candles."

Jax watched them warily. "Does that mean you'll all back away from Sunshine?"

"I'll send Stacey a bill. We answered her questions and got her insurance, even if we didn't find her computers." Reuben opened a chip bag.

"Mebbe we can write up a full report of our findings and send an invoice to the feds." Roark wished he could read auras, but he figured Jax's hadn't left red hot simmer. He wasn't buying the complaisance one bit. "Copy to Gump. We did a lot of work, saved them a bunch of time."

Evie lifted her tomato from the sandwich, ate it, and licked her fingers.

Roark wanted to howl his laughter as Jax got more uptight, trying his damndest to steer Evie into compliance.

"Can you make your witch app say, 'you got money'?" Evie asked.

Roark thought about it. "You have an evil mind," he decided once he realized where she was going with this.

"A hex is a hex." She shrugged. "They're not illegal. They only work on people who are already superstitious and paranoid." She got up and dusted herself off. "I'll work on spreading a little paranoia."

She walked back to the cottage.

Jax squeezed his beer can in two.

Roark cackled like his granny.

Only nerdy Reuben had no idea what had just happened here. Happily lost in producing reports and invoices, he looked up at the silence, shrugged, and finished his sandwich.

Twenty-five

EVIE PROWLED CITY HALL'S CONFERENCE ROOM SATURDAY morning, cell phone in hand. She couldn't sit still while waiting for scammers to call the numbers forwarded to her phone. Pris had received one of the first scam calls and was busily messing with the caller's mind in ways only Pris could do. Evie didn't expect everyone to be as Machiavellian as her family, but Roark's scripts gave the phone bank operators something to work with.

She'd much rather get in her new car and drive to New Orleans or wherever Roark's father was and put the fear of damnation in him.

Well, Roark's app might do that. She'd really like to be in the room as, one-by-one, the cackling witch shut down their phones and ate their money.

Dante had brought his laptop and was busily answering email as he waited for his phone to ring. Others were knitting or playing cards. They'd done a good job preparing everyone for a day of waiting.

Reuben had set up a study carrel on a table against the wall, essentially blocking him from the rest of the room. Evie stopped to lean over his shoulder to check on their own little scam. "Any luck yet?"

"Jax gonna kill us," he muttered.

"No worries. Either the miscreants kill us first, or we succeed and bring home the bacon."

"Ain't no bacon here," he warned. "No glory either. We succeed, a bunch of folks outta jobs."

"I'm no businessperson, but I'm willing to wager there are a bunch of good people in Sunshine willing to step up and keep things running. If we can freeze management's phones and their assets with Roark's hack, can we siphon off Sunshine's funds into a new account that we control to keep operations going?"

Reuben shot her an evil look. "Dream on, little girl. Ain't no bank, nowhere, gonna open an account without credentials. Go away."

Evie grinned and texted Ariel with her idea. Ariel texted a thumbs down. But Ariel had a curious mind. She'd toy with the thought.

Evie hovered behind Jax, who was apparently blowing up battleships online in a game with Roark. She kissed his ear, and he tugged her down for a toe-shivering real kiss. That blurred her mental processes for a while.

It was possible this was more than sex. She might be having an actual relationship. Who knew?

The forwarded number rang on her phone. She dropped into the chair she'd been assigned and checked the scam being played on this victim. Eighty-two-year-old Japanese widow with late husband's pension and social security, living in a boarding house in Memphis. She'd been threatened with deportation if she didn't pay debts her late husband owed. Or most likely didn't owe. Dirty, dirty, dirty.

Fortunately for Mrs. Ito, one of her roommates had set up the call forwarding at Pris's request.

"'Erro," Evie answered in a weak voice.

"Miz Ito, we gave you until today to pay this bill. We will have to garnish your social security and start deportation proceedings if you can't send us the money today." The male voice spoke sternly, although a hint of drawl lingered.

Roark wanted the scammer's phone lines tied up for as long as possible, if only to prevent them from calling more victims. They had little hope of catching the thieves or providing evidence against them, but driving them crazy, hexing them, and shutting down their phones offered an opportunity to consider a different career path.

To that end, Evie answered, "Soshuh secuity, yes, at bank. You pick up newspaper while you theah?"

Evie didn't have enough experience with Asian accents to carry this off well, but maybe the jerk didn't either. She had a vague recollection that "l" wasn't in the Japanese alphabet and "r" sounded like "l." and they didn't use articles the way Americans did.

Silence descended as the jerk looked for a place in his script to counter her inane request. "Ma'am, I don't think you understand. You owe us a thousand dollars. If you can't wire that money today, you will receive no more social security checks."

"Yes, yes, *moah*," Evie rasped excitedly as Roark sauntered over to listen in. "Soshuh secuity. Please, need moah. I need shoes."

Irritation made the scammer sound more threatening. "You won't have shoes or social security unless you send the money today. Can you get to the grocery store?"

So far, he seemed to accept her act. Grinning, Evie continued. "Glocey? You take me? I love go glocey."

The next command registered weariness and disgust. "Credit card? Do you have a credit card?"

Roark flipped the page of her script and pointed at a line.

"Cahd? I have cahd. Just one minute." As the script said, Evie put the phone down and leaned back in her chair to let the jerk stew. "No fun," she whispered at Roark. "Let me play with him, please?"

Another phone rang. Roark shrugged, gave her a thumbs up, and wandered off to annoy someone else. Pris was still enthusiastically leading on her scammer. Pris and enthusiasm seldom came together in the same sentence. Maybe her cousin should start her own call center.

Dante looked up from his email to frown as Pris emitted a series of whoops, curses, and stuttering Tourette's noises. Dang, the girl was good.

Evie returned to her own victim. "Zoom? You got Zoom? I show you cahd."

"Just read me the numbers, ma'am," officious voice demanded.

Evie summoned every bad accent she'd ever heard in old movies. Since she seldom watched TV or movies, it was pretty bad. "Me no lead numbah. Me show you. Big, big numbah. Husban's cahd. Melican. Black. Plitty." How in heck did anyone talk without "r"?

But the vague description of an unlimited American Express card had El Jerko salivating. "Yes, that will work. Can you ask someone else to read it for you?"

"Zoom," Evie insisted, although what she'd do if he agreed, she couldn't say. She didn't have any Asian lady to stand in for her. "Me show you cahd."

"Ma'am, I can't do Zoom. What is the name on the card?"

"Husband," she crowed. "Husban name Ito. Velly good name, Ito. You know him? He died."

Eavesdropping on Evie, Gracie cackled like Roark's voodoo queen at her sister's absurd accent.

"Ma'am, I just need the card number. This is a very serious situation. You could be sent back to. . . where you came from if you don't pay this bill. What is the expiration date on the card?"

"Send back to Califolnia?" Evie asked excitedly. "Yes, yes, my sister theah. I go."

Gracie practically rolled on the floor. At the other end of the table, Pris sounded as if she might be having an orgasm. The men in the room watched with interest, except Reuben. The professor was still industriously bent over the project Evie had given him.

"Asia, ma'am. We'll have to send you out of America if you can't pay your bills. What is the expiration date on the card?"

"Asia?" Evie tried to sound wistful. "Not since rittle gir." Really, she couldn't keep making up this accent. They needed to find people who could fake it. "Don know no one no moah."

"Just read me the date from the card, ma'am." He sounded as if he might be tiring of the game. That was the problem with crooks these days, no stamina, no perseverance.

Jax came over to massage her shoulders. Evie stretched. She'd love doing this more if she could catch the jerkwad.

"I know," she said excitedly, inspired by Jax's massage. "You call my flend from glocely. She give you cahd numbah. And I go Carifolnia!"

"Just give me your friend's number." He barely hid his triumph.

"No, no, she not answer." Evie had grabbed Jax's phone and was hastily looking up grocery stores in Roark's hometown. Hah, Shop-Rite. "She only answer call from Shop-lite. She got Zoom. I give her cahd to lead."

"Shop-Rite?" the voice asked dubiously.

"Yes. Her son work Shop-lite. She don' answer no strange numbah. I Zoom-zoom show her cahd. You call from glocely. She read numbah. I go Carifolnia." Evie thought she'd mispronounced the state three different ways by now.

"Shop-Rite, okay. Give me your friend's number."

Jax signaled Roark, who scribbled down a phone number.

Evie rattled off Roark's number, and crowing over her imaginary visit to the coast, hung up with regret. "I didn't get to hex him."

"If he has half a brain, he'll use a VPN to show Shop-Rite calling." Roark was already punching numbers into his cell. "But just in case, I'll file a complaint and see if they'll pick up the good ol' boy at the grocery. Good try. He'll be occupied doing one or the other for a while."

Another phone rang and he wandered off, still texting his official contact.

Pris turned her phone on speaker and the witch cackled at the other end of the line. Everyone in the room spontaneously cheered, and Gracie shouted "Score!"

And the race was on.

~

ARIEL WATCHED WITH GLEE AS ROARK'S WITCH APP SUCKED money out of Whiteside Fishing and back into the victim accounts the scammers had been robbing. Numbers fascinated her, so she'd fallen into her line of work accidentally, not because she was motivated by justice, like Jax.

So even though she knew what Roark was doing was illegal—the justice of stealing from thieves, then rendering their phones useless, brought unmitigated delight. So much so that she checked into the fake social media account Roark had established for his family to see if anyone was talking about the witch's curse.

She rocked in her chair and grinned as the first reports popped up—not from the phones that the witch had frozen, of course. But friends and family complained that their messages weren't being answered. Then when it became apparent a whole lot of phones weren't being answered, there was a brief flurry of panic. Followed by a lot of acronyms and emojis indicating frustration and fury.

And then, mysteriously, one by one, each of his family's social media accounts shut down. The chatter fell silent. Was his whole family in on the fraud? And now *all* their phones were frozen? They had no other computers?

She texted Evie to ask what was happening.

Evie replied a few minutes later with a video.

Roark was in front of a giant whiteboard scribbled with names, some of whom Ariel recognized as Evie's family. Like a giant scoreboard, each name had marks beside it, some more than others. Pris was busily turning the marks into exclamation points and stars while Roark screamed "Booyah!" and added still another point. If each point represented a phone, they'd taken out a whole lot of scammers today.

The entire room seemed to be screaming in joy and dancing around the long conference table. Even as Ariel watched, music began to play and a conga line formed. She was startled to watch joyless Jax grab Evie and tug her into the dance. Who was holding the camera now?

Reuben's face popped into view. "He did it, kid. Check the bank, then get out and clean your trail. The cops are moving into Whitesville as we speak."

The video ended.

Alarmed, heart rate higher than normal, Ariel opened the Whitesville Fishing account. She blinked at the amount of money being transferred out. The account didn't have that much—

It had overdraft protection. Roark's app had transferred everything in the account and then started drawing on its credit line. The amounts being returned to victims were miniscule in comparison to what had been stolen— but the crooks were out of business.

It was Saturday night. No one at the bank would notice.

Hastily, she cleared all traces of her computer from their files and cleaned out all her drives as well. Roark could do a better job when he returned.

Tentatively, she poked around his family's social media again, but no one was posting. She wiped out any trace of those searches and in a moment of creativity, checked power and internet outages in the vicinity of Whitesville.

The whole county was down.

He'd shut down the *internet?*

She tried to go back to her normal routine but kept playing Reuben's video, reassuring herself that all was well and Roark had won.

He could go home now, right? If the police arrested his father, at least. She didn't know how to hack police reports the way Reuben and Roark did.

She fretted until Roark finally returned.

Her security camera showed Jax's motorcycle dropping him off at 20:20. She hadn't eaten any supper. Had he? Should she go in the kitchen and prepare something?

She tried to focus on the work on her screen but listened for him to come inside instead.

Respecting her space, he entered through the kitchen.

She couldn't take it any longer. All the thoughts buzzing inside her head made her want to crawl under the desk. But she wasn't a child anymore. Roark was safe. Her routine was already shattered. She could leave her work for a few minutes.

She slid back the pocket door. He was nuking the leftover pizza he'd made yesterday. At her entrance, his whole harsh face lit up from beneath his riotous black curls.

"We won, bébé! We cleaned them out!" Without warning, he grabbed her waist and swung her in a circle.

She had to clutch his shoulders to steady herself.

In that second, he kissed her. A real, heart-stopping, mind-numbing exchange of germs that silenced all the noise in her head—for about thirty seconds.

When she realized her breasts were crushed against his chest, her brain short-circuited and she pushed away.

He took her hand and spun her in another circle. "Bébé, do that again, and I'll die of happiness."

"People wouldn't like it if you died," she said by rote, instinctively tugging free of his grip. She had to concentrate on physical action to keep from collapsing on the floor.

He released her but daringly leaned over to kiss her cheek. "You smell of heaven."

"Heaven doesn't exist and has no smell." Unable to think with all the fizziness buzzing in her head, she backed away to take the pizza out of the microwave. Her knees shook so badly she could barely tear off a slice before collapsing on a chair. Only because she had become accustomed to Roark looming over her kitchen did she keep from sliding under the table and banging her head on the legs.

Business. If she could stick to business—

He poured wine into glasses she didn't own. How had he smuggled the bottle in here? The wine effervesced in the glass, and Ariel watched in fascination.

"Larraine sent over the bubbly. She couldn't publicly endorse what we did, but Reuben told her about it. Everyone went home with a bottle." He handed her a glass.

Ariel sniffed it suspiciously before sipping. She wrinkled her nose as the bubbles hit. "A mayor endorses theft?"

"Not a mayor yet. Not theft to return what was stolen." He bit off a large chunk of pizza while she nibbled hers.

She tried to process everything, only the bubbly drink and the hot pizza and the hot man practically fizzing like his drink had her paralyzed.

"It's over then?" she managed to ask, because it was a question that had hovered for hours.

"Don't know." He produced a laptop from his backpack—ah, that's how he smuggled in the bottle and glasses.

"Whitesville blacked out," she said helpfully, while he pulled up whatever websites he was after.

"Booyah!" He pumped his fist in the air. "I didn't know if I could pull that off."

"You planned that?" She couldn't decide if she was more incredulous that he was capable or would do it deliberately. "That's criminal. Why?"

"Listen to the lady who hacks banks for a living." He opened a screen and grinned. "I didn't know if they could pass on the witch virus. Looks like they did."

"How?" She refused to look over his wide shoulder but remained seated.

"Doofi don't secure their phones or computers. Virus infects their email program, text, social media, anywhere it can get in. Link spreads. Idjits open it hoping for explanation and voila, they freeze. Wasn't sure it would work." He crowed, "Entire fam damily down!"

"Your mother? Your sisters?" So caught up in the horror, she forgot to process words.

"Wives, in-laws. They're all enablers." He turned the laptop around so she could see the screen.

It was merely a list of calls to the state police—from numbers all over the southeast. Ariel recognized most of them from the victim list she'd compiled. "The victims finally reported the scam?"

"The app did." He switched screens. "That many complaints couldn't be ignored. The guy I had following Cousin Omer called in da's location. The cops won't find many of them there, but they have names and numbers now. Da will have to lie low. His cohorts will scatter. Don't know if anyone will do time."

"You can go home now?" she asked tentatively.

"Hell, no," he replied without hesitation, before studying her. "I can leave here, if you want, move back to Evie's, mebbe. But I don' like leaving you alone."

It was on the tip of her tongue to say she lived to be alone. But that was a lie. She was learning to enjoy the company of a man who respected her idiosyncrasy. She didn't know how to say all that.

"If you don' mind, I'm stayin'," he said quietly, turning the screen toward her again.

An email addressed to Roark from the Candyman filled the screen.

I know it's you, was all it said.

Who was the Candyman?

Twenty-six

EVIE ROLLED OUT OF BED SUNDAY MORNING WELL BEFORE JAX was prepared to get up. He glared at her from under his arm. "It's Sunday. We don't work today."

"Mavis wants me and Loretta to go to church with her." She rummaged in her wardrobe—the house didn't have much in the way of closets.

"You haven't been to church all summer." He flipped over and propped his shoulders on pillows, always curious about Evie's family and their peculiarities. "Do witches go to church?"

"We have *psychic abilities*. We just like to occasionally wind people up by calling ourselves witches." She produced the ice-blue dress she'd worn the other day and gave that statement some thought. "I think even the Salem witches attended church. Or maybe they burned the ones who didn't. Oh well. You should come with us. Good for business."

Jax couldn't remember the last time he'd gone to church. With his upbringing, Sundays had been for golf. He had a suspicion that Evie's attendance might have the same reason as his golf—social networking. "So, what is Mavis up to that she wants a posse with her?"

She beamed at him and headed for the shower. "Mom is introducing Larraine to the congregation. We're all going to be there to show our support. Hank would have an apoplexy, but this is his big summer clearance sale at the hardware store. He'll be working."

181

Jax almost felt sorry for the other mayoral contender. Maybe he should show solidarity with the male candidate—except Larraine had her own grounds for sexual discrimination. The world was complicated.

To each their own seemed the simplest policy.

He got out of bed and joined Evie in the shower to take life back to the basics.

After a creative and satisfying session of shower sex, she dashed to dress while he lingered over shaving. By the time he dragged on his Sunday clothes of shorts and polo shirt and ambled downstairs, Evie was proudly ushering everyone out to her new car—including Reuben.

"Dude, you know her church is all white ladies, don't you?" Jax filled his coffeemaker while Reuben polished off his green smoothie.

Reuben shrugged. "Used to it. Wouldn't otherwise but Larraine asked me."

Jax grimaced. "Friends gotta be friends, got it. Anything I need to work on while you're socially occupied?"

Reuben waited until Evie led a chattering Loretta outside before replying. "Sunshine has called an emergency board meeting for tomorrow. There's a conference room in the office wing of the Azalea Apartments. You might ask Gump if he's bothered wiring that room. It would be beneficial."

He hurried after Evie before Jax could question.

Emergency board meeting? For why? And why would it be beneficial to bug it? He hadn't really believed Evie would drop the case, but what had she had time to do to result in a board meeting? They'd spent all yesterday in a phone bank!

Alarmed, Jax pulled out his cell, but he doubted if Gump had had time to obtain any warrants. On the face of it, Sunshine was completely legal. It might employ a few questionable employees, but the feds didn't waste time arresting penny-ante embezzlers and reformed counterfeiters. They'd need interstate criminal activity, and no one had evidence of that yet.

Reuben was telling him that Evie hadn't stopped interfering.

Shit. Drinking his coffee, he texted Roark. Then snatching a donut from the box Mavis must have brought over, he headed out to his Harley. Ariel would be sleeping at this hour, but it was probably best if they kept her out of Evie's machinations.

Barefoot and shirtless, Roark greeted him on the front porch, water bottles in hand. He'd built a pull-up exercise bar under the eaves and had worked up a sweat in the August humidity. Still early, the heat hadn't reached boiling yet.

"Celebrating?" Jax asked, rolling the bike up the last part of the drive to keep from waking his sister. "Did Pris jump your bones in jubilation last night?"

Roark snorted up the water he'd just swallowed. "I left her and your Italian geek shouting at each other in foreign languages. Does she really read minds? Because she didn't seem to like what was on his."

Jax accepted a cold water bottle. "Evie's family *knows* things the old-fashioned way, gossip. What's up next for you?"

"Waiting to see what the cops did with my da's nest of vipers. Needing action. You bring me some?"

"Depends. You know what Reuben and Evie are up to on the Gump case?" Jax settled on the front step.

"You told us to pull back." Roark handed him his cell phone with the message from the Candyman. "Reckon I'll have a visit from da as soon as he works out where I am. Probably ought to head out before then."

"The Candyman?"

"Yeah, my bros used to call him dat cause he'd bring candy when he wanted to wheedle somet'ing out of us."

Jax whistled. "What are the chances he'll find you?"

Roark shrugged. "Don' even know how he found that number. I reckon we stirred the sleeping giant behind his operation, someone with tech knowhow."

"Any of your family back online? Can you tell what's happening?"

"*Mais oui*, women are pissed. Lotta code words flyin'. My name came up a time or two. I called Mama, since my number out there now." He looked at his prepaid phone with regret. "Gotta get a new one."

"You've earned it. You should collect ten percent, minimum, of all that money you got back. Send a bill." Jax grinned at the idea of all those victims receiving a bill for services rendered. "What did your mother say?"

"Cops raided a bar in town. She thought da clowns were gambling and was cursing dem for shuttin' down the internet while her favorite show was playing. She said my cousins suddenly decided to follow my bros out of town. Now I gotta hope the rich honcho doesn't have an operation in Texas too. I can't keep doin' this."

"Well, if your father had a phone to text you, we'll have to assume he escaped the raid. And since you emptied his bank account, he can't get far. The security here is tight. You should be good."

Roark's look was almost wistful as he glanced over his shoulder at the cottage. "It's nice here. But I can't keep bumming off your sister."

"Stacey Gump will pay her bill, and you'll have a share of that. Shame there wasn't any big reward for catching scammers. That line of business ought to pay better."

Roark shrugged. "Gotta face facts. Can't get paid for illegal hacking, unless I want to turn criminal. I coulda made a bona fide bonus yesterday."

"Which is where I come in." Jax knew he hadn't had time to think this through, but time was of the essence. "You didn't have time to build in a transfer to your own account in yesterday's attack, but I assume that's doable?"

Roark squinted at him. "You mean, I should skim off the top of old ladies' stolen money?"

"I mean, you stopped a criminal operation and saved them hundreds, maybe thousands. Any lawyer would take 50%. You let it be known in certain circles that you and your app are available for a small fee, you've got your own sideline. Coming up with a phone bank to counter a phone bank might be truly. . ."

Roark snorted. "I got an AI almost done. I can do one scammer at a time with a robot talking. Why you tellin' me this?"

"Because I need all the help I can get to keep Evie from trouble."

Roark laughed. "You askin' the impossible, dude, but I'm all in. Give me work. Whatcha need?"

"To start with—bugging a boardroom while I research the legality of your new app."

Evie returned from church alone, leaving her family and Loretta to brunch with Larraine and take a tour of the mayoral candidate's designer clothing factory. She changed into a pair of frayed cargo shorts and a bulky work shirt she'd bought at the thrift store when she'd painted Loretta's room. Then stuffing flyers into her tote, she trotted happily down to the Subaru, hoping to steal a few hours of ghost talk with Marlene.

Reuben was leaning against the car. She'd lost track of him in the mob of family, but of course he had no interest in touring a factory he probably saw nightly.

"You goin' somewhere without me?" he asked with all semblance of nonchalance.

"Any reason I should take you? You can't talk to Marlene."

"You're gonna hurt my feelings, girl. Get in the van and pretend we're a team, okay?" He opened the passenger door of his utility vehicle.

"Jax told you to back off," she countered warily.

She'd really wanted to test her new car, but she supposed he had a point. The Subaru wasn't equipped the way the van was. "I just want to chat up a few old people. You know you hate that sort of thing." Glowering, she buckled into the van's passenger seat.

"Yeah, but I got to collect those cameras, remember? And now I've sent those messages you had me set up, Sunshine won't be so sunny. You need bugs in their offices. You were planning on visiting more offices, weren't you?" He took the highway toward the interstate but pulled off onto Ariel's side road.

"Are we picking up Roark too? I thought we weren't taking the van out there."

Roark stepped out of the woods and flagged them down. Reuben did a neat three-point turn in the middle of the empty road and halted so Roark could climb in back.

"*Ca va*, bébé?" he called as he settled in with the equipment.

"I have your seat," Evie grumbled.

"Nah, Reuben's got that. You got his. It works out." He began rummaging through drawers.

"Do I ever get to drive my car?" Resigned, she settled back and tried to plot how she could use the extra help, but plotting wasn't her expertise.

"If we need to split up, I expect you can drive. But you're talking to Mrs. Gump, and we're taking out cameras, and it's all one place, right? We need you as our cover. Ain't no one letting us in looking like we do." Reuben glanced at her outfit. "Although you ain't looking particularly professional today."

"That's because I wasn't planning on going in the front door." She crossed her arms and tried to reconfigure her thinking to take in these two over-protective clowns.

"Back door, even better!" Roark crowed. "It's got a keypad. I can do dat."

Evie wouldn't give him the satisfaction of asking *how*. For all she knew, there was an app for that.

"How'd Sunday go-to-meeting go?" Roark asked in amusement as he rattled around in the van's drawers.

Reuben just chortled.

Evie poked his shoulder. "It went just fine. Reverend Roberts is a broadminded man. He welcomed Larraine and let her speak at the coffee afterward. His brother-in-law, the deacon, is less accepting."

"The deacon told Mavis—you had to be there," Reuben was grinning ear to ear. "The deacon told Mavis he'd never set foot in her shop again. She told him he didn't have to; his wife ordered his keep-it-up supplements from her website. And if the pills didn't work anymore, he could guess who was to blame."

Evie grinned. "It was worth wasting a few hours of my Sunday to see Deacon try to drag his wife out and all the women blocking his path. Then Larraine tapped him on the shoulder. . ." She giggled, reliving the scene.

"Like I said, man, you shoulda been there. Larraine is a foot taller and twenty years younger and the deacon, he looked like he was about to get swallowed up and dragged off to hell. He dropped his wife's arm and fled and might never be seen again."

"And my mother got free advertising for her supplements and new website. Thanks for that, Reuben. She has Loretta taking the orders and Aunt Ellen packaging them up. It's giving my aunt something more useful to do than talking to conmen on the phone."

"Can I adopt your family?" Roark asked. "I want to be dem when I grow up."

"You're crazy enough to fit right in," Evie said solemnly. She made Reuben pull over at a fast-food joint so she could have a milkshake and salad. The men happily opted for the biggest sandwiches on the menu, with extra fries.

By the time they pulled into the rear lot of Azalea Apartments, she was feeling more charitable. She'd deduced Jax had set them to following her while he went about his own business, whatever that might be. The poor man still didn't grasp that she could take care of herself. She simply did it from a different plane than he comprehended.

Roark waited until a janitor approached the back door, then climbed out with his toolbox in hand. He politely stood to one side as the janitor programmed in the key number, then caught the door and entered with him. He texted the number back once he was inside.

"How did he do that?" Evie studied the numbers Roark had sent as Reuben keyed them in. She could barely read the pad in the bright light.

"Hears it. Each number has a slightly different tone. You ought to see him crack a safe. Fortunately, that's not our usual line of work."

"Huh, acute hearing? I thought only my family could do that. That's a for real thing?"

"Ain't got no idea what you're talking about. He's got good ears is all I know." Reuben held the door for her.

Inside, Evie gestured at a coat closet where employees left their work clothes as well as their outside clothes. She grabbed a maid's tunic that might fit and found a nametag in the pocket. Most excellent.

The guys opted for safety vests and pulled out their own name tags, as if they might be with a janitorial or repair service.

Pushing a rolling laundry cart, she followed them into the elevator and up to the fourth floor. She sensed a temporal disturbance that usually meant paranormal activity, but this was a retirement home, where old people died regularly. She really didn't want to investigate any extra ghosts just yet. Her focus was divided as it was.

"What are our main goals here?" Reuben demanded.

"Remove the cameras," Roark promptly replied. "Then bug their conference room."

"Talk to everyone we saw on Granny's camera the week she died?" Goals had never been in her game plan. Knocking on doors was more her style. Consulting the ghost, maybe.

Reuben rolled his eyes. "And just exactly what do you say to a potential murder suspect?"

"Does anyone here drink Gatorade?" she suggested. She had no clue beyond her flyers.

"Coroner hasn't verified Gatorade yet. Does that stuff even come in purple? You'd be as useful asking about Purple Passion Juice. And why would a maid be asking questions?" Reuben held the elevator door so they could all get off.

Marlene's door was open and the hall stank of fresh paint. Oh crap.

Twenty-seven

"You two go do what you do," Roark suggested, peering into the apartment through the cracked open door. "I got the cameras under control. Reuben, turn on your ears." He liked knowing where everyone was if they split up. He should probably teach Evie to wear a mic and ear buds.

"I'm off to bug a boardroom." Reuben said into his mic, testing it, before he took off down the hall with his tool bag.

"I need to talk to Marlene," Evie whispered.

"Then do it in the hall."

Once assured she wouldn't barge in, Roark straightened his shoulders and pushed open the door. He didn't normally use his size to bully, but intimidation was easy. A couple of paunchy painters sloppily throwing a boring beige on the walls glanced up at his entrance. Saluting a curt greeting, he set his toolbox on the counter and climbed up to remove his cameras, as if he were simply maintenance.

The painters didn't question. Or didn't dare.

From this angle, through the open door, he could see Evie leaning against the hall wall, muttering to the voices in her head.

When she abruptly wandered off, Roark cursed. He hurriedly removed the first camera. Climbing down, he could see her knocking on the door across the hall. He moved on to the next device.

188

Wait a minute. . . She was going into the old guy's apartment dressed like a laundress?

He peered into the hall again. She'd wrapped her distinctive orange hair in a bandana and donned spectacles. When no one answered the door, she slid a slick flyer under the door. Where the hell had she hidden that?

That blamed tote bag, of course. Probably hidden in the laundry cart, sneaky diva.

Leaving her performing the same routine at the next door—although this one answered and Evie got to chat her up—Roark returned to retrieving his equipment.

Once he had everything in his box, he left without saying a word to the painters. He almost felt the tension relax at his departure. From their whispers, he gathered they thought him some kind of spy for management. Which would mean they were afraid of management? Or he could be making that up.

Listening, he heard Evie talking around the corner. He stalked in that direction, peering around the edge to verify what she was doing. Then he pushed the mic to call Reuben. "You gonna tell me what the two of you up to?"

"Just drumming up a little paranoia the modern way. You do voodoo, we do tech."

"App is tech. Flyers ain't. Explain." He watched Evie chatter with a little old lady and hand her a paper. They had a nice little discussion and she moved on.

"I borrowed your app but ditched your witch and used one that would scare them more," Reuben responded. "I emailed the board and upper management a link to an app that says *You got money.* I figured that was the fastest way to catch their attention. They click it and get an official looking IRS letter saying Sunshine is being audited, and if they have any illegal activity they would like to report, it will release them from liability. A reply goes to a comment page on an official looking website, but just clicking the link gives me access to their devices. Even if only a few are stupid enough to click. . ."

"Paranoia ensues, the virus spreads, and the shouting begins." Roark chuckled. "I like it. If they're already calling an emergency board meeting, then sounds like a few did some clicking."

Evie disappeared from view. Roark hurried down the hall to keep up with her. "And what is our *petite sorcière* doing with the flyers?"

"Official communication from Sunshine headquarters announcing police are investigating the murder of Marlene Gump and several burglaries and asking for anyone who knows anything to report to a confidential phone number and/or e-mail address. Evie doesn't like websites."

Roark's brain screamed alarm. "Are both of you *crazy*?" He rushed to catch Evie before she took the stairs to the next floor. She looked miffed when he caught her elbow but waited explanation.

"Out of here *now*," he ordered both Evie and Reuben, holding her captive while heading down the stairs. "Every one of those little old ladies is calling every person they know. The real killer will know what we're doing in seconds."

"The Cajun speaks English," Evie complained, prying off his fingers. "Of course he will. That's the *point*. Were we supposed to twiddle our thumbs until the feds decide Marlene is important enough to investigate? How many other people will die in the meantime?"

"I've got the bugs planted," Reuben said into his ear. "Just leave the rest of the flyers on the desk and we can go."

"We're not going anywhere near the front desk. We didn't sign in. Just leave them in the break room or whatever. And those better be secure numbers you're using because Sunshine isn't my daddy's ignorami. They got skills." Roark blocked doors, forcing Evie to continue down the stairs.

Jax was going to have his head and probably his balls too.

And when had he ever cared what the head honcho thought?

When he'd moved in with Jax's sister. Damn.

"Your aura is flailing," Evie said with amusement as they came out in the staff hall. "It was easier when you weren't trying to please Jax."

"Not trying to please no one. Trying to stay alive." Roark glared at his partner in crime as Reuben trotted down the hallway, unpinning his plastic name tag. "You should have more sense."

"What? How? This is what we *do*. Since when did you become a Nervous Nellie?" Shaking his man bun in disbelief, Reuben headed for the door. "Paid good money for those flyers. Hate to waste them."

Roark grabbed the lot from Evie's hand and distributed them into the various cleaning carts. "There. Cleaning ladies can hand them out."

Evie resisted being pushed out. "Marlene says Mr. Charles had a party before she got ill. He had an alcoholic purple punch with fruit floating in it. She thought the third and fourth cups were stronger than the first ones but drank them anyway. I talked to some of the other ladies on the floor, and they remembered the party. They thought the drinks got weaker."

"So, the old goat wanted to seduce a drunken Marlene." Roark opened the door and dragged her out. "That didn't mean he was adding antifreeze to her cup. Why would he do that? Besides, the purple wouldn't still be in her stomach days later."

"Opportunity and means are a start, isn't it? Now we look for a motive." Evie glared and glanced wistfully back at the building. "I was just getting started."

"You were on your way to getting killed." Roark yanked open the van door and pointed inside. "I can heave you in easy enough."

"Bully. I'll tell Ariel on you." She climbed inside.

"Ariel got more sense than you. She'd cheer me on." He slammed the door.

"Ariel lives inside her head and not the real world," Evie retorted from the interior.

She was right, but Roark didn't care. He took his place behind the driver's wheel, leaving Reuben on the passenger side. He wasn't sure why he was so angry. This stunt wasn't anything different from all the others he'd pulled.

Maybe he was starting to see the world from Ariel's perspective—as a dangerous place.

Once Reuben was buckled in, Roark took off, turning left out of the parking lot instead of right, toward the highway.

"You forgot your way around?" Reuben asked, opening his phone.

"No. Shaking any tail. We need to get a South Carolina plate real soon if we're staying here."

"You'd have to give my address and that would lead right to us." Evie leaned against the driver's seat from behind. "Where does your Georgia plate lead to?"

"Jax's old office." Roark chuckled, thinking of anyone trying to track him down there. "And there he is. Black Mercedes, three cars back."

"Car wash." Apparently having opened a map app, Reuben pointed down a side street near a shopping center.

Roark judged the car wash line. "Mebbe." Swinging the van into the shopping center, he zigzagged through the parking lot to reach the car wash in back. He cut in front of a Ford heading the same direction and got in line.

The Ford fell in behind him, probably cursing. If he could get inside the wash before the Mercedes made it back here. . .

The car in front finished and Roark gave the pay machine the card Evie handed him. "Where did this come from?"

"Loretta. She was buying candy for everyone, and I had to take it away. We'll need an accountant to straighten out our finances at this rate."

Roark rolled the van into the car wash. "We either lost him, or he's out there waiting for us. Anyone want to place bets?"

"He's got the plate number. If they have connections, they might think that's enough." Reuben tried to look behind them but the mirror and windows were covered in soap.

"I'm betting he's waiting. Hope you got the wax." Evie opened the rear door as soon as the soap machine moved forward.

"What the f. . . friggin' hell. . ." Roark watched in dismay as the diminutive witch jumped out, closed the door, and vanished.

THE FIRST OF THE RINSE CYCLE CAUGHT EVIE AS SHE DASHED FOR the car wash entrance, but on a hot August day, she figured she'd just steam herself dry.

She really hated being bullied.

Not that the guys had threatened her in any way. They simply didn't accept that she was her own entity, just as entitled to do what needed to be done as they were.

She appreciated the idea of a team, as long as they all had equal roles. She was feeling disenfranchised.

She tugged off her old work shirt, uncovering a hot pink tank top. Then she unwrapped her distinctive hair from its bandana so she didn't look like the maid who'd climbed out of the van in the middle of a car wash. She ditched the shirt in a trash can and stuck the bandana in a pocket. Could she write the shirt off as a business expense?

Prepared to tackle baddies, she studied the parking lot. If she were tracking the van, she'd be waiting at the car wash exit. Keeping an eye on the parking lot, she strolled down the side of the concrete block building to the exit at the back of the minimart.

And there he was, black Mercedes with tinted windows backed into a spot by the store, catty-corner to the car wash so they could pull right out after the van passed. She didn't suppose they'd gone inside for a hot dog, but they'd be watching the windshield and not their backs.

Strolling the sidewalk toward the front of the store, she rummaged in the pocket of her cargo shorts where she kept her emergency supplies. Once she was behind the Mercedes, she let the bandana fall—then bent down to retrieve it.

Among other handy tools, she'd learned to carry a jackknife way back in childhood. It came in handy to cut brambles out of dog fur or slice string on kites or any of a million uses. She'd never used it for slashing tires.

She wasn't strong, but she knew where to strike. Turning her face away to avoid getting hit with a rush of hot air, she plunged the tip of the blade into the sidewall. It took a hard twist, but she heard the satisfying *pfft* of leakage. She angled the knife in a couple of directions to widen the hole. No point in giving them time to go far.

Standing again, bandana in hand and knife out of sight, she continued strolling toward the front of the minimart. If the guys were mad enough to abandon her here, she wouldn't go hungry.

Well, maybe she would. She'd given the credit card to Roark. She probably still had a little cash.

She smiled when the utility van roared past the front of the store and stopped on the far side, out of sight of the Mercedes. She opened the rear door and climbed in, barely slamming it before Roark hit the gas.

"That was slick, girl," Reuben crowed from the front.

"That was *sick*," Roark corrected. "Sick, sick, *sick* and never do that again without warning. I almost had to grab the dynamite."

"But he was stuck driving." Reuben laughed. "What else you got in those pockets?"

"Not dynamite." He had dynamite in the van? Evie didn't want to look. "You could see what I did?" That couldn't be good.

"Nah, when you dropped down behind him like that, we just figured sabotage was on the agenda and tires look easy." Reuben watched the mirror. "Mercedes didn't get far. Driver got out and is swearing up a storm. Don't know what he's complaining about. He's right there at a service station."

"What does he look like?" The van had no back window.

Reuben grimaced. "White guy, gray hair, kinda portly. Could be someone else in the passenger seat. Windows tinted, can't tell."

That probably described half of Sunshine's management. "Thank you for trusting me to have a brain."

Roark stayed ominously silent as he navigated the side roads back to the highway.

Evie whacked his black curls with a leftover flyer. "*You*, moron, may have military training, but I have street cred. I am not your family."

He grunted. "My family would have taken a machete to the driver. Jax gonna kill us."

"Yeah, well, get used to it. He and I are diametrically opposed on the battle ground. He's the privileged officer at the back of the line with a tent and maps. I'm behind enemy lines in a pink tutu. To each their own."

Even Roark sputtered at that image. Good. He hadn't completely lost his humor.

Jax wouldn't find it in the least funny. Evie thought she might be testing the poor guy, but she couldn't change to suit his role models.

"I thought we're a team," Roark said warily.

"We are. And when we can, we plan together. And when we can't, we have each other's backs however works for us. So, yeah, you're allowed to get mad at me, just as I'm allowed to get mad at you for going off without me or pushing me around. But I will still leap out of a moving vehicle for you."

The men thought about that as the van hit the highway.

"Don' like it," Roark admitted. "But we lost da tail."

Evie sighed in relief. "I didn't think I could make the hole big enough. Steel-walled tires are tough."

"Let me see your blade." Reuben held his hand over the seat. "We may need to get you a better one."

"This one fits my hand. Don't go telling me what to do already." Evie handed him the knife.

"Accept we know weapons better than you, and you know ghosts better than us. Did your ghost tell you anything useful?" Dropping his agitated accent, Roark kept his eyes on the road.

"Granny is furious about the antifreeze. She can't give me the names of the people at the party, just weird descriptions like *nosy old lady*, that aren't very helpful. But she's convinced the *nurse* knew about antifreeze poisoning."

"Makes sense," Reuben agreed. "But Savanna was never in Mrs. Gump's apartment according to the cameras. She's been out on sick leave, right?"

"Right, which is why Marlene was bouncing off walls. She was certain the nurse wasn't at the party. She wanted me to talk to her *old fart neighbor*. She even left her apartment to cross the hall with me. But Mr. Charles wasn't there."

"Wasn't he her boyfriend? Did he think she would leave him her things and offed her? This isn't about Sunshine at all?" Roark asked in consternation .

"You're worse than Jax. Quit speculating. This wasn't domestic. Marlene claims she *didn't* give Charles her phone. She didn't trust anyone. But she has no cognizance of the days she was ill or right after she died, not until Stacey arrived some time later. So there could have been a week or so when she wasn't aware."

"We have her camera cloud backup. Charles was in her apartment that week she was sick, as was just about everyone in the building at some point—except the nurse." Reuben was scrolling through his phone, reviewing the videos. "They brought her food she didn't eat. There's a couple of days when she let no one in—probably dead or dying at that point."

"The bossy blond director was the one who finally unlocked the door, presumably after someone reported Granny wasn't answering. Charles followed her in, as did a couple of old ladies. Unless the director forced poison down Marlene's throat, then called an ambulance, you have to figure Granny was dead by then." Roark checked his mirrors.

"But while everyone was crying and calling ambulances or whatever, any one of them had the opportunity to slip the phone into a pocket and pour evidence down the drain." Evie sat cross-legged in back, picturing the situation. "Could you see the whole place from her cameras?"

"Nah, just the doors and windows, mostly. People wander in and out of view. Her laptops were in sight on the one camera. That might have been deliberate. One of the ladies set her purse beside them. Can't see any phone." Reuben held up his screen for her to see.

Evie took the phone to examine the video. "I wish auras showed up on cameras. But this lot all looked suspicious when I saw them, so that probably doesn't help. Personally, I think they're casing the joint for what they can steal. Hard to squeeze a laptop into a purse with people watching, but a phone is ideal." She handed the phone back, disappointed.

"So, what are your plans for tomorrow's board meeting?" Roark asked cautiously.

Evie beamed. "Reuben, did you plant the ghosts?"

~

With Roark out of the house when she woke up, Ariel sighed in relief and returned to her routine. After that mind-bending kiss, she needed to recover her equilibrium.

She did her exercises and took her shower. She fed Mitch Turtle, sat down at her desk, and checked email.

Pris sent enthusiastic gratitude. After hearing from everyone at the phone bank, her mother had very reluctantly agreed to block her gentleman caller. She'd booked an appointment at the eye doctor.

Find her a boyfriend? Ariel emailed back, even though she thought phone smashing was the best solution.

Finding boyfriends wasn't exactly easy, Ariel knew. That had been a foolish thing to say.

Roark wasn't here to prepare her first meal of the day. She fixed tea and toast and ate a peach.

But when she returned to her numbers, she couldn't summon her usual excitement at watching a spider web of finance unravel. She had an inexplicable urge to know the people behind the numbers.

Roark knew how to research people. He could teach her. But he'd run off into the real world where she couldn't easily go. Or had any reason to go.

She had a bike now. She could ride into town. Why would she?

Oddly unhappy without Roark's energy vibrating her walls, she returned to tracking the cryptocurrency related to his father's nasty business. An unsophisticated person like his father wouldn't even know bitcoins existed. The trail was cold this morning, since Roark had emptied the bank account. But there had been other bank accounts buying cryptocurrency through this dealer.

She just hadn't been able to hack the dealer's password. But she could hack into the bank accounts buying from him.

She had quite an interesting list by the time Roark returned. Her mind instantly emptied of anything except last night's kiss.

No one had ever kissed her before. She usually didn't like being touched. She wanted to be kissed again.

Roark's touch—had awakened parts of her better left sleeping. He'd be gone any day. There was no purpose in learning what she couldn't have.

And still her stupid pulse picked up pace when she heard him enter the back door.

She had a right to be curious, didn't she? Maybe she'd never exhibited interest in others because they weren't interesting. Roark was. And exciting and annoying and. . .

Breaking routine, she printed out her bank account list and took it back to the kitchen where he was throwing chopped onions into a pot while texting one-handed. At her entrance, he glanced up, and a huge grin spread across his dark face.

"Cher! To what do I owe this honor?"

Honor? She studied him quizzically, then laid the paper on the table and repeated the words she'd memorized. "Your father transfers money to Bytes Unlimited once a week."

Roark flung a handful of garlic into the onions, then set down his phone. Stirring the pot, he gestured for her list. "Da knows not'ing of bitcoins."

"Someone empties his checking account down to the minimum balance." She handed him the list.

He frowned. "He don' know not'ing about minimum balances."

"Someone does. They clear it out once a week."

He frowned at her list, stirred his onions, and added more garlic. "And the money goes to Bytes Unlimited?"

"Bitcoin dealer, yes." She pointed at the list. "Other accounts buying from that dealer follow similar pattern."

Her strained effort at communication had his full attention, she realized with relief.

"These are the other accounts buying from the dealer?" Regularizing his speech, he brandished her list.

She nodded. "Once a week, excess is swept to the dealer. I don't know how to research these companies."

"I can do that. One of them on this list says *Sunshine Services*. Any chance they're connected to the retirement home?"

Ariel nodded. "Address in Savannah."

Roark whistled. "Eh, bébé, sounds like Evie got herself mixed up in money laundering. Jax ain't gonna like dis atall."

Twenty-eight

"WHAT DO YOU MEAN, YOUR FATHER'S SCAMMERS ARE connected to Sunshine Healthcare? He's a two-bit phone grifter in the Louisiana swamp. Sunshine is a perfectly legitimate nursing home in Georgia apparently into ripping off employees, patients, stealing identities. . ." Jax caught himself. "*Stealing identities*, damn."

"Exactly," Roark said cheerfully from the other end of the line. "We got a federal operation across state lines. Get Fuzzy Gump on this. Get my da sent up the river big time."

"That's a stretch." Jax ran his hand over his hair. He hadn't had it barbered recently, saving dollars and blending in. He grabbed a hank and yanked it now.

There was no way in hell he could tell the FBI about his sister's propensity for hacking bank accounts.

"Diplomacy." Roark said wickedly, reading his thoughts. "You gotta feed him just the right info so he can follow his own trail."

"Bureaucracy," Jax retorted with disgust. "How long will it take for the feds to connect their own data for warrants? Ariel's hacking is illegal and not permissible in court."

"Talk to Evie. She's crazy, but she's our kind of crazy. You just gotta funnel her onto the paths of righteousness before she sets people's hair on fire."

Evie had come pretty close to doing just that in the past. Jax rubbed his face. "Laugh, if you want, but she'll drag you in with her if you're not careful." He shut off the phone and stared at his laptop. He really needed a bigger monitor.

He couldn't afford a bigger monitor because Evie's idea of justice didn't pay. One of them really ought to consider consequences. . .

But his long buried super-idiot wanted to bring down the corrupt cretins *now*. Fraud could wait for formalities. Murder couldn't. If they got away with it once. . .

Setting aside the research he'd been doing on the legality of Roark's phone scam app, he closed up shop. It was Sunday, after all. He was entitled to a few hours with his girlfriend. His significant other.

He tried on various other descriptions of their relationship on the way back to the house. He'd never lived with any of his partners before. He didn't know the rules.

He found Evie innocuously trimming overgrown bushes in the backyard, like any normal person on a weekend. Except Evie appeared to be leaving long, drooping branches on top that looked like dreadlocks, while sculpting holes in the middle that might well be eyes or noses.

"Want some help trimming the tops?" Jax asked warily, just in case he was wrong.

"Nah, we're going to add blinking eyes and red lights for lips. Leaving flowers in their hair seemed reasonable." She turned and grinned at him.

Damn, but that grin turned his insides out. He shoved his hands in his pockets. "Are you using the grass-that-isn't-there for the dance floor?"

Her smile brightened. "Reuben insisted we have planks. It's Loretta's party, so it's coming out of her allowance. No idea what we'll do with a dance floor after."

"Party every week!" Loretta crowed from the porch, where she appeared to be planting flowers in coffee mugs. Or Toby mugs. They had faces: blue ones, red ones, black, brown—ethnically diverse Toby mugs. With flowers for hair, of course.

"You'd need heaters in winter," Jax reminded her. "And then you'd want a barn to keep out the rain and wind. Let's stick to just one party a year, okay? What's with the mugs?"

"Loretta found them in the attic—with holes carefully drilled in the bottom. You'd have to ask my great-aunt what that's about. I'm sure she thought they'd be useful someday. Or maybe one of her exes thought it funny."

"Your family, the ultimate recyclers." Having already learned that her wealthy great-aunt had no interest in the contents of the house, Jax examined the neglected backyard. Baked clay, overgrown mimosas and crepe myrtles, long purple flowering shrubs. . . That didn't leave a lot of opportunity for the manicured garden parties his adoptive mother once held.

She laughed. "We're not hoarders, mind you. We do actually recycle the junk eventually."

Jax wondered if he and Roark and Reuben might be recycled junk—useful when applied creatively. He could live with that. "Should I weed whack the fence?"

"Only if you know what's weed and what's not. Mavis grows stuff back there. Even I don't know what's weed, and some of that might be of the pot variety for all I know." Evie considered the jungle along the fence line. "I was thinking we could put lighted sticks in there and call them flowers."

"Ingenious." Giving up resistance, Jax circled her waist and kissed her just because he could. And maybe because her creative insanity turned him on.

"Ummm, yes." She licked a corner of his mouth. "What do you want and what will you do to get it?"

He chuckled. "If I thought there was any way to drag you from your fun and games to a nice, air-conditioned bedroom—" He kissed the frown forming over her nose. "I'll settle for making bush monsters if you'll give me a clear run-down on what you're planning with Sunshine. And tell me if you've received any response to your flyers."

"You're not going to yell at me for interfering in a federal case?"

"I did that. It didn't help. Now I'm just trying to run interference."

She handed him the clippers. "This calls for lemonade. You may need something stronger but beer is all I've got."

"Beer works." Jax studied the bush she'd been mutilating. He thought it might be called a butterfly bush and decided the long purple spiky flowers dangling from the "hair" made it female. He started pruning small features instead of broad ones, hollowing out leaves on the sides to indicate a jaw, leaving leafy "lips" plump. Trimming sticks into shape was torturous.

"This is pure nuts," he informed her when Evie returned with his beer. Sweat was already pouring off his brow.

"I'll turn the sprinkler on," she suggested helpfully.

"Let's go back to the fence and unbury the garden bench. Whacking the plants back should be good for them, shouldn't it?" Pressing the cold can to his head, Jax steered Evie toward the shade. He lopped off a few of the taller weeds so they could sit.

She sipped her lemonade once they settled on the crumbling concrete bench. "Okay, what did Grumpy Gump say this time?"

"Not a thing, yet." Jax explained how Ariel had found connections between Roark's phone scammers and Sunshine.

"Can't businesses all use the same bitcoin exchange without being connected?" She leaned over and yanked at a thorny weed. It broke off in her glove.

"Whoever is running this operation is uniformly sweeping the scammer bank accounts, plus the Sunshine accounts. They're related somehow. And then there's the question of who is supplying Roark's dad with the names and numbers of vulnerable old people."

"Sunshine, among others, I imagine." She sighed and sipped her drink. "Marlene really was onto something."

"Probably. Sunshine may only be one of many mushrooms cropping up under a huge rotting tree. Any way you look at it, they're dangerous. We've been warned off for a reason."

"More than one way to kill," she murmured, repeating Dante's earlier warning. "People lose their money to a scammer and feel stupid, depressed, neglect their health, kill themselves. Or they lose savings needed for necessary health care and die without medical attention. Although I blame that problem on the feds. Still, you have people being murdered by misery."

"Politics are not the problem here. Thieves are. Embezzlers, counterfeiters, murderers, tax evaders. . ."

"Yeah, yeah, bad guys, nest of, got it. So what is it you want from me?"

"Tell me what you're planning."

She shrugged and sipped her lemonade. Jax knew Evie was organizing her scattered thoughts, not easy when her overactive mind was planning parties, tonight's dinner, and sabotage.

"We're just gathering information. Sometimes, it's easier to persuade people to talk if we rattle their cages. I'm betting that everyone at Sunshine knows only a small piece of the big picture."

"But a few know the full picture, I get that. I doubt the ones on top are easily rattled."

"Oh, they'll rattle if the money vanishes. We need a lot more info to make that happen though. So I'm just hoping scared people have loose lips, and we can pick up a few nuggets when they all get together tomorrow. Is that what you wanted to know?" She gazed up at him through thick lashes concealing her crystal blue eyes.

"So you're just going to explode party favors and see what happens?" That would be typical.

"Well, if Reuben can dig into a few accounts with that IRS scam, it might be more than party favors, but yup. That's the basic game plan. I think our ghosts are quite creative, if I do say so myself."

Jax groaned and closed his eyes. "Ghosts?"

She patted his hand. "Not real ones, silly, although if Marlene can show up, that would be a bonus. Just think Halloween Haunted House with cute little ghosties popping from the walls and floating about a bit. Reuben is really into haunted houses. We'll have to have one this year."

Jax tried not to imagine a roomful of gangsters shooting at floating blobs. "You installed cameras?"

"Silly question. Of course, if we've made them paranoid, eventually they'll smarten up and start searching for equipment. We're probably blowing the fed's chances to bug them." She shrugged.

"It will be months before Gump can collect enough data to get permission. But how is any of this catching Marlene's killer?" That's what had Jax worried. He didn't want Evie anywhere near killers.

She looked pensive—an odd expression for Evie. "I don't know. Granny can't tell me. Auras are fickle. All we know is that she stuck her nose too far into Sunshine's business and someone took her out. The nurse had the knowledge and probably wanted her to stop snooping into her thefts. But Savanna wasn't there. So it has to be Sunshine, somehow."

"And a nurse won't be at a board meeting, so that won't help if she's your main suspect. It's a little hard to trace antifreeze purchases." Jax crushed the over-tall grass under his feet.

Evie laughed. "Anyone buying antifreeze in August ought to be suspicious, but who would notice in a city? I'll see if Reuben can trace Nurse Savanna's purchases, just out of curiosity. Where does one even buy the stuff?"

"Anywhere that carries automotive supplies. I don't think you'll persuade Wal-Mart to cough up the info, and she could have paid cash.

And since she wasn't there to administer it, she really isn't the killer, is she?"

"We need to take a look at that video again showing who visited while Granny was ill. Some of them brought food." Evie jumped up and headed for the house.

"A bunch of old ladies," Jax called after her. "You really think they're a mob of killers?"

"One of them is!"

~

AFTER DINNER, EVIE SAT IN THE CELLAR WITH REUBEN AND JAX, scrolling through her email while they played the videos from Granny-cam over and over.

"A covered dish means hot food, right?" Reuben asked, halting the video on blue-haired lady #1.

Evie called up her memory of meeting Blue #1, found the apartment number on the home's map, and ID'd her. "Leticia Mortimer, resident for five years. And yes, covered dish normally means hot food. Does antifreeze not work in that?"

"Imagine Gatorade in your scalloped potatoes." Jax clicked the video to the next visitor.

"Granny is still well enough to answer the door in these first clips. She's just not letting anyone in." Reuben stopped the film on Mr. Charles bringing saltines and Seven-Up.

"Seven-Up in antifreeze? Is it clear?" Evie added Mr. Charles and his contribution to her list.

"Don't think that would hide the taste, and no, probably not clear enough and not bubbly. We should buy some antifreeze and test it. Apparently it gels in gelatin salads. Does it cloud them?" Jax gestured for the next clip.

"Lucy Murkowski." Evie identified this visitor easily. "And Ursula, from HR. Why is *she* there? What's Lucy carrying?"

"Lucy is probably trained not to enter a resident's apartment without accompaniment for liability purposes. And if Marlene had already raised hell about theft, she'd be doubly cautious." Jax studied the open bowl Lucy held. "Cold food. Fruit, maybe?"

"With antifreeze dressing? How much fruit would it take to finish off Granny? There's a mess of it in there." Reuben zoomed up the image so they could all admire the neat slices of peaches and melons and grapes decorated with blueberries.

"I'll email Stacey and ask if there was any fruit salad left." Evie shot off the message.

"But Marlene actually did have a heart attack," Jax reminded them. "If the first attempt just made her sick, are we assuming a second attempt triggered the attack? Or maybe she didn't need any extra at all for her heart to give out."

"Are you saying we're not indicting anyone?" Reuben asked indignantly.

"I'm saying Murder One will be a tough call, even if we can prove who administered the poison—which is unlikely since Stacey threw out all the evidence." Jax didn't look happy as he gestured for the next image.

"Tall, thin, ascetic lady." Evie labeled her list. "That should be Mary Smith, Apartment 450. Can that be her real name? Maybe she's another spy like Granny."

"Looks like brownies," she continued, studying the zoomed-up image. "But they need butter and eggs. Antifreeze won't cut it. We don't know anything." She threw down her laptop in disgust.

"Chemistry lab!" Reuben hooted. "I'll look up how to test for poisonous levels of antifreeze and figure out the formula for antifreeze brownies."

"Who's going to taste-test them?" Jax took the remote and scrolled through the video, stopping long enough for Evie to identify residents, then move on.

They repeated the exercise through the days after Granny's death and Stacey's visit, but the culprits were all pretty much the same.

Once they had a complete list, Evie sent it off to Roark to research. "This doesn't feel as if we're getting anywhere."

"Any email from your flyers asking for suspects yet?"

"Anonymous gossip, mostly reporting the nurse for theft, suspicions about what Marlene did for a living, and then anything about their neighbors that annoys them." Evie hit her laptop keys. "Sending them to y'all."

Reuben scrolled through a website. "I'm looking at a page saying ethylene glycol is perfectly normal in prepared foods. I'm gonna give up grocery stores."

Jax looked over his shoulder. "So it takes a whole lot of the stuff to poison. Chocolate *frosting* contains glycol! Evie, were those brownies frosted?"

"Looked like it. Poisoning brownies? That ought to be cause for the electric chair."

"It's even in some whiskey and a whole lot of prepared baked goods. But I don't know how they'd add deadly amounts once they're already prepared. Was there whiskey in the apartment?" Reuben scrolled through search sites.

"Probably purloined before we got there. Since no one else has dropped dead, I'll guess any whiskey was safe. So from this, I gather antifreeze could have been added to any of the food brought in. I mean, if you can bake cakes with the stuff—" Jax grimaced.

"It's all about proportion. But if Marlene had already been poisoned earlier by purple punch, then it may have only taken a shot of the stuff in frosting," Reuben concluded.

"Text from Stacey," Evie shouted. "She says the fruit was brown, and she threw it out. She tried a brownie and concluded it was stale and tossed it. She refused to touch the tuna casserole, but it looked like Granny ate some of all of them. There was also grape gelatin with grapes in it! Stacey tossed that too."

"We didn't see anyone bring a gelatin salad. Isn't that usually mixed with water?" Jax opened his phone to look up recipes.

"Grape juice," Evie crowed. "Grape gelatin made with grape juice. Or grape power drink. Stacey said the fridge had both. Marlene liked grape."

"Scroll back the apartment video." Jax picked up the remote. "Gelatin sits around forever. I used to feed the asparagus aspic to the dog because it never went away."

"The camera doesn't show the kitchen," Evie reminded them. "Granny may have made it for herself."

"Using a previously poisoned drink?" And they'd have no evidence at all.

Evie held up her phone. "One of these emails says Marlene was suicidal. Gossip or someone leading us astray?"

"I read that one." Reuben hit the keyboard. "It was easy to trace. Came from a device owned by Savanna. Leading astray is my guess. She's looking pretty guilty."

Jax took the video back to the week before Marlene's death, when she opened the door carrying sacks of groceries. Behind her, Mr. Charles carried cartons of bottled water. "Right before the party. I wish this thing had audio."

"She was trying to catch thieves. They don't talk." Reuben zoomed up on the grocery bags. "Reckon there's a box of gelatin in there? I'm guessing those are the grapes on top."

"Uh oh, look." Evie tapped Jax's shoulder and pointed. "Halt it. See? Mr. Charles goes out to retrieve more bags. Isn't that Lucy Murkowski in the hall?"

"She has a Jim Beam bottle and more purple drink," Reuben crowed.

"But she doesn't come in. Did she have time to doctor anything on the way up?"

"Do we have the film from the camera in the hallway? Switch to that." Jax scrolled through grainy black-and white videos. "Lucy talking to Blue Hair #1. She's holding up the drinks and making a face. The whole building would know about the purple punch before supper."

"Lucy is part of management," Evie reluctantly pointed out. "I like her aura, but if Granny's death is related to Sunshine—"

"Lucy is the obvious suspect. Let's start digging there." Jax shut off the video and pointed at Evie. "Not by going through her trash or her office."

Evie shrugged and returned to her laptop. "To each his own."

Jax wasn't certain, but that sounded like a defiant threat.

Twenty-nine

ROARK KNEW HE WAS NO SAINT, BUT HE THOUGHT HE DESERVED A halo for his night's work. Showing Ariel how to use the search engines from Jax's old law firm had been torture enough. All that silky dark hair smelling of heaven right beneath his nose while he leaned over her desk had nearly scrambled his gray matter. But he'd resisted touching.

Spending these last hours in her inner sanctum, watching her work, answering her cryptic questions, while he tried to do his own research—was like setting an alcoholic in front of an open bar.

He ached to kiss her again, to feel her in his arms, to assuage some of his dangerous daydreams. He rationalized excuses for doing so.

But he'd been brought up by strong women who would sever his head and more valuable parts of his anatomy if he acted on his excuses. Ariel was an innocent. She had to be willing. More than willing. And she was too. . . Hell if he knew what. *Ethereal* came to mind. *Vulnerable*. Fragile.

And he was a big ox in rut.

So he spent half the night exchanging text and email with her—when they were right there in the same room—because it made her more comfortable. She hadn't objected when he'd taken over one of her desks to work. The air-conditioned front room beat the bug-infested humidity of the porch.

But he couldn't adapt to her vampire hours. He fixed her midnight meal, sent off a host of inquiries on their bitcoin research, and quit for the day. He

207

needed to get his exercise in the early morning hours, before heat stroke set in. His leg was healing, but it wasn't there yet.

Ariel didn't notice his departure.

Monday morning, Roark got in his run, took his shower, and debated moving back in with Evie and the guys. Ariel was seriously messing with his head. He'd stayed here because it was isolated, and if anyone was hunting him, they wouldn't find him this far off the grid. But apparently no one cared if he'd been blown to hell or set fire to the town.

And if his da really did have dangerous connections who might trace him, Ariel would be safer if he was out of her house, surrounded by ex-military like Jax and Reuben—and Evie's dotty witches.

But Ariel had him hooked. He simply couldn't leave her alone—especially not when she left him a recipe for beignets and ordered a deep fryer delivered to the door.

The woman was certifiable—but independent as all get-out. And she was *trying*. . .

That's what got him, he decided after he set out the dough to rest and settled at her desk to see what she'd found overnight. He had this niggling hope that Ariel was preparing to step outside her boundaries, and he wanted to be there when the chrysalis opened.

He dug into the wealth of detail she'd compiled, whistled softly, and decided the feds really needed to hire her. Although whatever she was doing for the bank probably paid better and was a lot safer. He wanted this secret weapon for himself. This was some heavy-duty shit.

He texted Evie and the guys. **SUNSHINE ALL OVER. INCOMING**

Then he emailed Ariel's elaborate spreadsheet.

Evie's tiny Subaru drove up half an hour later, spilling Reuben, Jax, and the Italian stranger like overgrown clowns from a toy car. Evie stepped easily from behind the wheel, following the clowns to the trunk. Under her guidance, they unloaded an enormous barbecue grill.

Roark hooted in delight. "Where'd you get dat baby? We ain't got a gas hookup but—"

"Already done." Jax sounded just the slightest bit surly. "I found it cleaning out the garage, polished it all up, and Evie waited until then to show me the dangerous propane modification."

"One of my aunt's boyfriends somewhere along the line nearly blew us up, maybe intentionally. He didn't hang around long after that." Evie turned to introduce the newcomer. "Roark, Cajun spy; Dante, Italian archeologist. Dante wanted to meet his cousin Ariel, and I thought you might fix the grill properly. And then we could have barbecues out here where Ariel could stay in her zone but still participate."

Roark held out his hand to the tall Italian but concentrated on Evie as they shook. "I love the way you t'ink, bébé. Let's take it 'round back, near the kitchen." He lifted one end of the heavy old grill while Reuben and Dante took the other. "Jax, ain't you got work to do?"

"After that spreadsheet of more aliases you sent? Are you kidding? This is the best I could come up with to prevent Batman and Robin here from committing felonies. It was either this or tie them up." Jax took a corner.

"Which one of us gets to be Robin?" Evie followed as they carried the grill around the cottage.

"Robin's prettier." Reuben grunted and eyed the jungle of the backyard.

"Do we need judges to decide which one of us is prettier?" Evie inquired.

Ignoring their idiocy, Roark tilted the grill and cursed. "Nowhere to set this."

Dante let down his side, glanced around, and strode directly to a patch of dirt and grass. "I'd say there are stones under here preventing the grass from growing."

Huh, maybe the pretty boy had some use after all. Roark waited while Dante and Evie explored.

Evie scuffled at the dirt spot, then yanked at the grass. "You may be right. Good eye."

"It's what I do for a living. Anyone got a shovel?"

"No garden, no shovels." Along with Reuben and Jax, Roark hefted the grill again and hauled it over. "This will do, if it's level." The ground felt pretty solid.

Setting his side down, Reuben returned to the earlier argument about Robin. "It's all about the muscle, not the pretty face."

Roark scuffed his bare foot over the grass, locating more stones. "Neither of you got brains, so that works. Brainless superhero dudes, what the hell you think you can do to catch a cartel?"

That's what Ariel's research seemed to have turned up—a banking connection run by an unknown entity who raked in the profits and turned them into untraceable cryptocurrency.

"It's a whole company of mafia across half a dozen states preying on old people!" Evie dived right in. "On sick people and their families! They're already buried in a world of hurt, and these... these..."

"Scumbags? Vultures?" Jax offered. "Ass rats?"

"Ass rats?" Roark laughed. "They got rats up their ass?"

"Not old farts," Jax said gloomily. "Asshat doesn't begin to cover it. How could the feds not have seen what was going on? Isn't there any oversight of nursing homes?"

"State." Evie joined Dante in pulling grass and uncovering flagstones. "And that's only inspection of facilities and whether they have trained personnel. And when it comes to places like the apartments—not even that, I imagine. It's like gathering all your victims in one place and having a license to systematically rob them blind. It's legal robbery."

"Theft isn't legal. But it has to be reported and ill old people might not even notice." Jax helped Roark test the grill level. "And on the surface, Sunshine is clean. They get their fire and health inspections and obey most laws. The illegalities start out as a penny ante local matter."

"Not when known criminals are stealing IDs, cheating on taxes, and laundering ill-gotten gains through cryptocurrency." Roark polished the grill's shiny hood with the hem of his tank top. "Ariel's got it all lined up so simple even a mongoose can trace the money."

"She did a pretty thorough job on uncovering management." Reuben sank down on the back step in the shade. "I thought numbers were her thing."

Roark shifted uncomfortably. "I been showing her a few ropes. She's got dis steel trap mind dat remembers details back to dinosaurs. She's the one remembered Mr. Charles appeared to be related to one of the managers and started digging."

"And here I thought he was just a muddled professorial type." Evie ripped out a huge hunk of grass. "Yeah, his aura colors are muddy, but that doesn't always mean anything. It could mean he had Alzheimer's for all I know. How did she discover Charles is an alias?"

"What do you mean, you've been *teaching* Ariel?" Jax didn't look happy. "I don't want her involved in your illegal hacking."

Roark rolled his eyes. "Man, what do you t'ink she does for a living? She's a federal charge waiting to happen. You can't leave brilliant minds cooped up with a computer and expect anything less. All I showed her was da legal ropes you use. But those search systems get their info from somewhere and she just kept digging until she turned up fingerprint databases and DNA data, and I can't tell what all."

"Fingerprint databases?" Jax asked warily.

"Don' ask unless you want to know," Roark warned.

Dante pulled a fancy tool out of his pocket and began digging around the stones. "I take it Cousin Ariel is not available?"

Roark grinned at the pretty stranger's dismay. "She works all night and leaves explosive Easter eggs on our doorsteps while we sleep. She's a magic Easter bunny, and she isn't even related to Evie's witchy family. You'll have to come back at suppertime. Jax was just using you for muscle."

Dante didn't look daunted. "Are you really working a dangerous case? Is there something I can do to help?"

"No buried carcasses to be unearthed as far as we know," Evie answered. "Jax will probably try to persuade you to keep me out of the way tonight. I don't advise it."

Dante sent them all a narrow-eyed look but contented himself with excavating the patio, while listening. Roark had to admire the man for keeping a low profile, not easy with a handsome phiz like his.

"Just notify Professor Gump that Sunshine's management and his mother's boyfriend are career criminals living under aliases and laundering money, then drop it," Jax advised.

"I'm sending the fed everything we find." Roark waved a dismissive hand. "But I can't tell him your sister invaded police records to match prints from the apartment with a database and dat in all likelihood, a retired swindler stole his mother's computers. The local cops should have done dat."

"Gump should have done that," Jax grumbled. "He probably did and didn't tell us. But we have no evidence on anything."

Reuben stepped up. "What we need is a strategy for tonight. The boardroom is bugged, so we can pick up what's happening there without leaving the van. I can dig into Mr. Charles aka Bernard Barouche to see if I can find a connection to Sunshine, other than his residency at the home, but right now, he's just a retired ex-conman. His bank account does not show millions."

"Granny didn't know his alias, did she? Unmasking him might be pretty strong motivation for murder." Evie yanked more grass.

"If we didn't, she didn't. She didn't know about any of the scum running the place. Ex-cons, ex Russian spies, all bad guys." Roark sat down with his tools and the grill. "You should do one of your séance t'ings, call all da ghosts in the place. Or pretend to. My granny shakes chairs and swings lanterns."

"Your granny is a fraud then. Although Granny Gump is getting good at rattling doors. What did you have in mind? We can't get in the apartment anymore."

"Sure we can. Dose locks are easy. Sunshine ain't big on security, now, is it? They'd already removed Marlene's bolts when we were there with da painters." Imagining the barbecues he could hold, Roark dismantled the faulty propane connection.

Evie still looked dubious. "I don't know what holding a séance would accomplish."

"We didn't find anything except patient files in your camera images from the nursing home. I'd like into HR's employee files or better, the VP's. Any way we can do that?" Reuben sipped his bottled water.

"I'm going to lock all of you up before the cops do," Jax protested, right on schedule. "Just wait to see what happens tonight before you go out on more limbs."

"I like the séance idea," Evie abruptly decided. "I bet Granny knows where the files are."

Roark snorted. He'd known being told what not to do would do the trick. Jax really had to lighten up.

Evie happily continued. "While fake ghosties are breaking up the board meeting, let's call on the real ones. Is there some way to invite all our other suspects like Lucy and Savanna? Roark, did your voodoo granny teach you how to create auras?"

Well, he'd walked right into that one.

Stepping out of her shower, Ariel heard the tap-tap of metal on stone. What was Roark up to now?

Last night had been unnerving, to say the least. Enervating. . . maybe, just a little. Her insides had tied in knots when he'd leaned over her shoulder, but then, she grew accustomed to him there. And when he'd left, the room seemed empty. Somehow, oddly, she felt connected to him.

She was pretty proud of the research she'd accomplished with his lessons and wished to hear his reaction. She'd thought he'd be digging deeply into his computer. Surely the fact that Sunshine was riddled with unsavory characters should be sufficient evidence to have people arrested?

Perhaps if she could hack that bitcoin exchange to see where the money went. . .

Tying her wet hair back in a ribbon, too eager to hear Roark's thoughts to blow it dry, she hurried out to the kitchen to see what he'd prepared for her.

Roark was nowhere around. A bowl of unpeeled peaches waited on the table.

Frowning, she stepped onto the back porch to determine what he was repairing.

A stranger sat in her yard, digging with a hand ax at what appeared to be stones near the azaleas. A shiny grill rested near him. She almost had a panic attack. *Had someone come to claim her home?*

She took several deep breaths as she'd been taught and considered it logically. Jax had said the cottage belonged to Loretta's estate, and he was paying rent for it. Jax was the estate executor and wouldn't allow a stranger to steal her home.

She should start paying the rent herself.

The stranger finally looked up. "There you are. I'm Dante. You must be my cousin Ariel."

Ah, now she remembered him from Pris's video. She'd even looked him up when Pris got so angry with him. "You should tell Jax who you really are."

He seemed startled. "What do you mean? I assure you, I am a distant cousin. My passport has my name. As you can see, I'm an archeologist comfortable digging in stone." He gestured at a flagstone patio emerging from the dirt and weeds.

"Only because Signor Rossi, Conte Armeno, lacks the funds to restore his villa and his project didn't receive the grant needed to continue. Where is Roark?" Ignoring the stranger's surprise, she waited for the answer she needed.

"They're setting up a sting at the retirement home. Roark asked me to keep you company. There is some concern that someone might be after him?" If he was relieved that she'd changed the subject, he didn't show it.

"A sting?"

"They're trying to catch a thief? Or a murderer? Is Roark a policeman?"

Ariel liked that he kept his distance and appeared as confused as she was. "No. Roark does not seem to like authorities."

Politeness required more, she supposed. She summoned the best she could without preparation. "I need to work now. You are welcome to help yourself to the kitchen."

She returned inside, ate her peach, drank her tea, and checked her game cameras. Only then did she think to check her phone.

BRILLIANT WORK, BABE. C EMAIL, read Roark's text.

With reluctance, she carried her tea to her desk and opened her email on a larger screen.

He thoughtfully kept his message succinct. *Evie setting trap. Links to Sunshine cameras enclosed. If you see trouble, call 911, give them the address, say murder, and hang up. Use burner app to call.*

Ariel blinked and read the message again.

Murder? He was anticipating murder? And thought the police might stop it?

How? Was he mad? Were they all mad? She'd just given them a list of dangerous criminals associated with Sunshine, and they were *setting a trap*?

Was Jax involved, too? Surely not. She texted him. **WHERE R U?**

SAVANNAH. U OK?

My word, they'd all lost their minds. Reluctantly, she answered, **OK**

She was very definitely not OK. Setting her phone aside, forgetting her calming numbers research, she plunged down the rabbit hole she'd discovered last night after Roark had shown her his databases. She knew his passwords. She knew how to find the link to his private website. And from there, she could follow him anywhere.

First, though, she checked the security camera link he'd sent. This appeared to be to the main security center of the retirement apartments that they'd been investigating. It opened on a screen of square blocks similar to a Zoom meeting. Each block contained a different scene. She could see the front desk, the entrance to the elevator, the halls of all five floors from above the elevator doors and also the stairway exits.

She was very bad at recognizing faces, so she memorized the movements of various hairstyles and clothing. A number of men in business suits or informal blazers entered from the rear of the lobby and continued off to an unseen corridor on their right. The board of directors must be gathering.

She looked, but the security cameras didn't cover the office wing. How odd. Wouldn't that be where the company kept its valuable files?

If Sunshine really was run by criminals. . . They might not want security watching them.

After verifying that she couldn't find Evie or Roark or anyone she recognized in the parts that she could see, she closed that link and opened the other one he'd sent.

It focused on the boardroom. R&R had set up four cameras, one in each corner so she could view the entire room. *That* was the way security cameras ought to be set up.

Remembering that Reuben had been keeping documents on the various board members, she called up that file on her laptop and began comparing photos and names. Sometimes Reuben had added question marks, so she understood that he wasn't certain that image went with that file.

She could hear rustling papers, murmuring voices, and she shivered. It was almost like being in the boardroom—and she didn't want to be there. Surely, Reuben was following this from his van.

She was just back-up insurance, she supposed. She felt a little let-down at that realization.

But where was everyone? If Reuben was monitoring cameras from the van, where had Evie, Jax, and Roark gone?

For that, she dived into Roark's website and started digging.

Thirty

TOO AWARE OF THE EARBUDS, MIC, AND CAMERA ROARK HAD made her wear, Evie scratched at her bugged ear while trying to round up her guests in Marlene's apartment.

Granny was bouncing off walls, as usual, and not quite as coherent as Evie would like. She turned her focus on the residents filtering in, drawn by the phone tree they apparently activated when anything entertaining was happening. All the people who had been in here after Stacey was robbed were present. Most of them were Granny's immediate neighbors.

The people who had brought food when Marlene was sick arrived, although Ursula was probably at the board meeting. Lucy wasn't high enough on the executive tree. She probably had to be present at the front desk so the board could see she was at work. Evie shivered when Mr. Charles arrived. She'd read his file—*Bernard Barouche's* file. He'd spent his early years in prison for gang activity, weapons assault, and car theft—of an entire fleet of cars. Murder wasn't on the list, but then, he'd not been caught again. He'd smartened up in prison and learned new tricks.

Since then, he'd only left a few sticky fingerprints connected to various high-end cons, swindling everyone from corporate executives with investment scams, to hospitals with miracle drugs and fake research under one alias or another. Would a man that worldly-wise risk killing a neighbor?

A man who knew how to steal identities was standing right there in a nest of blue-haired old ladies.

Well, to be fair, a few balding men and silver foxes joined them. Bottles of wine and other alcohol miraculously appeared. Evie felt as if she ought to be on the stage at Las Vegas pulling rabbits out of hats. "People, please, I don't think alcohol is conducive to our spiritual journey. If you'd set your glasses and bottles aside until later. . ."

Without furniture, they didn't have a lot of choice for disposal. The kitchen counter filled up. More bottles lined up along the newly painted walls. A few people suggested they should all repair to their better equipped apartments. Evie corrected that thinking. "We're here to speak with Marlene Gump. I don't believe she inhabits any other apartment but this one."

Although she suspected Granny could, if she wished. Evie just didn't want to walk into a trap.

She knew Roark was sneaking into offices, while listening for Reuben's warnings from the van. Jax had driven the Subaru and was out there attempting to reach Professor Gump to see if he'd received the files Ariel had compiled—and probably hoping for a raid before anything happened. As a lawyer, Jax had to distance himself from any illegal activity, and Evie was pretty certain everything they were doing was illegal as it got.

It took a crook to catch a crook?

"Please, folks, this is far more than I'd hoped would be here. I thank everyone for your eagerness to discover Marlene's killer, but you must understand that there are limitations on our communication. Do not expect television drama. If I could just have half a dozen or so of Marlene's closest friends or neighbors. . ." She gestured to where she stood in the center of the living area.

Letitia of the hot dish and Mary Smith of the brownies stepped up, as did Mr. Charles/Barouche and half a dozen other people. Evie sorted through to choose others Marlene suggested and had the others step back for now.

She really wanted the nurse and Lucy and Ursula here, but she had to leave them to the men. *For now.* She had plans.

Marlene hovered near the ceiling, just above the spirit circle forming without benefit of table or chairs. Sitting on the floor wasn't the best idea for this group. Besides, standing was faster for escape.

"Draw the blinds, please. I'll light the candle, then I want everyone to grasp their neighbor's hand and remain silent. Those of you who are watching, no whispering, please. It's difficult to reach through the veil between this world and the next, and I need your cooperation. Say prayers, think good thoughts, but please, don't speak." Evie recited some of the nonsense she'd heard her mother say over the years. In actuality, she didn't need any of that to reach a ghost she could already see.

She had no intention of summoning less predictable spirits if it could be avoided. That was too draining an exercise. She preferred Reuben's more controllable surprises. With all the bigwigs in the boardroom, the offices were ripe for plucking. She simply needed an excuse to break in.

The darkened apartment finally grew quiet.

"Marlene Gump, are you present?" Evie intoned in her best spiritual advisor tone. "Can you make your presence known?"

Marlene snorted and slammed a closet door, then rattled some of the wine bottles. She was growing stronger in ability, if not focus.

Her audience gasped and seemed to shrink in on itself.

"Don't release your grip," Evie warned. "Marlene, are there other spirits present who might assist us on our journey?"

"You bet your bottom dollar," Marlene muttered in Evie's ear. "They're pretty pathetic wraiths. Do you really want to call them up?"

Mentally, Evie laughed and said, "Not really." Outwardly, she intoned, "Marlene is calling on those who have passed before."

That produced titters and whispers. Evie slipped into third-eye mode and, through narrowed lids, observed auras. Charles/Barouche was as muddy as ever, his heart and spirit so shrunken that he barely had any colors left. He was rotting from the inside out. Evie almost felt pity for him.

She scanned the rest of the room, looking for fear or hatred or anything that might give her pause. *Fear*, of course, could mean almost anything, so she had to look deeper into those auras. Of the people who had carried food to Marlene, only Leticia Mortimer of the hot dish had a deep enough fear to be worrisome. But maybe she was just more afraid of ghosts than the others. Evie didn't see guilt.

Despite Evie's reluctance, Marlene and the candle drew other spirits. She had sensed paranormal activity throughout the residence. And here they were —insubstantial, faded auras reflecting anxiety and despair and a host of other wearisome characteristics not particularly helpful to her cause.

Still, she owed it to the spirit brigade to address them. It was only polite.

"Marlene has gathered a few of those who have gone before. Does anyone have a question for a particular person?"

Mary Smith, of the frosted brownies, spoke up. Her aura was fairly clear, although a bit gray with fear. "Is Mary North present? Her children were concerned about her jewelry. Did she sell it?"

Mary North had gone on to the next plane, but Evie figured it wouldn't hurt to answer for her. She closed her eyes and muttered a little—moaning really wasn't her thing. Then she nodded and whispered, "Noooooo."

Mary Smith looked indignant. "Do you know where it is?"

Evie shook her head, and in amusement, Marlene rattled a few more bottles. "They took it," Evie reported in what she hoped was an appropriately sepulchral ghost voice. "Gooooonnne."

"Does *Marlene* know what happened to the jewelry?" The tall ascetic lady asked.

Evie continued shaking her head. "Gooooonnnne. Found ring. Find killer."

Before the very insistent Mary Smith could ask about the ring, Evie pressed the button Reuben had given her. The candle blew out and a hidden black light came on.

Glowing letters on the newly painted wall read **HR OFFICE.**

Shrieks and pandemonium ensued.

Even Evie panicked. That sign used to read *VP's office.* She'd wanted to storm Bibb, the manager.

What had Marlene done?

Thirty-one

FINISHING HIS FRUSTRATING CALL WITH PROFESSOR GUMP, JAX glared at the residence home. In the late afternoon sun, through thickening clouds, the apartment house merely looked shabby, not sinister. Evie was in there, conjuring ghosts in an attempt to break into the VP's office. . .

While career criminals gathered in the boardroom, looking for tax escape hatches. A pity Jax couldn't send in the real IRS.

Gump had admitted that he had read the files Jax's team and Marlene had accumulated, but even *his* hands were tied. A nest of bad men did not mean they had evidence of Marlene's killer, especially since not one of Sunshine's directors had been in Marlene's room. Even Ursula had stayed outside.

The matter of interstate fraud was thornier and would take time to research. They couldn't use illegally hacked evidence.

Sitting in the tiny Subaru, Jax texted Reuben. The nerd was ensconced in the utility van at the other end of the parking lot, monitoring activities and probably wreaking whatever havoc he and Evie had concocted. Jax wanted to disassociate himself from illegal activities, but his curiosity and anxiety—and itch to act—were intensifying.

Reuben sent him a video of a dark room with ghostly writing on the wall and old people shrieking. Evie's camera must be working. Jax knew she was committing fraud right now, but it wasn't as if she were charging for it. Any haunted Halloween house could produce those effects with glue sticks and black lights.

What he worried about was her contact with real spirits.

Roark wasn't answering his messages. He texted Reuben, **WHERES CAJUN?**

Reuben's reply was sufficient excuse for Jax to slip his licensed Glock into his shoulder harness, don his blazer, and haul out of the car to enter the building. Roark incommunicado meant nothing. Mostly, Jax couldn't take being left out any longer.

Lucy Murkowski was at the reception desk, her posture stiff and her smile frozen. She gestured for Jax to wait while she answered the ringing phone. Her frozen smile turned to puzzlement as she swung her chair to watch the elevator.

Oh good, he was in time for the show.

The elevator door opened, and dancing lights bounced out. Reuben had explained how he'd created that effect, but Jax hadn't paid attention. Evie had wanted rainbow auras, but apparently the techno-geniuses hadn't been able to invent anything suitable in the time allotted. So Tinkerbelle lights bounced along the walls and floors as Evie stepped out—leading a parade of old folks.

Barouche was in the procession. What kind of moron named himself after a horse-drawn carriage? Jax suspected even the old crook's birth certificate was fake.

Jax performed a cursory inspection for weapons, but most of the people marching into the lobby were wearing sundresses or T-shirts and shorts. Afternoon attire on a summer Georgia afternoon didn't lend to coats and long sleeves, especially when the a/c wasn't cranked up. Even Barouche wore a short-sleeved white shirt, half tucked into his pants. If he had a weapon in his waist band, he'd have to struggle to reach it. Maybe the old con had actually retired.

Evie was performing her mutter/whisper routine that might or might not mean she was communicating with Marlene. Overhead, a modern chandelier swung, and Jax tried very hard not to imagine a plump, gray-haired ghost up there, laughing down at them.

The bouncing lights led toward the office wing—of course. A cadre of bad guys were meeting in the conference room, and Evie was leading a parade straight toward them.

At the front desk, Lucy panicked. She rushed to head them off, but there had to be nearly two dozen residents marching determinedly after Evie. Something had their backs up. In the interest of observation, Jax followed Lucy across the lobby. The parade filed into the hall. He watched as Evie tilted her head in front of one of the office doors, nodded, and turned to the resident manager.

"The spirits are. . . uneasy," Evie said. "They wish to check on Mrs. Stanislaus. Could you unlock the door and verify that all is well?"

Oh, that was rich. Jax held back and watched as a panicked Lucy Murkowski—and Evie no doubt was reading Lucy's terror—pulled out her key ring and unlocked the door to the Human Resources office.

Evie shoved in without invitation. Jax had thought Reuben had directed her to the VP's computer. He'd told her precisely where to plug the transmitter so they could start hacking passwords. Maybe they'd decided HR was easier.

Jax didn't want to watch whatever sleight of hand Evie performed. He understood that her family had learned to protect themselves and their weird abilities over the ages, but he didn't have to like their magic tricks.

What he did watch was Mr. Charles Bernard Barouche. The old man was frowning furiously, trying to elbow through Evie's audience, but they were all eager to watch the performance. They formed an impassable senior-citizen knot in the doorway.

Not liking the way Barouche pulled out his phone, Jax stepped up and jostled the older man as he tried to peer into the room. "What's happening?"

"Your girlfriend is a con artist," Barouche grumbled. "She shouldn't be in there."

"I'm her lawyer," Jax corrected, in his best we're-all-in-this-together voice. "She's pretty good at what she does, so she needs reliable witnesses. Have you seen her do anything illegal?"

Barouche didn't answer but glared at his phone. "Battery's dead."

That tended to happen around Evie and her ghosts. Maybe she really was on to something—

A shriek of horror accelerated that fear.

Without an ounce of civility, Jax shoved his way through the throng of senior citizens and their walkers. Evie had an unpredictable tendency to go into overload and drop like a rock.

If phone batteries were draining, she was on overload. He didn't bother checking his phone but used his greater height to see past the crowd.

Looking pale, shocked, and as if she really were seeing beyond the veil, Evie staggered backward into her league of followers, who were unhelpfully shrieking and backing away at the same time. Jax tromped a few toes, elbowed a few ribs, and reached her before she dropped.

There, at her feet, lay the drunken nurse. She wasn't snoring.

Jax was pretty certain she wasn't breathing either.

He reached for his phone to dial 911 and swore. The battery was dead.

CURSING HIS CARELESSNESS, ROARK SMILED BLITHELY AT THE tall HR director who knotted the drapery cords around his wrists. "FSB didn't pay well enough?" Their research had been thorough. Ariel had verified the Russian spy connection but not the reason Ursula had fled her home.

Ursula knotted the ropes tighter. "FSB as stupid as you and all cops. We are surrounded by idiots."

"We all make the occasional mistake," he said insouciantly, aiming for James Bond but too furious and terrified to restrain his temper much longer. He did not suffer confinement well.

He hoped Reuben tuned in to his camera soon, before Ursula found it. In the meantime, he had to convince her he was one of the smart ones. Concentrating on dropping his accent at least gave him stress relief.

"You have made your last mistake. You will go to the landfill along with that immense idiot who dares call herself nurse. My mother was a nurse. She saved the lives of thousands! That lump of alcoholic blancmange couldn't save her own." Looking triumphant, Ursula straightened and admired her handiwork.

Roark felt like a trussed turkey. "Blancmange, that's a gelatin dessert, isn't it? Does it come in grape?" If he had to die here, he at least wanted answers. He scanned the shelf-lined walls of the fire-protected vault. He could probably scream himself hoarse without being heard.

He'd thought he was so smart finding the door and opening the combination lock. . .

But that meant his concentration had been on the lock and not the female sneaking up on him.

"Gelatin," his jailer snorted. "People who eat this disgusting stuff deserve their fate. Boiled bones and skin—perhaps that is what we should do to you.

Dmitri would not like it though. He does not like killing people either, so I must do it for him." She climbed a stepstool to reach a drawer near the ceiling.

"So you killed Marlene with grape gelatin? Or the grape punch? The antifreeze was a good idea." Roark tried to wiggle his fingers into his back pocket while she had her back turned.

She hadn't bothered searching him, apparently because she thought he was too stupid to carry weapons. Or to reach them after she'd tied him up.

"Me? I am not so stupid! Why kill an old lady who knew nothing and would die soon anyway? She was amusing to watch." She carried down a small metal box. "It is that thieving alcoholic blancmange who caused all this trouble. We should never have hired her."

"Savanna? She was nowhere near Marlene's apartment. She was on medical leave. You were there, though. You brought the fruit bowl." While Ursula picked through a key ring searching for the one needed to unlock her box, Roark finally pried his knife out of his back pocket. The military had taught him many skills, most of them not useful in a civilian world. But every so often. . .

Ursula shot him a disbelieving look. "You think I waste my time cutting up fruit for a gray-haired old spy? Savanna fixed it. If it contained antifreeze, I did not know. The old lady was already ill. Just now, Savanna stupidly bragged about it, said she would get rid of me the way she got rid of the other spying bitch. She meant to pin the murder on *me*. I gave her my credit card to buy ingredients for the punch. She took advantage of my generosity! She said she'd give the receipts for the punch and the antifreeze to the police if I did not rehire her!"

"Ah, I see your point." Roark sawed at the rope, but he didn't see much hope of cutting free before she locked him in here. "So you bought the juice for the punch, Savanna doctored it, and gave it to who—Lucy?—to deliver. Then why wasn't the whole party poisoned?"

Growing frustrated, she sorted through her key ring again. "*My* juice went in the punch. Savanna picked up the groceries Marlene ordered, poisoned the juice, and gave them to Lucy to carry up. Stupid fool thought she could blame me because everyone knew I bought the punch juice. Dmitri will be very mad, but the bitch had to die. She was too stupid to live."

Cursing, she hooked the key ring on her belt and headed for the door. "I

224

will be right back. Do not think you will free yourself in time. Once I open the box, sarin works very quickly."

She slammed out, locking the vault behind her.

Sarin, the deadly Russian nerve agent. . . That gave him something to fear besides the walls closing in on him. Roark sawed at the thick cord.

Curled up and lying down on the narrow back seat of Pris's truck, focused on the horrifying video streaming into her phone, Ariel screamed in horror as the vault door closed, leaving Roark in blackness. He couldn't hear her, of course.

Pris and Dante in the front seat could, but they were concentrating on their own screaming arguments about speed and directions as the old truck flew down the highway. Ariel had shown them the video from Evie's camera of the dead nurse, and Pris's mental alarms had gone off.

The moment the Russian killer had caught Roark in the vault, Ariel had dialed 911, just as he'd instructed. It had taken interminable moments to reach anyone, and they had seemed dense as trees when she tried to give them the address. Why weren't the police already there?

Where was Reuben? Did he have a camera on him?

She called Jax but he didn't answer. She tried Evie. Where was everyone?

With a storm approaching, the day had gone dark early. She pulled an old raincoat over her head so the headlights flashing by wouldn't distract her.

If she wasn't already crazy, she'd be losing her mind now. She didn't know how to shout at the fighting pair in the front seat. She sent panicked mental messages to Pris, who usually understood. But Pris had her mind on driving fifty miles over the speed limit.

They might be there in half an hour instead of an hour. Sarin worked in minutes.

Where was everyone?

Her phone was too small to view all the home's security camera screens at once. And once the crowd had left the lobby to follow Evie down the hall, the security cameras became useless.

Roark was still in the dark. She could hear him cursing Reuben but couldn't see what he was doing. She tried calling his number, but she didn't hear his phone ring through the microphone. And of course, he couldn't reach it if it did. He didn't know she'd hacked her way into Reuben's computer. She had no microphone of her own to talk with him.

Why wasn't Reuben answering?

Pris asked her something, but Ariel had shut out everything but her phone. Pressing hard against the seat, she clung to this electronic salvation, her Gibraltar. She widened the images from the cameras in the lobby and tried to see if anyone was looking for Roark.

They weren't. She finally located Evie's camera. She and Jax were caught up in whatever drama was happening in that small office. Only Roark and Evie had been wired.

Tears crawled down Ariel's cheeks, and she wiped at them furiously. Tears were useless. She'd cried a million when she was little, and they hadn't returned her parents. They hadn't made her normal, either. They wouldn't save Roark.

How long before the Russian woman returned and opened the box with poisonous capsules? Where had she gone?

Evie's camera hurt to watch. It showed a crowd of shouting old people. Ariel left off the sound once she caught glimpses of Jax in the melee. Jax wasn't wearing any devices. She just knew he was safe and with Evie.

Reuben was supposed to stay in the van, listening to the board meeting. The board meeting. . . They had planted cameras in the conference room. Ariel played around with the screen, trying to call them up.

A siren screamed so close that Ariel could see the police car's strobe lights through the raincoat. She buried her head as Pris cursed and turned off the highway.

Ariel couldn't do three things at a time. She called 911 again, gave them the address again, shouted *two murders,* and hung up. She prayed she was wrong and that Roark wouldn't die, but the police needed to be at the apartment house, not following Pris.

Finally connecting with the board meeting cameras, she watched the Russian stride in as if she'd just taken a restroom break. She bent over and whispered to one of the men, who brushed her off in irritation. Russian lady didn't like that, but she took a seat.

Ariel switched back to Roark's mic and heard him still muttering curses. He was alive.

In the front seat, Dante spoke curtly into his phone. Ariel hoped he was explaining the situation to the authorities better than she could.

She'd never really spoken to Reuben, but he was Roark and Jax's friend. She had all Roark's contacts in her phone. She pressed his friend's number and heard it ring.

"Roark?" a whisper asked anxiously from the other end.

"Ariel." She fought through her terror for words. "Roark. Vault."

"I know. I'm following his dad. He's got a gun. Roark may be safer where he is."

Reuben's voice was so low, she had to strain to hear it over the chaos inside and outside the car. "Sarin kills."

Reuben cursed. "Papa LeBlanc is looking for a way in the back door of the office wing. I have to go."

Ariel wanted to scream. Screaming didn't help any more than tears. Or maybe it would, if it shut up the argument in front. She shrieked louder and longer this time.

Pris and Dante abruptly silenced, thank all that was holy. The police sirens didn't.

Ignoring Pris's question, Ariel returned to watching the board meeting. They were arguing, too, and her head spun trying to follow all the words. Her brain wanted to shut down. She moaned and rocked and tried to focus. The tiny phone screen helped.

A blond man with a receding hairline and weak chin called JP wanted to close down operations, sell out, and scatter. He tried to talk about the IRS and financial statements, but the others yelled over him. A more confident, bronzed man smirked at caution and demanded that the JP person bluff their way out of the audit, if the emails were legitimate. Two men named Bibb wanted the emails investigated. Smart men.

The Russian wanted to take the money, flood their offices with overhead sprinklers, and run.

Lost in a world gone mad, Ariel's focus disintegrated. Weeping and screaming at phones that didn't communicate, she ignored concerned questions from the front seat.

She wanted her closet. Roark was locked in a closet.

Roark—who laughed at fear, dived headfirst into trouble, and caught the bad guys, as she couldn't. Roark—who smelled of fresh soap and man and kissed her as no other had. Roark—who couldn't sit still for two seconds. . . trapped in a narrow vault, bound and tied.

She wanted him to have superpowers and burst through the ropes like in the comics.

Superheroes should not die from a coward's poison.

How could any of this be real? She had simply wanted to help bring bad guys to justice—

"We're here, we're here!" Pris shouted as the truck screeched into a parking lot, followed by angry sirens and flashing lights. Flipping off the ignition, she dashed out, followed by Dante.

Was it still daytime? It didn't seem possible. From under her raincoat, Ariel heard the angry bark of authorities. Pris and Dante's voices retreated into the distance, along with the shouts of the police. They would be running for the building. She didn't allow herself to feel relieved. No one knew where the vault was. She'd only seen glimpses from Roark's cameras as he'd sneaked around in dark offices.

Ariel couldn't force herself to join the turmoil. She needed her closet.

Reuben's van might be better. He wasn't in it.

She peered out from the raincoat. The sirens and lights had stopped. She heard no voices. Ascertaining the direction of the apartments, she climbed out of the truck on the far side, staying low.

The lot in front of the building where Pris and the police had parked was blessedly empty, for visitors only, she imagined. The utility van sat at the far end. Would Reuben have left it open?

Thunderclouds boiled, as they often did on late summer afternoons. She'd still be conspicuous covering her head with a raincoat. She had to walk across the strange space and try the van door.

The Russian had spoken to Silver Fox. Silver Fox must have the key to the sarin box that the Russian couldn't find. A vault wouldn't have keys, would it? How did one learn the numbers of a combination lock? Roark had acute hearing. He would have listened to the lock.

Concentrating on the problem of opening the vault, she made it to the van. It was locked, of course. She sat down on the curb, out of sight of the building, and called Reuben again.

"Van keys?" she asked when he answered.

He swore briefly. "You're here?"

"Yes. And Pris and Dante and policemen."

"OK, stay put then. Key is in box under the driver wheel well. Combination three one four one."

"Pi?" She poked under the car until she found a box. How was she supposed to see the lock? She crawled under and squinted at the keypad. There had to be a dozen better ways to do this.

"Yeah. Call me square. They took Roark's phone, but he still has his mic. Let him know he should stay in there." Reuben switched off again.

Reuben was the expert, but Ariel didn't think leaving Roark locked in a closet was a very good idea.

Obtaining the key, she let herself into the van and set about learning the equipment.

It took her much too long. Roark's camera still showed only darkness. She didn't wish to scare him by speaking through the van's microphone. Not yet.

She called up Evie's camera. Jax was holding her back, so he was safe—if Evie didn't gouge out his eyes once he let her go. The small room they were in was a little less crowded now. Most of the residents had been sent away. Policemen questioned a little blond lady and a man in a security uniform.

She could find no camera for Reuben. There was no camera in the office hall. She had to pray Pris and Dante were leading the police down it in search of the vault. If they led them into the board meeting—Roark would never be rescued. How much air was in a vault?

Before she tried speaking through the mic, she tuned into the boardroom again.

In a matter of minutes, it had turned to chaos. A tall, dissolute man with dark hair stood at the back door, holding an ominous-looking gun on the crowd. She recognized him from Pris's photo and his resemblance to his son.

Roark's dad.

Thirty-Two

"ROARK IS LOCKED IN A VAULT."

Evie startled at the unfamiliar voice in her ear. Ghosts didn't talk through earbuds.

Given that Jax was holding her, and a policeman at the door prevented her from going anywhere, and there was a body on the floor in the next room, she wasn't real focused. It took a second to recognize the impossible. . . *Ariel*?

That made no sense at all in any universe she could picture.

"Roark's dad is in the conference room with a weapon."

Panicking, Evie started to hand the ear bud to Jax, but did she really want him running into a gunfight?

Before she could say anything, Ariel continued in her precise, robot voice. *"A tall, balding man is sneaking out a side door near the van. He has luggage."*

"Barouche! How did he get away from the crowd?" Evie jumped up, but with so many different problems converging, she didn't know where to start.

Jax caught her arm. "What? What is Reuben saying?"

Problem four—where was Reuben? He'd been awfully quiet. And telling Jax that his hermit sister was outside. . .

"Barouche," she shouted, gesturing at the hall. "He's escaping out a side door. He has bags with him. What if they contain Marlene's computers? How did he escape the police? Shouldn't he be down here with the rest of us for questioning?"

She was practically hopping up and down, her mind running in circles. Roark in a vault? *Ariel talking!* From where? The van?

"Police followed Pris and Dante inside." Ariel was on a relentless roll. She must have made a list to read.

Jax would go berserk if she told him his sister was probably outside in the van, watching all this. But someone needed to stop Barouche. Roark sounded safe enough in a vault. Pris and Dante. . . What the fiery demons? . . . And Reuben, where was Reuben? She had to get past the police and find Reuben. Could she send the police to the boardroom with a mad gunman. . . ?

Jax looked ready to grab the ear bud again. She clutched his hand so he couldn't. "Catch Barouche. I'll try to persuade the cops he's dangerous, but I make no promises. Go!"

She didn't want him to go. She didn't know if Barouche would be armed or even worth chasing. She didn't want to stay here without Jax. She *hated* this. Even Marlene was dancing on the ceiling, flitting back and forth and cursing rather colorfully inside Evie's head—seriously not helping.

"Be careful." Evie shoved Jax toward the door.

He glanced at the cop guarding the small anteroom off the lobby and shook his head. He kissed her cheek. "Distract him."

He slipped behind her, against the wall. He was the military expert. Unquestioning, Evie walked up to the policeman blocking the exit. "Sir, I need water, please, and possibly a mint of some sort, if there are any. I suffer dehydration and low blood sugar, and I fear I'm about to pass out again. I think I saw a candy dish in the HR office but taking candy from a crime scene. . ."

He frowned down on her. Sometimes, Evie hated being only five-two. Other times, it helped to look pale and helpless. She clung dramatically to the doorjamb. She thought she heard a door open behind her. There was another door? Why hadn't she noticed?

Because Jax had distracted her. Of course an anteroom like this would have two doors—and Jax was trained to scout exits.

"He has a gun!" a woman's voice screamed on the far end of the corridor.

Pris? That sounded an awful lot like Pris. . . Except her cousin was in the hall, not in the conference room where she could see Roark's dad. . . Either she was reading minds or Ariel had given her an ear bud. *Bets on first.*

The policeman pulled his weapon and took up a defensive stance. Well, good to know she was protected. Except Roark was in a vault, Reuben was missing, and Pris. . . She wouldn't even ask what her addled psychic cousin was doing.

Slipping back into the room, Evie spoke quietly into her mic. "OK, Jax on his way after Barouche. Roark, if you hear this, all hell is breaking loose out here. Can you breathe?"

"Breathing," he muttered raggedly. "Combination one-nine-six-nine. Get. . . me. . . outta. . . here."

"If I knew where you were. . ." Evie slipped out the door Jax must have taken. She was in an office off the lobby where residents milled excitedly. Marlene returned to chandelier swinging, obviously clueless about vaults or Roark or anything else. A second later, the apparition flew down the office corridor. Okay, so maybe Granny wasn't entirely clueless, just causing a distraction. Everyone was staring at the creaking chandelier.

"Filing room off big office. Is that Ariel talking?" Roark sounded breathless and furious and. . . not himself.

"I can't go down that corridor. It's packed with cops and screaming cousins. Does the office have a window?" Evie slipped through the crowd in the lobby and out the front door. More cop cars were pouring into the lot, but they apparently didn't have enough men to station at the door, just in the hall.

Outside, she glanced around for Jax. . . and saw her Subaru flying down the drive at high speed.

What?

Covering her mouth to prevent screaming, she watched as Jax. . . it had to be Jax, he had the keys. . . drove her little car straight in front of a Mercedes leaving the resident parking lot.

A *black* Mercedes—one with a new tire?

Shattering metal and glass exploded as the big sedan crashed into the rear fender of her pretty car. She would have wept for the car, except *Jax was behind the wheel.*

She raced down the drive, catching a policeman stepping out of his car and pointing him that way. "Barouche! Barouche just tried to kill my lawyer!" She thought *lawyer* might sound less hysterical than *boyfriend*, but she kept running, not waiting to see if he'd listened.

Of course Jax had let the Mercedes hit him. It would have been illegal to hit the Mercedes. She was going to strangle him if he was still alive. The Subaru now blocked the parking lot exit.

Weeping, her heart stuck in her throat as the Mercedes backed up, apparently prepared to ram the smaller car out of the way. She'd never get there in time. . .

Jax dived out the car door, tumbled, rolled, and came up with a gun in his hand. She wasn't as shocked as she should have been. Jax was ex-military. She'd known he had weapons. She offered garbled gratitude to Whoever was listening for making him be all right.

The Mercedes slammed the Subaru again, shoving it out of the way. Jax shot the front tire.

Pushing ahead of her while unholstering his gun, the cop came up shooting, shattering the back window of the Mercedes. Thank all the heavens, someone had listened to her.

Halting to catch her breath, Evie whispered into her mic, "Jax is fine. He just caught Barouche. We'll find Roark next, okay?"

She thought Ariel might be weeping.

STANDING BESIDE EVIE'S SMOKING SUBARU, JAX COULDN'T STOP cursing. It was as if he'd saved up every foul word in his vocabulary all summer and unleashed them now. He caught Evie as she ran up and flung her arms around him. The world tilted back in order as he hugged her, hard. With soft curves cuddled against him and concern pouring over him like syrup, he could think clearly again.

He'd destroyed her brand-new car, and she was kissing him. Maybe the world wasn't all evil.

He shoved his gun back in its holster. He wanted to choke the dangerous old man in the Mercedes, but he let the uniform handle him.

"His name is Bernard Barouche, alias Mr. Charles, probably wanted on a dozen charges of fraud, and there are more waiting once this all comes down," he shouted at the officer. He was pretty certain that was a solid guess. "I need to take the lady back inside."

Without more explanation, he shoved Evie toward the building. She was jabbering something about Roark and vaults, but his pulse was racing too hard to listen until they were safely inside, using the side exit Barouche had taken and avoiding the mob scene up front.

"Roark locked himself in a vault? Let me talk to Reuben." He reached for her mic.

She slapped him away and babbled hysterically. "I think Reuben is following Roark's dad. It sounds like Ursula killed Savanna, locked up Roark, and is planning on killing him when she has time. I was busy being interrogated by police and listening to Marlene and didn't catch it all. But Roark gave me the combination. We need to get him out before his dad shoots everyone in sight, including Reuben and Pris and Dante and who knows who else. . ."

The horror finally sunk in. Roark in a box. . . Jax knew the hell Roark and Reuben had suffered in a prison box in the desert. Roark did not do confined spaces well.

"Direction," he demanded. Roark first. He'd hope the cops had the other situations in hand. There were certainly enough uniforms running through the building, shouting, and evacuating the residents. Poor sods, from all the screaming, they probably thought they had a hostage situation and a serial killer. They wouldn't be looking for one man in a vault.

"Big office, Roark said. One with a filing room on one side. How can we get down that hall?" Evie peered worriedly into the lobby.

Both their phones were dead. They couldn't link to Reuben's cameras or the ones in here.

"Outside," he decided. "Look for a corner office with big windows."

They retreated out the parking lot door. The officer and Barouche weren't in sight.

"Garden in back," Evie whispered. "Wouldn't a corner office have the best view?"

And possibly an escape hatch. Hand in the small of her back just to stabilize himself, Jax guided Evie along the sidewalk. He peered around the corner to the employee parking lot. Judging from the pricey cars, this was where the board had parked. They must have entered through the back of the lobby— or there was a side door into the conference room. He should have been in the van with Reuben, watching who entered and where.

He didn't see anyone loitering. No one flew out some hidden entrance, fleeing whatever was happening inside. A policeman guarded the back lobby entrance.

"Act innocent," he told Evie, dropping his arm over her shoulders and kissing her hair while he steered her through the darkening parking lot. Fat drops of rain had started to fall.

She wrapped an arm around his waist, and he wished they really were out for a stroll in the rain.

But Roark would be going insane somewhere inside this damned haunted building.

"Where is Marlene now, can you tell?" he murmured as they passed the policeman without interruption.

"No. I can only see her when she presents herself. Shouldn't there be more than one policeman back here?" She watched anxiously as they passed fancy BMWs and Porsches.

"No idea what's happening inside. Is Reuben back online yet?" Jax scanned the windows on this section of the building. The conference room had no windows that he remembered. Executive offices probably surrounded it.

"Reuben?" she spoke quietly into the mic. "Anyone?"

"Where are you?" Roark growled.

"Back of building, looking for way in. Place is crawling with cops."

Jax took the mic and ear bud away. "What happened to Reuben?"

"Don't know. He's not wired. Watch out for Ursula. She's former FSB."

Roark wasn't speaking Cajun. That was an ominous sign. Jax narrowed his eyes at the realization that Reuben wasn't in the van. Then who was? Someone had been feeding Evie information.

They weren't responding though.

"Here," Evie whispered, leaning against a patio door and peering in as the first gusts of rain hit.

"Bingo." Action over worry. Jax took out his gun, rapped the glass beside the lock, and with the security alarm blaring, cleared an opening for his hand and unlocked the latch. They stepped through in a flash of lightning and roll of thunder.

"We're inside," he told Roark.

"This is it, VP Bibb's office. We have a file room," Evie called, exploring behind a curtain.

From here, they could hear shouts and what might be gunfire. Presumably, security had better things to do than check on a break-in.

"We need a damned flashlight," Jax muttered as he followed Evie into a room filled with file cabinets. Who on earth kept paper files anymore? He hunted for a light switch. He'd come to rely on his phone too much. Hanging around Evie, he'd have to carry two chargers.

Evie dug through her plastic tote to find her key ring. She flipped on a tiny Maglite and ran it around the walls.

A rapping sound came from behind a panel. "Get me out!" Roark shouted in Jax's ear.

They pounded on the panel until they found a latch. It swung back to reveal the combination lock.

"One-nine-six-nine," a voice in his ear repeated as Jax spun the dial.

That voice wasn't Roark—or Reuben. It sounded distinctly like his sister. . .

Before Jax could take in this new insanity, the vault door sprang open, and Roark stumbled out, yanking ropes off his arm and feet, with a knife in his hand. He staggered against a filing cabinet for a moment, then shoved out of the room with a small security box under his arm.

Thunder rolled. Alarms blared. Another shot rang out.

"Let's roll," Roark roared.

Thirty-three

BLIND WITH EXPLOSIVE FURY AND FEAR, ROARK SHOVED PAST A stunned Jax and a worried Evie. Ariel frantically tried to communicate in his ear, but as much as Roark was in awe of how much his personal angel had risked, he'd given up on security precautions. This was ending. . . *now.*

He'd fought his dad all his life, rebelled against strictures because of him, got blown up and locked in jail, lost his job and his home, and had no life to offer a good woman like Ariel—because of the anger beaten into him by the criminal bully now holding a bunch of crooks hostage. The irony swelled.

He'd already sized up the head honcho's office before he'd wandered off into the file room and found the vault. He reckoned the FBI would have a real good time with that vault.

His goal now, however, was the fake fireplace he'd uncovered earlier. Without bothering with the nicety of looking for hidden hinges, he ripped the false front off the wall, then smashed his boot into the panel behind it. The destruction didn't satisfy him. He slammed his shoulder into the drywall of the next room.

"Marlene, swing the chandeliers," Evie shouted incomprehensibly behind him.

Apparently accepting Roark's rage, Jax reverted to their commando training. He pried open a light switch panel with his jackknife and used his rubber-soled shoe to rip out and jam the wires together. Electricity arced. Brilliant man.

As the lights blew, screams escalated in the room behind the wall, and chairs scraped.

"Well, now they can't see the fun chandelier," Evie griped. "I'll have to turn on the Tinkerbelles."

Fine, they were as insane as he was. Roark kicked until the bottom panel gave in.

Behind him, Evie's bubble lights popped on, playing through the darkness. She found a crouching position that had the tiny lights flashing through the hole he'd made. They bounced in sparkly rainbows off the conference room walls and illuminated the swinging chandelier. More shrieks and curses and a burst of gunfire. Yeah, right, good ol' da, shooting at haints.

From behind the wall, Jax lowered the hand holding a powerful flashlight, shining it through the crawl hole into the larger room, blinding the occupants. Stooping down to see through the panel, Roark thought he caught a glimpse of Reuben with a small automatic and a handful of cable ties hidden by a credenza along the back wall. Cautious Reuben wouldn't take down his da. . . yet.

The blinding light brought more screams and chair scraping. Over the chaos, Roark could hear his father bellowing, "*Tais-toi* you *putain de merde* and give me my son so I can whack his sorry tail. . ."

Mon dieu . . ! At least now he knew where the bastard was lurking.

"Stay back," Roark ordered, before shouting through the hole. "Claude Roark LeBlanc, I damn your cretinous hide to a hell of your own making."

Sure enough, his da swung around, blasting his pathetic automatic in the direction of Roark's voice, except at chest height. Entering the office in a crouch, Roark rolled under the hail of bullets, jumped up, and flung the sharp-edged metal box of sarin at his father's head. He'd had a mean pitch when he was a kid. He'd not practiced lately, but big box, big head, hard to miss. He heard Claude grunt. His father was out cold and not going anywhere.

Roark shouted into the uproar, "Sarin! The box is filled with poison gas! Run!"

Ursula's screams resounded loudest, Roark noticed in satisfaction, swiveling in her direction. He tackled her before she could reach the door. He

238

didn't know where everyone else was, but he was personally taking down the murderous bitch.

Tinkerbelle lights played over the room. Chimes tinkled. Big police lights finally flashed on, spotlighting the board of directors cowering under the conference table. Obviously, the money-grubbers had no idea what sarin was and were hiding from Stupid Man with his gun.

"The whole damned lot of you are under arrest," a voice of authority shouted.

Not him. No more prison cells for him. Roark slammed his palm under Ursula's jaw, and she went limp. If he was lucky, he'd broken a bone. If he wasn't, oh well, she was unconscious and not going anywhere. Keeping to the darkness of the floor, he slid backward and through the panel he'd crashed. Jax and Evie helped him up.

He wasn't in the least surprised when Reuben crawled through after him.

Feeling more wiped than he ever had in his life because this time he had to think of others, Roark whispered into his mic. "Ariel, *cher*, bring the van around to the back. We're going for ice cream."

"*Sarin*, you crazy man!" Reuben whispered as he hit his feet running, joining Evie and Jax who had fled out the patio door ahead of them.

"Sarin deteriorates. If she stole that from the FSB, it's been rotting for decades. And the box was pretty tight. They can't say I didn't warn them." Roark dashed into the parking lot as the van turned the corner.

He opened the driver's door, scooped Ariel out, hugged and kissed her, then handed her to an irate Jax. "Full house. Let's get outta here."

He hopped into the driver's seat, turned the ignition, and didn't wait for the rear door to close after the last person scrambled in back.

This was one shit storm his da wasn't dragging him into.

"WHAT THE HELL IS ARIEL DOING HERE?" JAX SHOUTED, slamming the rear door as the van rumbled into traffic.

"Helping." Ariel hoped she'd helped, maybe just a little. She was shivering and wished she'd brought the raincoat with her. "Where are Pris and Dante?"

"Pris and Dante? They're back there. Oh, hell." Roark hit the brake. The van fishtailed on the wet road.

Ariel handed her phone to Evie. "Call?"

Evie pounced on it, hit Pris's number, and put her on speaker. "Do we need to rescue you?"

Pris's voice filled the car. "The Great White Savior is pontificating with a police chief and a federal agent. I have the car keys, so if he wants out, he'll have to follow me. And I'm leaving. I do not want to know what just happened in there."

"You do, too, but I'm not telling you unless you fix us lunch tomorrow. I want all the pretty spiraly veggies on crackers you fix for customers."

"Those are for Loretta's birthday party." Pris clicked off.

Ariel took the phone back. The men were arguing. She clasped her hands anxiously. Were they mad at her? Jax probably was.

She huddled in a corner behind the driver's seat, trying to make herself small while processing what couldn't be processed. The phone. . . Her window on the world. She opened the screen to the cameras in the conference room and showed it to the others.

Jax whistled and passed it around. Hazmat was boxing up the still-sealed sarin box. The police were cuffing everyone in sight, including Roark's dad. He was holding his bleeding head and shouting about frauds and cheats and demanding that everyone be arrested, except himself, of course. Ariel thought she'd have to send the evidence against him to the local authorities.

Roark swung the van off the road into a shopping center parking lot. He halted in an unlit corner as the rain unleashed a torrent. "Plate, sign," he ordered. "Take no chances."

He and Reuben leaped from the front seat, opened the back of the van, and began searching through their drawers. While he was drawing out a magnetic sign, Roark found a tarp and threw it in Ariel's direction. "Ain't got blankets, cher, but if this helps. . ." He dashed off.

She gratefully pulled the tarp over her head and relaxed in the darkness. Jax wouldn't yell at her when she was in here. She could just hug Roark for his understanding. . .

She really wanted to hug Roark the way Evie was hugging and kissing Jax, although Evie was also beating his big arm with her fist and shouting about her car at the same time. It was a little difficult to determine if she was more upset about losing the car or almost losing Jax. Ariel could appreciate that.

"Plate switched," Reuben called into the van. "Ice cream orders?"

"White chocolate raspberry," Ariel said from under her safety net. She had people she trusted around her. If she could stop all the fights and lights. . .

she'd be just fine, she discovered. She was feeling a little. . . giddy. . . but she didn't have to focus right now.

"USB plugs, panel behind you," she told Jax, hoping to stop the argument and feeling remarkably confident now that she'd memorized her surroundings.

Evie instantly swung to examine the equipment. Once she had her phone plugged and charging, she texted Ariel's phone. U OK?

Ariel thought about it. She'd watched chaos—but that had been on a familiar computer screen and hadn't affected her. She'd never worried about others before, so her fear had muddled her thinking very badly. And then she realized. . .

"*Barouche.* The numbers for Barouche are 2-1-23-15-21-3-8-5. That's the bitcoin wallet number. . ."

Frantically, she poked her phone, hoping to reach her computer so she could pull up the account she'd been working.

The door beside her opened and Roark lifted her canvas. "Ice cream, bébé. Numbers can wait. I'm gonna kiss you now, if dat all right."

"*That*," she corrected in distraction, reaching for the ice cream and almost losing her phone as he leaned over and overwhelmed her with his masculine size and musk. Ice cream and kisses. . .

Worked. It all worked beautifully to pull her shattered pieces together into one whole bundle of nerves.

❀

"THEY ARRESTED URSULA FOR MURDER, FOUND THE KNIFE WITH her prints all over it." Sitting on the floor, Jax showed Evie his notebook computer while she wrapped Loretta's birthday presents in the privacy of their bedroom. "They found the antifreeze in Savanna's apartment, and Ursula's griping about the nurse's stupidity pretty much concludes the investigation into Marlene's death. Reuben is sending Gump a sizable bill."

He lifted Psycat off the colorful gift wrap on the floor and placed the Siamese in the box the gifts had arrived in. The cat gave him a baleful look, meowed something that sounded like *murder,* and curled up in his cardboard bed. Psychocat might have been a more apt name.

Sitting on the floor amid the debris, Evie sent him a mischievous glance. "Will the FBI pay for all the files we sent them showing where to find the stolen funds? I'm hoping that leads to catching all the rest of the Sunshine hydra."

Her T-shirt today read *Keep Talking, I'm Diagnosing You*. Jax had bought it for her.

"Gump said he'd file an expense report for independent contractors. We'll see. We need incentive to keep Roark here now that his dad is safely behind bars." Jax held his finger on the ribbon so she could knot it.

"Oh, I don't think keeping Roark here will be a problem," she said airily. "You might ask Loretta if it would be okay to expand her rental property so he doesn't get too claustrophobic."

Jax clenched his molars and tried not to roar too loudly. "There's no need for him to stay with Ariel any longer. She needs her privacy."

Evie nudged his toes with hers. "She's not a baby any longer. She gets to decide who lives with her. And last I looked, she's pretty happy sharing the house and the business with him. If you're really, really lucky, Roark will figure out how to make what she does legal."

"She's working in cryptocurrency!" he shouted. "Unlocking Barouche's account and revealing all those illegal transactions spun heads. The old con was stealing from his own conmen to set up all his girlfriends. Messing with criminals is dangerous."

"Well, Ariel stole the funds back, which means she probably needs Roark as a bodyguard. Of course, cleaning out his dad's bank credit line with that witch app is what set Claude off." Apparently not caring that she was exploding his head, Evie admired the clutter and reached for the next present to wrap.

Jax took back his computer. "Well, Barouche robbed him first by siphoning funds into bitcoins. The feds don't know what to do with all the information. We're damned lucky Ariel hasn't been arrested."

The image of two hacker geniuses living out there in the woods. . . Gahhh!

"Maybe the feds or banks or whatever have hired her by now," Evie said reassuringly. "Your sister is a grown-up. Leave her be. Lucy Murkowski's twisted aura apparently reflects her learning disabilities and self-doubt, but she's honest. Did they put her in charge of Sunshine? I hate to see everyone lose their homes."

She studied a plush snowy wizard owl, then began building a box for it by taping together an assortment of Blu-Ray fantasy videos to expand Loretta's horizons beyond Harry Potter.

"Lucy is pretty much incapable of running anything, but she's good with people." Preferring this positive topic, Jax flipped through his emails to show her the images he'd been receiving. "Sunshine will probably go into receivership; the assets are frozen. But she's organized a group of tenants to act like an HOA and operate the place with expenditures approved by the court. There's a lot of talent in that home, so the judge sanctioned it, for now. It will be a little difficult to refund the scammed money, so using it to house seniors seems best."

Evie grinned at the picture of Mary Smith and Leticia Mortimer sitting at the head of the conference table. "They can handle it. When I stopped by the other day, the auras of Granny's neighbors were almost transparent with delight. I think they'd been worrying about unlawful activities, but only Granny had been willing to investigate."

"Mary Smith is a retired CPA. She's setting up a legal payroll, and the court has authorized me to help their staff get real IDs." A steady income of sorts would tide Jax over until his other cases paid off. And this was the kind of income he could appreciate. He held the video boxes in place as Evie finished taping them. "Are any of these gifts from me? Or is this a joint effort?"

Evie leaned over and kissed him, giving him a nice view down her T-shirt. "You contributed the cash. I contributed my creative talent. Let's call it joint."

"Together, we make one whole, right." He tugged her head down to where he was sprawled on the floor so he could kiss her more thoroughly.

She rolled on top of him, covering him in a blanket of sumptuous Evie. Before he could carry this to the next stage, child-sized feet pounded up the stairs in accompaniment to a dog's barking.

"Head her off at the pass, partner." Evie rolled off and pushed him away. "I'm not done yet."

He wasn't in any condition to confront a ten-year old. When Loretta pounded on the door, Jax just shouted through it. "You can't come in. Presents in progress."

Evie kicked him with her bare toes for revealing her activity.

"Ms. Murkowski from the nursing home is on the line," Loretta called through the heavy panel. "She wants Evie to exorcise Marlene and the other ghosts. Can I come, too?"

Evie laughed and tucked the snowy owl into the box of videos. "Sure, why not? Marlene won't leave unless she wants to, but that place needs a good sage burning."

She leaned over and whispered in Jax's ear, "Do you think the court will approve witchcraft-related expenses?"

Thirty-four

SITTING ON A CORNER OF HER BACK PORCH RAILING, PAINTING her toe nails a flaming red, Evie admired the college boys setting up their equipment on the other end of the sprawling Victorian porch. They'd probably blow out every ancient circuit in the house once they got going, but they sounded good for now.

Top-knotted Reuben climbed out of his cellar wearing cut-offs, tank top, and cowboy boots. Evie whistled at him. He waved absent-mindedly and inspected his handiwork. He'd built a platform just beneath the porch as a kind of an elevated proscenium between the stairs and cellar, then covered half the lawn with a pine plank dance floor.

In the back of the yard, the neighbors had pushed together picnic tables from every house around. They'd been decorated with colorful birthday tablecloths and balloons, and gifts had started piling up—as if Loretta needed gifts. The kid could buy anything she wanted. Jax and Evie just wouldn't let her, so maybe that worked out okay.

Larraine, Afterthought's fashion designer mayoral candidate, strolled out of the house, laughing and fanning herself with a feathered fan. "Those girls will be the death of me! Were we really that silly at that age?"

"Us? Probably not, and I doubt Loretta has been before, but I'm pretty sure it's normal for eleven-year-olds to be silly at birthday parties. Are they all covered in sequins and glitter?" Evie capped her polish bottle. She didn't want to out-do the birthday girl's glamor, so polish was all the dressing up she'd do.

"And rhinestones and capes and even a tutu. They have creative ideas of what to wear to a dance. And you, girl, can't dance in bare feet. What are you thinking? Where's your boots?" Larraine frowned in disapproval at Evie's toes.

"I'm in charge of guarding the kids' punch. This crowd can get rowdy real quick. The adult punch stays in the kitchen. I'll boogie in the grass behind the picnic tables." She swung down from the railing. "Hey, Reuben, you and Larraine need to test the stage. Let's see your moves!"

Pounding a loose nail into the planks, he gave her the finger and returned to work. The nerd was finally emerging from his shell. She thought the shoot-out at the Sunshine corral had given him back some of his confidence.

Larraine sighed in anticipation. "He's good. He just needs a little motivation." She wiggled her skinny hips in their skin-tight sequined blue jeans and set off down the stairs.

Evie was pretty sure Larraine's alligator boots had heels high enough that she almost reached Reuben's six-foot height. Reuben stood up straight the instant she approached. Afterthought could only benefit from having the nerdy computer engineer and fashion designer in their midst.

With Mavis's golden retriever on his heels, Jax emerged from the carriage house where he'd been tinkering with the new/used cherry-red Subaru he'd found for her. The insurance proceeds had almost covered the cost, and he'd chipped in the rest. Evie stood on the top step and leaned over to kiss his hair all over. "I do love a manly man who can stoke my engines."

He laughed, pulled her head down until their lips met, and proceeded to show her real kisses. The band struck up a raucous chorus in accompaniment. Honey settled in the shade and waited for Barbecue Man to start the new grill. The retriever had been following Jax ever since he'd set it up.

Neighbors yahooed from the alley gate, and Evie broke away to greet the guests. Parents poured from the kitchen door bearing Pris's legendary hors d'oeurves, although it appeared people had already been sneaking tastes.

"I have to start the hot dogs and hamburgers," Jax murmured into her hair. "Meet you by the punch table later."

Butterflies flitted in her insides. Evie was pretty certain no one had given her butterflies before. She'd been so positive six months ago that Jax was the kind of man she loved to hate. . . but all that managing authority had benefits she'd never known. She squiggled all over thinking of the evening ahead.

"Here we come," Loretta hollered from behind the screen door.

Laughing, Evie held it open.

Loretta emerged first, dressed in a billowing rainbow-striped gown with a purple cape covered in silver stars and bearing a flashing light sabre she treated as a wand. Her new purple-rimmed glasses matched the purple streak in the bangs she was growing out and had pinned to one side.

Her indigo aura was practically put to shame in all that drama.

Behind her streamed a gaggle of sixth graders of every gender, all garbed in costumes Larraine had her workers help sew together. The bullied, heckled queer kid Larraine had once been now had the confidence to help other misfits find their pride. Evie got out her phone and snapped photos as they paraded past, down the steps, across the dance floor, and to the food.

It was good that Loretta's friends were forming a place where everyone could be accepted. Her Indigo child was changing the world, one sliver at a time.

"Let the games begin!" Mavis's shout came from the side gate as she shoved it open, bearing a flaming citronella torch. Behind her marched a contingent of flame-bearers singing an off-key Happy Birthday song, which the band picked up in screaming guitar and drum rolls.

As the torch bearers spread out around the perimeter, slipping the poles into waiting holders, they were followed in by Roark and the sheriff carrying a table of cakes with flaming candles.

"How do they keep those candles from blowing out?" Gracie, Evie's sister, whispered as she emerged from the kitchen with her wide-eyed daughter.

"Special candles that glow forever, I think. Ariel found them online. Which reminds me. . ." Evie got out her phone and texted Jax's sister that it was party time. Roark had set up video cameras around the yard so she could watch. She'd been right about Ariel's aura—she was the Crystal Key to accompany Loretta's Indigo awesomeness.

The band rocked out. Roark and the sheriff found space for the cake table and stood back as Loretta attempted to blow out the candles. Evie beamed as her once solemn ward crowed with delight when the flames wouldn't die, and all her guests had to huff and puff with her.

Roark waved at the camera. Ariel texted a laughing emoji and fireworks to all their phones.

Pris strolled out of the kitchen covered in flour and wearing rainbow stripes in her hair. She leaned against the wall, observing. "Days of work, and I give it half an hour before the tables are wiped clean. Birthday cake first?"

"Yup. That's what Loretta wanted, and it's her day. I figure they'll be starved after an hour of line-dancing. Reuben's a demon on heels." Evie nodded toward the prof in his cowboy boots. This new Reuben could be right entertaining. "Where's Dante?"

"He booked his flight before he knew about the party. Good riddance," Pris said stiffly.

Iddy climbed the steps with her raven on her shoulder. "La Chusa saw them fighting last night. Make her tell us what that's about."

"He's gone. Who cares?" Pris marched off to supervise the picnic tables.

Ariel rang up on FaceTime. "Dante has problems."

Huh, so Roark had the cameras wired for sound. Evie looked around, found the nearest one and gave Ariel a thumb's up. Ariel added, "Pris knows."

Evie wanted to hug Jax's sister through the phone. She loved this addition to her family. "We'll let them fight it out. I'm taking you to the party, new sis." Leaving her family to size up the band, she worked her way through the buzzing kids on the dance floor to the tables where she was supposed to be guarding the punch, letting Ariel see it all.

Jax was waiting for her. He waved at his sister on the phone, then tugged Evie against him so they could watch as Larraine and Reuben got up on the proscenium to order the kids into line.

Roark grabbed Evie's phone and took Ariel out to the dance floor. He'd ordered a new state-of-the-art fancy smart phone with the promise of payment from Gump, but it hadn't arrived yet.

"Sometimes I'm really dense," Jax said as they settled on the concrete bench they'd uncovered earlier in the week.

Evie laughed. "Focused. The word is focused. Goal-oriented. What did you work out?"

"That this is what I've been missing." He gestured at the rowdy, laughing mob of kids and adults chowing down on food and drinks and grooving to the music. "I was only twelve when my parents died, and I spent so many years trying to be the well-behaved child that our adoptive parents wanted, fitting in with their country-club set, that I repressed earlier memories."

Evie gazed up at him in concern, but his aura was lovely and content. "Your real parents were a little less. . . puritanical?" Given her family's history, that was a word that held generations of meaning.

He nodded. "My parents' parties looked like this—all ages, colors, gender. They had philosophical and political arguments over casseroles and cheap wine with crazy music in the background. I remember eating potato chips and kicking a ball around the backyard with kids I'd never met before. I don't know who they were or where they are now, but I felt at home." He turned and looked at her. "The way I do now. You make me feel at home."

Evie thought her heart might explode with joy. "Your aura isn't red anymore. We'll have to ask Loretta if your walnut is growing."

Jax laughed. "I love you, Evangeline Malcolm Carstairs. I've never said that to anyone, but I'm pretty sure if I don't say it, I'll burst holding in the words. I love you, and you make me happier than I've ever been."

"Even when I tell you those torches contain illegal fireworks timed to go off at dark?" Evie kissed the corner of his lips and felt them turn up in a smile.

Laughing, he hauled her on his lap. "Even then. Maybe because of them. I love you even more."

"That's good then, because if you hadn't said it first, I was going to say I love you the instant they fired off and the band starts playing 'Witchy Woman'." She tugged his head down and kissed him so he didn't laugh too hard.

ARIEL HAD ENJOYED WATCHING THE PARTY WHILE SIPPING A bubbly wine Roark left in the refrigerator. Now she calmed herself by nibbling her toast and scrolling through her game camera videos in the silent dark of midnight. She noted the arrival of the possum with her babies. Instead of continuing on to the lake out of sight of her cameras, the new family stopped at a small pool beside the newly widened trail.

A raccoon emerged from the shrubbery to dig into the cat food basin on the other side of the path. And to her delight, a fawn nibbled at field corn in a hay rack built into the trees. The squirrels usually emptied the rack before night arrived, but she enjoyed watching them at daybreak.

Accessing the camera settings, she turned the camera to the platform rigged between trees.

Roark sat there cross-legged, content to be in the open air while he worked. He'd already drawn up schematics for a more elaborate tree house made out of old window frames he'd salvaged from a farmhouse being torn down nearby.

As if sensing her presence, he glanced at the camera, grinned, and waved. A text zinged into her phone.

YOU GOT NIBBLES. JOBS YOURS

She didn't have to click the link to know he was talking about an operation they'd applied for testing internet security. He was helping her set up a legitimate business with connections Professor Gump was sending their way.

She wasn't a lone operator anymore. She didn't miss the loneliness.

MUFFINS BAKING, she typed back. **JOIN ME?**

He was out of the tree and at the back door in a flash.

He needed a home, and she was ready to share hers with a man as damaged and lonely as she was. In time, maybe their parts would adjust and fit together and make one whole.

They had time to find out.

Characters

MALCOLM FAMILY—Afterthought SC

Evangeline Serena Malcolm Carstairs—sends spirits to light, reads auras
Mavis Malcolm Carstairs—Evie's mother; reads crystal ball
Gracie— Mavis's elder daughter; telekinetic; daughter—**Aster**, age 6
Idonea (Iddy)—Evie's cousin, veterinarian who talks to animals
Priscilla—Evie's cousin; telepathic
Loretta Aurora Post—ten-year-old heiress; sees souls
Aunt Felicia—Mavis's sister; Iddy's mother
Aunt Ellen— Mavis's sister; Pris's mother
Great Aunt Evangeline Valerie Malcolm Brindle—Aunt Val, Civil War re-enactor

BOOK THREE:

Damon Ives Jackson (Jax)— fraud and family lawyer; parents, deceased
Ariel Jackson—Jax's sister
Roark LeBlanc—Jax's hacker friend, former military intelligence
Reuben Thompson—Roark's partner; degrees from MIT and Duke
Marlene Gump—grandmother and retired FBI; age 80
Stacey Gump—Marlene's granddaughter

CHARACTERS

Lucy Murkowski—director of Azalea Apartments
Mr. Charles—professorial resident of Azalea Apartments
Savanna Johnson—resident nurse of Azalea Apartments
Ursula Stanislaus—wife of Dmitri; HR director of Sunshine Healthcare
Dmitri Stanislaus—owner of Savannah's Best Cars
Claude Roark LeBlanc—Roark's dad
Professor James Gump—Marlene's son, Stacey's father
Bill Bibb—VP of Sunshine Healthcare
J.P. Peterson—manager of Sunshine Home Care
Kurt Calder (aka Sam Reilly)—VP of Patient Relations at Sunshine's assisted living facility
Dante Alfonso Ives Rossi—distant Ives/Malcolm Italian cousin of Jax
Laura Evans—annuity stolen; deceased
Mary North—ghost
Mrs. Decker, Mrs. Lopez, Mr. Wong —went to Sunshine nursing home
Leticia Mortimer—resident of Azalea Apartments
Mary Smith— resident of Azalea Apartments

TOWNSPEOPLE of AFTERTHOUGHT

Mayor Arthur Block—resigned office over land fraud
Gertie—elderly owner of Oldies Café
Sheriff Troy—unmarried, older sheriff of Afterthought
Hank Williams—hardware store owner; town council member; mayoral candidate
Larraine Ward—fashion designer; mayoral candidate

The Crystal Key
Patricia Rice

Copyright © 2021 Patricia Rice
Cover design © 2021 Killion Group
First digital edition Book View Café 2021
ISBN: 978-1-63632-055-7 ebook
ISBN: 978-1-63632-056-4 print

This is a work of fiction. Any references to historical events, real people, or real locales are used fictitiously. Other names, characters, places, and incidents are the product of the author's imagination, and any resemblance to actual events or locales or persons, living or dead, is entirely coincidental.

Published by Rice Enterprises, Dana Point, CA, an affiliate of Book View Café Publishing Cooperative

Book View Café
304 S. Jones Blvd. Suite #2906
Las Vegas NV 89107

About the Author

With several million books in print and *New York Times* and *USA Today's* bestseller lists under her belt, former CPA Patricia Rice is one of romance's hottest authors. Her emotionally-charged contemporary and historical romances have won numerous awards, including the *RT Book Reviews* Reviewers Choice and Career Achievement Awards. Her books have been honored as Romance Writers of America RITA® finalists in the historical, regency and contemporary categories.

A firm believer in happily-ever-after, Patricia Rice is married to her high school sweetheart and has two children. A native of Kentucky and New York, a past resident of North Carolina and Missouri, she currently resides in Southern California, and now does accounting only for herself.

Also by Patricia Rice

The World of Magic:

The Unexpected Magic Series

MAGIC IN THE STARS

WHISPER OF MAGIC

THEORY OF MAGIC

AURA OF MAGIC

CHEMISTRY OF MAGIC

NO PERFECT MAGIC

The Magical Malcolms Series

MERELY MAGIC

MUST BE MAGIC

THE TROUBLE WITH MAGIC

THIS MAGIC MOMENT

MUCH ADO ABOUT MAGIC

MAGIC MAN

The California Malcolms Series

THE LURE OF SONG AND MAGIC

TROUBLE WITH AIR AND MAGIC

THE RISK OF LOVE AND MAGIC

Crystal Magic

SAPPHIRE NIGHTS

TOPAZ DREAMS

CRYSTAL VISION

WEDDING GEMS

AZURE SECRETS

AMBER AFFAIRS

MOONSTONE SHADOWS

THE WEDDING GIFT

THE WEDDING QUESTION

THE WEDDING SURPRISE

School of Magic

LESSONS IN ENCHANTMENT

A BEWITCHING GOVERNESS

AN ILLUSION OF LOVE

THE LIBRARIAN'S SPELL

ENTRANCING THE EARL

CAPTIVATING THE COUNTESS

Psychic Solutions

THE INDIGO SOLUTION

THE GOLDEN PLAN

THE CRYSTAL KEY

Historical Romance:

American Dream Series

MOON DREAMS

REBEL DREAMS

The Rebellious Sons

WICKED WYCKERLY

DEVILISH MONTAGUE

NOTORIOUS ATHERTON

FORMIDABLE LORD QUENTIN

The Regency Nobles Series

THE GENUINE ARTICLE

THE MARQUESS

ENGLISH HEIRESS

IRISH DUCHESS

Regency Love and Laughter Series

CROSSED IN LOVE

MAD MARIA'S DAUGHTER

ARTFUL DECEPTIONS

ALL A WOMAN WANTS

Rogues & Desperadoes Series

LORD ROGUE

MOONLIGHT AND MEMORIES

SHELTER FROM THE STORM

WAYWARD ANGEL

DENIM AND LACE

CHEYENNES LADY

Dark Lords and Dangerous Ladies Series

LOVE FOREVER AFTER

SILVER ENCHANTRESS

DEVIL'S LADY

DASH OF ENCHANTMENT

INDIGO MOON

Too Hard to Handle

TEXAS LILY

TEXAS ROSE

TEXAS TIGER

TEXAS MOON

Mystic Isle Series

MYSTIC ISLE

MYSTIC GUARDIAN

MYSTIC RIDER

MYSTIC WARRIOR

Mysteries:

Family Genius Series

EVIL GENIUS

UNDERCOVER GENIUS

CYBER GENIUS

TWIN GENIUS

TWISTED GENIUS

Tales of Love and Mystery

BLUE CLOUDS

GARDEN OF DREAMS

NOBODY'S ANGEL

VOLCANO

CALIFORNIA GIRL

Urban Fantasies

Writing as Jamie Quaid

Saturn's Daughters

BOYFRIEND FROM HELL

DAMN HIM TO HELL

GIVING HIM HELL

About Book View Café

Book View Café Publishing Cooperative (BVC) is an author-owned cooperative of professional writers, publishing in a variety of genres including fantasy, romance, mystery, and science fiction — with 90% of the proceeds going to the authors. Since its debut in 2008, BVC has gained a reputation for producing high-quality ebooks. BVC's ebooks are DRM-free and are distributed around the world. The cooperative is now bringing that same quality to its print editions.

BVC authors include New York Times and USA Today bestsellers as well as winners and nominees of many prestigious awards.

Made in the USA
Las Vegas, NV
19 July 2022

51869483R00148